T0666287

Books by Terry C. Simpson

AEGIS OF THE GODS
Etchings of Power
Ashes and Blood
Embers of a Broken Throne
Forges of Creation
The Shadowbearer (Prequel)

THE QUINTESSENCE CYCLE
Game of Souls
Soulbreaker
Crown of Souls
Soulsworn (Sidestory)

THE FROST FILES
Void Legion

THE ARCANUS ARCHIVES
ShadeBorn

VOID LEGION

THE FROST FILES

1

TERRY C. SIMPSON

Void Legion is a work of fiction. Names, characters, places, and incidents either are a product of the author's imagination or are used fictitiously. Any resemblance to actual persons, living or dead, events, or locales is entirely coincidental.

Golden Arm Press

Copyright © January 2019 Terry C. Simpson

Mapwork by Terry C. Simpson

Cover Art by Julie Nichols

The right of Terry C. Simpson to be identified as author of this Work has been asserted by him in accordance with sections 77 and 78 of the Copyright, Designs and Patents Act 1988.

All rights reserved. No part of this publication may be reproduced, stored in retrieval system, copied in any form or by any means, electronic, mechanical, photocopying, recording or otherwise transmitted without written permission from the publisher.

www. terrycsimpson.com.

Printed in the United States of America

First Edition

ISBN: 978-1-939172-25-9

To Kai: your love for writing and seeing your Daddy write and always asking me when my next book will be done is what made this possible. You are the reason I keep going.

Be sure to visit terrycsimpson.com for free book offers and to join Terry's Facebook reader group. Just search for Storyteller Terry C. Simpson's Void Gate. Free swag, updates, chapters, ARCs, regular chats with Terry, beta reads, input into Terry's worlds and books. You might even get towns, creatures, and people named after you.

So come on over and join up.

Map of Mikander

CHAPTER 1

A madman with a sword quoting what sounded like Shakespeare. Three cops with handguns aimed at the madman's head. Desperate yelling. Screaming. People scrambling away, hiding behind pillars. Such was the chaos that greeted Andre Taylor when he stepped off the Maglev at the Neptune Avenue train station on a frigid October day in New New York.

Transfixed more by the man than the confrontation, Andre huddled into his thin jacket behind a pillar. Most people had their cellphones out, recording the incident. Three drones hovered several dozen feet above the debacle, one emblazoned with News 7 on its underbelly, the other with POLICE, and the last with NAIL. Some people shouted for the cops to shoot. Others stayed as far away as the platform allowed, many covering their mouths and noses with their hands or scarves.

The man looked as if he had bathed in filth. Froth spilled from his lips. His clothes were nothing more than rags, yet he seemed oblivious to temperatures in the teens. Sword in hand, he paced back and forth, a dozen feet of space between him and the cops as he muttered to himself one moment and yelled profanities the next. He stopped

1

abruptly, pointed the sword at his imaginary foe, and then paced again.

Andre's cellphone vibrated.

"Mom calling." Bixby's resonant voice piped through Andre's Bluetooth headphones.

"Answer," Andre said to the virtual assistant. A soft click. "Hey, Mom. What's up?"

"Dre, are you almost home?" Mom's voice was strained as usual.

"Just got off the train."

"Hurry up, okay?"

Dre frowned. "Everything alright?"

"The twins are kicking my ass," Mom said.

Dre smiled with the thought of the baby brother and sister he'd soon have. "That's like every day." He chuckled.

Mom laughed weakly. "Ain't that the truth. Regi and Rayne can't get here soon enough. What's all that noise?"

"The usual Coney Island madness."

"Be careful and don't get caught up. Hurry home."

"On my way. See you soon."

"See you soon." Mom hung up.

"You have sullied my queen, Lancelot," the madman yelled. "I, King Arthur, challenge thee to a duel." He brought his sword up, hand waist high, then he turned, and paced away.

The cops followed but kept their distance. The man rounded on them. The cops stopped, Glocks not wavering from the madman's head.

Dre wondered why they didn't shoot. Or at least tase the man. Another part of him was glad they were showing restraint.

The madman pointed the sword at the cops. "Bastard, I fart in your general direction. For honor!" He swung at the air and then parried an imaginary return blow.

Dre gasped when several people said the madman was a DeGen. It explained the presence of the North American Immigration Logistics' drone. And why the cops had not engaged. They were afraid. They weren't equipped to deal with DeGens. Not with standard-issue Glock 60s. They needed pulse weapons. Something that would cauterize immediately. Weapons that were the territory of NAIL and the Special Defense Force.

Dre shivered. And it was not from the cold. A very real possibility existed that the DeGen carried a plague. He could not see any bloody lesions covering the DeGen's face, but their absence did not matter. The sores could be all over his body, hidden by his clothes.

Covering his mouth with his hand like many other people, Dre desperately sought another way off the platform. None existed. Not unless he wanted to jump down onto the tracks.

Left with no choice but to wait for NAIL or the SDF, Dre wondered if the madman was the same DeGen who'd tried to kick in his building's front door a few weeks ago. Dre shuddered to think of the possibilities had the DeGen gotten inside. As far as he was concerned, DeGen appearances in Coney Island were becoming too common now. Ten times in the last five months since his family had moved here. Ten times too many.

"Do not flee now, vermin." The DeGen dashed to his right, away from the police. A cop yelled. The DeGen leaped. The incoming Maglev train struck the DeGen. Thud. The body burst like a melon.

Wincing, Dre turned his head. As a few idiots rushed toward the tracks, Dre and many others made for the stairs as fast as they could through the crowds. He'd be damned if he got stuck in the aftermath of this mess. The next thing would be calls for a quarantine.

Hunched into his jacket, Dre left the station and hurried home. He sought to clear his mind of the DeGen and the cold with thoughts of playing Ataxia Online. Smiling, he envisioned his sorcerer fighting a Giant Ugly Mofo. Dueling players. Raiding. Getting epic loot. He dreamed about the game daily, more so since he quit playing as part of a promise to Mom and Pops.

Rushing home to throw on Virtual Reality goggles and jump into an adventure had been the height of his days after school and then college. Back in Barbados, before his family emigrated to America, he played Virtual Reality games and simulators of all sorts. Pops had encouraged the habit. In fact, Pops had created many of the sims and made certain Dre spent hours in them every day. Dre had lived to game.

But no more.

Now, he was stuck walking all the way to and from the Neptune Avenue train station every day to go to a job with no future. A job Pops had gotten him. An off-the-Grid job. Airbus Guide and Customer Service Rep for some obscure company in Downtown Brooklyn.

Pops had told him about the job during one of Pops' frequent talks about being a man. Dre recalled Pops' deep voice and Bajan accent like it was yesterday.

Experiencing the struggle… overcoming it. Hard work. It makes you a man. Teaches you the value of things. Makes you understand why you gotta be wary of things that sound too good to be true… why I don't take handouts, and you shouldn't either. They come with a catch. Next thing you know, you're trapped. Learn to stand on your own two. And remember that nothing worth doing is easy.

Dre scowled at the memory, and more so at his current life. If this was what being a man was like then life could keep it. At least in Ataxia Online he was somebody. Someone important. Rather than a useless Bottom Warder no one cared about.

4

Dre stepped in shit. He blew out a breath and shook his head. "Great. Just fucking great."

He turned up his nose at the stench and hoped it was only dog shit. Cringing at the thought that it might be human, or worse yet, a DeGen's, he muttered to himself, and found one of the few patches of dirt and grass outside his building and wiped his foot repeatedly. He considered tossing the sneaker, but these were his only good pair.

Stop bugging, dawg. It was only dog shit. With a sigh, he continued down 17th Street.

Thoroughly disgusted, he again wished he could work from home. But switching to Virtual Reality meant missing out on the rich folk who could afford actual trips to the city. Every credit mattered. Although, now that he considered it, working from home meant having the company's language translation eye and ear wearables. He could claim he lost a set and sell them. He dismissed the idea, as tempting as it seemed.

A soft tone echoed in his Bluetooth headphones. He pulled out his cell and took a peek. Green notification bubbles lit up the UI. He poked the air above them. His OneWorld newsfeed displayed several new comments on the thread for Void Legion, Ataxia Online 2. Shit forgotten, he poked the notification box.

Ten minutes until the most anticipated trailer of 2050.

He hurried up the steps and along the catwalk. His mind flitted through a dozen possibilities Void Legion could offer. Even the new game's name was epic. Upon reaching the front door, he pulled it open and entered the vestibule.

"Identify yourself to gain access," the Voice ID chimed.

He opened his mouth to comply. And stopped. The mere thought of standing there, saying Andre Taylor twenty times until the ID caught the right inflection made him want to punch the thing in its virtual face. He had no time for that. A moment to fiddle with his keys at the inner door and he let himself into the lobby.

Bunch of worthless security measures. He huffed.

"Good night, Mister Taylor." The MX1 guard behind the desk waved with an arm whose metal was pitted, the paint peeling.

Dre snorted and shook his head without acknowledging the android. *Don't even know why management bothered with that fossil. Fucking obsolete AI. Worse than my old Samsung phone and tablet. Can't protect anyone from my nine-year-old sister. Much less if another DeGen tries to break in.*

He pressed the elevator button and waited. A notice on the wall asked tenants to sign a petition to complain about building upkeep and security. Or the lack thereof. Another was to demand that the city extend the Maglev beyond the Neptune Avenue train station.

"Good luck with that," he muttered. Stillwell Avenue hadn't seen a train since Hurricane Donald wiped out much of Coney Island in 2020 back when there was only one New in New York.

One of the more ridiculous petitions was for Governor Morrison to pay for rezoning, completely evacuate Coney Island, and move them all to a higher Ward. Or to petition one of The Seven, preferably Sunrise Systems, to take up their cause.

Dre almost laughed. Unless the Corps saw some benefit in revitalizing the area, perhaps as the tourist attraction it once was, that idea might as well be dead. The Seven had more important things to do in New New York and the North American Republic than worry about a ghetto on a strip of land below sea level.

He returned his attention to his phone and swiped

the Void Legion thread. The post opened up. The last comment was from GamerGod. It read, 'There gonna loose a lot of players if we gotta start from scratch.'

Andre grimaced. He thought about leaving the comment alone. For about two seconds. He poked the air over the reply button. A text box opened. With his pointer finger, he swiped over the letters to form words. They're. Lose. Then beneath them, he added: People like you shouldn't be allowed to turn off the AI or Language Assistance. He clicked enter. Grinning, he imagined GamerGod's pissed off response.

The elevator bell dinged; the door slid open. He stepped in, pressed 5, and headed up. He wrinkled his nose at the smell of old food and sweaty armpits. And shit. When he got out, he wiped his feet on the faded green carpeting then hurried to his apartment door.

The moment he got inside, he shouted, "Mom, I'm home."

He dropped his backpack on the floor, slipped off his sneakers, and reminded himself to disinfect them later. Or soak them in bleach. He shrugged out of his jacket and put it in the hallway closet.

A moment to rummage through the backpack and he had his trusty Samsung tablet in hand. His heart ached for a moment. Every time he looked at the old thing, he was reminded that Mom had forced him to sell his VR headsets and even his Holotab. Right now, he would've settled for the Holotab. Its projections were better than watching the Samsung's regular old video as if he were back in 2025.

He touched the screen. The tablet lit up. A promo for new Airbuses automatically began. Shane Constantine, CEO of Sunrise Systems, was promising that his Corp would make New New York a prime tourist destination again by increasing investments in the city and revamping

7

AI for all Airbuses.

The admins chose that moment to post the Void Legion trailer.

Andre's breath caught. He clicked on the video just as he heard a noise. With a wave of his hand, he paused the playback. Frowning, he looked toward the hall that led to the rest of the apartment, waiting to see if Mom had called him. Muffled voices echoed outside the front door. *Probably those badass kids from next door going to smoke weed in the stairwell again.* He waited a moment, but when he heard nothing more, he gestured. The Void Legion trailer played.

The narrator's voice piped through his headphones. "Here at BioGen Studios we had put our very best techs behind our Virtual Reality Massively Multiplayer Online Roleplaying Games, or VRMMOs, because we knew your time was precious. But now we have taken VR to another level.

"We introduce Simulated Reality. With advances like you've never seen before, you'll live your fantasies, become more than a player, become part of the world of Mikander, a home away from home in Void Legion, Ataxia Online 2, a redefining of the genre."

New additions to the game popped onto the screen, boasting the new Simulated Reality tech they called Total Immersion.

Attention riveted, Dre nodded his approval for the changes to come. He had thought VRMMOs were better than sports. Better than movies. Better than books. Better than sex. Although he'd never had real sex yet. But who needed real sex when you had VPorn? He had enough experience with the stuff to be a pro, just like he did playing VRMMOs. He was willing to bet VRMMOs were the closest thing to the most perfect entertainment ever created and not just the best games.

Where else could you live in your own world and not

need anyone else? Where else could you literally lose yourself for days on end? Be whomever you wanted? Not have to worry about girls making fun of your looks? Discover incredible abilities? Where else could you fling the sickest magic, rescue damsels in distress, go on epic quests, rule a kingdom, lead raids into the most dangerous dungeons to defeat massive bosses, collect the best loot, or revel in the sheer joy of soloing a Giant Ugly Mofo?

And the best game of the lot? Ataxia Online. It was a masterpiece; Mikander, a revolution of world building.

And now they had improved upon it with Simulated Reality. Testers claimed you could *feel* in the game. They said they couldn't differentiate between the game and real life.

The promised changes sounded too good to be true. Immediately, Dre heard Pops telling him there was a catch.

Frowning once more, Dre looked up from the old tablet toward the hall. Again, he could have sworn he heard his mother over the narrator. *Probably wants you to take out the garbage. Or wash the dishes.* He groaned.

When Mom said nothing more, he headed to the couch and plopped down. He returned to listening and reading about Void Legion. Some cool shit was coming.

A new weapon popped on the screen. Some draconid tech. An aether cannon. Its Damage Per Second, or DPS, flitted above the weapon. His first thought about the cannon was Big Fucking Gun like the BFGs in DOOM.

Dre marveled at the new items. New skills. A new class: cannoneer. Increased level cap. Two raid dungeons. A world boss. Two zones: a beginner island for noobs and another with end game content.

There were several new Giant Ugly Mofoes, or GUMs, the massive boss-like monsters that roamed the world. Best of all was the Player Vs Player improvements. There were some stiff new penalties to dissuade Player Killers. As well as bounties to encourage the community to hunt down said PKers.

Then, of course, there were the castle sieges.

Oh, man, the castle sieges. He shook his head, imagination running wild. *In the right guild, I could rise up the PVP ranks, maybe become a Nomarch. Better yet, an Exarch.* He grimaced at the idea of being in a guild again. *Or I could play a merc, do the shit by myself. Yeah, solo would be the way to go. Far more epic. Epic players do epic things.*

The scatter of thoughts and the little smile he wore lasted about five seconds before they faded. He sighed; his shoulders drooped. None of that was to be. Between taking Kai to school and working every scrap of OT, he had no spare time. Add cooking and cleaning since Mom could no longer manage, and his day was completely shot.

And then there was his promise to Mom and Pops. A promise he regretted but would also keep. A man's only as good as his word, Pops always said.

Dre let out a deep breath. He couldn't wait for Mom to have the twins, for things to be easier, to have free time again, to quit his job, and have everything return to normal. To get away from this shithole of a building, go back to college. Although it would only be a college on the Grid. But the Grid meant VR, which suited him just fine. He wanted to disappear. To game.

Life had become so different since they lost Pops. He immediately saw Alphonso: light-skinned, a gray beard that would give Santa Claus a run for his money, and smiling eyes that seemed to know everything. *Why'd you have to get yourself killed?* Dre shook his head.

He remembered the times Pops would talk about his own days gaming. Pops loved the old classics like World of Warcraft, Lineage 2, Fortnite, Red Dead Redemption, Horizon Zero Dawn, God of War, Zelda, and Final Fantasy.

10

He'd even mention games Dre couldn't imagine playing and had only seen in old videos. Ancient pixelated 2D games like Castlevania and Contra.

Pops bragged that his favorite gaming company before it went belly up was Konami. He often complained that today's companies had killed the joy of gaming. He would go on and on about back in the day when there would be Easter Eggs, puzzles, and hidden code within games.

Dre missed Pops so much. He often imagined they were in a VR world. Those days and worlds had been as much about fun as they had been about learning. He and Pops had spent countless hours in VR, whether it was for academics, fitness training, mixed martial arts, or shooting.

There was a time he had hated the educational aspect. Sometimes it was a bore. But now, with Pops gone, Dre wished he could do it again. His heart grew heavy.

He recalled how Pops and Uncle Kim would test him after every session. Physically or mentally. Repetitions of MMA styles and moves. Hours spent in real life target practice or shooting courses. Dismantling and reassembling guns. The tests became a game of sorts. They'd try to trick him into a mistake. Or try to outdo him.

Andre smiled. He got the better of them more often than not. He even won several 3-Gun competitions. His reward would be to play VR games. Driving simulators, military shooters, adventure, or role-playing games. When Dre started playing Ataxia, he had found his love.

The night they got the fateful call rose fresh in Dre's mind. They'd been living in the Mid Ward in Prospect Heights. Pops had been on his way home from another late night at work, designing AI for some Corp he never spoke about. He'd lost control of the company car; it had struck a median and burst into flames. Not even the traffic drones could put out the fire.

That was six months ago. To this day, Dre's main questions about the accident went unanswered. *What caused it? Why was Pops' car off the Grid?*

Dre chased away the memory. *If you were here, we wouldn't be living in this shithole, Mom wouldn't have needed to work eighty-hour weeks, and I coulda stayed in college. Well, you always talked my head off about being a man, not taking handouts, not letting people take advantage of me, about standing on my own two feet. I'm my own man now.*

Life was difficult enough before. And had grown near impossible since. No matter how Dre tried, he couldn't make up for Pops' salary or for the hours Mom wasn't getting paid while on bed rest. Even with his OT, they barely managed credits for rent, food, gas for Pops' old car, and their cell phone plan, despite the benefits of living in a rent-stabilized building and having a Rental Assistance Voucher from the city. Anything else was a luxury. New clothes were out of the question. Christmas was two months away, and it might be the worst one ever. Thanksgiving? He didn't want to think about. And he might as well just forget about his seventeenth birthday in a month.

Whenever he complained about their shitty building or the even shittier neighborhood, Mom would say that at least they had a roof over their heads. If he mentioned how many hours she worked, she'd say that when you work hard for things you need, you appreciate them more. That there was honor in hard work that can't be earned any place else.

Sometimes, she'd point to a newsflash about the crazy stuff happening in the First Ward: the killings over food and water, the gangs, the human trafficking, the disease-plagued DeGens who called the place home, and say he should be grateful they weren't living there.

He snorted as he recalled Mom's struggle to find and get accepted into this building as if it were some prize. As if she forgot the last time they lived a few blocks from the sea when Hurricane Perol had destroyed everything. He still remembered the horror of swimming through water up to his neck, thinking he was going to drown. Just like the time in Barbados. If Pops hadn't been there… Dre banished the thought before it festered.

Despite all that, Mom had refused to give up Regina and Rayne. Stubborn as ever, Mom had also refused to ask for help from any of their family or friends. She'd also made him promise not to contact any of them. Ever. Not even Uncle Kim. He'd cut off every friend but one.

She'd been forceful about it, which he chalked up to a few things: pride, shame, and fear. Pride in that she felt they could manage all on their own. Shame at their fall from Mid Warders to barely Bottom Warder status. Fear of the Better Tomorrow Law. Getting pregnant again meant a knock on the door from the Family Planning Corps. A visit from NAIL. Sterilization. Or worse. He didn't want to think about the worse.

He spent days dreaming they could win the Massive Millions Lottery. He could buy their Citizenship and solve all their problems. Each day he'd short himself a bagel or coffee before work so he could drop a credit on a ticket. A dollar and a dream. That was Pops' old saying.

The Massive Millions might have been the only type of easy money Pops might have accepted. And in truth, it wasn't easy money. Dre snorted, driving away thoughts of real vacations to some exotic island, living on the hundredth floor in the Mid Wards, or better yet, past a hundred and fifty in the Upper Wards. Preferably some place Downtown Brooklyn. And well away from the ocean.

Forget all that, he thought. *Right now, just earning a hundred more credits sounds good.*

Mom had spent their savings on secret doctors to

ensure Regina and Rayne would be born healthy. He didn't blame her. They were the last things she had of Pops, of thirty years of marriage.

It was the same reason he cherished the aether ring replica Pops had given him for his sixteenth birthday. Pops had called it the Two Ring. Dre smiled as he recalled that day, and the fact Pops had known to buy him a replica from Ataxia Online. The ring was perfect, down to the engraving of a two and his name, the patterns, and the black metal.

He made to rub the ring when he realized it was missing from his pinky. *Where'd I put the damn thing?* He checked the couch to either side of him and atop the stained and cracked glass center table. The Two Ring wasn't in either place.

"Mommy calling you, Dre," Kai said from the start of the hallway.

"Tell her I'm coming." He waved off his little sister.

A video of a new Giant Ugly Mofo popped up on his tablet screen. Dre smiled at the beast's size and features, the very reason GUMs were Giant Ugly Mofoes. This GUM was a void revenant the size of a house. The nebulous creature threw its bird-like head of white bone and whiter beak to the sky and screeched. It held a storm lance in one clawed hand. Dark tendrils of void energy coiled between the curled horns on its head.

A full group battled the void revenant. One was a human, two were eradae who reminded Dre of horned succubi, one was a giant crimson-skinned gurash, and the other was a winged yurid. Their class choices were dementer, mystic, marksman, marauder, and cutthroat.

Dre studied their tactics and set up. The marauder was the tank, trying to soak up the GUM's damage while generating threat with attacks meant to keep the void revenant aggroed or targeting him rather than the weaker players or glass cannons in the group, namely the marksman and the cutthroat. The damage dealers or DPSers were the cutthroat, marksman, and dementer. While the mystic could do some damage, her main role in this fight was as a healer and buffer.

Shoulda been the dementer as tank for this GUM.

The dementer had the best gear, and with his insane damage, he kept pulling aggro, which meant the GUM would turn to attack him. Normally, this wouldn't be an issue because dementers had high Hit Points. But the void revenant's Shadow Lightning was jumping from the dementer to the cutthroat and the marksman. The mystic was having a hell of a time healing all three when that happened. They nearly died several times.

The encounter finally went to shit when the cutthroat pulled aggro, causing the GUM to turn to the three DPSers just as it was casting Shadow Wave. The ability stunned them all. The GUM finished them with Black Storm, a hail of shadowy bolts from the sky.

Dre smirked at the group. *Bunch o' noobs. Bet I could solo that bad boy with my sorcerer. Full end game hierka gear, genesis grade? Pfffttt. The damage would be insane.* He frowned, contemplating the GUM's abilities. If he was also fully sharded, both for weapons and skill effects, his sorc could pull it off. He envisioned his tactics: a glowing chakram in each hand, he fired off spell combos and used stuns, leaps, and Flickers to avoid attacks while kiting the monster. The idea made him smile.

His cell vibrated on the glass table. He leaned over, took a look at the name, and then flicked his finger across the screen. "What up, dawg."

Hughey's nasal, excited voice piped through the Bluetooth headphones. "Yo, Dre, tell me you saw it?"

"Saw what?" Dre grinned. "The argument in the

store between Habib and the gangsta?"

"Nah," Hughey began.

Dre ignored Hughey and continued, "Yo, the expression on homeboy's face when Habib told him to shaddup was an instant classic." Dre chuckled, reliving the incident. "With that accent, too. And when homeboy tried to drop a threat and Habib doubled down with shaddup, shaddup. Talking about eyes popping outta someone's head."

"No, fool, that's not what I meant," Hughey said.

Dre grinned wider this time. "Ah, you mean the De-Gen at the train station. That Maglev–"

"I don't mean any of that," Hughey blurted, frustration in his voice.

"What you talking about then?" Dre could barely stop himself from sputtering. "The new Star Wars trailer?" He hoped his best and only friend didn't hear the laughter in his voice.

"You playing around right?" Hughey asked.

"Huh?" Dre frowned. "The biggest movie fanatic I know hasn't seen–"

"Come on, man, I *know* you saw it."

"Hugh, if it ain't Episode 13–"

"The Void Legion video, fool!"

"Void Legion?" Dre fought the urge to burst into laughter.

"Stop playing. It's the Ataxia expansion! How could you–"

"Oh, thaaat." Dre shrugged.

"Oh, that? Oh, that? You can't be serious."

Dre could picture Hughey turning red. He guffawed, unable to keep up the act. "Shaddup," he said. And laughed even louder. "Of course, I saw it. And it's not an expansion. It's almost a different game. Yo, did you see the new weapons? The damage is insane."

16

They chattered away, breathlessly exchanging opinions on one new feature or another, sharing insight on the many possibilities. One of the main points was how would BioGen compensate the old players who wanted to keep their characters. There was talk about giving them boosted stats at the start and perhaps credits, special armor, a rare mount, and titles. Perks to mark them as veterans.

Kai's small brown-skinned hand appeared in front of Dre's face. Dre faked as if he were about to pounce on her and said, "Rawrr." She scurried away, stopped at the hallway, and stuck her tongue out. With a smile and a shake of his head, Dre got to his feet with his phone in hand and strode over to the window.

Some ten floors below, the glare of NYPD emergency lights brightened the intersection of Mermaid Avenue and 17th street and the garbage-filled alley beside the building. A few more of the fixtures were spread about the property, particularly in a parking lot rife with empty spaces, and next to the long-abandoned basketball courts and playground. Rats the size of small dogs scurried about a dumpster in their nocturnal foraging.

Another three thousand feet from the building was the massive sea wall. The ocean beyond it was a black soup as was the sky. Dre couldn't imagine swimming in the stuff. He'd rather forget any contact he ever had with the ocean. Or any sort of deep water. Only nightmares waited there.

Several red and yellow blips marked the path of patrolling EVTOL aircraft equipped with smog vacuums. The wall made Dre wonder after Pops' stories about the old days before Hurricane Donald. Pops had come to New York City on vacation multiple times before 2020 and claimed Coney Island was known back then for its theme park, concerts, the MCU stadium, and Nathan's Hot Dogs. People were actually able to go down to the beach and swim in what was now polluted water infested with mutated fish.

Dre shook his head. The 20th century and first quarter of the 21st mostly sounded like heaven when compared to this era. The last twenty-five years had seen a glut of super storms, the Climatic Shift, the Global Energy Crisis, the Great Migration, and the Second Civil War, quickly followed by the War of the Americas. He could only imagine a time when the country was the United States of America rather than the North American Republic.

He reminded himself to prune the Grid for video of those days. If any still existed. Which reminded him of Pop's stories about a time before the Grid, when the internet connected everyone in the world.

"This means you coming back, right?" Hughey asked, breaking Dre from his thoughts. Dre remained silent as Hughey continued, "I signed up for the free trial. You should too." Dre still refused to answer. "Just Blaze been talking a lotta shit on the forums. Said you're lucky you quit."

"And you believe that nonsense?" Dre grimaced. "Come on, bruh, I'd still be top dog across all servers if I was playing."

"I said the same thing, but she said you needed to come prove it. Even said you were shook."

"Me? Scared? Please. I'd have no probs with her. She don't want no smoke with me. She still running that cutthroat... ummmmm... Gilda Mordian?"

"Yup."

"I'd make light work of that chick."

"I don't knowww. She bust your boy's ass."

"Which boy?" Dre frowned. Hughey was the only one he'd played with in Ataxia after their guild broke up.

"Dante Blackblade and his marauder."

"Blackblade? My boy?" Dre scoffed. "Pffffttt."

"Shaddup." Hughey chuckled. Dre laughed in turn.

"I know," Hughey continued. "Still, the duel wasn't even close, homie. Just Blaze straight slayed him."

"Damn."

"She's definitely a prob. She's gotten some real skills since you left, even beat what you couldn't. Castle Dhoom on Heroic. She off-tanked the two chimera guards while the rest of the guild killed Emperor KiGyaba."

"*The* Emperor KiGyaba? As in the last boss? The hydra god?"

"Hmm hmmm."

"Shit. Two GUMs? At the same time? With a cut-throat's HP?" Dre envisioned the class' Hit Points, Gilda's health meter. "Nahhhh, I'm not buying that one, Hugh. Splash damage from their AOEs woulda killed her."

"I'm telling you, dawg. I watched the video. She had no probs. *And* it's on the forum kill list. Check the link I sent you."

A notification popped up on Dre's phone. He swiped. A video ran, showing Gilda Mordian's duel with Dante Blackblade as well as the battles throughout Heroic Castle Dhoom. It was a guild run, but she was the leader, the focus, and made everything so much easier. Her skill was breathtaking. Beautiful. She wove her way through enemies like a dancer gliding across a crowded ballroom.

At Emperor KiGyaba, she was even better. The Emperor was a hydra boss known to drop aggro, stop attacking the tank or whomever it had generated the most hate toward, and target whomever was fighting the guards. Gilda employed Escape perfectly every time, vanishing to erase her threat level while avoiding the splash damage of Emperor KiGyaba's Area of Effect spells, dodging the numerous snake-like heads, and still picking up the chimera guards before they charged into the raid to wreak havoc. Her HP never dropped below half. Dre couldn't recall seeing anything so amazing.

"Wow," he whispered.

"Exactly."

"But she still needed her guild." Dre shrugged. "I was doing it with randoms."

The idea of a return was tempting. So tempting. He did have several email invites to alpha test. One of them had even offered to pay him. Dre started to count hours and credits in his head, then stopped and took a breath, chest aching.

He remembered his promise to Mom and Pops to stop playing. For now, his gaming days were done.

"Dre!" Kai shouted.

He turned from the window to face his little sister.

She was standing at the hallway entrance again, hands on hips, impatiently tapping one foot. "Mommy wants you."

Dre didn't move.

She turned her hands, palms up, and stuck her head forward with all the attitude of a nine-year-old. "Nowwww." She disappeared back the way from which she'd come.

"Andreeeeeee!" Mom's wail echoed.

Dre shook his head. *What is it this time?* he thought, then he said, "Yo, Hugh, I gotta go. Holla at you later. And... Shaddup." Hughey repeated the goodbye. Dre smiled, sighed, pressed the disconnect button on his headphones, and dropped his cell on the couch.

"Yes, Mom!" he yelled.

Before he took another step there was a rumble, a thump, and a stifled cry.

"Mom?" Frowning, he crossed the living room to the hall.

Little Kai was standing in front the bathroom door, her mouth forming an O. Her eyes bulged. And then her face contorted. She burst into sobs.

"Mommmyyyyy," she bawled, one hand extended to the open bathroom door.

CHAPTER 2

Heart thundering, Dre rushed down the hall. When he reached the bathroom and looked in, he froze and stared. He choked back a curse.

Mom sat with her back against the tub, legs stretched in front of her, while she clutched her round belly. Her nightgown was soaked. Pinkish fluid covered the tiles. Her face was bleak, her brown hair a mess. "No, no, no, please, God, no." Sobs wracked Mom's chest.

A pit opened in Dre's stomach. "Mom!" he finally managed, inadvertently rubbing his pinky where the missing Two Ring belonged. Uttering that one word set him in motion. "Kai, get my phone off the couch."

He made to rush to Mom's side across the tiles but slipped on the viscous fluid. Grabbing the sink saved him. He glanced over to his sister. She was still standing there, in shock, crying.

"KAI," he hollered. She jumped. Her watery eyes focused on him. "Get my phone off the couch." Sniffling, Kai wiped her eyes, nodded numbly, and ran down the hall.

He got down on his knees beside his mother. She was sniveling now, still clutching her belly, muttering under her breath. He reached a hand up to brush away strands of brown hair from her sweaty face.

She started, but then her eyes focused on him. Her mouth opened a little, and was completely downturned as if she were about to bawl, but she just shook. Tears streamed down her cheeks.

"What-what happened?" He wiped away the tears.

"My water brooooke."

He frowned. "But that's a good thing, right?"

"Nooo, it's three months early."

It took a moment for realization to dawn, for the thought of a miscarriage to develop. "The babies… Rayne and Regi." His chest hurt. "They gonna be alright?"

"I don't know; I don't know; I don't knowwww." Mom broke into prayers.

Dre tried to think of a way he could offer immediate help. But faced with the situation, there was little he could do. He cursed himself for not paying attention, for not coming when Kai first called him, or even checking on Mom when he got home.

Kai appeared at the door with his cell. Dre gingerly got to his feet, stepped across to the wet rug, and took the phone from her. He dialed.

"Nine-One-One, what's your emergency?" asked a female operator.

"It's my Mom. We need an ambu–"

"NO!" Mom yelled.

Dre snapped his head around, the operator's voice forgotten. Mom stared at him, her expression so fierce, so determined, that it scared him. He hung up. Dre opened his mouth to question the decision when realization dawned. *Better Tomorrow, you idiot. You fucking idiot.*

Dre's phone rang. The screen read 911. His stomach knotted. He held the screen up toward Mom.

"Answer it. Tell them you made a mistake," she said with a grimace. "Tell them we're on our way to the hospital already."

He did as he was told. After he hung up, he looked to his mother. "What now?"

Mom beckoned him over to her. "First, help me up. Then help me change my gown. We'll take the car to Dr. Rozanta."

"The car?" He reached for the rug and dragged it closer to her. "You can't drive in your condition." He got his hands under Mom's armpits, and after a bit of a struggle where Mom teetered, he helped her to her feet.

"Not me. You."

"Me?" His eyebrows shot up even as he let her use his shoulder and arm for support. "But I don't have my license yet. And ever since Pops, you said–"

"I know what I said. None of that matters now. We have to get to Dr. Rozanta."

"Can't we just call her? Make her come here?" He guided Mom toward her bedroom.

"No. All calls are on the Grid. Any calls to gynecologists or midwives are reported to the Family Planning Corps."

"W-we can call–"

"There's no one we can trust," Mom said. "I know you're scared of the car. You hate it, hate the idea of driving ever since your father died."

"It's not that. That's not it at all." The idea of driving left a sour taste in his mouth, but he wasn't about to admit it.

"I remember when Alphonso wanted to move down from the Tenth Ward and I didn't. I hated the idea." Mom's voice was tender despite the pain she had to be in. "And he said to me, 'Theresa, sometimes you have to do something you hate to save the people you love.'"

Dre took a deep breath. "Alright. I'll go for Dr. Rozanta by myself. It won't be a prob. But it's best if you stay here."

"So Regi and Rayne are gonna wait, huh?" Mom chuckled painfully and then grunted. "By the time you got

24

back, they'd be out already. I'm not sure I could survive that. Or the police would be here. And they'd alert Family Planning. Especially after the call you made. So, we stick together, get this done together. As we always have. As family. Okay?"

"Alright." Dre nodded. He looked toward his little sister. "Bunny, go put on some jeans, a hoody, a coat, and some sneakers." Kai hurried toward her room.

Dre sat Mom on her bed, got a fresh wooly gown from the closet, helped her out of the old, and into the new. Mom's breathing had been heavy and labored the entire time. It changed. She sucked in great breaths of air and blew them out. Sweat poured down her face. Dre had seen that before. It ended with Kai born on the couch at their old apartment.

"How bad is it? Are the babies coming?"

"It's bad enough," Mom wheezed. "They aren't coming yet. They're as stubborn as you. But it hurts. It hurts." She moaned. "Hurts so bad. We gotta hurry."

"Just hang in there. Keep fighting."

Dre shoved a pair of fur-lined boots on Mom's feet. Then he led her from the room, down the hall, put her on the couch, and told Kai to sit with her. He hurried to the door, put on his sneakers, and grabbed his and Mom's coats.

Kai was holding Mom's hand and speaking in a soothing voice when Dre turned from the closet. "It's gonna be alright, Mommy. Rayne and Regi are gonna be fine. You gonna be fine. I love you, Mommy."

Mom stroked Kai's hair, a smile breaking through the pain etched on her face. "I love you too, Pumpkin."

Dre smiled and said, "And I love you both. Now, let's go." He took the car keys off the little hook by the front door and hurried to help Mom off the couch.

He got Mom into her coat. He slipped his on. With Mom using him for support, they left the apartment, made their way to the elevator, and down into the parking lot, the frigid October night reeking with the recent passing of a garbage truck.

Mom was breathing hard, moaning, mist puffing from her lips by the time Dre got her into the passenger side backseat of their beat up 2017 Toyota Camry. Wary of Mom's belly, he fastened the seatbelt across her lap and tucked the top strap behind her shoulder. Kai got into the seat on the other side. Dre secured his sister's seatbelt.

He opened the creaking front door, eased in, and slammed the door shut. The car was freezing. Dre blew on his hands several times then adjusted the side mirrors and did the same with the rear until he had a good view of Mom. He shoved the key in the ignition. *You got this, dawg. It's no prob.* He turned the key. The car coughed as the engine tried and failed to start. He groaned and tried again with the same result.

"Please, not tonight of all nights." He shuddered as he fought against the urge to cry.

If there was one time he truly wished they were well off again and could have afforded an electric car, or better yet, a Hover Type or a Personal Transport, it was now. But Pops had insisted on this piece of shit that wasn't even registered or connected to the Grid.

Dre waited a moment, took a deep breath, and whispered, "Come on, baby, come on, baby, come on, baby." Just the way Pops used to do it.

He turned the key. The car sputtered to life. "Yes!" He fist-pumped.

Dre put the vehicle in gear and drove out of the lot and onto Mermaid Avenue. A weight that he hadn't realized he carried eased off his chest. He breathed easier. And then he frowned. "Mom? What if we get pulled over?"

"Just tell the cops I'm your aunt... I'm in labor and we're on our way to a private clinic. They'll rush us there before they do an investigation."

Dre smiled, both at Mom's shrewdness and the idea of racing to the doctor under a police escort. "How're we doing back there?" He glanced at the rear-view mirror.

Mom was taking long, slow breaths again, one hand gripping the overhead handhold, the other on her round belly. Her face was contorted. "Not bad. Not good. We just doing."

Dre stopped at a red light. "Then just keep doing. We gonna be there soon." He glanced at his sister in the mirror. "You alright, Bunny?"

"Yeah." Kai was turning something between her fingers.

Dre frowned. "Hey, that's my Two Ring." He smiled at the sight of the black ring, relieved that he'd found it. "I've been looking for that." He pressed the gas.

Something slammed into the car. Glass shattered. The world spun. He heard Mom and Kai screaming. *How'd I get outside the car?* His entire left side hurt so much. He couldn't lift his arm. He was cold. Freezing. He groaned. Teeth chattering, he struggled to his feet in agony and stumbled to the open passenger side door of the mangled Camry.

Mom was no longer making any sounds. She was slumped to one side, barely held in by the seatbelt. Kai was still crying.

"I'm coming, Bunny. I'm coming." He crawled inside. He reached toward his little sister, who was somehow still holding the Two Ring, her hand stretched toward him even as she bawled. Dre grimaced at a whiff of blood and shit.

And then, blackness took him.

CHAPTER 3

Dre woke to a growling belly, a hammer pounding the nail that was his head, a soft bed, and cold air. Soreness radiated down his lower back, his left shoulder, his left side, and leg. He groaned. An incessant beep worsened the headache. *What the hell is that sound?*

He opened his eyes to a coral-colored ceiling and recognized the coldness as air conditioning. He frowned. Neither was right. He figured he was still in the same recurring nightmare of a strange room and a car accident.

He sat bolt upright, a sudden chest pain multiplying his agony. *Mom! Regi and Rayne! Kai!* Frantic thoughts made the hammer become a blade driving into his skull. With his right hand, he covered his right eye and part of his forehead, hoping to make the migraine go away, hoping to ease the hurt, chase away the memory of the accident.

But the black Two Ring was there on his pinky finger below his eye. Then it was in Kai's hand. Mom was on the bathroom floor. He was taking Mom and Kai to the car. Driving. The crash. He sobbed as he relived seeing Mom slumped to one side. Kai bawling. He didn't know how long he sat there, mired in grief, but eventually the stabs in his head subsided to a hammer again… and eventually a throb.

Sniffling, he clung to the possibility that if he were alive, so were they. *But how are they? Are they here? I gotta find them. How did I get here? Where's here? I know I shouldn't have driven.* Amidst the frantic thoughts and blame was his fervent prayers for their well-being. And a need for answers.

"Hello." The words echoed, his voice a hoarse thing. "Hello."

White walls surrounded him in a room that screamed sterility. On one side was a tall, wide, tinted window, and a solitary door. There were two comfortable-looking armchairs and a polished wooden center table. Hovering above the table was a holo display running a commercial for Equitane Holdings' Electric Vertical Take Off and Landing Personal Transport. The acronym EVTOL PT flashed above the vehicle.

Dre glanced down. He was wearing a gown, pale blue against his caramel skin, and was sitting on a decent-sized bed. An IV was in his left forearm, its lines running to several bags of solution. The beeps originated from a series of other monitors at his bedside. On his shoulder was a biometric tatt.

Gotta be an expensive hospital, then. Not some shithole. Hospital? He gaped.

His mind conjured horrid images of Mom in custody of the FPC, forced to have an abortion, and then sentenced to sterilization or death. Pops had barely managed to pay the fines for Kai's birth. No such recourse existed for additional babies under Better Tomorrow. Not for Bottom Warders. The best he could hope for was that they'd let her live, but then NAIL would deport her for the crime. And he was likely to follow.

"Nurseee," he called out in desperation. "Doctorrrr... anyoneeee!" No one answered.

He forced himself to think. Maybe, this wasn't a hospital after all. Maybe, Mom was fine. So was Kai. His racing pulse and heaving chest subsided.

Wincing at the soreness along the left side of his

body, he rolled his neck and massaged the outside of his bicep, elbow, and upper forearm. He stopped and peered at the tender area. A barely discernible line ran from the top of his bicep, down to the elbow, along his forearm, to his wrist. Like an old scar. He reached for the I.V.

"I would wait for the doctor if I were you, Andre." The woman's voice was cool, the accent, cultured.

She filled the open doorway, attired in a black curve-hugging dress with a deep V at the neck, white trim, and heels to match. Her raven hair was cut in a short bob, every strand in perfect place, framing a tan face straight from Celebrity Style magazine. Hawkish obsidian eyes studied him. They made him feel small, unimportant, like his boss did when he called Dre into the office to chastise him for lateness. He averted his gaze and cleared his throat.

"You probably have a dozen questions," she said.

"I-I do. First—"

"I'm Sidrie Malikah. CEO of Equitane Holdings." She strolled across the room, long tan legs and strong calves taking her toward an armchair.

Dre tried his best to hold in his shock. Here, he was, speaking to the owner of one of the top Corps in all of New New York. One of the infamous Seven.

"You're Downtown Brooklyn in the Equitane Towers' medical wing." Sidrie gestured with an open palm.

"Thank you, Miss Malikah." He clasped his hands and dipped his head in a show of appreciation.

"Call me Sidrie," she said. "I insist." Dre nodded. "Theresa and Kai are safe here also."

A little pressure eased from his chest. "How are they? I mean… their injuries… the accident."

"Your little sister is fine." Sidrie took a seat and crossed her legs.

"And Mom?" Dre swallowed.

"She's in a coma."

Dre squeezed his eyes shut. He took a deep breath and opened them. Warm tears trickled down his face. "Rayne and Regi... the twins—"

"They're still in your mother's belly for now. At the moment, they're fine." Sidrie leaned back in the chair, a finger tapping her thin lips. The finger stopped and gestured. "My doctors aim for them to remain that way. And while under my protection, there is no need to worry about any of the authorities."

A tiny smile touched Dre's lips and he whispered, "Thank you." He cleared his throat and spoke much louder. "Can I see them?" He paused. "If it's not a prob, that is."

"Certainly." She flicked her hand up across her face. An implant's blue light flashed in her eyes and then was gone. She pointed to the holo display above the table.

Jet engine whining, the EVTOL PT lifted straight from a rooftop, hovered in the air, then zoomed off between skyrises in Times Square. The image changed to a room identical to his. Kai sat at the top of a bed with her back against a pillow. Her attention was riveted upon a projection floating above a Holotab. It was her favorite show, Munsters and Minions. Dre smiled.

The display blinked. Dre's breath caught in his throat. Mom was lying on a bed in a pristine white chamber. Several tubes and lines trailed from her mouth, nose, and body to various machines. Five holos several feet above her displayed readings.

"Mom," Dre whispered, his hand extending of its own volition toward the projection. He let his hand fall to his lap. "I know you said she's in a coma." Mom's chest rose and fell. "But how's she doing? When's she gonna wake up?"

"She is better than one might expect, given the trauma of the accident combined with her pregnancy. She is a tough woman."

"But—" Dre began.

"I have the best facilities and people at my disposal," Sidrie Malikah said. "And not just here in the Republic, but in the entire world. They can't say for certain when she will wake, but given time, and the proper treatment, my doctors are confident she *will* recover fully."

Dre nodded. "I understand, Miss Mal—" Her arched brow stopped him. "Sorry, Sidrie. I can't thank you enough for all you've done." The woman was risking life in prison for them. The idea of it was overwhelming.

Miss Malikah tilted her head. "Give me a moment, Andre. I have to take this call. Yes, go ahead," she continued even before he answered. She paused for moment, perfect brows wrinkling. "Now? I'll take a look."

A newsflash replaced the holos of Mom and Kai. One of the DeGen gangs from the First Ward had somehow gotten hold of XM-25 grenade launchers and HK433 assault rifles. The DeGens were a bedraggled, filthy group, faces covered with lesions. Quite a few of them were taller than anyone had a right to be. They had managed to sneak past the police and NAIL drone patrols and had robbed or destroyed two hydroponic silos in the Tenth Ward and killed several Citizens.

The Special Defense Force and police had been first to respond. North American Immigration Logistics soldiers wearing tactical armor with NAIL emblazoned upon it soon joined them. Armed with NGSAR5 assault rifles and AVP41B pulse guns, they were in a fierce firefight with the DeGens. They drove the DeGens back down into the First Ward's old streets and dilapidated buildings. Drones fired several missiles into the structures.

Much of the talk afterward involved questions as to how the DeGens managed to infiltrate not only a Mid Ward location, but also one owned by the Sunrise Systems Corporation. Pundits suggested hackers had got into the Grid to disable surveillance. Was the Grid truly impenetrable? A discussion ensued about the very real possibility of a severe food shortage and the governor's announcement concerning rations.

The reporter also spoke of a full-scale assault on the First Ward. Under pressure from their Citizens, politicians were demanding a cleanup of the crime and disease-riddled place. They stated it was past time to correct the errors made during the Great Migration, to kill or capture the glut of illegal aliens who called the First Ward home, and destroy the thriving gangs that followed orders of the cartels that ran the South American Conglomerate. They wanted to be rid of the general depravity of the people who had abandoned society to become DeGens, living in squalor with little to no heat, light, food, or fresh water. The most outspoken among those politicians was a round-faced, pudgy man named Senator Kirkland.

The scene switched to Governor Morrison, who blamed the crisis on past mayors for declaring New New York a sanctuary city during the federal crackdown on immigration dating back to 2018. He extolled the virtues of continuing the change begun after the Second Civil War to resolve the problem. After all, it was such illegal aliens the cartels of the SAC had relied on to begin the war that had seen the end of the U.S.A and formation of the North American Republic. He swore to ask President Rashaad for more NAIL troops and promised to keep the SDF mobilized. As usual, the name rat was flung around when discussing the DeGens. The holo display winked out.

"Keep me posted," Sidrie said. Her hawkish gaze returned to Dre. "Where were we? Yes, your questions."

"How did we end up here?" Dre dragged his eyes

away from her face.

"Luck? Fate?" Sidrie shrugged. "A bit of both."

He made to say if they were lucky Pops would be alive, Mom wouldn't have gotten sick, and they wouldn't have been in an accident. But he bit his tongue instead.

"And of course, there was you," Sidrie said, gesturing to him with an open palm, "bravely trying to take your mother to a doctor."

He shook his head. "I was doing what any son would."

"What do you recall of the crash?" Sidrie raised a quizzical brow.

Dre closed his eyes, his thumb and forefinger absently stroking his Two Ring. Images flashed of buckling Mom's seatbelt and doing the same for Kai. He'd driven down Mermaid Avenue on his way to the Belt Parkway. He remembered stopping at a red light, checking on Mom through the rearview, then Kai playing with his aether ring.

He cringed as the crash itself came roaring to life. *I was thrown out the window?* He crawled back to the car. The sensation of a useless arm. Screams. Mom unconscious. Reaching for Kai. He tilted his head to the side, squeezing his eyes tighter as he tried to recall something in the background. *A whine of some sort?* Then blackness.

"Something hit us. I was tossed from the car." He shook his head and opened his eyes. "Then I woke up here."

"One of my employees was surveying a bit of property in Coney Island near 17th Street," Sidrie said. "His hover car struck your vehicle."

Dre's sense of gratitude vanished. His eyes opened wide. "He caused this?" Nostrils flaring, he folded his lips. His mind spun. He stroked his Two Ring even harder.

"In so much as he hit your car? Yes. But it was you, Andre, who ran the red light and caused the accident." The

34

blue light flashed in Sidrie's eyes.

"No," he said through clenched teeth. "That's a lie. It has to be." He shook, hands balled into fists.

The holo changed once more. This time, it showed Mermaid Avenue near Dre's building through a traffic drone's lens. A weather-beaten Camry he knew too well stopped at a red light. Seconds passed and then the vehicle drove into the intersection. The light was still red.

A blue hover car smashed into the Camry's driver side and sent the Camry spinning with its passenger side door flung open. The driver was tossed from the car. The drone hovered above the smoking wreckage. Long minutes passed. The driver clambered to his feet, his left arm and side a mangled, bloody mess.

Horrified, Dre looked away. *That's wrong. That's not true. It can't be true. Someone faked that video.* He felt sick.

"But," Sidrie continued, "as I said, it was both fate and luck. The accident was destined to happen as was this meeting with you. And luckily, it occurred with one of my associates at a time when your mother was in dire need of help, a moment when she or the twins, or all of them, all of you, could have died. Or could have been discovered by the Family Planning Corps."

If the words were meant to soothe, they accomplished little. He felt empty inside, his mind running through all the different scenarios, creating gruesome images. He didn't know how long he sat there, stroking his Two Ring, but eventually he calmed. Sniffling, he wiped his eyes.

Sidrie was still sitting in the chair, face impassive. A clean-shaven man in a doctor's white robe stood beside her. He gazed at Dre over his glasses.

It was your fault, Dre. He fought against the truth of the words. "A-again, thanks for saving Kai, Mom, and the twins… for helping us. There's no way I can repay you, but one day–"

"Actually, Andre, there is a way."

Dre perked up. "Tell me. And could you just call me, Dre? Only my mother uses Andre... and only when she's mad at me."

"Certainly, Dre." Sidrie inclined her head and stood. "As for the assistance you can provide, it should suit you rather well. It's an alpha test for an SRMMO."

There was only one SRMMO Dre knew of. *She couldn't mean Ataxia Online 2, could she?* He made to speak.

"It's better if I show you. But first, let Dr. Redmond take a look at you." She indicated the man beside her.

"Hello, Dre. I'm glad to see your progress has gone so well." Dr. Redmond was all smiles, even his eyes. He strolled toward Dre's bed. "You were in pretty bad shape when they brought you in. Your arm was broken, the flesh quite mangled. You'd broken several ribs. And was suffering a severe concussion.

"Although, I must say I'm surprised it wasn't worse. Someone else might have died. Or at the very least suffered internal bleeding and life-threatening injuries. Like your-never mind."

Dre recalled the video. Brows furrowed, he touched his head, his side, glanced at his arm, and then looked at Sidrie and the doctor. "My arm... my ribs... how long have I been here? How did you–?"

"A week," the doctor said.

"A week to fix broken bones? How's that possible?" Dre turned his arm, noting the tiny scar again. "Why don't I remember any of it?"

"You were unconscious throughout the process. We healed your injuries by way of nanotech. In this case, Tissue Nanotransfection. Or TNT. In a nutshell, nanochips containing genetic code are delivered to cells, transforming those cells into other usable cells of our choosing. It allows us to grow anything. Bone. Tissue. Organs."

"Wow," Dre said.

"Yes, wow, indeed. And here at Equitane we are foremost in TNT." Dr. Redmond puffed up his chest. "We expanded the tech to include things we learned from extensive study and cloning of axolotls."

"Axolotls?"

"A type of salamander." The doctor waved casually. "Cancer resistant and capable of regenerating any body part. Even its brain. They've been the key to us developing near perfect clones. Now, let's see what we have."

The doctor gestured in front of his face. A holo appeared at eye level between him and Dre. It showed Dre's arm and ribs.

"Yes, yes," Dr. Redmond said absently. "Very good. The biometrics are very good. Another few hours of TNT and that tiny scar will vanish completely." He turned to Sidrie. "He's more than ready." The projection blinked off.

"Excellent," Sidrie said. "Dre, I'm certain you're hungry. Have a bite, change into something more comfortable, and meet us outside."

Dr. Redmond stepped forward. "Here, let me get the IV." He plucked the line from Dre's arm and passed Dre a bit of gauze from a small drawer on one of the nearby monitors.

The door opened and an Automatic Guided Cart rolled in, its tabletop laden with several dishes. On its single arm was a change of clothes, what appeared to be sweat pants, and a T-Shirt. Mouthwatering aromas drifted on the air. Dre's stomach rumbled a complaint. Sidrie and Dr. Redmond departed. The AGC stopped next to the armchairs.

"Hey," he called to the cart, "can you bring that over here?" The AGC didn't respond. Dre sighed, disappointed that the AGC was as it seemed: an older model with an out-dated AI.

Dre swung his legs over the side of the bed and stood. He strode to the armchair next to the AGC but chose not to sit. A large bowl contained strawberries, plums, and mangoes. There was a pitcher of orange juice. But his attention was riveted on the long platter with two types of rice, some potatoes, salad, jerk chicken, curry chicken, and fish. And none of it was the cloned, artificial, or canned stuff. This was real. Organic. He couldn't believe his eyes. The last time he tasted real food was when Pops snuck some home from work. Dre heaped a helping on a plate and dug in.

The holo display blinked on. A commercial for a Virtual Vacation ran, this one toting the functionality of newly designed eye implants rather than wearables like smart contacts or glasses. When the ad ended, Ataxia Online's theme music piped into the room.

The display changed to Void Legion. Storm clouds gathered; lightning flickered; thunder let out an ominous rumble. A maelstrom formed. At its core was a black void from which lightning poured. The voidstorm swept across Mikander before ending above an ocean. When the waves subsided, there was an island surrounded by the voidstorm's remnants. The deep NPC voice announced a free trial and the new Simulated Reality feature, Total Immersion.

Dre watched, all the while imagining he was playing the game.

CHAPTER 4

"Well," Sidrie said, "now that you've seen the demo, what do you think? Are you ready to sign on? Time is of the essence."

Grinning, Dre pushed the Smart Glasses up on his forehead. "Is this real? This can't be real. You gotta be kidding."

A part of him was in awe of the possibilities before him. Another begged caution. But experiencing Void Legion firsthand was like playing VR for the first time. A dream come true. A rush. Dre could not help thinking that Pops would have loved it.

"No, I am not kidding," Sidrie replied dryly. "This is all very real. This," she gushed, gesturing to the room below them and its numerous Simulated Reality pods, "is Total Immersion, the culmination of decades of research, work, and billions of credits. This is the future, not just of gaming or entertainment, but of humankind."

Dre, Sidrie, and Dr. Redmond stood on an observation deck, overlooking the pod chamber with its pristine white walls and technicians wearing smart glasses and sterile coveralls. The silver polymer pods were at least the length of an average man, built like reclining coffins, with glass covering the portion where one might see a person from the waist up.

A tech at the closest pod studied her personal holo screen that hovered in front of her face before she touched a button on the projection. Along the length of the pod, a door slowly swung up. Dre pictured himself climbing into the thing. He rubbed his arms against a sudden prickle.

"It reminds me of Virtual Vaycays. A better version, but still–" Dre's memory of his first and only Virtual Vacation to Barbados with Mom and Pops was one he cherished. The experience had felt so real, down to the wind blowing through his hair, the smells, the music, the Crop Over carnival. Even the sun's heat. Despite avoiding the beach in VV, he had returned so tanned his skin had been like coffee for a few weeks.

"*That* is an insult." Sidrie's lip curled, her perfect face becoming an ugly twisted thing. She took a deep breath and clasped her hands. Her features smoothed. "If you must insist on such an inferior comparison, then multiply your Virtual Vacation experience by a thousand and you *might* get an inkling of time spent inside our game under Total Immersion."

"Does it replicate language like VV?"

"Almost every dialect, tongue… every nuance ever recorded." Sidrie beamed with pride. "We were meticulous. It's all part of what we call Information Memory or IM. You think of a thing and it's there, available to you as in real life, a part of your mind, a part of your knowledge."

"Impressive." Dre nodded appreciatively.

"And yet I haven't scratched the surface," Sidrie said. "The Total Immersion engine allows you to affect the physical game world itself. Spells can literally blow things up. Players can do something as massive as destroying a city, or as simple as leaving ruts in the road with their wagon wheels or footprints. Players tear up the very earth of a battlefield. And those effects remain until some other aspect of the world changes them. You aren't stuck with one way of doing things. Want to enter a dungeon? You don't have to go through the door. Tunnel into it.

"For all intents and purposes, you *become* a part of the world, a part of the game. Everything you do, from questing to leveling, from stats like the knowledge of a weapon's Damage Per Second or a tank's armor, is intuitive, as natural as simply living."

"Get the hell outta here. Oh, I'm sorry," Dre said to Sidrie's raised brow and disapproving glare. For the first time, he noticed the redolence of her perfume and the perfect mounds bursting from the V of her dress. They were as good any he'd ever seen in VPorn. He felt himself rise until his gaze met those dark, hawkish eyes. Face flushing, he looked away.

"This is more than a game," she said, mouth downturned in distaste. "More than life. Down to the AI, which adapts. She is ever learning, ever changing with her inhabitants. But without the flaws and issues that come with emotion."

"She?"

"I like to call her Estela." Sidrie's face brightened. "Because of her, the non-player characters have as much effect on the world as the players themselves. And not just the non-player characters who dole out information or help, but the monsters, the mobs themselves. You might still call them mobs, but they are no longer mindless cretins. Like you, they also change… grow.

"They are mostly autonomous. Leave villages or areas unchecked and one of the non-playable races like the dryads or nalarr might raise a queen or king of their own and declare war on others. Our world is truly persistent."

"We're talking about non-player characters and mobs here." Smirking, Dre gave her the side-eye. Sidrie nodded once. "NPCs and mobs," he repeated with a shake of his head, countless possibilities running through his mind, "doing things outside mere programming. Sounds like a recipe for more RNG rather than controlled situations. I got a love hate relationship with RNG."

"But isn't life one big Random Number Generator, most of the times?" Dr. Redmond asked.

Dre shrugged. "Is it? I never really gave it a lot of thought."

"That's a discussion for another day," Sidrie interjected.

"Agreed." Dr. Redmond nodded to her then returned his attention to Dre. "All this is made possible because of our combination of AI and TNT. Think of TNT as the life-blood of Total Immersion." He sounded like a proud father. "Our nanites circulate through every device and through the subject's body by way of the blood. Any stimuli experienced is passed along to the brain... the muscles... to the AI itself. The subjects then learn, whether they're artificial or organic. It's a delicate ecosystem, which has to be experienced."

"The demo wasn't a version of the game you'll play, just an idea of the capabilities. The game itself is far more advanced under Total Immersion. Testers have been known to forget they're in game. One of the reasons we request that players have a keepsake, a memento of the real world, something they hold dear, one we can replicate to keep them grounded."

Dre arched an eyebrow and muttered under his breath, "Y'all been watching too much Sci-Fi."

"Think about your time here," Dr. Redmond said. "You were unconscious for a week and hadn't used your extremities in that entire time. No walking, standing, holding anything... you get the idea. You had a broken arm. Yet, not long after you woke, you were able to get off the bed and walk, grab a fork and eat. No stiffness, unfamiliarity from muscles that hadn't been used in a week. You experienced no disorientation. No malnourishment. Why? Those dreams you had of doing normal activities? Some of them were not dreams at all. They were part of an environment conducive to the effects of TNT."

Dre studied the pods. "So, if I lift weights and exercise in Total Immersion, I'd be diesel in real life?"

"Diesel?" Redmond repeated with a grimace.

"Jacked." Dre flexed his bicep.

"Oh." The doctor cleared his throat. He regarded Dre with raised brows. "And you just said we watched too much Sci-Fi?"

Dre shrugged. "Won't know if you don't ask."

"Total Immersion is an experience," Sidrie said. "One in which a person could live out his life, his dreams, and never need the real world."

"Really?" Dre didn't quite know how to feel about the idea.

"Definitely," Sidrie said.

"The NDA and the waiver mentioned injuries and death," Dre said. "How's that work? Isn't it supposed to be a game?"

"Call it insurance," Sidrie said. "Like any NDA."

"I understand all that." Dre furrowed his brows. "What I'm asking is how do injuries and death work that makes a player and Equitane need the waiver?"

"Because some of your experience can affect real life." Sidrie gestured to the doctor. "Dr. Redmond can explain the details better than I."

"In-game wounds are visible, must be healed or treated, and recovery time depends on severity," Dr. Redmond said. "Your real-world body won't have the physical signs of injury, but as we mentioned, the nanites are receptors and can and will transfer an approximation of your pain from the game.

"However, we control the process, and while we limit the pain intensity to make the experience mostly enjoyable, we feel the stimuli is necessary for realism and to push the mind. Pain. Fear. The idea of injury. Threat of failure. The euphoria of victory. The adrenaline rush that comes with such things are all vital facets. Since we shoot for the full gamut of emotions, pain is a part of the process. Even limited."

Dre nodded. "I guess that could work."

"Some type of pain also serves an additional purpose," Dr. Redmond said. "Just like life, pain is a warning that you might be doing something incorrectly, protection of sorts against stupidity. If there were no consequences, players would attempt ridiculous things. We've seen it first-hand."

"Trying or doing the ridiculous is a draw for many," Dre argued. "Power fantasy. If we wanted everything the same as in reality then we wouldn't game."

"There's more than enough of the fantastic to satisfy any appetite," Dr. Redmond countered.

"Alright." Dre nodded. "How does HP work with this system of yours?"

Dr. Redmond turned his hands palms up and shook his head. "Do you have Hit Points in real life? The amount of damage a player or NPC could take is directly affected by their armor, strength, fitness, proficiency in certain skills, and a number of other factors, but there is no metered indicator."

"No indication for damage done or received at all?" Dre narrowed his eyes.

The doctor shook his head. "Numbers and meters? No. Information Memory will tell you the overall damage a weapon can deal and its Damage Per Second or DPS-"

"I know Damage Per Second means DPS," Dre said.

"I'd say I'm not a noob, but you know this already."

"Point taken." Lips pursed, Dr. Redmond nodded once before continuing, "As I was saying, you'll know a weapon's total damage and DPS when you initially possess it, but when you're fighting you won't see the damage delivered in numbers. Players must be diligent and look for the physical signs. We believe this particular twist on gaming adds realism, more tension, a heightened sense of danger."

Dre nodded. He could understand the thought process, particularly where danger was concerned. But there was a certain rush a player got when a boss was on its last few percent that he felt would be missing. Or the fear instilled by visibly depleted HP. Which was better? More enjoyable? He couldn't say, but it could make for an interesting discovery.

"And death?" He was still trying to wrap his head around no HP. *How would players know when to heal?*

"In-game death means loss of items in your possession at the time," Dr. Redmond said. "You're given an automated respawn location, and you can return to the spot you died to reclaim the items if someone hasn't found the remains."

Dre wasn't sure how he felt about the idea, but he guessed it could work. Something else bothered him. "Is there a real-world effect of dying?"

The doctor hesitated and glanced toward Sidrie, who nodded. "Respawning in-game after death can take a few hours for players under Total Immersion."

Dre shook his head in confusion and annoyance. "Didn't answer the question, but I'll bite. Why so long to respawn?"

Dr. Redmond took a deep breath. "Real-world recovery time. In-game death causes a disturbance in real-world brain function and can make the heart stop for a few seconds." Dre opened his mouth but was at a loss for words as the doctor continued, "TNT kicks in to fire your brain impulses and heart. Think of it like a defibrillator for both organs. The result is a short period of debilitation. We ensure the player is fully recovered before returning them to the game."

Dre snapped his mouth shut. Grimacing, he said, "No wonder you didn't wanna mention it. Who the hell would volunteer for that?"

"The right motivation can make a man try anything," Sidrie said.

"The recovery process has yet to fail," Dr. Redmond said. "We could shorten the recovery time, but it's possible for too many in-game deaths close together to cause loss of some brain functions in real life due to continual revival."

"Why even tell potential players about the side effects?" Dre watched the techs continue to work. He was thinking of refusing the offer, but these people had helped his family in his time of need. Mom would be dead if not for them.

"It's in the waiver," Dr. Redmond said. "But to be perfectly honest, we withheld such information at first. However, as with pain, we found testers were more likely to play recklessly, thinking they could simply revive indefinitely and continue on. We were forced to put a stop to that."

Dre thought of his side and arm. "Earlier, you mentioned recovery time for wounds. Mind explaining?".

"In game, minor cuts and bruises last seconds, healed by a mystic or by a health or rejuvenation potion. Something more serious takes longer. You'll suffer comparative debilitation. Use of sayyy, a broken arm or leg would be impossible until the mind outside the game says its healed, which is generally induced through TNT within minutes. The more you play, the better your body and TNT adapts, and the faster the process. Although, I must say that handicaps do make for interesting and challenging combat."

Dre smirked. "Challenging, maybe. Interesting? Fun? No."

"Depends on your idea of fun." Dr. Redmond shrugged. "For some people, such challenges *are* fun."

"If I said yes, how long are the sessions? A few hours?"

"Weeks for the first few. Then we expand to months," Dr. Redmond said.

"Weeks without ever coming up? And you control when I come and go?"

"Yes," Dr. Redmond said.

Dre took the Smart Glasses off his forehead. As good as the game and Total Immersion seemed, the idea of flatlining if he died in game bothered him. As did the time spent in game per session. The rest sounded too good to be true.

"At any other time, a chance to test this kinda tech would be no prob," Dre said. "A dream. I'd jump at it. But not with the way things are with Mom and Kai. Spending that long in game and the side effects of dying means I'm gonna have to say no. Sorry."

"Your mother and Kai are in the very best hands," insisted Dr. Redmond. "Any risk to you is minimal."

"I guess, but still, I gotta be here for them. To take care of them."

"By doing this, you will be," Sidrie said. "You'll be their hero."

"I'm not trying to be any kinda hero. I just wanna do right by them. And that means Mom seeing my face when she wakes up. Kai being with me. Not strangers."

"You could think of it like a job," Sidrie said. "A job that pays a million credits."

Dre opened and closed his mouth. The offer was

tempting. The money would solve so many problems. But there was his promise to Mom and Pops. He frowned as he considered it. *Playing the newest version of my favorite game, with tech that makes VR even better, and I get paid a mil?* It was too good to be true.

"Thanks, but I can't," Dre said without further hesitation.

"Think about where you live," Sidrie said, voice flat, eyes cold. "Coney Island is the last remaining place with a First Ward not overrun by DeGens. But it will be, soon enough. And it will be like all the rest of the First Ward, filled with crime and disease. More than it already is." Dre made to speak but she overrode him. "Alphonso did not leave you much when he died. And Theresa spent it all trying to keep those twins alive in defiance of Better Tomorrow. You had to drop out of college, work a dead-end job. A job you acquired only because the people hiring you owed your father. You have no money, you cannot afford—"

"Bullshit." Dre ground his teeth, his face hot. He would rather be anywhere than here. His mind reeled as he considered just how much the woman knew, how much she was playing him all along. He rubbed at his Two Ring even as the cruel knife of betrayal stabbed him in the gut. "It's all bullshit. All the caring for them, and saving us… it's all bullshit so you could run a guilt trip?"

"Watch your mouth, boy," Dr. Redmond began.

"I'm not anyone's boy," Dre shot back. "I'm a grown man."

"I'll take it from here, doctor." Sidrie gestured to the man. Dr. Redmond nodded and made his exit. The door to the room slid open then closed behind him with a whisper.

"Look," Dre said.

"You're right. You have Theresa and Kai to consider." Sidrie watched him with those hawkish obsidian eyes, her face expressionless. The blue light flashed in her eyes.

"Good, so—"

"Dr. Redmond is on his way to remove Theresa from the life support and transfection machines," Sidrie said in her monotone. "I'm tempted to have them remove any organs we cloned. Or should I let her keep them?" Before Dre replied, she carried on, "Someone will get Kai for you. My driver will drop you off together in the First Ward. Or he can turn Theresa over to the Family Planning Corps first, and *then* drop off you and Kai. I will also inform NAIL of her crime and make certain they refuse to renew your green cards."

Dre tried to process her words. Images spun through his mind, each one more gruesome than the last. He saw himself and Mom led away by NAIL agents, deported back to Barbados. Kai was bawling the entire time as FPC took her, most likely to have her sent off to a foster home. He saw the FPC doctors performing an abortion, sterilizing Mom. DeGens attacked him and Kai, dragged them both into tunnels beneath the city. His legs became like jelly.

"Good luck." Sidrie turned on her heels to leave.

Dre grabbed her arm and squeezed. "You can't do this!"

Sidrie hissed. She tried to pull away but could not. Her face became a mask of rage. And pain.

For all of a second, Dre considered putting her in a chokehold. *But then what? It won't get Mom the help she needs. It won't make our situation better.* He let go, his arm quivering. "I-I'm sorry. Please, please, don't do this."

Grimacing and rubbing at her arm, Sidrie stared at him. Those black eyes were pitiless beneath blade sharp brows.

Dre deflated. "Just promise you're gonna take care of my family and I'll do whatever you want. I swear."

Sidrie smiled, a cruel, twisted curve of her lips. "Deal. Now, sign the waiver and the NDA. And if you ever touch me again, I will have you and them killed slowly."

Shoulders sagging, Dre put on the Smart Glasses. He gestured in front of his face. The virtual screen popped up. With his eyes he navigated down to the waiver and the NDA. He hesitated. And then took a deep breath and signed. The glasses took a retina scan to add to his signature.

"Thank you." Sidrie's expression actually seemed sincere.

Dre ground his teeth at the woman's depravity. *Don't thank me, bitch,* he thought. Something inside him swelled. Something primal, dark, and craving violence. He thought of what it would be like to toss her out of a moving PT or beat her bloody and drag her down into the First Ward and watch DeGens feast on her body. He squeezed his eyes tight against the urge to smash her pretty face.

He found solace in the idea of playing Ataxia Online again, but this time to help himself and his family. He was among the best. It would be one of the easiest things he'd ever done.

"Any regrets you harbor now will be gone when you're in the game," she said.

"Whatever." Dre shrugged. He wanted to ask why she was doing this but didn't bother. Her reasons were of no consequence. Only her actions. "Can I at least see Kai and Mom before I begin?"

"Of—"

"Not through a holo. The real thing."

Sidrie regarded him for a moment, and then smiled, but it did not touch her eyes. "Certainly." She indicated the door. "One of the guards will escort you." He made to move. "Dre?" He stopped. "The better you do, the more time I will grant you with them. Do exceptionally well and I will also see to it that NAIL renews your green cards. Impress me. Reach level ten and clear Imanok Sanctum in the new zone on Maelpith Island within a few days." She smiled mirthlessly. "At that level, you should find the GUM pairs quite interesting. Not to mention our updated Emperor KiGyaba." She left through the opposite door.

Dre followed a gray-uniformed security guard down a long hall whose air carried a whiff of disinfectant. The guard had to be in his early twenties and did not seem to pay much attention to anyone or anything. Dre wondered how capable the guard was with the Glock 60 sidearm he carried.

Techs and business men and women bustled by, lost in their conversations and thoughts. Other than the occasional AGC, there were no other robots or androids, not even the latest models with eerily realistic skin. Dre supposed they were relegated to specific halls and paths to keep them away from humans.

To Dre's left, a line of windows offered a view of Downtown Brooklyn. The sky directly above was clear and blue, but farther out, at the city's outskirts, smog formed a gray fleece that stretched to the ground to obscure the world beyond. Vacuums atop the buildings kept the murk at bay. As did the numerous massive EVTOLS that roved along the edges of the smog wall, equipped with similar technology.

Equitane Towers were among the tallest skyrises, boasting two hundred and forty floors. PTs zipped along the invisible skylanes of the Upper Ward levels in an endless stream between the cluster of shiny building facades. A bulky Airbus maneuvered toward a docking bay in the Fifteenth Ward.

Down in the Tenth Ward, which housed most of

the shops, condos, and apartments for the middle class, pedestrians traversed glass-covered skywalks. A Maglev pulled into a station housed within a building's belly. Hover cars glided along the broad, alloy thoroughfares at that district level.

Far below, beyond blocks worth of empty space around the bases of each skyrise, emergency lights flickered on police drone patrols. Beneath the drones were the dark, ancient streets of the First Ward. Dre shivered.

The guard turned the corner into a quieter portion of the Equitane Towers. He led Dre to the far end of the carpeted hall and stopped before a door. The guard put his eye to a retina scan, and the light above the door changed from red to green.

"In you go," the guard said.

Kai was sitting in an armchair, playing Munsters and Minions. "Dre!" she exclaimed when she glanced toward the door. Dre broke into a wide grin. She leapt to her feet and dashed to him.

"Hey, Bunny!" Dre snatched Kai up, pulled her close, and hugged her tight.

Kai clung to him, her arms around his neck. She buried her face into his shoulder. She was warm, so alive, and smelled clean and fresh with a hint of vanilla.

Unbidden tears trickled down Dre's face. "I missed you sooooo much. I love you."

"Me too."

He held her like that for a bit before he set her down. "Let me take a look at you."

Kai was wearing blue jeans, a pink Margo the Minion-Master tee, and a pair of sneakers. She watched him with those big brown eyes.

Dre nodded to her head. "Who braided your hair?" The cornrows went straight back and fell past her shoulders.

"The android that comes to clean my room and bring me food every day. You like it?" Kai smiled and turned so he could see the back.

"I love it."

"Dre?" She faced him, mouth downturned.

"Yes, Bunny?"

"Where's Mommy? When are we gonna see her?"

Dre smiled. "We're gonna do that right now."

"Yay!"

Dre took her hand, headed back the way he came, and knocked on the closed door. It slid open. The same guard led them.

Dre memorized their route through the building to an elevator and up ten floors, an entire Ward level, then a few turns along carpeted halls to a wing busy with doctors in robes and techs in coveralls. The guard passed them off to Dr. Redmond, who took them to an area where they had to put on sterile coveralls. From there, they traversed another hall past a few guards armed with G60 pistols and NGSAR5 assault rifles. They stopped at a silver door. Dr. Redmond let them in.

The room was the pristine white chamber from the holo. It smelled of medicine. Mom was in the same position on the bed, body mostly covered by a blanket. Tubes and lines trailed from her mouth and nose to several machines. Floating above her were the holos displaying her vitals.

"Mommy!" Kai pulled away from Dre and ran to Mom's side, her little feet pattering on the white tiles.

It took everything for Dre not to follow suit. But he was certain Sidrie was watching. He refused to give the woman the satisfaction of seeing how vulnerable he was in this situation. He breathed deep, swallowed against the lump in his throat, and crossed to Mom's bedside.

Mom's eyes were closed. She looked... peaceful. If

not for the steady rise and fall of her chest, he might have thought she was already gone.

Kai stroked Mom's cheek and whispered for her to get better. Dre leaned down, past his sister, and kissed Mom's forehead. Her flesh was cool.

He stepped to Kai's other side and bent again to kiss the covers atop the swell of Mom's belly. Then he took her hand in his. Kai moved as close as she could to rest her little hand on theirs.

"It's Dre and Kai, Mom," he said. "We're here for you. We love you. Squeeze my hand, move your eyes or something if you hear me." He waited, ever hopeful, but her eyeballs didn't shift beneath her lids and her hand remained limp. He hung his head. "I'm so sorry this happened. If I'd been paying attention to the road… Forgive me.

"You're gonna get better. And Regi and Rayne will be fine. I'm gonna make sure of it. You and Pops always said never let anyone take advantage of me, and I'm not, but these people want me to play the new version of Ataxia. If I do it, then they'll make sure you're all well taken care of. I know I promised not to play anymore, but I gotta. It's the only way to keep y'all safe.

"I'm sorry, Mom. I really am. One day, when this is all done, I look forward to seeing you smile, and holding the twins, and hugging Kai. I love you so much."

He stood there a while, holding Mom's hand. He ached. Imagining a world without her or Kai was a world without color, without life.

At some point Dr. Redmond told them they had to go. Kai kicked and screamed and cried. Dre picked her up by her underarms and pulled her in close, hugged her tight, and whispered soothing words. Eventually, Kai calmed. Dre took Kai back to her room, comforted her again, kissed her forehead, and told her he'd soon return. Then he left with

Dr. Redmond.

******

Dressed in spandex shorts, a shivering Dre rubbed his bare arms against the coldness of the pod room. If not for the Two Ring, he might have felt completely naked. He was glad the techs had accepted it as the memento to help with the transition to and from the virtual world.

Sidrie Malikah was up on the observation deck with a line of doctors, senior techs, and several men and women in expensive suits. Her last words stuck with him. 'The better you do, the more time you get to spend with your family.' *Reach level ten and clear Imanok Sanctum.* He repeated the goal.

The pod room bustled with purposeful activity and the breathless murmur of expectancy. A few of the pods were no longer empty. Several people around Dre's age, or perhaps a few years younger or older, waited their turn. Dressed as he was, some chattered with techs or amongst themselves while others preferred to be alone. Like him, a myriad of biometric tatts covered the exposed portions of their bodies like corrupted data.

Dre frowned. "Hughey?" He headed to his best friend who appeared as comfortable in underwear as a cat was in water. "What're you doing here?"

"Dreee!" Hughey smiled bashfully. "I signed up for the free trial. Remember?"

Grimacing, Dre glanced from Hugh to the pods and back again. "Oh."

"Isn't that why you're here?"

"Not exactly."

"They invited you to alpha test, didn't they? Dammmmmn, homie." Hughey clapped Dre on the back. "I shoulda known. You being the man and all. This should be a breeze for you."

"Maybe. We'll see."

"We'll see?" Hughey deadpanned. "Really, dawg? You feeling alright?" Hughey shook his head. "Shit's gonna be sweet, just like old times. There're rumors that Just Blaze is here. So is Dante Blackblade. All the top players."

Dre opened and closed his mouth. He glanced up at Sidrie, who simply watched him with those predatory obsidian eyes. *How many others did you force or trick into playing? Does anyone outside know?*

Two techs stepped up to him and Hughey. "It's time."

"Hey, Dre," Hughey called as he followed his tech, "I know you're Mr. Solo, but if you want some company this time around, or run into some probs, look for me in Kituan. The same old char, Meritus Killgain, doing what I love."

Dre nodded glumly and then allowed the tech to lead him to a pod. A200 was stenciled into the side. He hesitated when the pod door swung up. "This doesn't fill up with some kinda fluid, does it?"

"Does it matter?"

Dre licked his lips. "Yeah, it does. I have a thing about being underwater."

"No need to worry about that here."

"Alright." After a deep breath to calm his heart, Dre climbed in and lay down facing up, the polymer cold against his skin.

"Remember to relax," the tech said, hovering over him. "You'll feel a few pricks, and then you're all set."

"Try telling that to yourself when you're the one in a fucking plastic coffin," Dre muttered.

The tech smiled and left. Dre waited, stomach fluttering the entire time. The long door to the pod swung down slowly and smoothly, the world growing smaller and smaller above him, until it was just him peering through the glass at the blank white ceiling. A helmet with a transparent visor slid down over his face. The visor slowly dimmed until he was left in complete darkness.

A whirring sound echoed all along the pod. Dre started and had the sudden urge to get out, to punch the glass and hope it broke. Even as he had the thought, a hundred needles stabbed into him from beneath his back, his neck, his ass, his legs. Dre screamed. And then the pain faded.

A light appeared. *Is that in my mind? Or the ceiling?*

The NPC voice from the trailer said, "Welcome to Ataxia Online 2, Void Legion."

The world shot forward. The light swallowed him.

CHAPTER 5

Dre stood in a room surrounded by mirrors. He was rendered in graphics impossible to differentiate from the real world, from his low fade haircut and impeccable waves, his broad nose, thick eyebrows, down to his caramel complexion, loincloth, and black aether ring. Knowledge clicked in the back of his mind. Information Memory. It told him this was character customization.

He considered his possible resemblances. Immediately, his features shifted through countless iterations drawn from Mikanderan races. *Holy shit.* Dre grinned. And then froze.

Wide-eyed, he touched his face. He *felt* his face. Reveling in the smoothness of his skin, and the sensations of actually *being,* he ran his fingers along his cheeks, his nose, his brows, his mouth. He pinched himself. And gasped at the sensation. A small twinge. Barely noticeable but noticeable all the same.

Get. The fuck. Outta here.

He looked down at himself, elbows bent, palms up, head shifting from side to side to take it all in. He took off the aether ring. The engraving with his name was there. As was the 2. It *was* his Two Ring. Shaking his head in disbelief, he put it back on.

He sucked in a deep breath and blew onto his palm. The air was warm. Placing a hand on his chest slightly off center to the left revealed a steady heartbeat.

And then he farted. It smelled like rotten eggs.

He burst into laughter, the sound echoing. If he harbored any doubts as to how real Simulated Reality could be, then the ability to push from his stomach, fart, and the subsequent stench, blew them away. He frowned. *If I can fart...* He shook his head. *Nah, having to take a shit in game would be taking it a little too far.* He hoped there'd be no such need.

Now, what should I play this time? A gargant?

Information Memory responded. His eyes widened at the scope of it. He was a walking encyclopedia. Whether lore or other practical aspects, IM was there to be accessed by mere thought in a seamless transition as if he'd been a part of Mikander all his life. No longer was there a Heads-Up Display or User Interface. Everything was in his brain, presented visually, like a holographic recollection.

His reflection shifted and grew to one of the twelve-foot colossuses. There was a bit of disorientation, but no pain or any other type of feeling as the change occurred. Fur covered his body, shifting from shades of brown, to blue, to black, to gray. Background for the race rippled through his thoughts.

Originating from the southeastern continent of Korbash, the gargants are descendants of the original colossus race, the titans. By refusing to join the Colossus Alliance in the Slave Wars, the gargants avoided their progenitors' doom during the first Void Cataclysm. Smart fellows. Gargants are naturally a hardy people, their prevailing traits being intelligence, endurance, skin like stone, and brute strength. The combination makes them resistant to stuns.

Contrary to their appearance, gargants seek peace and knowledge. The greatest libraries and schools in Mikander belong to the gargants. Told you they were smart.

Despite their practice of pacifism and tolerance, it would be a mistake to overlook the gentle gargants in a fight. How one could overlook a giant is still a mystery. From two years old, every gargant trains extensively in combat to put their strength to use and balance their great intellect. Like the gurashi, the gargants hate slavery and are willing to defend the weak.

The gargants control the Ostenia dominion on the continent of Korbash, their lands mostly lush and bountiful, their mountains rugged.

He always liked the gargants, especially when the chosen class was a marauder equipped with a quaker: a specially-crafted massive double-bladed axe almost as large as the race themselves. In Ataxia's old version, most people who chose a gargant used them as a tank: a high HP, high defense player who soaked up damage and held the aggro or hate of the monster, preventing it from attacking other party members.

Those same people preferred reaver and marauder classes for the tank role. They had taunts and various skills to generate threat, or hate, as some called it. These skills got the monster's attention or aggro, forcing it to attack the tank. They also had abilities to pull the creature back to them should some other weak player, a glass cannon like a sorcerer or cutthroat, happened to pull aggro from doing too much damage or attacking too soon. Although the best tanks prided themselves on not allowing any player to pull aggro from them.

After a long look at himself as a gargant while considering its advantages, he decided against the race. For the playstyle he had in mind, which involved agility and speed as well as survival, their size seemed too cumbersome.

He noted that the game now intuitively assigned four starting attributes. Strength, vitality, agility, and aether.

Fiddling with his appearance changed the first three, determined by some unknown algorithms. The last, aether, the power used to wield magic in Mikander, was determined by racial bloodline.

He nodded his approval for the attribute change, as it meant no two characters would ever be the same. The verdict was out on lack of bars, meters, or numbers to indicate damage or health. He still felt their absence meant diminished excitement or fear factor.

Information Memory confirmed Dr. Redmond's words. Signs of health depletion would be reflected in debilitation, injuries, and such. Lack of aether meant an inability to cast spells until the required replenishment.

He tried to imagine healing with the changes. *What would the signs be for Heal over Time spells?* HoTs gave a small tick of health every few seconds, like an IV drip, easing the pressure of constantly casting larger, direct heals. The difference made it easier for mystics to conserve aether. Now, healing would be that much harder and required another level of skill, focus, and perception. In ways, the change made for more engaging play. He liked it.

Dre thought of the many players he knew who lived for knowing their Damage Per Second. DPS had also been a love of his when he first played his sorcerer. He smiled as he pictured one of his old raid leaders yelling for the DPS to burn a boss down when it hit five or ten percent of its HP. An undeniable thrill existed in that call.

Often, the reason for the call to burn was due to a mechanic where the monster in question had a trigger, activated either by time or by health. When the trigger activated, the monster would enrage or grow so powerful it would kill everyone in the raid in one shot. A wipe. To prevent a wipe, the monster had to die within seconds of reaching that critical point before it unleashed its raid-killing ability.

He frowned. *How would players deal with all these situations now? Look for a tell?*

He pondered the answer before he dismissed the thought and returned to the matter at hand. Deciding on a class. *You could always play a skinny colossus. A skinny colossus?* He frowned. The idea sounded ridiculous. The projection showed exactly how ridiculous. Too strong a wind might topple him over. Not exactly a fear-inspiring look.

Maybe, a gurash?

Again, the shift, IM, and this time he was the distant cousin of the gargant, measuring some eight or nine feet in height, with a more muscular build. Gurashi sported long bushy manes and had faces like lions, including canines. Typically, they were brown, green, or red, the red an indication of noble bloodlines. Some were a mixture, like marble, and considered impure. He shook his head.

Dre considered the centaur-like dresdori and winged yurids. He didn't bother with humans. *Who played a game like this to be the same?*

Finally, he settled on an erada with dark magenta skin, slender body, wedge-shaped ears, and thick curled ram-like horns to either side of his head. The average erada was just over six feet tall. Eradae always fit his image of succubi and incubi and gave him a body with which he was more comfortable. IM kicked in.

An air of mysticism surrounds the eradae, children of the assassin goddess, Nif and her lover, the god, Jerad. Once, they were a part of the kora race. But when Jerad chose the enemy's cause in the Divinity War, Nif did not agree and fled with those korae loyal to her and renamed them the eradae. She chose the Khertahka dominion as their new home. There, they hid for over a thousand years, keeping to the night.

Such action brought about an evolutionary change.

Their ossicones, two horny (not that type of horny) protuberances on either side of young erada heads, shed their hair and became pure bone. Not only did the newly-formed horns maintain the race's echolocation ability, but they gained healing properties when ingested. As such, the eradae became a hunted race when the gods disappeared after the Divinity War.

In that vacuum of power, the colossus races, led by the titans, rampaged and plundered much of Mikander. They allied with the newly named grand korae. Together, they enslaved the eradae, the dresdori, the nalarr, and the dryads.

But then came the human general, Aureliano Grendesh, the formation of the Grendesh Coalition, and the Great Slave Wars. And a lot of kicking ass and taking names in which the Coalition was victorious. In the end, only two colossus descendants survived: the gargants and the gurashi. The grand korae were dealt tremendous losses and fled to the Ouroboros and Isfet Mountains.

Over the past centuries, the eradae have worked hard to become strong, and have sworn to never be enslaved again. To this day, they fight their arch nemeses, the grand korae.

He thought about being a female erada. The shift occurred, and he was a blue-skinned woman with longer elegant horns and breasts. Breasts! Pretty, perky ones, to be sure. He giggled and shook his shoulders, admiring the youthful bounce.

Brows furrowed, he reached down to the loincloth. His eyes grew wide. *Nope. This ain't right. I like my dick. Thank you, very much.* He reverted to his former self.

For his actual features, he thought of himself: triangular face with a defined chin, high cheekbones, no facial hair, deep brown eyes, bushy brows, blob of a nose as if God took a gob of clay and used his face for target practice on a bad day. Not the best-looking guy at a party but not the ugliest either. Pretty boys drew too much attention. As did the grotesque. The right amount of each, though, and one goes unnoticed. Perfectly fine. Rather than his fade and waves, he added long cornrow braids that fell straight back past his neck.

He nodded his approval at the changes and then considered which class to play. Only to discover a big change in Void Legion's class mechanics. No longer was a player restricted to the class they picked. They could learn the skills of any class. The problem was acquiring the skill shards, the necessary effective attributes, mastering the weapons, and the time needed to become proficient in the skills, which made it preferable to stick with one class, but later down the line, given time, the possibilities were near limitless. It would take years, decades, perhaps, but the power... he could only begin to dream.

Skill shards piqued his interest. They didn't exist in the old version of Ataxia. With the thought came the knowledge. Skill shards looked like gems and contained the skill in its pure aether form. They could be obtained in a variety of ways: killing particular monsters until the player found one on the corpse, treasure chests, the Auction Market, or they could be traded between players or NPCs. He liked the idea.

Another change he noted was for stat points. Their allocation now happened automatically. Speed, strength, aether, and vitality were basic attributes given a set amount every level per ten levels with the earlier bloodline considerations part of the calculation. Those base sets gained one point every ten levels. Additions to those bases, as well as any other attributes gained, like knowledge, endurance, and charisma were all determined by practice and personality.

If you wanted to become good at anything, then you did that thing. If you wanted to increase will and heart then you had to take risks. Be brave. Want more stamina? Run your ass off. You could start off at a disadvantage in aether pool and spell ability but surpass someone whose genealogy supported it.

This idea was also reflected in skill effect shards. These had been in the old version of the game and were crafted by hierkaneers by way of Genesis Engines. They added attributes to a skill. These effects could now be further enhanced by constant practice. The examples were exhausting. He liked the idea, although he cringed to think about the grind of exercise, strength training, research, spell chucking, and the like.

IM clicked.

Strength: Levels 1 − 10:
Physical power increases at +2 per level
Vitality: Levels 1 − 10:
Health increases at +2 per level
Agility: Levels 1 − 10:
Speed and Haste increases at +2 per level
Aether: Levels 1 − 10:
Aether power increases at +2 per level

He had three available innate skills, but first came the knowledge on the part aether played.

Aether is Mikander's blood, flowing underground in fault lines like veins and spilling into the air. Aether is the key for all abilities. Aether is life. Some claim aether is alive.

Replenishment:
All Mikanderans siphon aether from the air. Although this happens naturally all the time, actively focusing and practicing this ability increases collection and the amount stored.

Aether Absorption:

When a monster is killed, it releases some aether back into the world. This aether automatically seeks out the killer and seeps into his skin if he is within five hundred feet of the corpse, adding to his storage of aether.

Aether Overload:

Mikanderans are born with the ability to store a small amount of excess aether beyond normal capacity. Overload also serves a second purpose. Beginning at level 10, Mikanderans can use powerful skills that can only be activated by way of Aether Overload.

Dre made to choose his favorite class in every game: sorcerer. And was handed yet another startling difference. Although a player could pick a class he desired, as was typical for most games, he did not start off with any of its skills. He had to acquire the shards first.

Furthermore, a skill requiring a weapon could not be utilized until the player had the corresponding weapon in his possession, which activated the innate connection between aether, said weapon, the player, and the skill. It was the same for any Mikanderan. The one difference were abilities that did not rely on such a relationship. Hand-to-hand combat, Concealment, various types of dash abilities, and others like them.

The idea of such an ecosystem was quite impressive. Although starting without a weapon was unlike most games he'd played, he relished the challenge. Even if he had to steal a knife or a sword, he would get *something*.

He cycled through the classes, immediately dismissing the melee. Being up close to monsters wasn't his thing. Neither was healing, which ruled out the mystic. He had no interest in the use of Damage Over Time skills or DoTs, the hallmark of a shadowmancer. As DPS, he loved direct damage. Burst damage. Sorcerers, windwalkers, and stormcallers were his favorites. The newest class caught his attention.

Cannoneer

As a cannoneer, you're a heavy-armor-wearing, big-weapon-toting, running-circles-strafing, get-some-yelling, high DPS son of a gun. Woooo! You have massive Area of Effect skills and a constant supply of aether-generated firepower.

If you want to nuke a battlefield and your sorcerer is off wooing some crafter to get a new chakram, then a cannoneer is the class for you. In fact, a cannoneer would argue that with him in your group, you don't need no stinking sorcs.

In PvP, your victims will cry that you're Overpowered. They'll run to Mommy. But are you really OP? Or is it skill? Are you just so nice, they should've named you twice? Grab an aether cannon and find out.

Dre smiled as an example of a cannoneer bloomed in his mind. He held an aether cannon, the weapon epic in size, its barrel the length and width of his body. He had the weapon waist high with his left arm outstretched, hand tight around the topmost horizontal handle, while the fingers of his right gripped a matching handle to the cannon's rear above a circular ammo drum. His index finger hovered over the trigger built into that rear assembly. Beside his left forearm was the battery pack that powered the cannon, allowing it to fire korbitanium projectiles or energy bursts generated by aether. If someone made a cross between a BFG from the latest DOOM game and a minigun, it would be the aether cannon.

It was strange to behold a regular Mikanderan with an aether cannon. Like the quaker axe, it belonged to a group of relics called hierkas that were specially crafted in Genesis Engines. Such items possessed the capability to harness greater amounts of aether than normal. The best hierka items were typically reserved for Grendesh Coalition Vindicators.

Originally, the advanced tech could only be found on the scaled monstrosities, the draconids, who reminded Dre of the rare humanoid dragonkin, except draconids were gray with fluorescent colors threading through their bodies like infected veins. Armed with such empowered magic and weapons, the draconids had taken a chunk of Northern Mikander, defeating countless Coalition armies dating back to the very first Draconid War when the creatures had emerged from a voidstorm and began the first Void Cataclysm. They had a firm grip of their territory, where they not only used the Genesis Engines to craft more powerful items, but also to terraform the world to suit them.

On cue with his thoughts, the cannoneer recollection shifted into a gameplay demo. A cannoneer strafed, dived, and rolled, all the while firing the weapon. An array of skills was on full display, first in single shots, then in combos. The demo ended with ultimate abilities accessed by Aether Overload. Apocalypse at level one hundred. Aether Fusillade at level fifty. At level ten, there was Stand and Deliver.

Grinning, he imagined wielding them all. The DPS would be epic. He didn't need any more convincing. He'd found his new baby.

Next, he checked the list of basic life skills and professions. There was alchemy, herbalism, mining, blacksmithing, woodworking, woodcutting, leathersmithing, skinning, jewelsmithing, tailoring, weaving, scavenging, and so much more. If he wanted to be a bibliophile, that was there too. The premise, as with everything else, was for the player to practice whatever it was he desired and he'd automatically build the skill. Dre had no real interest in any of them. He wouldn't be playing that long.

For starter armor, he had a basic tunic and pants

whose colors he could change. Of note was that armor and inventory did carry weight impediments at some point. But again, increasing his strength would help alleviate the restrictions.

Or you could wear lighter shit. Or not try to carry around every single damned thing you find. He shook his head.

As with most things, the inventory itself was activated through Information Memory. Thinking of and acting out the part of removing or placing an item in the inventory made it so within an instant. It was odd they'd chosen this method, having attempted to stress a realistic feel, but he understood there were some things about gaming that needed to remain as they were for sheer convenience and enjoyment. Sometimes, you didn't need to remake the wheel, just enhance it.

Finally, he settled on an In-Game Name, the one he always used. Drelan Frost. He smiled at the IGN, ready to enter the world of Mikander and Ataxia Online in all its glory, ready to do the thing that came naturally. Pops often said that each man had a calling, something he was born to do, and those who found theirs were lucky.

"I was born to game," he said aloud. "Watch me work. Begin."

Everything faded.

Drelan Frost woke to the malodor of burning wood. Coughing, he cupped a hand over his mouth and nose and scrambled from his bed. Smoke poured from beneath his closed door, crept through the sides, rising, coiling like a serpentine specter. The crack beneath the door glowed a smoldering, demon-eyed red.

A part of him wanted to treat this all as just part of

a game. Something not as dire as it seemed. His racing heart screamed otherwise. The heat, the smoke, and the stench screamed otherwise. The *feel* of the warm and rough wood beneath his feet, the way his chest heaved, the fact that he *breathed,* screamed otherwise.

With coughs wracking his chest, he grabbed his boots from near the bed and tugged them on. By the time he stood, the thick gray smoke was filling the room, an expanding blob creeping across the ceiling. His eyes stung; his throat dried. Hunched over, he tried to reach the door. Only to be driven back by the encroaching heat and the crackle of the hungry fire out in the hall.

Forced onto all fours, he crawled toward the lone window. Smoke seeped through floorboards that were hot to the touch. And growing hotter.

"Mom! Beketia!" he yelled upon reaching the window.

He frowned at the names. Images bloomed. Mom was an electric blue erada whose eyes always smiled. Beketia, his sister, was royal blue. He had memories of them, feelings about them. An entire life's worth. The need to find and save them pressed down on him.

"Mom! Beketia," he shouted, louder this time.

No one replied. Or had they?

Brows furrowed, he waited, and let out clicking noises with his tongue. It was a strange thing to do, yet felt natural. An echo sprang up. A reverberation within the room that he couldn't quite place. With it, he swore he could make out certain objects. Wondering about the noise and the effect brought the knowledge that it was echolocation at work. An erada trait.

Thoughts racing, he considered his options. The best bet? Through the window. From there, he could get to their bedroom across the sloped roof of the makeshift veranda.

70

Out in the hall, the fire was a monster now. Roaring. He raised up, felt past the curtain, unlatched the window. And stopped. The dawn sky bled.

Rising heat reminded him of the fire, knocked him from his momentary lapse. He climbed through onto the veranda roof. He was greeted by char's effluvium, the hellish hues of several other fires that lit the town of Niba, gouts of smoke pouring into the sky, the discordant chorus of chaos from desperate throats, and the first gong of a bell's mournful dirge.

He stood transfixed for mere seconds, as people dashed down the street, before he remembered the task at hand. Balancing himself against the roof's slant, and the slippery wooden shingles, he hurried as best he could to the other bedroom window, a shiver running through him as he considered the ground yawning below. He pushed on the window. The damned thing was locked.

"Shit."

He got on his tiptoes and peered in, but thick smoke obscured his view. He could just make out the bed. Frost rapped on the windowpane and waited. When there was no answer, he looked around, hoping to find a piece of branch from the nearby tree or any other thing with which he could break the glass.

When the search proved fruitless, he pulled off his tunic, wrapped it around his fist and lower arm, and punched. The glass shattered. Smoke poured out. Shielding his eyes, he took care not to cut himself, reached in, and unlatched the window. He hoisted himself up and in.

"Tia? Mom?"

No answer. Again, he made the clicking sound, the action as normal as speech. He thought he could make out something in the murk. Objects. Impressions brought about by more than his sight.

71

The smoke was billowing black now. Choking. He staggered his way over to the bed, but neither his mother nor his sister was there. He spun in a circle, thoughts frantic. *Where could they have gotten to?* There was no way they could have made it out the door with the infernal flame beast waiting to feast.

He got down on his knees again, hoping the lessons in school had been right, that the position could truly help against the stinging, stinking smoke. He spied a mound in a corner near the closet. His breath caught in his throat. He swallowed even as he scrabbled toward the shape, pleading for the wellbeing of whomever it was.

When he reached the person, he turned them. It was Beketia, her royal blue skin flushed. Her chest rose and fell, but her eyes were closed. Pressure eased from him. Barely.

"Drelan," Mom croaked from the closet's dark confines.

Squinting, he made out her arm, head, and horns. Frost scrabbled to her. She was sucking in great breaths, the sound of each one a hoarse moan from deep within her chest. Cold fingers crept down his spine.

He squeezed her closed fist. "I'm here, Mom. I'll get you out of here. You and Tia."

"Bek... Beketia first. And... and take this." She pulled her fist away and reached up.

He opened his palm. She dropped a pouch into it. He stuffed the pouch down the side of his boot.

"Your sister," Mom said. "Save your sister then come back for me."

Frost nodded reluctantly. He squeezed her hand again. "I'm gonna be back. I promise."

He crawled back to Beketia. Staying low, he grabbed her by the armpits and dragged her toward the window, his throat burning now with every cough, eyes mere slits that

72

watered nonstop.

A crash echoed from the direction of the room door. It hung on one hinge. Flames licked all around it, clamored to enter, to devour all within. Heat beat from the opening.

A quick glance at the closet revealed his mother as she crawled toward him. He wanted to drop Tia and help, but Mom shook her head.

"Go," she mouthed.

Teeth gritted, stomach roiling, Frost complied. He pulled his sister up and onto the window sill, letting her hang with her head and upper body outside. He squeezed through the space beside her and out onto the roof.

Flames surged through the window to his room, the heat making him throw his hand up over his face. His lapse was momentary. Spurred on, he grabbed his sister and pulled and shifted, almost slipping and falling on several occasions before he finally got her through and onto the roof. He pulled her halfway down, away from the windows.

"Tia. Tia." He shook her desperately. "Beketia! Wake up! Pleeease."

But her eyes remained closed. He had to get back to Mom now. He knew it. But he could not leave Tia on the roof.

A crash echoed as something inside the house fell, sending shudders through the structure. Left with little choice, he turned Tia until her legs pointed toward the roof's edge. He hurriedly got a hold of her nightgown before she slid down. Positioned above her head, he hooked his arms under her armpits, and lowered himself.

Inch by creeping inch, he shifted his butt and legs and worked his way down the roof until her feet dangled in midair. In moments, she became so heavy that his arms and shoulders burned. He refused to let go. He could not give in. Not now. *All I gotta do is lower you down, then I can go for Mom.*

73

He was almost at the very edge, Tia's slender form like five hundred pounds. *A little more. Just a little more.* His grip gave way. He snatched for Tia. And missed. The move pitched him over the side.

Yelling, blood thundering in his ears, he tried to twist, to somehow cushion his fall. The impact knocked the wind from his body. A jolt of pain shot through his shoulder and side, but luckily, he'd somehow avoided landing on his head. Lights danced in his vision.

He gathered himself and crawled to Tia. She seemed to have landed feet first, as they were no bruises or broken bones he could pick out. She was still breathing.

"Over here!" Someone yelled. There was a rush of blue-sleeved arms as Azureguards helped him and Beketia, dragging them to safety.

Fire devoured the house's innards and vomited acrid black and gray smoke. Wood creaked and cried. The blaze writhed with life, becoming a roaring infernal of pure flame, the windows its demonic eyes, the front door its gaping red and orange maw. It swelled as it consumed, until it shot through the roof, leaped to the adjoining homes, reached to the sky. Crackling. Popping. The front of the house collapsed.

"Mom!" Frost cried. He tried to rush toward the inferno, but several people held him back. He struggled against them but to no avail. "No. No. No. Please. No. Someone help her."

"Anyone in there is beyond help, young man," said one of the Azureguards, her voice stern. "They're in Nif's hands now."

"This is what happens when four or five families try to live under one roof," another person said. "And a shitty roof at that. Nothing more than shacks stacked on top of each other. Damned sceeves, I tell ya, the whole of Coppertown is. Bunch of nasty bastards. Don't even know why we stopped to help. Hope this fire burns it all out."

"Nomarch Setnana did say the town needed a cleansing," said a Blackguard, while he leaned on his crescent axe. "But who would've thought it would be by the hands of our hated cousins the grand korae?"

"There'll be less beggars and thieves now, for sure. Less work for you Blackguards, less work for us," the first Azureguard said.

"It ain't all good," the Blackguard grumbled. "It means less whores too. A lot less fun. Probably lost a whore or two in every house." The others murmured their agreement and continued on with their nonchalant conversation.

Frost barely heard them anymore, such was the heat flushing through his body. Quivering, he opened his mouth to let the bastards know they were pieces of shit. That was his mother in there. And other families. People he grew up with, who struggled every day to eke out a meager living in the shithole that was Coppertown.

But Tia woke, coughing and sputtering. She sat upright and looked around, wide-eyed. Her gaze fell upon their home. She unleashed a wail, an unrestrained sea of sorrow that threatened to drown him.

IM activated. Two quest lines became a part of his knowledge.

Khertahkan Trials

Family Trials

With them came a long list of sub quests, the first of them more prominent than the others.

An Infernal Fire

Objective Complete

Escaped burning building:

250 experience points

Sister saved:

1000 experience points
Extinguish fire:
Fail
Mom saved:
Fail
Level 2 gained
Gained 50 Khertahka dominion credits.

He sat down beside Beketia and rubbed his aether ring. For a moment he'd completely forgotten that he was inside the game. Everything had felt like it did in real life after waking from the accident. The smoke, to the fire, to the throbbing in his side, to the fact that Beketia resembled Kai. But all that paled in comparison to the hurt, the hole deep inside himself, in his heart, the numerous thoughts that suggested he could have done something differently, the gut-wrenching sorrow of loss.

And so, he hugged his sister and wept. Because it was the best comfort he could offer.

And in that moment, there came a whoosh.

"Another volley incoming," yelled an Azureguard.

Frost glanced up in time to see lances of fire arc up through the air. The dawn sky turned bloody. Old instincts kicked in. He dragged Tia to her feet and half ran, half stumbled away, hoping to escape the rain of death that was an Aether Flame Bombardment.

CHAPTER 6

Frost fled, dragging Tia with him. Aether flame hurtled down like bloodied lances, reddening the sky. Sporadic at first, the lances exploded through homes, blasted the ground, scorched stone, melted metal, impaled people, and animals. He swore he felt the lances as he ran. Sensed them somehow. Soon, the bombardment increased in frequency until it was a deluge of destruction.

Chest heaving, he did his best to shut out Tia's whimpers and cries, the screams of nearby Khertahkan folk, the burning bodies that staggered by. Men, women, and children batted at the greedy flames and danced a macabre dance as if caught in a bee swarm. The air became a miasma of smoke. Burned meat. Char.

Almost blinded by the billowing smoke, he found himself making the clicking noise again as he ran. He abruptly became aware of the objects around him, the impressions of those falling toward him.

The aether flame lances.

Concentrating on the impressions and the telltale sound of the wind buffeting the flames of any falling lance in close proximity, he veered this way and that. He zigzagged through devastation, gritting his teeth against hair-singing heat. More by sense and will, he strove to stay ahead of the main onslaught.

Desperation was a snake in his chest, constricting his heart. Explosions and heat wiped away any thoughts of his experience being just a game. As did the tiny details, the lingering fires, dryness in his throat, the thud of his boots, the roar of blood in his own ears.

Stumble or fall, he drove forward, not allowing himself to stop, not releasing his grip on Tia. Not even when the lances ended. Not when the heat diminished with distance. Not when they met a formation of Battleguards.

Foremost among them were Azureguards, cloaks emblazoned with the Coalition's Mountain and the Aetherstream. On their sleeves was Khertahka's insignia: triangular-shaped dual katars. They rode majestic crevids with sawed off antlers, each creature at least a foot taller than a draft horse, but whose visages had more in common with rams.

The second rank of Battleguards were the namesake Blackguards, many with large crescent axes. Their mounts were maned lupines larger than any crevid, looking for all the world like giant wolves, slobber leaking from elongated jaws filled with rows of teeth meant to shear through meat and bone.

An IM message slid across his mind.

Death From Above
Objective Complete
Survived Aether Flame Bombardment:
500 experience points
Sister kept alive:
1000 experience points
Other people saved: 0
50 Khertahka dominion credits

He stopped and flopped down on the steps of a shop in the Rose Quarter and drew in ragged breaths, making hoarse sounds with each inhale and exhale. Tia collapsed beside him, covered in soot and grime, blisters showing on her exposed blue skin, the bottom of her feet a bloody blue. He, too, had similar blisters along his arms and a few on his face, making his purple skin a darker hue. The stench of his singed hair filled his nostrils.

Finally able to think, he considered the objective completions so far. And the quest lines. He liked the seamless acquisition of quests and the fact Information Memory kept them hidden until he thought of them or until a completion or failure. He understood Sidrie's love for the intuitive gameplay. It helped with the immersion. He would have to pay careful attention to his surroundings and conversations with NPCs.

He thought of the current main quest, the Khertahkan Trials. Another objective, Escaping Niba, popped into his head. The sub quests were blurs, shrouded things at the edge of his mind.

Back toward Coppertown, infernal hues lit the sky while billowing gray, white, and black smoke shrouded the distant wall behind which the grand korae were surely readying their main assault. Battleguards galloped down Masha Avenue on their way to defend Niba.

"We're gonna rest here for a few minutes, then find some clothes for you and bandage those feet of yours." Frost wished the game had started him out with some healing potions. Those would have been a blessing now.

He pondered the sensation from the blisters and burns. They stung, but it was more discomfort than pain. He didn't like the feeling despite recognizing it as a warning against recklessness.

An idea popped into his head. "Maybe we should go to the Temple of Nif. Some mystics should still be there."

Beketia said nothing. She hugged herself, her body shaking, hands trembling, as she stared off in the direction of Coppertown. Tears brimmed in her blue-rimmed eyes and trailed down her cheeks.

"Everything will be fine. I promise." Frost squeezed her shoulder, but the attempt at comfort did not elicit a response of any kind from his sister.

When he looked at Tia, he tried not to see Kai. The resemblance was undeniable. *Sidrie, you wouldn't have been so heartless as to have thrown my sister into the test, would you?* He shook his head against the possibility. He decided Tia had to be a non-player character. But even if Tia *was* an NPC, using Kai's likeness was a cruel reminder of the lives at stake.

Exhaustion bore down on him even as the morning's events replayed repeatedly in his head, the realness of all he'd experienced. *You coulda saved Mom if you were a lighter sleeper. You shoulda pushed Tia out the window then grabbed Mom.* Scenario after scenario popped up with the blame falling squarely on him each time. He tried not to think on it, but that was like asking himself not to breathe.

Remembering the pouch, he dug into the side of his boot and came away with the last thing Anefet had given him. Made from rough cloth, the pouch was cinched closed with a string. He loosened the string and poured the contents into his palm.

There were three skill shards and a folded paper. The shards had the appearance of two-inch-long marquise cut diamonds. Each contained an azure tendril of aether, which shifted, coiled, and caressed the glassy insides like a nebulous serpent. A mere thought of his willingness to use them caused the shards to seep into his skin, disappearing completely.

Skills acquired:

Cannon Kata
Passive
Consumes: Nothing
Effect: After killing an enemy, movement speed increased by 50 percent for 5 seconds. Adds 5 percent Aether if level 20 or above.

Korbitanium Projectile

Cast time: Instant
Recharge Time: none
Consumes: Korbitanium Shells
Available shard slots: 3
Effect: Fire a burst of projectiles which explode on impact with an enemy or obstacle. Accurate up to 300 feet. Available during Stand and Deliver.
Requires aether cannon

Aether Shot
Cast time: Instant
Recharge Time: 2 seconds
Consumes: Aether
Available shard slots: 3
Effect: Fire a bolt of aether energy which explodes on impact with an enemy or obstacle. Accurate up to 500 feet. Available during Stand and Deliver with no recharge.
Requires aether cannon

Frost nodded his approval, particularly for the Korbitanium Projectile being an instant cast ability with no cooldown or recharge time. Instacasts of that sort were his favorite type of skills on his sorcerer. They were generally weak but still very effective due to the speed at which they could be used repeatedly.

He took a look at the paper. When he unfolded it, he saw writing as well as a copper chain with a black ring attached. Engravings on the ring caught his eye, and he recognized it as the twin to the one on his pinky. He slipped the chain around his neck, tucked it under his blackened tunic, and then checked the message. It was Mom's handwriting.

Dear Drelan,

If you are reading this, then I am dead.

Which means you must leave Niba and never return. Not to the Kadi nome nor anywhere else in the Kher-

tahka dominion lest you end up the same way. Know that I did the best I could for you and Beketia. Take care of her.

My death was always a possibility living in Coppertown. But it wouldn't have been at the hands of one of our own. They all knew better.

Discover the circumstances, and then seek vengeance. But only after your sister is safe. This, I ask, above all else. Promise me.

The aether ring is for you to present to Adesh Hamada, an erada of some import. You will find him in Kituan. You can be certain it is him if he has a ring like this one on his left thumb. Tell him your name, and with this ring as confirmation, he will help you with whatever you need, and answer any questions concerning my death.

Beware the Blackguards and Nomarch Setnana Botros. Beware the Black Hand. Go to Adesh. As soon as you can.

Do not speak of this to anyone. Trust no one. They are always watching.

Love, Anefet.

Overcome by emotion, Frost bowed. *I promise.*

IM advised him of newly acquired quests. Khertahkan and Family Trials had shifted to third and fourth in the main branch behind two of the new ones: The Black Hand in second, below another which he could not discern. The others were Escape from Niba, Arrive Safely in Kituan, A Sister's Safety, Find Adesh Hamada, and Circumstances of Anefet's Death. Deciding not to think about them made the recollection go away.

He read the letter again before he tucked it into his boot. He frowned. *Who wanted you dead? Why? Who's Nomarch Setnana Botros? Who's the Black Hand? Who the hell is Adesh*

Hamada? And who is watching? What were you into? Kituan… the capital of the Ignis dominion in the Ad Mauros nome… why there?

The questions and implications assailed him. Worst of all was being placed on a Blackguard bounty list. Azureguards were bad enough. But they paled in comparison to the Black. Few survived the Black's hunts.

He could think of no answers. Unlike many of the vagrants who called Coppertown home, his family had not turned to thievery, whoring, or running swindles. Instead, they begged for alms along the roads leading to the Rose Quarter. He'd also sneak into the Rose Quarter from time to time for better handouts. Once, he'd even dared to enter the Vermillion Quarter to petition the richest of the rich, only to be chased by Battleguards. Those were minor crimes, nothing worth Mom's death.

As for his father, the man had abandoned them before Frost was five. Tia's father had succumbed to the Gray Death months ago. He shook his head, baffled by the letter's implications.

Those implications grew more acute as he considered that the road northeast across the Khertahka dominion, from here in Niba to Kituan in Ignis, was a long arduous trek by foot and fraught with danger. Even begging a ride on a wagon when the opportunity presented itself might still take weeks.

Maybe, I could scrounge together enough credits to buy passage on a kirin. He imagined riding atop one of the scaled, horned beasts with manes that flowed upwards. He shook his head. A drake or a simurgh would be much faster. It would take days then. *Pfft. Might as well pee in a cup and call it beer. I'll be lucky to afford something on a crevid or lupine.*

Still, those last two were better than walking. Anything was better than walking. Especially if he hoped to avoid marauding GUMs, slavers, and poachers. Those last two sent chills down his spine.

Frost paused, his mouth falling open, struck yet again by the realization that he possessed an entire background. A history with all the intricate details. They were as much a part of him as anything in real life.

Pondering how to proceed, he studied his surroundings. Survivors streamed by, bedraggled and soot-covered, with tear-streaked faces. Some helped the wounded. Too many to count had charred and peeled skin, mottled in red, blue, and purple, exposed flesh glistening wetly.

A human priest strode among them, pausing to offer kind words where one person or another wept over the unmoving body of an injured loved one. At some stops he said prayers for the dead and made the sign of the Circle on his forehead.

"It's just a game," a man said.

Frowning, Frost glanced toward the voice's origin. The man was walking with two girls. His kids, Frost assumed. They were sobbing.

"This will all be over in a day or two. The gods will return your mother to us when they're done playing," the man said. He continued on with similar reassurances.

It was an odd conversation. Typically, gamers wouldn't be reassuring any other player or NPC that it was a game. Frost almost tried to stop the man and ask him to explain but thought better of it. He assumed the man's wife was a player who died and had returned on some prior occasion. Frost listened and watched for anything similar.

Rose Quarter residents who owned homes or shops along Masha Avenue were preparing to evacuate. Some were eradae like himself, a few gurashi towering over everyone, and a sprinkling of humans. They packed valuables onto wagons, four-wheeled drays, crevids, tentacle-nosed unguls, horses, or carried what they could in sacks and bags.

He tried to discern how many of them were players, just questing, and how many were NPCs. The interactions were beyond anything he expected. NPCs had patterns. Even when the game tried to make them random, you could still pick them out. But the people on the street acted no differently than if he was in a town in real life. The portrayal left him flabbergasted. It made him understand why Sidrie bragged about the AI. And had even named it Estela.

The people were so real he wondered if GMs were among them, actively manipulating events. *And if there were Game Masters, what were their capabilities? Were they human admins or the game's AI?* He wished there was a way to tell, to even discern something as simple as a player's level.

Those questions led to others. He pondered how many were playing the old VR engine. And which ones were a part of the SR Total Immersion alpha test. *How many are like me? Forced to play?* He grimaced at a sudden pang of sadness for his mother's plight and simmering rage when he considered Sidrie's deception. Reliving her threats, he stroked his aether ring.

The boom of erada war drums broke him from those thoughts. His mind immediately leapt to the battle. He could imagine the lines drawn. Erada Battleguards formed ranks, females in every shade of blue, standing proud beside black, brown, and purple males, facing off against their pallid cousins from the Puria dominion.

He frowned. *How'd the grand korae manage such an attack without warning? There's no way they eliminated every sentry between Niba and the Isfet Mountains.* With a shake of his head, he dismissed the thought and stood, but one glance at Tia, at her bloodied feet, told him she would be unable to walk at any great pace. If at all.

"Take me to Nebsamu," she said, voice a hoarse croak. Her distant gaze remained upon Coppertown's burning, smoking remnants.

"I'm not leaving you in this shithole." Frost shook his head. "And definitely not with Nebsamu. Mom's friend or not."

Nebsamu Tadros was an erada with skin so black it glistened, but there'd always been something about the one-horned man that made Frost uneasy. He fancied himself as a relic dealer, but in truth, Nebsamu was little more than a scavenger.

"Mom said don't trust anyone. We're gonna do this alone." Frost wondered if his mother's warning not to show anyone the letter included Tia.

"I know what she said. I also know we have to go. He can help us. He *will* help us."

Frost frowned at her insistence. "Did Mom tell you why we had to leave?"

"Not the details. Just that someone might try to kill us." She burst into tears.

"Maybe, we should just do as she asked," Frost said. "We don't need anyone. I can take care of any prob."

Sniffling, she wiped at her eyes. "You always think you can do everything by yourself," she blurted. "What happens if these killers find us? How are you going to fight them? With your hands?"

He sighed. Tia had a point. Even if he wasn't one to openly admit it.

Nebsamu had survived poachers. His scarred face and one horn were a testament to that. And his reputation with a knife preceded him. Mom wouldn't have invited the man over to share their meager dinners if she hadn't trusted him. Or so Frost hoped. Besides, Nebsamu's shop wasn't too far away. They could go there, get some supplies, a change of clothes, and perhaps a weapon, and then be on their way.

A previously obscure objective uncovered in IM. It

was called Relic Hunter, the goal for Frost to take Tia to Nebsamu Tadros' shop, Odds and Ends. Frost smiled inwardly at such a vivid history for the scavenger. The man had to be an NPC.

"Fine. Let's go to him." He strode down the steps and squatted in front of Tia. "Climb on."

She grabbed his shoulders and wrapped her arms around his neck, hissing in pain, no doubt caused by the blisters rupturing. A quick glance at his arms revealed that hoisting her onto his back had broken some of his blisters, but he suffered no sting from the exposed purple flesh. He stood, hooked his arms under her legs, and set off down the road.

"I hope we don't end up regretting this." He'd barely gone a few steps before questions popped into his head. "Tia, you aren't Kai, are you?"

"Who's Kai?"

"Never mind." A weight lifted from his shoulders. "Are you an NPC?"

"An NPC?" She frowned.

"A non-player character."

"Not you too, brother," she said, her voice brittle. "Not you. You can't be going mad like them."

"Like who?"

"The dreamers. The ones who think we're a part of a game played by the gods."

"No, I'm no dreamer, Tia. And I'm not going mad."

"You promise?"

"I promise, sis." Frost couldn't help but to wonder about the dreamers.

The erada war drums continued to roll.

CHAPTER 7

Chased by the beat of the distant erada war drums, they arrived at Odds and Ends as the sun bathed the streets in gold and afternoon heat. Exhaustion and Tia's weight bore down on Frost. He was grateful to see Nebsamu's salvage shop. Odds and Ends meant a chance to tend to the raw patches of his purple skin and to get some rest.

IM alerted him of a quest completion.

A Relic Hunter
Objective Complete
Arrived safely at Nebsamu's shop:
100 experience points

Nebsamu was overseeing the loading of an open-backed wagon attached to four male crevids with sawed off antlers, their fur a mix of blue and black. Thumbs tucked into the loops of his belt near his long daggers, the ebony erada scavenger paused in the act of giving orders to his workers. Blue eyes narrowed, he studied Frost and Beketia.

A litany of scars and raised scar tissue crisscrossed Nebsamu's face like a road map of torture. The scars had gifted him a permanent grimace and the appearance of lips longer on his left side than his right. His stump of a horn peeked from behind his left ear, partially hidden by his shock of dark hair, in stark contrast to the long curled horn on the other side.

Nebsamu said a few words to his helpers and sent

them scurrying to Frost and Tia. One helper was a gurash, a walking shed of a man with green and brown marbled skin, marking him as an outcast among his people. The other was a lithe, young, cerulean erada. Numerous rings adorned her fingers. Frost was instantly drawn to her long slender horns.

The gurash plucked Tia from Frost's back and sat her on one arm as if she were a pet bird. Frost shooed away the erada's attention and walked with his back a bit straighter, his gait more purposeful.

"Frost, Beketia. Nif be praised," Nebsamu said as the gurash cleared a space on the back of the wagon with his free arm, and with care, set Tia down. "I hoped to see you. I had also hoped to see Anefet, prayed to Nif that the reports I received were wrong." He shook his head, slow and solemn.

Frost hung his head, more from the statement and hearing Mom's name, rather than for any real grief it might have sparked. He frowned, searching inside himself for deep sorrow. He hurt but not like earlier.

"It was brave of you to carry your sister all this way," Nebsamu said.

Frost shrugged. "She's my sister. I did what any older brother would."

"Before we talk." Nebsamu gestured to the erada. "Gilda, fetch some clothes, bandages, and vera ointment." He turned to the gurash, who was setting up Tia with cushions behind her back and head. "Melori, fetch them something to eat." The two helpers dipped their heads and hurried off.

Frost eyed the cerulean erada, intrigued by her nimble form and her name. There was something about her long legs, coloring, long red and black hair... and horns. They were elegant. Beautiful. They curved out, then in, then out again. He couldn't pry his eyes away from them. His brows climbed his forehead at a growing firmness in his pants. He glanced down. Then back at her horns. He grimaced. *Over horns? Really? That can't be normal.*

"She's a pretty one, isn't she," Nebsamu said.

Frost jumped. His face flushed. "Um… I guess." Nebsamu's scarred face killed any arousal. It hurt to even look at the man.

"In Nif's name, don't be modest with me, young man. I know that look in your eye. But I'd be careful if I were you. I've been teaching her the blade." Whip quick, one of Nebsamu's daggers appeared in his hand. He twirled the weapon and re-sheathed it. "She's an incredibly fast learner. And not afraid of blood." Nebsamu's gaze shifted down for all of an instant.

Frost swallowed. "I'll remember that."

In a quest to ignore the gruesome images running through his head, he noticed Tia's resting spot and became envious. His back and weary legs cried for such comfort. But he refused to let it show.

"You can join your sister." Nebsamu gestured toward the wagon. "If I survived an Aether Flame Bombardment, dressed in night clothes, I'd sleep for several days. By Nif, I'd probably kill anyone who woke me early."

"I'm fine. We don't plan to stay. Tia was the one who suggested we come here… that you might help us."

Nebsamu arched the eyebrow on his hornless side. "You're not fine. You don't need to convince me of your strength. The fact that you're here speaks on its own."

Frost gave in. And in so doing, a load lifted from him. He clambered into the wagon beside Tia and leaned back onto a cushion, his body only too glad for the respite. Tia was asleep. The war drums had grown louder. They beat faster and faster. Frost imagined the battle, and hoped the erada Battleguards were winning.

"Whether or not you stay," Nebsamu added, "is up to you."

"I'm not trying to impose on you, dawg," Frost said. "As soon as Tia wakes, changes, and eats, we're gonna be on our way."

"If you insist." Nebsamu shrugged. "And I'd prefer if you didn't refer to me as your dog."

Frost opened his mouth to explain but changed his mind. He sighed. He had to remember he was in the game now, particularly when speaking to an NPC. But certain things came naturally.

Wishing to change the subject, he said, "You sounded as if you knew what happened to my mother."

"I received word of Anefet's passing not long ago." Nebsamu bowed in a show of respect. "Whether she was directly targeted remains to be seen. But there's no doubt her death was a result of our work together. As is this grand kora attack."

"Your work? The grand korae?" Frost sat up. The war drums beat in earnest now.

Nebsamu's lips curved; the corner of his eyes wrinkled. A stranger might have ran away screaming at the nightmarish expression. Frost recognized it for a knowing smile.

"Anefet was a woman of many secrets," Nebsamu said. "She was a high-ranking member of the Blue Sky Network."

Frost opened and closed his mouth. He couldn't believe his mother had been involved with Blue Sky much less be a top member of the organization that split the opinion of many. And yet there was the curious letter.

Still, Blue Sky were either terrorists or freedom fighters. Classification depended on which side you were when you encountered them. And whether to believe the Coalition or the common people. Blue Sky was originally formed to fight poachers who hunted eradae for their horns. Horns coveted for the healing properties when ground to powder and added to certain potions or prized as collector's items and art pieces among grand kora nobles.

Countless slaves owed their liberation to Blue Sky. Poachers and slavers owed their deaths. To the Coalition, Blue Sky's fight to see Khertahka return to an independent erada dominion was a threat to their hold on the continent of Marang.

"Without her, and her people, I would be dead." Nebsamu touched his stump of a horn. "Your mother was the Hand of Freedom."

Frost gasped. *Mom had been the Hand of Freedom?* He couldn't envision it. None of it. Even with the letter. The Hand of Freedom had gained notoriety in battles all across the Khertahka. Either against injustice, at slave camps, or helping to defeat many a Coalition company in the hunt for Blue Sky members. The Hand had gone into exile when rumors abounded that the Coalition would dispatch Vindicators to stop him.

Most assumed the Hand had been a man. He represented the poor, the destitute, the seedy underbelly of society that people called the sceeves. He was known for his ability to make anyone disappear, whether foe or people in need, those wanted for crimes they didn't commit, or who had been declared enemies of the Grendesh Coalition.

"Ah." Nebsamu gestured toward his helpers. "Food and something to wear have arrived. We'll talk again soon." He shuffled off to a stack of boxes.

Gilda and Melori strode over. Melori placed three bowls next to the cushions, one filled with rice, another with stewed crevid, and a third with fruit. Then he headed over to Nebsamu. Frost's stomach protested as if he kept a massive lupine imprisoned within him, rumbling and growling deep in its throat. Gilda passed Frost a few sets of tunics and trousers.

He held the tunics up to get a sense of their sizes. "Which one?"

Gilda shrugged even as she studied him with eyes like green phosphor.

"Gilda," he continued, "would your last name beee… Mordian?" She nodded. "Strange name for an erada." He chose the larger clothes.

"No stranger than Drelan Frost."

"So, it *is* you. The infamous Just Blaze." Frost smiled.

"Only my friends get to call me that."

"If that's how you wanna play it. I can respect that. Here with a group?"

"Nope."

Frost nodded his approval. "Solo is definitely the way to roll."

"I wouldn't go that far," she said.

Frost lowered his voice. "Why would a famed cut-throat be working as a scavenger helper?"

"A girl's gotta do what a girl's gotta do." She paused and looked him up and down, her phosphorescent green eyes and expression saying she was thoroughly unimpressed. "I go where the quests lead." She produced a dagger from the folds of her shirt, twirled it between her be-ringed fingers, and replaced the blade deftly in an eye-blink. "And you didn't fare much better for choice. At least I know what to expect, what I'm supposed to do."

Frost's brows shot up. "What to expect? You're questioning my skills? I've been playing Ataxia longer than you."

She pursed her mouth into a smirk. "No doubt." She strode away.

Frost studied her, a dozen questions running through his mind. He wanted to go after her, but she shot him a warning look over her shoulder. Frost shook his head in exasperation.

He woke Tia. She got up and stretched, a bewildered expression on her face. She looked around and burst into sobs. Frost comforted her the best he could until Gilda came to take her to change inside the little hut that was Nebsamu's shop.

Frost got out of his night clothes and pulled on the tan trousers and a deep gray tunic. The fit wasn't the greatest, but it would do. Then he proceeded to apply the ointment to his blisters. They disappeared within seconds and his skin returned to its deep purple tone. Tia returned dressed similarly to Frost but also sporting a floppy wide-brimmed hat.

The two of them sat down to eat. Frost marveled at the taste of the food, its spiciness, at the very act of tasting. And the *feel* of it. Everything about it was real, down to the tingling on his tongue. He was again awed by the replication. Frost was wiping his mouth with the back of his hand when Nebsamu strode over.

"Now that you've eaten and feel a bit better, I'll continue," the scavenger said. "Much of this began when Anefet got word of a treasure sought by the grand korae. An artifact of some type hidden deep within Imanok Sanctum on Maelpith Island."

Frost perked up at the mention of the place and loot. An objective for exploration of Imanok Sanctum revealed itself.

"She discovered that Nomarch–" Nebsamu squinted up at something beyond Frost.

The scavenger's expression grew flat. He extended his arm. A moment later a large raven fluttered down and landed. The erada plucked a missive from its leg and flicked his arm up to send the bird on its way. He unfolded the bit of paper, head shifting from side to side as he read.

Nebsamu's brows furrowed. "Nif, blind them. We must go. Now. Battleguards are on their way here with orders to arrest or kill me. And both of you."

"Us? Why us?" Frost stroked his Two Ring.

IM revealed another quest. Battleguard Pursuit.

The idea of being on the Blackguard bounty list left a sour taste in his mouth. Their bloodlust was renowned, their proficiency, legendary. The war drums echoed his heartbeat.

"I was wrong," Nebsamu said. "Your family *was* one of the targets for this attack. As well as any other Blue Sky members. When you arrived, I'd hoped the destruction of Coppertown would hide that you still lived. It seems a Blackguard captain recognized you two. I intended to go to the Aviary, but they'll most likely expect that. Instead, we'll go to my men at the East Gate."

Frost tried to think. He did not want to go with Nebsamu. But in his current condition he could not outrun the Battleguards. Especially not with Tia.

They stood no chance without mounts, food, or an abundance of credits. Hiding was also out of the question. If they had his scent, the lupines would sniff them out. The sense of helplessness made him wish he was his old sorcerer.

Melori and Gilda retrieved weapons from the shop. The gurash toted a wide-bladed, two-handed sword. He rested the blunt side on his shoulder.

Gilda held two silver, star-shaped chakrams, the size of dinner plates, the interior hollowed out to leave only the band of metal two inches thick. Frost frowned at Gilda's choice. Chakrams were a sorcerer's weapons.

Nebsamu searched a trunk in the wagon bed not far from Frost. When he stood, he was holding a black and silver aether cannon and an extra magazine.

"Normally something like this would cost you several hundred KDC. Knowing your mother as I did, and seeing that we might need your help, I'll let you borrow the weapon. If you decide to keep it, we can discuss payment later. It's already loaded." He handed the weapon and ammo to Frost.

"My man," Frost said, smiling.

IM clicked when Frost took the aether cannon.

Acquired weapon:

Noobstick

Level: 1

Damage: 25 – 50

Force: 10

Special: Extends Cannon Kata by 2 seconds

Available shard slots: 0

Skills unlocked:

Korbitanium Projectile

Aether Shot

"Finally." Frost hefted the rare hierka. He'd still have to get used to carrying the thing, but with its size, he'd expected the cannon to be heavy and cumbersome. It weighed perhaps a few pounds. Grinning, he nodded to Gilda, who rolled her eyes.

Holding the cannon by its carry handle located midway down the top of the weapon, he ran his hand down the barrel, which was double the length and width of his forearm. The battery pack was housed behind the handle. On the cannon's underside was the magazine of korbitanium projectiles. At the rear was a grip with a trigger assembly as well as a lever to control the power of its Aether Shots. An easy squeeze and he'd be wreaking havoc.

The cannon had a familiar feel to it. Frost was reminded of the extensive time he spent in target practice and 3-Gun sims as well as first person shooters DOOM EVERLASTING.

By way of IM he was able to use Noobstick's overall damage combined with his skills to get an idea of its Damage Per Second. The DPS was underwhelming, but it was to be expected for a beginner weapon. Even a genesiswork like this one.

He also doubted if the amount of force would stagger or stun any enemies. The Cannon Kata special got a nod. An extra two seconds with a fifty percent increase in movement speed might come in handy.

"Let's go," Nebsamu yelled, taking a seat across from Frost and Tia. With those words, Frost became aware of himself as part of a group. As with everything else, there were no physical or metered indications, just a sense.

A whip cracked, the crevids bellowed, and the wagon lurched forward. Frost was admiring the weapon when Nebsamu spoke again. "You *do* know how to use that thing, right?"

With his left hand holding the carry handle, Frost slid his right hand to the rear grip, one finger near the trigger. "You could say I've had some practice. Not with this exact weapon, but I'm a quick learner."

"I supposed that will do for now."

"Just watch me work. Any more ammo?" Frost placed the spare magazine into his inventory with a mere thought.

Nebsamu shook his head. "Not until we reach a supplier. So use the projectiles sparingly. Rely on Aether Shots instead."

"That... might be a prob."

"Prob?" repeated Nebsamu.

"Problem."

Nebsamu arched an eyebrow. "Let me guess... your Replenishment is lacking."

Frost nodded.

"Dear Nif, nothing is ever easy." Nebsamu looked to the heavens.

"At least I have the cannon and korbitanium ammo," Frost protested. "I had nothing a little while ago."

CHAPTER 8

Tapping a finger to her lips, Sidrie Malikah peered through the observation window at the pregnant woman lying on the bed. Theresa Taylor was still the definition of average. And the weight gain of pregnancy was not helping the matter. The caramel complexioned woman could be dressed for a ball and go completely unnoticed.

Sidrie sighed. Her hand fell to her side. It was not as if an upgrade had been beyond Mrs. Taylor's means these past fifteen years. The woman had chosen to deny herself one. For Sidrie, choosing anonymity was incomprehensible.

What was it that Alphonso saw in you?

Sidrie recalled her visit to Barbados to recruit Alphonso Taylor. That trip, the first of many to the Caribbean island, had offered a few surprises.

First had been the fact such a tiny island produced *two* of the world's greatest minds. One in AI engineering. The other, Hank Kim, a bioengineer.

Second was that no superstorm had struck the island during the Climatic Shift. Third was discovering the vast majority of Barbadians were your average people. Quite unlike the exotic beauties populating Virtual Vacations to the island. Still, she'd expected a man such as Alphonso to have a significant other who somehow matched his brilliance. A reflection of himself.

Sidrie shook her head. She could not imagine partnering with anyone of a lesser stature than herself, a person who could not measure up in multiple ways. Perhaps, it was the reason she was still single. No such person existed. And if they did, she had no desire to fall in love, become so attached that she'd want to reverse her infertility. After witnessing the continual weakness mothers had for their children, she counted her inability to bear children as a blessing.

She rubbed her arm where the Taylor boy had squeezed it. The area was still sore. *How dare he touch me!* She grimaced. He'd been unusually strong for his age and slim stature. She would have to be more careful around him in the future. But for now, he needed a lesson in action and consequence.

"Remind me why you are trying to save her. And why I should allow it. The little sister is adequate enough for the boy to do our bidding."

"Additional insurance," Dr. Redmond said, standing a step behind her to the right.

"But I already have that with his immigration status."

"More motivation is always better," the doctor argued.

"Always?" Sidrie raised a quizzical brow. "It depends on the motivation. It has to be the right one. When too much emotion is involved, it can be as much a hindrance as a help. Emotion is a flaw, a weakness, too often blinding a person to an obvious mistake. The very reason we're culling it from the gameborn, making them better than humans in every regard."

"Killing her now doesn't make sense," Dr. Redmond said. "Saving his family drives him. And Imanok Sanctum is only one of numerous extremely difficult challenges we suspect hold the keys to the protocols. Suppose he achieves what no one has and clears it, but returns to find them dead? It might destroy his will to carry on.

"There's also the chance Alphonso confided in her.

She might have knowledge or insight into *exactly* where he hid all the protocols and the rest of his research. As well as Hank Kim's brain emulation work. Or she might even know where Hank is hiding. We wouldn't need to rely on the testers then. We could perfect the gameborn."

"Estela, show me 2041's controls," Sidrie said under her breath.

Her optical implants flashed. A Heads-Up Display appeared in the air before her face. Numbers rolled across the HUD, calculating the cost of the attempt to heal Theresa. The forecasted result was still uncertainty. The time and money seemed a waste for such an unremarkable piece of flesh.

"There is a chance she could die anyway," Sidrie argued. "No matter which choice we make."

"Then we must be extra vigilant," the doctor said.

Sidrie scowled. Ending it now was the better option. Perhaps, the more merciful. She could then divert the resources to other programs in need of TNT. Killing the woman was so tempting.

Alphonso had earned that much for breaking her trust, stealing from the company that had given him a new life in the Republic, for ruining her plans, costing Equitane hundreds of millions of credits. And for locking her out of the brunt of Void Legion's controls. She could not yet make the bastard himself pay, but taking the life before her was the next best thing.

And it served the purpose of showing the boy he could not touch her. Ever. Just as upsetting was that the boy appeared as temperamental and stubborn as his father. She seethed inside. Not only at the similarities in character, but that Alphonso had also challenged her authority.

She shook her head at the thought of the boy turning down a million credits. *What was he thinking? The income could have solved his problems. Well, except for his mother's plight. But to discard such a windfall over a promise? Over a set of misguided morals? Emotions? The boy was naïve like his father had been years ago.*

Why am I surprised? Is that not a typical human failing?

She wished she had found the boy sooner. But Shane Constantine had done well to secretly employ the boy at one of his many obscure companies. There, Andre would have remained. If not for fate.

Sidrie smiled at her good fortune. After so much time spent searching for Alphonso's family since they disappeared soon after his crash, they had landed in her lap due to an accident involving one of her employees sent to search Coney Island for them. The chance of such an occurrence were one in a million.

But she would take it. As she would take this chance for a measure of satisfaction. She raised her hand.

But what if Theresa knows about the protocols? The files? The location of Hank Kim's research on Whole Brain Emulation? The location of Hank himself? What if she was the key to regaining full access to Ataxia? No. Alphonso wouldn't have been that stupid.

"You might also consider that her babies would make great additions to the gameborn," Dr. Redmond said.

Sidrie paused. She had not given much thought to the twins. *What had the boy named them? Regi and Rayne?*

Dr. Redmond cleared his throat. "Using them would save us the trouble of contacting our people in the FPC for new subjects over the next few months. Or trying to rely on clones whose growth constraints have hampered progress. With the latest scandals and Governor Morrison's anti-corruption campaign, it might be best to keep a low profile. Not expose ourselves."

"I was thinking that very thing," Sidrie said. "Now wouldn't be a good time to have the authorities looking into us, particularly the FPC or NAIL. Even if we could stymie any investigation, it would still interfere with our schedule." Reluctantly, she swiped her hand across her optics. The HUD disappeared.

Her aurals beeped. Estela's voice piped in through the implants. "Incoming from the Ataxia control room, madam. It's Zhi Yin. Do you wish to take it?"

"Yes."

The HUD flashed on. A smiling render of Zhi Yin's moon-eyed, goose-egg face popped up in a small box at the top left. Beneath it was her title: Head of BioGen VR development. "Sorry to bother you, Miss Malikah."

Sidrie tensed at the nervous titter in the normally jovial, girlish voice. "No bother, Zhi. What is it?"

"Anomalies have popped up in Void Legion again."

Sidrie ground her jaw. "Show me."

The HUD changed to a full view of the Ataxia Online control room as seen through Zhi's smart contacts. A holo map of Mikander encompassed the entire front of the room. Techs worked feverishly at holographic computer consoles. The buzz of conversation filled the air.

But it was the map that held Sidrie's attention. Green dots indicated Total Immersion testers. Blue were those playing the old version of the game. Red dots represented the anomalies. Off the top of her head she knew the locations of several aberrations: the cities of Deshem and Aprunis in Khertahka; Kituan, the capital of Ignis; Kesharai in Puria; Imanok Sanctum on Maelpith Island.

"Have we managed to identify the cause?" Sidrie asked. "Or what they mean? Are any of the systems compromised?"

"We've been unable to tell exactly what they are, but we know the cause," Zhi said.

"Go on."

"A study of the data in those areas and a bit of reverse engineering has revealed them to contain snippets of the code Alphonso uploaded."

"He placed them there?"

"We believe so. And that's not all. They move."

"Move?"

"Yes, since identifying the code, we've been able to track them at times. The one from Aprunis is now in Deshem."

"So, they're either players or NPCs."

"Of that, we're uncertain. We haven't been able to get a team near them when they're active. Surveillance and GMs found nothing out of the ordinary in their vicinity. They're like ghosts."

Holographic feeds popped up near each anomaly. Sound piped through Sidrie's aural pods, the sound of the living, breathing world of Mikander. Players and NPCs went about their business as normal. The murmur of a thousand conversations filled the air.

On another display the words from every conversation flitted by in a constant stream. Estela worked to pick out any keywords pertinent to her learning or that hinted at illicit activity, particularly hackers. The AI filed immediate profiles for players who triggered the latter, then assigned Game Master NPCs or gameborn to hunt down and eliminate the offenders. Yet, for all the information collected, Estela was unable to derive an obvious connection to the aberrations.

"Continue monitoring," Sidrie ordered. "Tinker with the algorithms used to track them. And send me a reminder of the full recordings around these anomalies. Whatever they are, whomever it is, they're bound to make a mistake."

"Yes, Miss Malikah."

On a whim, Sidrie said, "Show me the Taylor boy, A200."

Estela opened another holo feed ringed in green.

Andre had chosen an erada with dark magenta skin as his avatar. He was in Niba, in the company of two more of his kind. One of them was another alpha tester, a girl who'd dominated the previous version of the game after Andre had stopped playing.

Just Blaze.

Sidrie growled under her breath. She hated mysteries. Research into Just Blaze's past had revealed too little.

The girl was an orphan. Her parents had died during Hurricane Ezra fourteen years ago. From three, she'd been raised by her grandmother, who was also dead, killed five years ago during a DeGen raid in the Second Ward. In the immediate years afterward, she'd eked out a meager living by playing Ataxia Online and selling her services in game as a mercenary.

Sending agents into Just Blaze's home and subsequent surveillance had done little more than expose her as a thief who frequented the Mid Wards to ply her trade on unsuspecting shoppers and tourists. The crimes had been her undoing. Faced with prison or join the alpha tests, Just Blaze's choice had been obvious.

No records existed of a proper name for the girl. Knowing she was Asian was of no help.

Sidrie grimaced at the lack of complete information. She wished she could return to a time when such details were readily available, a time before the storms of the Climatic Shift, the Second Civil War, and the War of the Americas. A time when the internet connected everyone before the Chinese had corrupted it and America had turned to creating the Grid.

All these events had conspired to rip apart the country, destroy countless databases and knowledge. One day, she would be able to brave the First Ward to retrieve some of what was lost.

"Whose quest line are they on?" She was certain she knew but confirmation wouldn't hurt.

Estela's voice replied, "Setnana Botros."

Sidrie smiled. The Nomarch should prove quite the challenge. Setnana was one of the more advanced and newer gameborn, designed after Sidrie herself. "Good. Manipulate the emotional levels as needed and keep me updated."

"Yes, madam," replied Estela.

The two gamers had intrigued her ever since the first Ataxia. Frowning, she tilted her head to the side and began to tap her lips with her index finger, struck by a sudden niggling suspicion. She couldn't quite think of a reason for the feeling, but she'd achieved her success through intelligence, ruthlessness, and instinct. She wasn't about to ignore any of them now. With a wave of her hand, she dismissed the HUD.

"Is everything okay?" Dr. Redmond asked.

"Yes, for the most part. The anomalies appeared again. Zhi's team has linked them to Alphonso's work with the protocols." She gazed upon Theresa and lauded herself for discerning the importance of keeping the woman alive for now. And the added boon of two new gameborn. "The Taylor boy is playing the Botros line."

"The Botros line?" The concern in the doctor's voice was palpable. "You think he can handle that? Wouldn't he be better off—"

"We're not here to coddle, Dr. Redmond." She looked upon him piteously. "I know you have a soft spot for the testers, but I need them at their best to achieve our goal, to improve upon our current gameborn. If that means some testers die, then so be it. Grow a spine."

"Yes, Miss Malikah."

"Now tell me, have you made any progress with Hank Kim's work?"

He shook his head. "Not a great deal. The closest we've gotten is by having clones in Total Immersion repeatedly interact with recordings of the subjects. They return with those thoughts and mannerisms."

"That's simple learned behavior. Someone who knows the person intimately would eventually see the difference. Try harder." She turned away from the observation window, and strode down the hall.

As she walked, she envisioned the day when she had the protocols and the accompanying file in hand, making Estela, the TNT system, Total Immersion, and Equitane completely safe. The day when she would have the secrets of Alphonso and Hank Kim's team. When she would have eliminated all competition and every person who'd conspired to stop her. The day when not only New New York, but also the entire North American Republic was under her control. And the DeGens and South American Conglomerate were at her mercy. She smiled.

CHAPTER 9

They headed down Killiam's Avenue en route to the East Gate, the war drums fading behind them. Their pace was slow at first, particularly when they encountered another wagon.

Nebsamu instructed Melori to veer off onto the lesser traveled lanes. That brought them a few streets over from Niba's wall, the stone structure curving its path around the city. They trundled at a steady clip, the wagon jerking to-and-fro, Melori bellowing at the folk trying to flee the city. When a seven-foot gurash with a voice like thunder screamed at your back, and four snorting crevids bore down on you, you got the hell out of the way.

"So," Frost yelled over the churn of wagon wheels on cobbles, "I thought the Coalition had given up on the Hand of Freedom after her self-imposed exile. What changed?"

A cheerless expression crossed Nebsamu's face. "Not long ago, Nomarch Setnana had the Azureguards pass word throughout Coppertown that the mystics in the Temple of Nif would offer coin, food, clothing, and medicine to the poor and needy. Many went to accept the offer. Many never returned. Most of the missing were unreported. We assumed some of them had used their newfound good fortune to move to smaller villages or towns or to travel to bigger cities like Aprunis or even to another nome or dominion.

"The truth was far worse. Nomarch Setnana had

made a pact with the grand korae. She was sending poor folk off to grand kora slave camps that fed their korbitanium mining operations. Poor folk who had no family, no one to investigate their whereabouts, no one to care for or miss them.

"At the camps, those unfit for work were killed. The slavers harvested the horns of the eradae among those taken. So, your mother took up the fight again." Nebsamu's hand brushed the stump behind his left ear.

At a loss for words, Frost stared at the man and shook his head. Finally, he asked, "Why the hell would the Nomarch do that to her own people?"

Nebsamu shrugged. "The same reason she would send the Battleguards to defend against an assault she allowed. To hide the truth. She cares only for power. All she knows is what she wants. She will do anything to get it. Murdering your family or mine is nothing."

"Why didn't any of you warn the people in Coppertown?"

"We tried. But the promise of wealth proved too tempting for most." Nebsamu heaved a sigh. "And Setnana used her position. You see, Nomarchs have ever been the shepherds of common folk, leading the flock to lush pastures, protecting them from the wolves.

"But oftentimes, the wolves are the land's own nobility as much as they are a foreign enemy. The sheep love the shepherd for his protection, accept a meager existence, even as they're led to the slaughter."

"But some of you knew better," Frost said. "Why didn't you report her to Exarch Bakui Assam? Or hell, go above him to the erada Kalarch." The drums had picked up again, but uneven, with less rhythm.

"We sent word to the Exarch. We've yet to receive an answer."

"This doesn't make sense. Did you try the Coalition? They mighta hated Anefet because of her past, but they put an end to slavery and outlawed it."

"We sent ravens and messengers to them. None returned."

"I'd have thought a famed relic hunter like yourself woulda gotten your hands on a Communication Orb," Frost said.

"I could only wish I had such a hierka. I doubt there are even five of them across the Network."

Brow pinched, Frost stroked the aether ring on his little finger. He thought about mentioning the letter. "Any idea why the Coalition hasn't answered?"

"We assume they had their hands full with the draconids and their Void Legion at the Dagoda Front. We lost a major battle there. And there was also an outbreak of the Gray Death."

Frost's brows shot up at the news. "The draconids defeated the Vindicators?"

"Yes. In fact, all of this began soon after. And the strangest thing happened a few days before we got word of the defeat. A wave of blue light swept across the heavens. The clouds boiled. A maelstrom formed that could be seen from halfway across the world. Within moments, it became a voidstorm, its center spewing lightning as it swept across the land before settling over the Empyrean Sea. When it dissipated, there was a new island off the eastern coast of the Ignis dominion within sight of Kituan. The Coalition named it Maelpith Island.

"The storm left devastation, famine, and disease in its wake. The Coalition burned entire cities and villages to prevent the spread of the Gray Death.

"Then came word of renewed draconid activity. Not just along the Front, but there have been sightings of draconids and void monsters in Puria, Khertahka, Ignis, and Nimri."

Frost frowned. "How's that possible without anyone seeing them at the Front? Concealment, maybe?"

Nebsamu shrugged. "No one knows for certain, but I suppose it might be possible."

"Frost," Tia said. She'd been so quiet for so long that he'd forgotten about her. She was pointing back down the road.

There was a telltale shift, a commotion in the crowd some distance away. It resolved into several Blackguards and Azureguards on crevids and lupines, galloping for all they were worth. With the sight of them came a matching sound: the drums from minutes ago. Crevids' thundering hooves. People cleared ahead of the animals like insects scurrying for cover.

"In Nif's name, faster, Melori! Faster!" Nebsamu yelled. He yanked a dark cloth across his face, drew his daggers, and crouched.

"Tia." Frost pointed toward the wagon's rear. "Get all the way in the back." After she complied, he turned to Nebsamu. "Help me throw out some stuff to make a space." Frost grabbed a box and tossed it over the side.

The scavenger stared at Frost. "My precious things? Are you mad? Just pile them up."

"And have something fall on me when I'm letting loose with this?" Frost gestured with the cannon.

Nebsamu closed his eyes, took a deep breath, and shook his head. Then he opened his eyes, grabbed a metal container, and threw it over the side. They continued in this vein until they'd cleared a large enough space.

The Battleguards were closer now, to the point Frost could single them out. A dozen were Blackguard marauders and dementers. A dozen of this nome's deadliest fighters in

their nightmare armor, bearing huge crescent axes or korbitanium fists or vambraces. They rode atop lupines whose
maws gaped.

Six were sword-bearing Azureguard reavers, cloaks
flapping behind them. He was glad it was them and not
sorcerers, marksmen, cannoneers, shadowmancers or some
other ranged attackers. He still had the advantage. At least
until they got to the wagon.

Perhaps three hundred feet separated them. The gulf
was closing rapidly. The hooves beat to match the drumbeat
of Frost's heart.

He shifted a cushion on the wagon bed, placed
Noobstick beside it, and then got down on his belly, legs
stretched behind him. It was the same position he'd used
countless times in sims. He took the aether cannon by the
handle and front grip, rested his elbow atop the cushion, and
sighted down the barrel. With his finger over the trigger, he
flicked the lever to full power with his thumb, aimed at the
charging warriors, and targeted a Blackguard.

The distance closed. He took a breath. Squeezed.
Korbitanium Projectiles burst from the flashing muzzle
with a vibrating whine that was equal parts hammer drill and
buzzsaw. The sound stretched and faded.

The shots flew across the distance in streaks of
fire. Empty shells spewed out and pinged as they fell to the
wagon bed. Smoke vomited. The recoil jerked his arm. All
almost simultaneously.

Cobbles exploded a hundred feet ahead of his target. The Blackguard did not falter. If anything, he dug in his
heels.

"Shit. That's supposed to be accurate up to three
hundred feet."

Frost adjusted, took aim again, braced for the recoil,
and this time chose Aether Shot and its five-hundred-foot

112

range. The ensuing sound was a deep whomp, or a croak, like a giant bullfrog.

Cyan light pulsed from the muzzle. It streaked through the air. Right by his intended target: an Azureguard who wore no armor. An explosion echoed somewhere behind the Battleguards. A dust cloud kicked into the air.

The Battleguards were within two hundred feet.

He repeated the process, faster this time. His target's torso exploded. All that was left was legs attached to a bloody stump and a spine atop a lupine. IM made Frost aware of group exp gained. The lupine stopped, threw its head to the sky, and howled. Its brothers and sisters repeated the cry.

"Yes!" Frost fist-pumped.

His elation was short-lived. There was no way he could get them all in time. To worsen matters, another group had appeared behind the first.

Remembering Sidrie's claim of actual lasting physical effect on the world, he took aim at the ground just ahead of the Battleguards. Whomp. Blue streak. Recoil. The impact blasted a hole in the ground, sent cobbles and dirt flying, stone ricocheting in a hundred directions.

Frost stared. *That was incredible.*

The crevids and lupines closest to the explosion leaped into the air above it. Stone and pebbles struck them but did little to slow their advance. The ensuing blast ruffled thick fur and hair and illuminated snarling visages. Shrapnel bounced off the Battleguards' armor. The mounts landed and bounded forward. The lupines howled for blood.

"The buildings," Nebsamu shouted above the tumult of wagon wheels, thundering hooves, and howls. "Strike the buildings with Aether Shots."

Frost scowled at the man. "You gotta be kidding. I can't do that. People are in there. Fellow Khertahkans. Innocent people."

"This isn't the time for morals." Nebsamu glared at Frost, scarred features bunching. "This is life or death. Them or us."

"I can't!"

"Give it to me." Nebsamu held out his hand.

"No. Hell, no."

Nebsamu snatched Noobstick and knocked Frost aside. "I'm *not* dying today because you're too weak and emotional to do what needs doing."

The Blackguards had closed the gap to where Frost could make out their scowling visages, the slobber flying from their lupines' jaws. For a moment Frost considered kicking the scavenger off the wagon but then he glanced over at Tia. And saw Kai. He hung his head.

From his knees, Nebsamu aimed to the left. A clicking noise issued from his mouth. He squeezed the trigger. Whomp. Blue pulse. The sound hadn't faded before the base of the building exploded. Whomp. Another blue pulse. Another detonation. The structure toppled.

Nebsamu fired at the street's other side. He continued like this, from side to side every few seconds, a cyan glare lighting up his scarred features and single horn. Buildings exploded. Brick and wood and dirt tore apart, careened into the air. People screamed. When he expended all his aether, he turned to Korbitanium Projectiles, firing wildly into the cloud of dust and smoke.

Lupine howls cut off. The drum of hooves stopped. So did Nebsamu.

But Frost still saw the cyan light. Still heard the whomps. The bullfrog. Echoing in his head. The screams. He wanted to be anywhere but there. "You're a murderer," he spat. "A damned murderer."

"So are they." Nebsamu stood. "But we are alive."

"Killing innocents shouldn't come so easy."

"It never does," Nebsamu said softly. He shook his head. "In Nif's name, it never does. May she embrace them." He stared toward the devastation left in their wake. "This is war, boy. There isn't any clean ground to stand on. It's all death and dirt. To play in dirt, you must be willing to get dirty. Don't die over a ridiculous conviction."

Within the next few minutes they reached the East Gate and were rushed outside by Nebsamu's men. There were perhaps thirty of them. Fresh crevids were at the ready. Nebsamu gave instructions for a wagon train to be made for his valuables.

Gilda approached Frost in those willowy strides of hers, a smirk on her face, her phosphorous green eyes mocking. "I had expected more from the former top dog." She shook her head, disappointment thick in her tone. "Hope you don't chalk up that performance to playing a cannoneer. The class rocks."

Frost sighed. "I did my part."

Smiling warmly, Gilda raised her hand, an inch of space between her thumb and forefinger. "About this much. I bet the action was more than you expected. A little too real. Too intense."

Frost said nothing. He was disappointed in himself. But he wasn't about to admit it to her.

She continued, "Reminding yourself it's a game and that most of them are NPCs helps, but whatever they're pumping into us takes over at times. Took me a while to get used to it also. This is my third alpha with Total Immersion."

"Third?" Frost whistled.

"Yeah." She turned a ring on her middle finger. "Which is why I knew where to find you."

"Find me?" Then Frost chuckled. "I remember now. My boy, Hughey, told me you said I was lucky I quit. If you wanna duel, at least wait for me to hit max. Then it's no prob. With all your rep, I don't see you as one for killing noobs."

"You'd already know if I was here for that, trust and believe."

"Really?"

"No doubt." She deadpanned.

Smiling, Frost nodded. "You don't back down from anyone. I like that. I really like that." He glanced at the medium-sized chakrams hanging from special quick release metallic belt loops on her hips. "What's up with those? I thought you were a cutthroat."

"Maybe, I am. Maybe, I'm not."

Someone yelled a warning. A clash of weapons and spells echoed from just inside the gates.

The battle spilled outside the gates. Most of Nebsamu's fighters engaged. Spells, projectiles, and explosions lit up the area.

"Follow me." Nebsamu hurried to waiting crevids, and he, Frost, Tia, Melori, Gilda, and a few others fled, abandoning the scavenger's precious wares.

Behind them, Niba burned.

Escape from Niba
Objective Complete
Escaped Niba:
1000 experience points
Sister kept alive:
1000 experience points
Defeated Battleguards:
1000 experience points
Level 3 gained
200 Khertahka dominion credits

Nebsamu slowed a bit until he rode beside Frost. "I intended to sell these, but now they might be better used to help us keep ahead of these bastards," he shouted over the beat of their mounts' hooves. He tossed a pouch to Frost. "Think of them as your reward for helping to save me."

Frost caught the pouch. Inside were two skill shards. He was able to absorb one.

Skills acquired:

Divergence
Cast time: 1 second
Recharge Time: 8 seconds
Consumes: Aether
Available shard slots: 3
Effect: Fire a five aether shot spread up to 250 feet. Gain 1 percent aether for each successful hit, up to a maximum of 5 percent aether.

Aether Bomb
Requires level 4

Though he appreciated the gifts, Frost's thoughts wandered to his experience so far. A part of him wished he could log out, wished it was a dream. Another part of him swore to see it through. He would save Mom, Kai, Regi, and Rayne. And make Sidrie Malikah pay. Thoughts of the future made him stroke his aether ring.

He would bide his time, but when the chance presented itself, he would ditch this group and play the game the way it was meant to be played. Solo. He hefted Noobstick. With the power of the aether cannon at his disposal, it would be a breeze.

CHAPTER 10

Nomarch Setnana Botros could not stop dry washing her hands. Neither could she stop her lips from quivering. Nor the weakness in her knees, the urge to flee. She tried. And failed every time she looked through the glass at her son, at the blood and broth dribbling from Perihy's colorless lips, at skin that was once a deep glowing chocolate but was now rife with gray splotches, drawn tight until she could count each rib, see the outline of bones along his elbows, shoulders, and face.

His face! Perihy's once beautiful face! Instead of the disfigured skeletal features before her, she pictured the son she loved: intelligent golden eyes, full cheekbones, a brilliant smile, and dark horns polished to a shine. The gorgeous boy who had every mother of station across the Kadi nome vying for his affections on their daughter's behalf.

She clung to that last image. *That* was her Perihy.

Until a year ago. When he contracted the Gray Death at the tender age of nine. Nine! *What had he done to the gods to deserve this? What have I done, dear Nif?*

She remembered when the first splotch appeared. It was the same day a deep blue wave of light slithered across the sky, spread like a disease, seeped into the clouds. Thunderheads had formed, swirled into a great maelstrom, a voidstorm, its center a gaping black maw from which shot lightning bolt after lightning bolt.

The voidstorm tore across the land, devastated cities

and towns, ravaged forests, turned savannas and lush plains into wildernesses before it came to rest over the Empyrean Sea. The ocean boiled and bubbled, rising into mountainous tidal waves that destroyed any coastal habitation without stormcallers to protect them. When the voidstorm died, leaving behind its volatile remnants, it had birthed Maelpith Island.

And her son had become this… this hideous *thing*. She grimaced.

On the other side of the glass in the sealed room, five grand kora mystics worked feverishly. Dressed in specially designed germ suits, complete with hoods and cloth masks over their noses and mouths so only their eyes showed, they seemed like something out of a nightmare, one of the stories of strange beings who worshipped the vampire god Bodek and siphoned aether from bodies by drinking their victims' blood. Hands moving in tandem like some exotic dance, they hovered over Perihy, pooled their aether. With their power magnified, they cast Purifying Touch, Vitalize, and Suppression. Nomarch Botros felt their power, envied it, and was tempted to draw from it to see how much she could strengthen her own sorcerous abilities.

Perihy changed. Transformed. The splotches shrunk until they disappeared. His flesh reinvigorated. Atrophied muscles and tissue swelled with life. Deep chocolate crept across his body, flushed across his skin like the sky at the birth of a new dawn. He became the son she remembered. Beautiful. Perfect.

Setnana tentatively brushed her hand on the glass. She trailed her fingers down it as if she caressed Perihy's face. She lingered on one shiny horn and then the next.

Perihy gasped. His eyes shot open. Beautiful and golden.

Smiling, eyes brimming with tears, Nomarch Botros

pressed her palm against the glass. She craved to enter the room, to hug her son, to kiss him, talk to him, laugh with him. "Nif, I beg you. Please let it work this time. As your humble servant, it is all I ask." She made the sign of the X on her forehead.

She'd scarcely uttered the prayer when Suppression faded. Perihy sucked in a breath. His eyes bulged, his expression one of abject terror. He clawed at the air.

Through the glass, Setnana heard the choking sounds he made, as if something sucked the very life from him. His body deflated. Healthy skin grew diseased, riddled with gray splotches. She cupped a hand over her mouth despite having witnessed this reversal on other occasions. Unable to watch the rest of it, she fled the room. The door slammed shut.

Objective Ended
Heal Perihy Failed

As if I don't already know. Chest heaving, head down, her back against the wall in the long lamplit hallway, she hugged her arms and wished she could wipe the thought from her head, tear the memory away. She ignored the next thought, the one that recommended burning. She still felt the heat from a thousand pyres, the odious fumes of burning flesh after they had gathered almost every person in Aprunis afflicted with the Gray Death. A few had managed to escape. Most had been recaptured later and burnt. Others disappeared.

A door opened down the hall. She took a last quick breath to compose herself. And grimaced at the reek of decay and disease that had not been in the air moments ago.

One of the grand kora mystics stepped through the doorway, dressed in hooded white robes trimmed with blue, the back emblazoned with the Coalition's tan and blue insignia, the Mountain and the Aetherstream. The mystic closed the door, turned, and flipped back the hood to reveal Citri

Madiga's pale yellow face. A face that was middling at best. No wonder the woman could not rise above her current station.

And no wonder she loathes me. Setnana brushed her hair behind her right horn, one of two that personified elegance. Citri Madiga dipped her head in recognition of her betters, ears twitching behind her hairy ossicones.

Setnana offered a tight smile. She would not confuse Citri's show of respect as genuinely offered. The grand kora would much prefer to have Setnana as a slave, or have Setnana's horns to grind to powder to be used in some ointment to keep Citri's skin glowing and light, or as part of one of the infamous art displays cherished by grand korae. As evidenced by the way Citri's eyes shifted to Setnana's beauties as Citri approached.

Citri seemed to try to fight the urge, but it came as natural as breathing. As was the jealousy grand korae harbored because their ossicones would never develop into coveted horns.

Savages, Setnana thought.

"Your son's condition is deteriorating," Citri said when she reached Setnana, her voice echoing like a wind chime.

"I saw."

"Another attempt like the last could kill him."

Setnana clenched her hands behind her back and fought the threatening quiver of her lips by picturing the Perihy she loved. *I will show no weakness. I am a Botros.* "Could kill him." She shrugged. "But he *could* also survive, yes?"

Citri's eyebrow arched. "Possibly. However, it wouldn't improve his health. He wouldn't be cured."

"What are the other options?"

"We'll keep him stable for as long as we can, but curing him requires power we don't possess. Not even linked."

121

Setnana allowed her face to go slack. She dropped her hands to her sides. When next she spoke, her voice was flat, her eyes dead. "That is not the deal I made with Exarch Chaten. I did not betray my people for failure. Promises were made. Promises will be kept."

Citri licked her lips. "I... I didn't say the task was impossible, but that the mystics here lacked the power."

"Who among you has this power?"

"Exarch Chaten knows. She's arriving here soon to inform you."

"Soon?" Setnana felt as if she had just been slapped in the face. "How soon?"

"After the noon hour."

Nomarch Botros reached for the timeorb hanging from a chain around her neck. The dial was halfway to noon. She hissed. "You knew of this visit and did not inform me?" Something boiled within her.

Citri threw up her hands in a gesture of helplessness. "I was sworn to secrecy!" Her voice was shrill.

"Secrecy?" Setnana repeated softly. "By whom? In Nif's name, we're supposed to be at war. Your people are currently destroying Niba. How do I explain this visit to the Coalition?"

There would be no way for her to hide it as she had done with the five mystics. *Exarch Bakui Assam might kill me for this. Well, I will not die alone.*

"An explanation by you isn't necessary," Citri said. "Exarch Aishani Chaten isn't coming on her own. Exarch Bakui Assam is bringing her."

Setnana shook her head. "Exarch Assam is bringing her?"

"Yes."

Information Memory provided Setnana with an objective: Meet the Exarchs at the Acropolis' Aviary Landing.

Setnana's mind worked. *Does he know about Aishani and I? About Perihy? About the mystics? He does not. If I were in danger, Aishani would have sent word by Communication Orb. Or a messenger.*

For the first time, she noticed the blue-white glow highlighting Citri's too high cheekbones and thin lips, the ashen face, the sweat beading Citri's brow, the whiff of piss, and the soft crackle in the air. She glanced down. Arcane lightning danced up and down her hands. She released her hold on aether. The glow vanished. The crackle cut off.

As if she had not come within a heartbeat of taking Citri's life, she said, "Return to Perihy."

"Thank you, Nomarch." Wringing her hands, the grand kora bowed from the waist. She turned and fled down the hall.

After the door to Perihy's chamber closed, Setnana raced up the hall in the opposite direction, the objective filling her head. Although Exarch Bakui Assam knew she had been unaware of the visit, he would see her absence from his arrival as a slight. A failing. Incompetence. In his eyes, a person should expect the unexpected. *I cannot afford his wrath. For Perihy's sake.*

She exited the compound at the rear of the Temple of Nif and squinted at the gray murk above Aprunis, the sun a bleak blot within it. Scarlet banks swelled in the southwest like bloodied waves. There was no sign of the great beast-bird, the simurgh. Breathing a bit easier, she strode across the flagstoned courtyard toward the waiting lupines, making every effort not to run in the presence of her personal Battleguards.

"We're returning home. Exarch Assam is on his way."

"Yes, my Nomarch," said Ihuet and Khafra as one.

The three lupines perked up, tails wagging, as she

and her personal guard approached. That she had brought Wenet instead of one of her other mounts was a relief. And a blessing. Wenet was as fast as he was magnificent, his mane a mixture of silver like lightning itself. *Nif still smiles on me.*

Wenet got down on his stomach as she drew near, massive paws stretched before him. He regarded her with his head tilted to one side, gold and green eyes radiant, tongue lolling as if he anticipated the race to come. She climbed into the harness atop his back, stuck her feet into the bolsters along his flanks, leaned forward, and took a hold of the two grips braided into his mane. Wenet stood, towering some eight feet.

"Yah! Home!"

Wenet bounded forward, great strides taking him out the wide entrance to Nif's Temple where the patron goddess' statue stood in full cutthroat regalia, complete with a katar in each hand, the triangular daggers matching the insignia on the chests of Setnana's Battleguards. Down the Circle of Vespers they galloped, unwary mystics scrambling from the lupines' path. She glanced up at the square time tower in the heart of Aprunis upon which stood the Great Timesphere, the globe always rotating. It would be a close thing, but she would make it. She encouraged more speed with coaxing words and a kick of the bolsters.

Soon, they were darting through streets filled with patrons of every shade, erada and non-erada alike, the lupines' cracked bays giving warning. Wagons and carts pulled to the side. The roar of voices lulled as folks scattered. People looked on in consternation or annoyance. None of which mattered.

Nomarch Botros left the Radiant Quarter and its numerous shops and pushed hard down Caligin Avenue and into The Obsidian Quarter, the black flagstoned road like a tenebrous river. Her trepidation eased when she was surrounded by the marvelous architecture of taverns and inns whose bricks were streaked with chips of volcanic glass.

They rounded Caligin Avenue's final corner where the long stretch through the Noble Domain began. Smiling, she breathed in the sweet fresh air, relished the cool wind against her face as it whipped her hair, billowed her cloak. The avenue slowly climbed, and at its crest rose the walls and spires of the Aprunis acropolis.

The sprawling estates and walled villas with manicured gardens were a welcome sight. Laborers toiled in orchards. Here or there, a crevid grazed in a field, the males with horns so curled and majestic one might worship them.

Flightmaster Wedjedhi's oldest son, Ahmose, was out in a field working with his pet lupines under the tutelage of Wedjedhi's beast trainer. She remembered when that was her and Papa. Before Adesh Hamada, Anefet Frost, and their Blue Sky operatives had killed him. She grimaced.

The Great Timesphere gonged the twelfth hour.

A simurgh's high-pitched screech echoed. Another answered. A bevy of lower-pitched gurgling cries followed.

No! A knot formed in Setnana's stomach. She kicked the bolsters. "Yah! Yah! Faster, damn it, faster!" Wenet surged forward.

One of the colossal beast-birds plunged through the solemn gray quilt above the acropolis, its furry feathers silver, white, and red. Whenever she saw the creatures Setnana always thought of a winged lupine some two hundred feet long with a wingspan to match. But she had no time to enjoy such magnificence. Three people were atop its back, and she knew the one in the middle would be Exarch Bakui Assam, the other two his personal guard. Another simurgh followed, similarly mounted.

A dozen scaled drakes speared through the clouds, their calls trapped between gurgles and shrieks. Half of the drakes carried Azureguards. Blackguards rode the other half. Exarch Bakui Assam's simurgh banked and circled on its final descent.

Objective Ended
Reach the Aviary before the Exarchs
Fail

Nomarch Botros deflated. She could hear the Exarch's deep scathing voice, picture the disappointment etched on his violet face. Without hope of arriving before him, she was resigned to her fate. At least Aishani would be there to advise her on who had the power required to cure Perihy. In that, she took solace.

And then, she frowned. All was not yet lost. Information Memory provided a way to remain in Exarch Bakui Assam's good graces. She almost grinned as she considered his awed expression. And his words. "Bakui, just call me, Bakui, Setnana," he would say while bowing and fawning to her.

She rode up the tree-lined avenue and through the acropolis gates. Instead of dismounting there for the servants to take Wenet, she kept going all the way through the courtyard to the fortress. As she'd anticipated, Resena was waiting at the top of the stairs with six maidservants instead of the normal three. The seneschal and the servants shied away as Wenet took the stairs in a single bound and came to rest on the landing opposite them. He lay on his stomach, and she climbed down.

"Hada!" Nomarch Botros gestured to the lupine with her palm out.

Wenet trotted down the stairs and headed toward the far side of the grounds where the kennels were located. Khafra and Ihuet had dismounted at the bottom of the steps. Their mounts ambled after Wenet.

Setnana took a look at her timeorb. Although Exarch Assam should already be on the ground, he would not be seen without his entire retinue. And he would make certain his simurgh was properly stabled. With the right distraction, the rest would take a little over a half an hour to land, stable the simurghs and drakes, and walk from the Aviary to the fortress. Just enough time.

"Resena, we have some creamed mango cake, correct?"

"Yes, Nomarch."

"Take platters of it and greet Exarch Assam," Setnana said. "He finds it irresistible. And some red wine. His favorite is Kituan's Kelsial Valley vintage." The seneschal bowed. "Quickly. Use a wagon and intercept them at the Aviary. I need time."

Setnana glanced up. The second simurgh carrying Aishani was circling. The drake riders hovered above it, leathery wings beating the air.

"The rest of you." She regarded the maidservants. "Make me more beautiful."

With that, she swept through the great oak double doors. She strode down the carpeted hall and entered the changing room she had designed for times such as this. The room was well lit by way of bloomglobes imported from Kituan. She always thought the expense would come in handy one day.

Mirrors adorned parts of the four walls and the ceiling. On one side were several gowns on wooden hangers. On the other was a table covered with various face paints, polishes, and powders. She indicated the dress she had in mind: a gorgeous piece in royal blue and white, offset with gems around the opening of the short sleeves, flared hem, and teasing V neckline. On her feet would be a pair of satin slippers. She ordered the servants to get to work.

Not long after, she stood resplendent in her choices,

turning this way and that, spinning to see the gown twirl where it flared at the bottom. *I am the epitome of beauty. Flawless.* The gown followed her curves just right, made her pale blue skin stand out in contrast.

Her snow-white hair was done in a tight bun. Her elegant horns shone. And her face! It was as if she were already Kalarch, a definition of glory.

She wanted to touch her face but resisted the urge. She spun once more to see herself from every angle, giggled, and headed to the door. A quick glance at her timeorb said the visitors should be nearing the fortress.

She strode toward Khafra and Ihuet. The dementer and the stormcaller bowed before falling in line to either side of her. Head high, shoulders back, Nomarch Botros glided through the fortress, keeping her expression flat despite the gasps of servants and other visitors. Inside, she exulted at their adulation.

They arrived at the rear entrance moments before the Exarchs. She ordered her servants to line up with fresh platters as was the custom, and she went outside to offer greetings. Chest up, she stood at the head of the two lines. The Exarchs were perhaps thirty feet away, striding through the courtyard with a full Battleguard complement in tow. She called for silence.

"Remember to greet Exarch Assam the same moment I do," she said.

Her chest swelled as Bakui approached, his hands behind his back. He was dressed in all black: a jacket that fell to his ankles, one side buttoned from left breast to inches above the waist, the rest left open to reveal trousers and polished boots. Gold tassels adorned the jacket's right side from the topmost button diagonally to his shoulder. Bakui's violet skin glistened. And his horns. They were even more magnificent than she remembered, long and curved, as thick as a forearm, and practically glowing.

Her palms grew sweaty. Her hands shook. She clasped them in front of her just below her belly, which fluttered like a schoolgirl.

Calm yourself, woman. It was Papa's voice in her head as usual. *You are a Botros. We show no weakness. The weak have no place in this world. Any sign of weakness and the lupine will tear out your throat.* She put on a dazzling smile.

Time seemed to stretch as Bakui approached. Yet, she couldn't help but to shoot a glance at Aishani Chaten. The woman was stunning in lavender offset by her creamy skin. The look more than made up for her ossicones. And then, Bakui was there, right in front of Setnana. She opened her mouth to offer a greeting.

He looked right through her. And strode on by.

She was left standing, her words stuck in her throat. She felt lightheaded. Her face, neck, and ears grew hot. She stared at his back.

How dare he? This is not happening. He did not just—she could not finish the thought. She clenched her fist. Exarch Assam entered the fortress and his Battleguards blocked her view.

Objective Ended.

Impress Exarch Bakui Assam

Fail

She cursed the reminder and gazed at her servants, who all averted their eyes. She hung her head and trudged after the Exarchs. The failures were a weight on her thoughts. She was accustomed to success. The trip to the Grand Room was a blur, a flood of jumbled emotions she fought to control.

As she walked, her shame grew to something else, something hot and red and terrible. Despite the knot in her belly, she refused to let tears come. She hated herself for even allowing the man to affect her the way he had.

In her head, she repeated Papa's mantras. *Know who you are. Know your beauty. Know your worth. No one can take that away from you. Botros show no weakness. Strength always.*

She found her spine again. Even if it were less rigid than before.

She made her way past Exarch Assam's personal guard, who demanded that Khafra and Ihuet remain behind them. She nodded to the two Blackguards. Scowling their disapproval, Khafra and Ihuet stalked away, but she knew they would only go but so far.

As she followed, she eyed Exarch Assam's rather broad back, the slight hitch in his gait, the blemishes on the rear of his horns, the thinning of his hair. She smirked. The servants opened the door to the Grand Room. Exarch Assam waited outside while two of his personal Blackguards checked the room.

Setnana scowled. *As if I would allow harm to come to you under my roof.*

The guards returned and bowed to the man. He strode in first. Aishani followed. And then Nomarch Botros. The door closed with a thud. The Exarchs turned to face her.

Exarch Bakui Assam's hard blue-eyed gaze roved over her, but his face remained impassive. He seemed thoroughly unimpressed. Aishani's thin lips formed a tight line, her green eyes pitying.

Setnana was taken aback by Aishani's thinly veiled disappointment. From the day they met she had been drawn to Aishani despite the old enmity between their races. Aishani was a kindred spirit, in her early twenties, a woman who could appreciate beauty, as was evidenced by her lavish red locks done in intricate braids, lavender dress, and buttermilk skin. Setnana doubted the day could get any worse.

"I'm sorry I was not there to greet you upon landing, Exarchs." Setnana dipped her head in a perfect imitation of an apologetic person of status. Not too much to seem a grovel. Just enough to satisfy. She thought of saying they could have sent word via a Communication Orb, but obviously their intention had been one of surprise. "I was investigating a report of Adesh Hamada here in Aprunis."

Exarch Assam spoke. "We'll talk about Blue Sky operatives in a moment, but first, some news. You're going to Maelpith Island."

Setnana opened her mouth to protest. To mention Perihy. His ailment. And immediately snapped it shut. Aishani's eyes flashed a warning moments after Setnana had already decided. Exarch Assam cocked his head, gave Setnana one of his scathing looks, and then preened like a bird that his stare had silenced her.

You can never tell him about Perihy, Setnana thought. Clinging to the small victory, she bowed from the waist. "Yes, Exarch Assam."

CHAPTER 11

Nomarch Setnana Botros stood before the Exarchs with her head high and back straight despite how small she felt inside. Not once had Exarch Assam mentioned her absence from the Aviary. He directed his wrath elsewhere.

"You were supposed to be in Niba to oversee our efforts before Exarch Chaten's forces attacked." Exarch Assam glowered at her from the chair he'd taken. One arm rested on the oak table.

Setnana met the man's hard eyes with an unflinching gaze. "As I said before, I received word that Blue Sky lieutenant, Adesh Hamada, was here in Aprunis."

"Was he?"

"He had fled before we arrived."

Exarch Assam scowled. "As I said, you were to be in Niba. Those were my orders."

"I thought it best to remain far from the conflict," Setnana said. "To avoid the Coalition blaming us for failing to defend Niba."

"You thought wrong," Exarch Assam said in that grating voice of his. "Even the greatest commander makes mistakes. Any story we told the Coalition in response to a report would involve such an error. Or we could have simply blamed the failure on surprise. After all, the grand korae killed the sentries in and around Kirin Pass."

"In turn," Exarch Aishani said, "My Kalarch would blame the renegades, General Asamar, Umesh Madara, and their Redthorns, for the invasion. Revenge on a town controlled by Blue Sky, whose members have once again begun raiding Coalition caravans and mining operations.

"We would all be absolved. And this meeting was to be the sign that Puria and Khertahka were working on a peace treaty."

"But–" Setnana began.

"But nothing." Exarch Assam pounded the table with his fist. "Nif take you, woman. You were well aware of the importance of the mission in maintaining our pact with the grand korae."

"Yes, Exarch Assam. I apologize." She kept her posture stiff and met his scathing gaze.

As much as she wanted to point out the flaw in his reasoning, that the other Isfet Mountain sentries would have seen the grand kora army as it made the short journey across the Powder Grass Plains to Niba, she decided against it. Whether or not the Redthorns and their forsaken grand kora general or his second, the gurash outcast, Umesh Madara, were in the area was another story.

"Luckily for you, the mission wasn't a complete failure. We killed several high-level Blue Sky operatives, including one Anefet Frost, better known as the Hand of Freedom."

Setnana's eyes opened wide. "THE Hand of Freedom?"

Preening like a bird again, the Exarch nodded. "The very same."

Setnana deflated. She'd been robbed of vengeance. For over a year she'd hunted Anefet Frost. Ever since the woman, Adesh Hamada, and several other Blue Sky operatives had killed Papa when he'd cornered them in their hideout in the Ouroboros Mountains. She'd taken over from Papa then, becoming Nomarch, and had sworn to make Anefet, Adesh, and Blue Sky pay. In that, she had partially failed. Anefet's death had not been by her hand.

The Nomarch let out a slow exhale. Other parts of her quest still remained. Adesh Hamada being one. Exarch Assam himself was another. His incompetence was the reason Papa did not have enough Battleguards on that fateful day. She ground her jaw. It took everything to remind herself in whose presence she stood and to fight back the inadvertent summoning of arcane lightning.

"She'd hidden among the sceeves." Exarch Assam shook his head, disbelief thick in his tone. "Some claimed she'd gone so far as to become a whore and a beggar like them."

Setnana cringed. She couldn't begin to contemplate stooping so low for any cause.

"But one of our captives say her children escaped, most likely with instructions that can upset our plans." His expression was ice once more. "He was certain they'd flee Niba by way of a Blue Sky captain. A so-called relic dealer who turned out to be a scavenger named Nebsamu Tadros."

Setnana perked up, the news presenting certain opportunities. "I assume the Battleguards captured this Nebsamu?"

Exarch Assam scowled. "You assume wrong. He was one of those who escaped. A feat I'm sure you could've prevented had you been in Niba as I ordered. Instead, you were here chasing ghosts."

"But it was Adesh Hamada!"

"I don't care who it was." Exarch Assam sneered. "I give an order; you follow it. I swear to Nif if you fail me again, I'll have you stripped of all titles and your status.

You'll be just another sceeve."

She made to challenge the Exarch, to tell him only the Vizier or the Kalarch had such authority. But Exarch Assam's blue eyes were expectant little beads. Aishani gave an almost imperceptible shake of her head. Setnana acted as if she hadn't seen. Exarch Assam was daring her to make such a mistake.

Setnana took a deep breath and bowed ever so slightly. "Yes, Exarch Assam."

"Good. I'm giving you a chance to redeem yourself." The Exarch's expression softened. "That is the reason for your trip to Maelpith Island. As usual, draconids appeared in the wake of the last voidstorm. A Coalition expedition to the island discovered a draconid stronghold: Imanok Sanctum. Before the draconids wiped out the expedition, our people reportedly found two hierkas and hierka schemas." He was smiling now, eyes shining.

Setnana's mouth grew slack. "By Nif, such a find means the Sanctum is the only place outside the Akufa dominion with direct access to draconid advanced science. Assuming the stories of a Genesis Engine in the Aetherium are nothing more than rumors." She shook her head. "There would be no immediate need to fight or sneak past the Front."

"Exactly." Exarch Assam nodded. "Believe me when I say no one really wants to be at the Front. Much less go beyond it. No one truly wishes to face draconid legions or fight the high-level void lords and void revenants guarding the Genesis Engines. But some brave souls like myself have done what they must." A distant look encompassed his face before he caught himself. "Your mission is twofold. One is to search for hierkas or schemas for our hierkaneers. Second: Blue Sky is sending its best to Maelpith for the very same reason. They must not succeed."

Aishani cleared her throat. "You can also be certain every dominion will be sending its own expedition to the island. As well as another large one from the Coalition itself. Not to mention mercenaries, relic hunters, and scavengers."

Information Memory outlined objectives in a chain beneath Imanok Sanctum.

The implications were all too clear to Setnana. Anyone who came away with hierkas or schemas stood to either make a fortune or would have the upper hand against any other dominion lacking the empowered items and weaponry. So far, the Coalition had made certain such genesiswork items were spread evenly among the dominions, that the most powerful ones, those of genesis grade, remained with the Coalition forces in their fight at the Front and beyond. With the Void Legion having recently defeated the Coalition in several clashes, it was equally or even more important for the Coalition itself to retrieve schemas and weapons to stymie the Void Legion invasion.

And yet, despite all her reasoning, she did not want the mission. Perihy was all that mattered.

"I'm surprised the Coalition hasn't put its foot down and declared the island off-limits as they did to Akufa after the first voidstorms." Exarch Assam stroked his chin.

"They could try, but it would incur the wrath of the yurids and gargants," Setnana said. "The Accords declared the Empyrean Sea and the Endless Ocean as neutral territories to appease both races and attain their help in fighting the draconids. It is mainly because of them that the draconids have not advanced beyond the Front in a century. Even if the Coalition formed a blockade around the island, does anyone really wish to fight colossuses who could walk the ocean floors? Or yurids who would swarm us from the clouds, more adept at sky combat than we could ever be on drakes, simurghs, and zephyrs?"

While Aishani nodded in agreement, Exarch Assam's color darkened to a deeper purple. His nostrils flared. Setnana braced for an angry outburst that she'd shown up the man. None came.

"They could call an assembly and come to some agreement." Exarch Assam regarded her with eyes like flinty pebbles. "It's been done before."

"True. A very astute observation." Setnana inclined her head. She kept a straight face but chuckled inside at the man's petulance and at having to educate him on politics he should have known. *Why would you expect anything more? Unlike you, he hasn't been educated at the Aetherium, the greatest Academia in all of Mikander.* She flicked her hair behind her glorious horns.

"This works in our favor anyway," Aishani said. Although Aishani's expression was grave, she had a twinkle in her eye. One Setnana recognized. One that warmed Setnana's heart.

"It does," Exarch Assam said. "Setnana, gather a small group that would go unnoticed, perhaps twenty warriors, those you believe will succeed in the mission, and prepare to leave before nightfall."

The Nomarch paused for a moment. She hadn't expected the orders to be this soon. There had to be a way to change his mind, to make herself unavailable. Pressure tightened her chest. She couldn't be away from Perihy right now. She tried to think of something even as Aishani shot a warning look her way.

Deflated, Setnana bowed. "Yes, Exarch Assam." In the back of her mind, she swore to find a reason for Exarch Assam to pardon her from the mission before he left. She turned to depart.

His grating voice stopped her. "Have your servants bring me some of that creamed mango cake. And was that

Kelsial Valley Blood Red, I saw?" Setnana nodded. "Great. Send a full bottle. Indulging myself before I go is the least I can do since your failure forced me to make this trip." His attention turned to Aishani, who smiled with everything but her eyes.

Setnana's insides curdled. She had the sudden urge to spit. Exarch Assam dismissed her with a wave.

She left the chambers, preoccupied with ideas that might result in her exclusion from the mission. Setnana ordered the servants to bring food and drink for Exarch Assam but stopped short of telling Ihuet and Khafra to assemble ten Blackguards, to prep the Sky Swords, and the next two best Azureguard companies. Instead, she had them keep an eye on the chambers with instructions to send runners should Exarch Assam leave.

Though deep in thought, she made a show of passing instructions to her servants as if she intended to depart within the next few hours. She often peered at her timeorb as she headed through the fortress making certain Exarch Assam's people saw her go up to her quarters. She paid extra attention in long hallways, noting any vibrations, any forms behind her. No one was following.

Once inside her quarters, she found the nearest mirror. The one that encompassed the entire living room wall. She looked for a flaw. And found none. Not in the beautiful royal blue and white begemmed dress with its teasing V neckline that brought out the paler blue of her skin and her pure white hair, nor in her face, exquisitely powered and painted. Not in her satin slippers. Not her painted nails. Her polished horns completed the perfection.

The idiot let anger blind him.

Even as she thought of Exarch Assam, she remembered the lust in his eyes before she left. Lust not directed at her. She had that sickening feeling in her stomach again. Yet, there was nothing she could do but wait. She plopped down on a soft, cushioned chair and tried to ignore the images spinning through her head.

After raising the timeorb from her neck to take another look, she left her rooms by way of the secret passages within the walls. Making certain to use the reverberations of her steps in utter darkness for echolocation rather than to issue her natural clicks, she made her way down several floors and emerged in a spacious guest room that smelled of orchids. She hoped to find the room occupied. It was empty.

Disappointed, she took a seat on the large feather bed with a view of the room's main door by way of a mirror. She settled in to wait. It was not long before the door swung inward.

Aishani entered. The woman pressed the door shut, turned to face the room, and let out a deep breath with her eyes closed. She proceeded to disrobe immediately as if the clothes were the last things she wished upon her body. She hurried to the bedroom.

"You did it again, didn't you?" Setnana scowled at the woman for whom she'd come to care deeply. The areas where Exarch Assam's filthy hands had touched Aishani's buttermilk skin were bruised and glaring.

Aishani stopped and regarded her with a smirk. Her hairy ossicones twitched in annoyance where they poked through her red hair. "In Jerad's Light, what choice did I have? You disobeyed his orders. And then you weren't at the Aviary. I did it to save you from his wrath. Despite what he said before you left, he fully intended to send his personal guard after you and have you thrown out on your ass."

"I-I apologize." Setnana hung her head.

"As you should. Dressing as you did in a vain attempt to seduce him… like some young slut who knows no better." Aishani snorted. "As if he wouldn't see through the ploy. He laughed at you after you left. Called you a fool. At first, I thought you'd worn the dress for me. Only to be disappointed." Aishani grimaced and shook her head.

Setnana's shoulders slumped further. She averted her eyes from Aishani's condescending glare. The same piteous expression from earlier.

"And then you wish to be upset with me for doing what I had to?" Quiet anger filled Aishani's voice. "For protecting you? Tell me, if he'd accepted that which you so obviously offered, how would you have handled the situation? Considering the very reasons we're here, why we're doing as we are? You would be praying to Nif and Jerad right now had he accepted."

If she'd felt horrible before, Setnana was absolutely miserable now. She would have done anything to be in Exarch Assam's good graces and to stay with Perihy. Tears welled up in her eyes, but she refused to cry. *Never show weakness. Strength always. You're a Botros.*

"I would have done as you do… allowed Exarch Assam to have his way, thinking it is all his plan, and that he stands to benefit most." She straightened and looked into Aishani's eyes. "Until the day I killed him and was named Khertahka's Exarch."

"Praise be to Jerad. There she is." Aishani's loathing became a smile in an instant. "The fiery woman I adore. I was wondering when you would show up."

Setnana returned the gesture. And then frowned. "Why didn't you send warning of his visit by way of our Orbs?"

"Too risky. The man watches everything. Now, come, wash my back. And rub me where I like it most." The ossicones twitched with Aishani's longing. The Exarch headed toward the bath, her red braids falling past her shoulders.

"Did you manage to convince him to let me stay

in Aprunis?" Setnana followed, admiring Aishani's willowy curves and the intricate braidwork, which appeared to have gold strands woven within them.

"No." Aishani shook her head. "Unfortunately, your mission hasn't changed."

"But Perihy!"

"I know. I will have Citri and the others stay and take care of him." Aishani climbed into the large tub, which the servants kept filled with warm water in case of surprise visits such as this one. She sat a little forward and leaned. "This is for the best and works in our and Perihy's favor."

"How so?" Setnana took the long-handled sponge, dipped it in water, and proceeded to scrub Aishani's back.

Aishani took a bar of perfumed soap and lathered herself. "The power we lack to cure Perihy can be found on Maelpith Island. In Imanok Sanctum, to be exact."

"The hierkas?"

"Yes. One is a mystic's zhua, called Benediction, said to have been crafted by the titans while they drew directly from the Aetherstream. It is kept in Emperor KiGyaba's treasure room. The others are rare shards to empower Ameliorate, Suppression, and Rejuvenate. They can be had from GUMs and treasure chests before the emperor. The Coalition hierkaneers believe the boosted spells combined with the zhua will solve the recent Gray Death outbreak, but they wish to keep it secret to prevent thousands of people from flocking to the island."

Information Memory added an objective for the spells and one called Benediction. They fell under a line called The Cure. Setnana immediately saw the zhua, a long stave topped by a clawed hand, all made from polished korbitanium. The mystic's weapon was breathtaking.

Setnana stopped scrubbing. "Empowered Ameliorate and Rejuvenate would mean bringing in one of the Vin-

141

dicators. Can they be trusted?"

"Leave that to me, my love. I have one in mind. A grand kora who will be in my service by the time I'm done with her."

"I do not know—"

"Trust me, dear." Aishani turned so she could peer over her shoulder. "Perihy means as much to me as he does to you. We will see him well again. He is the key to our desires, our dreams of becoming Kalarchs. As is your mission.

"Think it through. Don't let emotion blind you. Our names will ring out across Mikander if we cure the Gray Death. With this zhua in our hands we can see our dreams of ruling come true. Most overlook us because we are young. More so because we're women. Let them make that mistake.

"Now, come, join me. I've washed myself of Exarch Assam's filth. We can discuss our plans among pleasure." A longing smile graced her lips.

Setnana slipped out of her clothes, all the while wondering if she was making the right decision. When she climbed into the water and caressed the ossicones on either side of Aishani's head, and Aishani stroked Setnana's horns in return, all was forgotten.

CHAPTER 12

They rode nonstop for hours, alternating between gallops, trots, and walks until afternoon's milk-soft clouds molted into evening's fiery sky. Frost was only too happy to find that riding basic mounts had not changed. He'd retained memory of his old ability. He also noted an increase in his endurance due to the length of the ride.

Despite the long travel without incident, he still stole looks over his shoulder from time to time. Noobstick was in a special harness within easy reach if he slid his right hand to the side and a bit behind him. The weapon's presence was a comfort.

Nebsamu had sent riders off in three directions to confuse any pursuers while he kept their original group together. He had a chestnut dresdor marksman named Saba Nerubi follow in their wake to hide the group's actual tracks. They avoided any major roads and kept to the shadowy uncharted foothills of Apep's Belly, a wall of slopes and peaks clothed in greens and browns to their right as they headed north.

Frost remained a bit off to the side from the others. He stole a glance at Gilda. She was riding up ahead, talking to Tia. He couldn't help thinking it was one hell of a coincidence to have met her at Odds and Ends. *Was she an NPC added by Sidrie as a challenge? Or a spy of some sort?*

Yet again, he wished for some way to immediately tell the difference in characters. At the same time, he had to admit that not knowing added to the game's intrigue. With questions in mind, he dug his heels into his crevid's flanks and sent the beast lumbering forward to catch up to Nebsamu. The one-horned erada was atop a black crevid, having a chat with Melori, who rode a lupine.

"Nebsamu, can I ask a question?" Frost fell in beside them.

"Certainly."

"What's the deal with this strange story I heard on my way to your shop? A few stragglers were claiming none of this was real, that it was one big game. Even my sister mentioned something about them."

Nebsamu hawked and spat to one side. "Damned dreamers. Nif blind them. There's been too many of them lately."

"Second time I've heard about dreamers," Frost said. "Care to explain?"

Melori spoke, voice like a deep bass drum. "Over the last year there's been talk that Mikander is a plaything for the gods. A shevla board. And we, the cards. Dreamers believe this with all their hearts. They're fervent in their worship of the gods and their game."

Frost frowned. He could understand such an interpretation of the trading card game. A shevla board was a map of Mikander, the game itself consisting of cards representing creatures and peoples of the world. He'd been a decent shevla player in the old Ataxia. Some players used the game to gamble and win tons of various dominion credits.

Shevla was often serious business. People had been killed for cheating or simply because they couldn't handle a loss, especially to a player whose deck was draconid faction. If the need arose, he would start building a deck again, but he did not intend to be around for that long.

"Just myth and wild imagination, then," Frost concluded. "Not something any of you actually believe."

Nebsamu snorted. "All nonsense. Only the staunchest among them stick to this idea when death comes calling. I give Nif her respect and praise as any god-fearing erada should, but not for a moment do I think she will come to save me." He absently brushed his stump of a horn before returning his hand to his reins. A wolf howled. "Night comes. And a storm's brewing."

Frost took in the sky. The sole clouds looked as if they were afire. "How can you tell?"

"I feel it in the air." Nebsamu shrugged. "A storm's always coming. Just like death."

"You brood too much."

"So I've been told. But does that make what I said less true?"

Frost shrugged. "Guess not. I just prefer good thoughts."

"Everyone likes good thoughts and a good life. Happiness. Prosperity." Nebsamu shook his head. "No one wants to struggle, to suffer, to live with adversity."

"Of course not," Frost said, grimacing.

Nebsamu continued, "But you can't have spring flowers without rain, and where there's rain, there's bound to be clouds, and where there are clouds, there's the likelihood of a storm."

"I guess." Frost still didn't see these storm clouds, but he wasn't about to argue. It might lead to another speech. It was clear to him that Nebsamu liked to hear himself talk.

The scavenger pointed ahead of them. "There's an old mine up in the hills where we can make camp and hide a fire. Saba should be there already. She will take first watch. Melori, you have second. Tell Gilda she will be third. Keep

145

your eyes open for plague wolves." He peered at Frost. "You won't be on watch duty tonight. Not with all you've been through. Take this time to rest." With a kick of his bolsters, Nebsamu surged forward.

Frost followed Melori to Gilda and Tia. Melori relayed Nebsamu's orders. They trailed after Nebsamu, who turned off into a narrow pass, where cliffs rose to either side of them, the way ahead falling into gloom even as the sun's fiery glow lit the upper slopes and peaks.

A wolf howled again. Several others picked up the dirge. The crevids snorted in displeasure.

Eventually, they came upon an old overgrown path, which they followed up to an excavated area and the black mouths of several mineshafts. A campfire lit one of those mouths. Saba Nerubi stood near the flames whose capering hues highlighted the chestnut hair covering her equine half and the lighter bronze of her humanoid upper body. Her hair was cropped short and the color of dark honey. The centaur was turning game of some sort on a spit. Frost's stomach grumbled.

Melori took their mounts off to graze and fed his lupine while Nebsamu, Gilda, Frost, and Tia got their waterskins and sat down near the fire. Nebsamu provided bread from his supplies.

Saba gave them some dented tin plates. She sheared off meat from the animal's haunches, the juices dribbling into the fire and giving off the most righteous scent of roasting. Frost licked his lips. The dresdor served Nebsamu and Tia first then walked over to Frost, her hooves clip-clopping on the hard ground.

"Cervin." Smiling, Saba handed the plate to Frost. "Cousin to the crevid. They have no horns, but are untamable. Some of the tastiest meat you will ever have."

"Thank you." Frost blew on the meat, then picked

146

it up and tore off a chunk with his teeth. It was soft and succulent. And tasted like chicken. He paused, once again amazed by taste and texture. *Incredible. Simply incredible.* He resumed chewing.

"This is really good," he said, words garbled. "Where'd you catch it?"

"The forest over that slope." Saba nodded toward the hill. "Was easy enough to snag one with my bow. I'd stay away if I were you, though. It's infested with plague wolves. You're not ready for those."

"I'll remember that." Frost nodded.

Soon after the meal, Frost sat with Tia. They chatted about Anefet and the times they spent together. They chuckled about stories of begging for alms and running from Azureguards who acted more as town watch than the warriors they'd become. He and Tia had pulled their share of pranks on rich kids who'd bullied them at one time or another. Such implanted recollections amazed Frost.

"Remember the time I filled dried crevid bladders with piss, tied them off, and threw them from rooftops as those bastards walked by." Frost chuckled.

Tia laughed. "The expressions when the bladders burst! I won't ever forget it."

They reminisced until Tia fell asleep. Frost put her to bed on some old sacks. He placed Noobstick next to him and sat with his back to the wall where he could keep an eye on everyone. Then he pulled out the letter and read it by way of the campfire. When he was finished, he tucked it away in his left trouser pocket.

Gilda came over. "Mind if I sit?"

"Knock yourself out." Frost shrugged.

She took a seat and folded her legs under her. She got to turning that aether ring of hers again. "Your sister sleeps as if someone dosed her with dreamweed."

"Might be her way of coping with all this."

"Might be." Gilda nodded. "You've been acting funny."

"Funny how?" Frost asked, frowning.

"As if you don't trust me."

Frost arched a brow, and then stared her directly in the eye as his father had taught him. "I don't know you. And I'm not the trusting type."

She didn't flinch or avert her gaze. "I can relate. But if there's one thing I learned, it's that sometimes you have to do things you don't like to get what you want. Or to save those you love."

"You mean like Nebsamu killing all those innocent people?"

"There's that. But I was thinking more along the lines of playing with others. Looks like you can't wait to ditch us."

"It's crossed my mind."

"And?"

"And nothing. That's as far as it's gotten."

"Okay, but I wouldn't advise it." She climbed to her feet. "You'll understand when you see how much harder this version of the game is. I'll leave you to get some rest." She strode away in that willowy walk of hers.

Frost couldn't help but to watch her body and horns until she disappeared into the night. He lay back on the sacks and stared up at the moon and her court of stars. He thought of Anefet's letter and how he would fulfill her last wish. His mind soon drifted to real life, to getting the help Mom needed, then finding a way out of Equitane Towers. He imagined the day they were free. He smiled. Sleep called to him, his body only too happy to oblige. A wolf howled.

Frost woke to the twitter of birds and the gray pearl of dawn. The air was cool and smelled of smoke from the now dead campfire. Frost sat up. Nebsamu and Melori were asleep against the mineshaft's opposite wall. Saba was a few feet outside the entrance, lying on her side, also asleep. Of Gilda, there was no sign. He assumed it was her watch.

He glanced at his slumbering sister. Tia seemed at peace. Her face reminded him of the letter. He felt his left trouser pocket, but it was empty. Frowning, he checked the right. And felt the paper. He pulled it out to be certain. And let out a relieved sigh.

He looked to Tia once more. If there was ever a time for him to go solo, find this Adesh Hamada, and make it to Maelpith Island as he felt he should, it would be now. Tia was in capable hands.

Not dealing with other people sounded like bliss. As did not having to wait. *I could make much better time.* Yet, a part of him argued against it. If he were to survive solo, he needed to level up and improve his skills.

With a sigh, he got to his feet. Noting his aether was fully replenished, he picked up Noobstick and headed outside to the hill Saba had shown him. He chose a part of the incline that didn't look like much of a challenge. He climbed it. On the other side was the forest. Trees spread below in a hundred shades of green, early morning mist worming its way among trunks and brush. Birds piped high and low in a euphonious serenade.

Frost worked his way down the rock-strewn slope and along the tree line, picking out the telltale signs of plague wolves: green droppings, decaying grass where slobber landed, and the fetor of mold. He encountered a cervin's half-eaten carcass, rips in the body rife with poisonous saliva. When he found a good spot to enter the forest, he flicked the power down on Noobstick so as not to draw attention when he fired. He became aware of an objective for curbing the plague wolf threat.

He wove his way among the trees, ears twitching at

149

padded footsteps, eyes tracking blurs of movement, flashes of green-gray past trunks. A moldy stench hung in the air. His heart sped up. His skin tingled. The anticipation built the same as if he lived it outside the game.

Near a tree trunk, he found a pile of tattered clothing, bones, and a rusted sword. On the fingers were two rings. A bracelet adorned the wrist. Frost assumed it was a dead player who'd not returned to reclaim his belongings. A quick rummage through the remains netted him a skill shard.

Skill Acquired

Concussion Blast
Skill cannot be absorbed due to attribute deficiency

"Bah." A quick calculation of the needed strength and agility told him he wouldn't be able to utilize the skill until level five.

He took the rings and bracelet. The rings were identical. IM was there in an instant.

Braided Loop: +1 attack power
Steadfast Bracelet: +1 stagger resist

With a sigh, he slipped them on. He'd hoped they would have increased his stats so he wouldn't need to wait to use Concussion Blast. Or at least been something less basic.

Something is better than nothing, he thought.

The crack of a branch made him snap his head up. Some four hundred feet away, a plague wolf stepped from behind a tree. Nearby birdsong halted. The plague wolf bared its teeth. Slobber leaked from its jaws. Its fur was a mottled gray and green.

Frost sighted down the barrel, took an easy breath, and fired. The pulse was low, almost inaudible. The Aether Shot's cyan pulse streaked toward the plague wolf. And flew right by. Its impact kicked up dirt and detritus far beyond the animal.

The plague wolf snapped its head around for a moment at the area of impact. But then refocused on Frost. It growled.

He adjusted his aim and fired. This time he struck the plague wolf square in the chest. The animal collapsed. Frost smiled. Aether drifted into the air, swirled for a moment then zipped toward Frost. He felt a bit refreshed as it seeped into his skin.

IM made him aware of experience points gained.

"A hundred exp. Not bad. Seventy-eight more kills to level. Time to grind."

He spent the next two hours hunting and killing plague wolves. The forest and its denizens would be better off with a lesser number of the invasive beasts. An extended two seconds of Cannon Kata after every kill proved to be better than he thought. The fifty percent speed boost for seven seconds helped him chase down the next target or flee when a second plague wolf tried to ambush him.

He also started to notice something peculiar when he walked. Reverberations that resolved into forms. Now that he considered it, he'd sensed the same during the fire and the Aether Flame Bombardment. If he focused, he could feel, could use the sound of his footsteps to pinpoint things. Extending the sense, he vaguely discerned trees, animals, and other objects without actually seeing them. He smiled. This had to be another facet of echolocation at work.

Recalling the clicking sound common among eradae, the sound he'd made so naturally on several occasions, he emulated it with his tongue. And stood in awe. The forest was revealed to him as never before. Not just the things he could see but also those hidden or beyond his actual vision. They might as well have been right before him. He could tell where a plague wolf was hiding, know the limb from which a beardbeak sang. With his eyes closed he could weave a path through the next two hundred feet of forest. It made hunting even more fun.

As the rising sun burned off the mist, he got a much better handle on the aether cannon and good practice at stopping to focus on Replenishment. A dozen shots were all it took to completely diminish his aether even after Absorption. Thirty minutes focused on nothing but the air, willing his mind and body to replenish aether brought him back to full.

His capacity was a sense. A natural sensation similar to a full belly. When he ran out of aether, he kept Korbitanium Projectiles handy for any surprises. He repeated the process.

On rare occasions when he was full, he felt aether gained by Absorption or Replenishment shift into a reservoir. IM told him it was Aether Overload at work. The ability gave him a sense of euphoria.

Curbing Plague Wolf Threat
Objective Complete
Depleted plague wolf threat in Snakewood Forest: 1000 experience points.
Gained 100 Khertahka dominion credits

Frost grinned. He loved the idea of miscellaneous quests. He continued to grind. Slowly, his accuracy improved. As time wore on, the plague wolves became harder to find. He wondered about the respawn rate. But there was something else more disturbing. The ones he did see avoided him now.

He clicked and waited. For a moment, he thought his echolocation caught something close by, but he saw nothing. He strained his eyes. Spun in a circle. Echolocation said something *was* there.

"Grinding is the absolute worst way to level," Gilda said from less than three feet away.

Frost flinched but tried to act as if he'd known she was there the entire time. "It's also the best way to improve my skills and attributes. You're lucky I didn't shoot you, dawg." He scowled. He made a mental note to practice echo-location until it became as easy as breathing.

"I'm not your dawg." She appeared out of thin air. "And trust and believe you couldn't shoot me if you tried." She gave him a smug smile.

"Don't tempt me. What level are you, anyway?"

"Almost ten."

"Damn. How the hell did you level so quickly?"

"Told you this was my third Void Legion alpha under Total Immersion. I didn't need the extra prep you noobs did. I was logged in hours ahead of you. Also, a lot of the noob stuff is the same. I know the easiest way to level, the easiest quests to do."

"Makes sense," he said. "Maybe you can help me with something."

"Go ahead."

"I've been trying to find ways to tell a player's level outside of waiting for them to use a particular skill. Or by their weapons, armor, and the like. Are there any?"

"Nope."

Frost sighed. He stopped to think. "Been having a hard time separating NPCs from players, too. I know to start with playable races, but beyond that, how do you tell the difference without a HUD?" Although he liked the IM aspect, he did miss the familiarity of a Heads-Up Display.

"You can't really," Gilda said. "Not without talking to them, discovering who's aware of certain game mechanics. Like you did with Nebsamu. And that can still be guesswork because of role players who won't reveal themselves. BioGen says it's to make the human experience as real as possible."

"Fair enough," Frost said. "Don't know how much I like it, though. I see you used Concealment, but you're walking around with chakrams. What class are you exactly?"

"My main is a sorcerer. But I used KDC to buy the first few cutthroat skills for the Concealment and Hand-to-hand Combat."

Frost smiled inwardly at the choice. And almost said he didn't blame her for walking in his footsteps as a sorc.

Her eyes narrowed. "You can wipe that look off your face."

"What look?"

"The smugness. I know what you're thinking. Trust and believe, it ain't even like that."

"You're in my head?" Frost widened his eyes, but a grin leaked through his feigned shock.

She blew out an annoyed breath. "Whatever... dawg." That last word leaked sarcasm. "Anyway, although a lot remained the same, just as much has changed. Some more important than others. Like weapons themselves might not necessarily define a class. Later on, we'll have to start looking at players as being classless or multiclass."

Frost nodded. "I loved the idea when I ported into the game. Really looking forward to that sort of development."

A plague wolf popped out from the brush several hundred feet to their right. Frost took quick aim and fired. The animal ducked out of the way and leaped into the brush. Frost gaped.

"Did that plague wolf just... nah... did you see that?" He stared at the spot. Perhaps, it was his imagination.

"I did." Gilda chuckled. "That's another thing you'll need to get used to. The game learns. You won't be able to kill the same type of creature too many times with the same exact tactic. Variety is key. You'll have to use every advantage you can find, like our echolocation. The higher the level, or stronger the monster, the better its AI. Elites and GUMs are the worst. Or maybe the best. Depending on how you look at it."

Though shocked, Frost was no less intrigued. And excited. "Let me guess, I can't tell the difference in AI until I engage them and see how they react, right? The same way I can't tell their strength."

"Exactly. Just like IRL."

"Cool and scary all at once," Frost said. "And challenging. Players will need to be really creative. Especially when the game's been out for a while. Things will only get harder. Since you mentioned echolocation... got any tips?"

"Use it as much as possible," Gilda said. "That's the only way to grow accustomed to it, or to master anything in the game. It reveals most things within a certain range, which can get annoying and distracting in places with lots of people. You have to learn how to weed out the unimportant stuff. Takes some practice."

Gilda bent and picked a few green weeds with red tips. She collected them by the bunches and tucked them into a little pouch on her waist. Then she set about doing the same with a blue bush.

"Dreamweed, I recognize," Frost said. "But what's the other one?"

"Bloodroot." Gilda grabbed another handful. "Considering the danger we're going to face, and our lack of a mystic, we'll have to take care of any wounds the old-fashioned way. Pots and what not."

"I always thought about maxing one of those life skills like herbalism." Frost shook his head. "I tried, too. But it got boring quick. Even mining. I always preferred to buy what I need. More time to kill stuff and to grind."

"It isn't that hard to do." Gilda stood. "Just takes

155

time. And it's not like you have to find a skill shard for them. When you start doing certain things, you begin developing the skill."

Frost made to say he didn't intend to play for that long, but another plague wolf slunk from behind a tree. Frost took better aim. He squeezed the trigger, shifted the cannon to the left, waited two seconds and fired again.

Two pulses streaked in the plague wolf's direction. It dodged the first Aether Shot as before but leaped directly into the second.

Frost grinned in Gilda's direction, proud of his own adjustment. "A few more to level."

She smiled in turn. "You're learning fast. I'd expect nothing less from the second-best player."

Frowning, Frost glanced from side to side. Shading his eyes with his left hand, he peered into the trees. He spun in a circle.

Gilda snatched one of the star-shaped chakrams from the loop on her belt. A red arcane glow lit up the weapon and her right hand. "What's wrong? What is it?"

"Trying to find this second-best player." Frost shrugged. He dropped his hand from shading his eyes.

Tension bled from Gilda's face. She rolled her eyes. The arcane glow vanished. Frost chuckled.

"That wasn't funny." Shaking her head, Gilda replaced the chakram.

"Yes, it was. The only reason you don't agree is because the joke was on you."

A glint down the hill among the forest's dappled shadows caught Frost's eye. He squinted. The glint disappeared.

"Playing your silly game, again?" Gilda asked.

"Not this time." Frost ducked low among the brush. He signaled for Gilda to follow his lead. "I saw something...

like sunlight reflecting off metal."

"Either someone's leveling or the Battleguards are on our trail," Gilda said.

Confirmation arrived moments later. Two Azureguards on crevids worked their way up through the forest. They were still far below and were more concerned with several plague wolves stalking them.

"As much as I'd love to fight them, it's time to go. There's bound to be more of them." Gilda tugged at Frost's shirt. Staying low, she headed uphill toward the tree line.

Shouts echoed from below. Frost snatched a look behind them. More mounted Azureguards were pointing up at him and Gilda. They dug their heels into the mounts' sides and bounded uphill.

Despite knowing it was impossible to outrun the mounts on foot, Frost scrambled after Gilda. The tree line and the sunlight's glare beyond it was a long distance away.

CHAPTER 13

Frost and Gilda burst from the tree line. Branches snapped behind them. The Azureguards' shouts were close now. Too close. With Noobstick cradled in his arms, Frost dashed after Gilda uphill in the direction of the mines. Saba was galloping toward them, hooves kicking up dust.

"Battleguards found us," shouted the dresdor marksman as she drew to a halt before them. She pranced impatiently and pointed to their right where the mountain curved away and up. "Your mounts are on the other side of that rise. Go!"

"My sister," Frost exclaimed.

"Run!" Saba raced in the direction she'd indicated.

From below came the bloodthirsty whoops of their pursuers. Frost ran for all he was worth, his heart a booming drum. Gilda was a step ahead of him. They dashed up the rise.

The moment they gained the top, Gilda halted. She spun and snatched her chakrams from her belt loop. A red arcane glow lit up one weapon. Blue surrounded the other.

"What the hell are you doing?" Frost stopped beside her, chest heaving. "Your spells are useless at this range."

"But your cannon isn't," she snarled.

Frost glanced down at Noobstick, cradled in his arms, as if just remembering the weapon. Hefting it, he grinned. This was the stuff for which he lived. For which he gamed. He lowered Noobstick, waist high, flipped the lever to full power, and leveled the barrel at the tree line. The clop of hooves announced Saba's return to them. The marksman had a massive bow.

Frost clicked several times, the sound revealing other forms in the forest below. Trees rustled. Brush shook. Frost made out seven erada Azureguards rushing through the spaces between the trunks.

Five were armored reavers, if the two-handed great-swords were any indication. One of the powder blue females wore robes. A caster. The last carried a longbow and handled his lupine as if he were born atop it. They crashed through the brush at the forest's edge.

Saba's bowstring thrummed. Three wooden arrows blurred across the distance. Two took one reaver in the throat and eye. He pitched sideways from his mount's back. The other arrow flew harmlessly by another reaver.

Aiming at the Azureguard marksman, Frost gauged the distance. He breathed easy and squeezed the trigger. Whomp. The pulse zipped down the hill toward the marksman even as he'd nocked an arrow and loosed. Blue energy exploded into the marksman's chest.

By sheer instinct, Frost dashed to one side. Cannon Kata's effect saved him from the arrow. It whistled through the space he had vacated. His eyes widened.

Gilda was standing next to him, a circular red Aether Shield about four feet in diameter extending from her chakram. An Ice Pillar the size of a man was on Frost's other side. A broken arrow shaft was on the ground inches from them. Another was stuck into Gilda's Ice Pillar. The Pillar dissolved.

"Thanks." Frost let out a slow breath.

"You're welcome." Gilda smiled.

Saba's bow thrummed as she loosed another Triple Barrage of wooden arrows. She fired two Aether Arrows an instant later, their cyan arcane glow leaving trails in the air. A sudden wind gusted, much too powerful to be natural. It whisked the wooden arrows off target.

The first Aether Arrow streaked into the reaver she had missed previously. He crumpled.

The second Aether Arrow had sped toward the caster. The caster yanked hard on her reins. Her lupine shifted. The Aether Arrow flew into the forest behind her.

Choosing Divergence, Frost fired. The sound this time was more of a whine. Five blue pulses blazed a trail down the slope. Two found their marks, blasting reavers from their mounts. The other three exploded into the trees. Frost loosed an Aether Shot, but his intended target, the caster, bounded to one side and dodged it.

Knowing they were well within range, Frost switched to Korbitanium Projectiles. The barrel spun, issuing the buzzsaw whine. The shots spewed out. A stream of fire. It cut through leaves, brush, and branches, tore into trunks. The Battleguards dived for cover.

Gilda Flickered from beside him. She reappeared sixty feet down the hill.

An armored Azureguard sprinted uphill to meet her, so fast his churning legs and body blurred. His abrupt speed burst was a definitive sign he'd called upon Onslaught. A reaver skill.

The enemy caster reached behind and came away holding a warfan the size of her torso. White arcane energy lit up the weapon.

Frost yelled a warning, "Windwalker!" He aimed at the caster and snapped off an Aether Shot.

The white arcane energy had almost finished coalescing around the windwalker's warfan. The cyan of Frost's Aether Shot had only covered half the distance.

Gilda swept her left arm up, the blue energy leaving an afterimage, while she made a throwing motion with the red one, unleashing a Flame Globe. An Ice Stalagmite flashed up from beneath the windwalker's lupine. It burst through the beast's belly and back and impaled the windwalker. They died in place. Frost's Aether Shot struck the dead windwalker a moment later and blasted her to pieces.

Gilda's Flame Globe crackled through the air and exploded into the onrushing reaver's chest even as he had leaped toward her, sword cocked back to strike. Smoking, the reaver flew backward, slammed into the ground, and bounced several times. He remained where he stopped.

Gilda Flickered back up the hill. Frost and Saba finished off the reavers who had been victims of Divergence but had not suffered direct hits. Breathing heavy, pulse racing, Frost took in the damage and marveled at the rush from the combat, the sense of danger. And the thrill of victory. The fight had been so intense he hadn't noticed the group exp gained after each kill.

"That was some good work." Frost gave Gilda a pound, thumping the bottom of his fist atop hers.

She smiled. "No doubt."

"A little rash on your part," he added, "but good."

Gilda shrugged. "A girl's gotta do what a girl's gotta do. But trust and believe I thought it through."

A rumble in the direction of the mines made him snap his head around. He squinted, fully expecting Battle-guards to come plunging over the distant slope.

"They found one of my Traps." Saba chuckled. "It should buy us some time."

"But my sister," Frost began, remembering Tia and the others.

"She left with Nebsamu and Melori. Either we catch them on the road or we meet them in Soleb, a little-known village well north of here in the Akhmis nome."

"Suppose they—"

Saba rounded on him, gold eyes ablaze with fury. "How about doing as I tell you? You're lucky I came for you. And even luckier those weren't stronger Battleguards. It's your fault they found us."

"How?" Frost indicated his weapon. "I turned the power down so as not to make any noise."

Saba turned away and clip-clopped down the hill toward the two waiting crevids. "The forest is on a slope. Why would someone need sound when they can see the Aether Shots from the plains below us?"

Frost snapped his mouth shut. *You idiot. You fucking idiot.* With his shoulders slumped, Frost followed the dresdori marksman, cursing himself for a fool the entire time.

A Test at the Mines
Objective Complete
Defeated Azureguard hunters:
2000 experience points
Escape from the mines:
1000 experience points
Rescued entire group:
Fail
Level 4 gained
Gained 200 Khertahka dominion credits

Frost hung his head. He cared little for any rewards. The failure grated at him, the feeling that he'd let Tia down, put her at risk. He took out the Aether Bomb shard and absorbed it.

Skill available:

Aether Bomb
Cast time: 1.5 seconds
Recharge Time: 1 minute
Consumes: Aether

Available shard slots: 3

Effect: Launch an Aether Bomb up to 200 feet. Explodes on impact with enemies or obstacles. Conflagrates enemies within a 10-foot radius of impact, causing disorientation. Gain 5 percent aether on a successful direct hit. 1 percent aether for each additional enemy in area of effect.

He nodded, for the moment brightened by the skill. From his memory of the demo, it was potent.

They rode on, stopping only to water the crevids or let them graze for a few minutes. Saba led them from the steep foothills down onto rolling plains.

"I'll cover our trail." Saba pranced beside them. "And then scout out up ahead and return."

"That's a lot of distance to cover and not be seen," Frost said dubiously.

Saba puffed out her chest. "Not for a dresdor. Not only are we fleeting like the wind, but my Concealment is sharded. It doesn't negate my speed. Combine that with Streak allowing me to dash several times my normal speed and the feat won't be a problem. It's how I got ahead of you on our way to the mines."

"Nice." Frost nodded. He found himself wondering if Saba was a player or NPC.

"Gilda, lead the way until I return." Saba galloped off behind them, cutting a swath through the grassland.

Frost and Gilda continued on in silence. During the ride, Frost practiced echolocation. Eventually, it came naturally. Not only did he hardly notice the clicking, but it grew muted. A part of him.

He still often marveled when the ability triggered. It gave him an entire new outlook on the world, revealing critters and objects he might have missed otherwise. He also practiced how to focus it on specific things while ignoring others, which proved more difficult than expected.

With the way Total Immersion felt, he began to question the need for real life. His experience so far had surpassed his dreams.

Frost found himself wondering about Gilda's real-life appearance and where she was from. *Was she even a girl?* His mind conjured images and scenarios, each more outlandish than the next. She was black; she was white; she was Spanish. She was some tall exotic beauty who just happened to like games. She was a midget. Then she was a three-hundred-pound girl who could barely move off her bed. She was a man.

He grimaced at that last, considering how her avatar made him feel. Although he much preferred to keep to himself, there was something about her that made him want to speak to her, get to know her.

After drumming up the courage, he went for it. "What's your story in real life? Where're you from? What do you do? How'd they get their hooks into you?" Almost immediately he cursed himself for sounding like a little school boy.

She chuckled. "Just like that, huh?"

"Won't know if you don't ask." He shrugged, trying to play off his embarrassment.

"No doubt." She nodded. "I'm a Second Warder. Straight from Downtown Brooklyn."

Frost whistled. "That means you've seen your share of DeGens. I couldn't imagine living so close to them."

"Most DeGens aren't what you think," she said, scowling. "You shouldn't believe everything you see on the news or OneWorld."

"True, but–"

"There aren't any buts."

Frost snapped his mouth shut. It was the second time in the last few days a woman had made him feel small with a mere look. He averted his eyes and reminded himself to tread lightly around the topic of DeGens and the First Ward.

Gilda continued, "After my grandmother died, I had to fend for myself. So, I got into Ataxia. I sold gear for IRL credits at first, but that didn't pay the bills. Then I tried my hand at shevla but wasn't very good at it. Too many damned rules and cards. That's when I became a merc."

"I remember that." Frost smiled. He recalled seeing her name on the Player Killers bounty list in a few towns. "You had a pretty bad rep as a PKer."

"I was never a PKer." She scowled. "I was into PVP. I hate when people confuse the two."

"Sorry."

"And If by 'bad rep' you mean I was a bad ass who made most players run away like little boys or shit themselves when they heard I had a contract for them, then yeah, I guess so."

Frost chuckled. "That's because too many of those maxed-out players bought their gear rather than earned it."

"And I made them pay an even steeper price." A distant look crossed Gilda's face. "PVP was my thing. If you wanted another player dead, I was the cutthroat to hire. As long as it wasn't some noob. IRL, I was a thief. It's mostly how I paid for Ataxia, my apartment... it's how I survived."

"You lived by yourself? How old are you?"

"Seventeen."

"A seventeen-year-old Second Warder who lives alone and was a thief in real life... I can't picture it."

She shrugged. "A girl's gotta go what a girl's gotta do. My crew and I had the Downtown Mid Ward shopping zones on lock."

"Wow."

"Until I got caught." Her dainty lips curled. "Some

bitch snitched."

"How much time did you get? Did they send you off to work the smog machines?"

"No. BioGen lawyers showed up at the precinct and gave me a choice. If I became a tester, they'd save me from jail and a long sentence of hard labor that would likely end with a cancer I couldn't afford to have cured."

"Not much of a choice."

"Even offered steady credits doing it. Seemed like a good deal at the time."

"Equitane has you by the balls, too," Frost said softly.

"If I had a pair, then, yeah."

Frost paused and frowned. "Wait. So, you *are* a girl in real life?"

"How should I take that?" She smirked. "I did say a girl's gotta do what a girl's gotta do. More than once."

"Sorry." Possibilities ran through Frost's head. "I didn't mean anything by it... like I wasn't trying to say... when you said a girl's gotta do what a girl's gotta do, I didn't take it literally... us being in the game and all. I just... forget it. I'm making it worse, aren't I?"

"Pretty much. But it was cool to see you flop around like a fish." She smiled.

"I–"

"It's okay." She waved him off. "Trust and believe, I know how I come off. How I sound. Even IRL, people who know me find it hard to believe. The fact that I don't wear dresses and makeup and other girly stuff doesn't make it any easier. The joke used to be that I'm a trans man or non-binary. Some even called me pansexual." She huffed. "Whatever. I'm just a girl who likes what she likes." Her dagger appeared in her hand. She twirled it.

"I swear I wasn't thinking any of that," Frost protested. "I've seen plenty of epic girl gamers." *But you've never*

166

considered being with any of them in real life. He swallowed at the thought.

"No doubt," she said. "Now you know about me, what's your deal?"

"Long story." He sighed.

"I'm listening."

"I guess I can start with my parents and I coming to the NAR from Barbados when I was six. My father got sponsored by a Corp because he was one of the best AI engineers."

"Barbados?" she repeated.

"An island in the Caribbean," he answered.

"And you came here? It's beautiful out there. Especially since the hurricanes seem to miss them ever since the Climatic Shift. I've always dreamed of being able to buy a VV to one of those islands."

Frost shrugged. "Pops had to follow the work."

"Is the ocean really blue?"

"When it isn't overrun with seaweed, yes."

"You must have loved swimming."

Frost shook his head. "I actually hated it. I almost drowned just before my sixth birthday. I've had this deathly fear of the sea ever since. Of water, period. Having the same thing almost happen in Brooklyn during Hurricane Perol only made it worse."

"Sorry to hear. I know how it is. My parents drowned during Superstorm Ezra."

Frost winced. "Damn. My condolences."

"Thanks. Now, back to your story before you get all sentimental on me."

"Alright." Frost smiled. "Life in the city was great at first. We lived in a Middle Ward apartment in Prospect Heights. Things changed a bit when my little sister was born a year later."

"The FPC allowed that?"

"Pops paid the fines beforehand so we were covered."

"Oh." There was a slight pause, an uncomfortable silence, and then she asked, "When did you get into gaming."

"I've been gaming for as long as I can remember. Pops said I was two when I first put on his VR headset." Frost smiled with the thought. "The first things I played were VR sims. Pops used them to homeschool me."

"Oh, okay, that explains a lot."

"Yeah," Frost said. "I was hooked. I'd play every and anything in VR. Pops even had me get into MMA and firearms. I was sick when it came to first person shooters. Won my fair share of MMA and 3-Gun tourneys both in VR and IRL."

"3-gun tourneys?"

"It's basically a shooting obstacle course," Frost said. "You run through it as fast as you can, using rifles, shotguns, and pistols, to hit pop up targets, trying to be as accurate as possible."

"Sounds like you can handle yourself." She nodded, lips pursed. "I'll have to put you to the test one day."

"First, you wanna duel me in game. Now outside of it." He smiled. "No prob."

"I'll hold you to that," she said. "What made you play Ataxia?"

"A friend in high school. I never looked back."

"Why'd you stop playing?"

"At first, it was a promise to Mom and Pops. Then soon after that we got a call that Pops died in an accident."

"My condolences."

"Thank you." Frost sighed, a throe gripping his heart. "Everything went to hell after that."

He continued on, reliving not only the night of Pops' accident, but also his own with Mom and Kai. He told Gilda about the day he woke in Equitane Towers to discover his mother was in a coma, only alive due to TNT, the same process BioGen ironically used in Void Legion. Then came the torment of mentioning Sidrie's threats. He didn't know why he told Gilda so much. Maybe, he shouldn't have. But it felt good. A release.

"I'm sorry they put you through all that," Gilda said. "Equitane has a lot of people fooled."

Frost nodded. "I see that. There were other top players testing Void Legion. I wonder how many went through what we did."

"A lot, I'd bet."

They drifted into silence. The crevids' frequent snorts became loud amid the susurrus of long grasses. A wind sighed through the branches of a nearby tree, the breeze a welcome respite against the blazing coin of a sun.

An idea came to Frost. "You said you were almost level ten... that you alpha-tested before. You musta been to Maelpith Island and Imanok Sanctum at some point. How hard are they?"

Gilda's brow furrowed. "Too hard for so-called noob zones. At least for soloing. The entire island's full of elite mobs."

"That should mean better gear than other noob areas," Frost said. "Nothing worth doing is easy."

"While both of those are true," Gilda said, "it makes more sense to risk it after leveling elsewhere. Then you can pay the island a visit when you're stronger."

"I guess." Frost heaved a sigh. "It's just that I really wanna get back to my Mom and my little sister."

"We don't always get to do the things we want or get to do them how we'd like," Gilda said. "Everyone I know

169

who was level ten or below died when they went to Maelpith Island. Myself included.

"And the weather's the worst. Clouds often blot out the sun. There's always thunder and lightning. One minute, it's a pretty decent day, if a bit gloomy, and in the next few minutes you're caught in terrible winds and rain. Even tornadoes. They say its remnants of the voidstorm.

"As for the Sanctum, it *can* get you some decent early shards and schemas off GUMs. Some people claim the new Emperor KiGyaba's treasure room has a hierka like your aether cannon. And you can find some rare shards. But no one's beaten him, so who knows what the truth really is."

The thought of empowered genesiswork equipment got Frost pumped. Perhaps, he might be lucky enough to land an epic or a legendary hierka. Hell, maybe something genesis grade. There was also the challenge itself. And what completing it meant in the real world.

He cocked his head to one side, brows knitted. "You beat the old Emperor KiGyaba in Heroic Castle Dhoom, right?"

"Yes."

"Did you reach this one?"

"Unfortunately, yes. Our group didn't come close to beating him."

"Anyone tried out-leveling the Sanctum?" he asked.

"The difficulty scales to match average group level."

"So gearing up to beat it at max would be the best option," he mused

"Who knows?" Gilda shrugged. "The dungeon might scale with power too. And whether or not he'd drop hierkas worthy of max level is another mystery."

"What about going the other way?" Frost asked. "Instead of trying to out-level it, bring a zerg." Frost imagined the zerg: a full fifteen-man raid of low-level characters trying to clear the place.

"A zerg wouldn't work either. It scales for numbers as well."

Frost's brow furrowed. "Any idea on the strats?"

"Throw away every old strategy you could think up, especially since there's no Hit Points to tell how well you're doing," Gilda said. "I told you Estela is always learning. I assume she has the logs of every failed attempt to call upon. I died so many times in the alphas that I'm beginning to think it's impossible."

"Yet, you're here."

Gilda shook her head. "You said it earlier: what choice is there? Plus, I live for the challenge." She grinned. "Trust and believe, I'm going to beat that bastard."

Staring into those bright green eyes, Frost believed every word. Abruptly remembering Tia, he frowned. He hoped she was fine. The moment he had the thought brought a fresh surge of worry. It made him wonder if he was better off without such real-life emotions and experience.

"So, this easier leveling you spoke about… think you could put me on?"

"You're doing it right now," Gilda said. "By following early quest lines. But avoid Maelpith Island until after level ten."

"Alright."

The beat of galloping hooves reached him. Saba appeared up ahead. Frost smiled wryly. *Damned dresdori sure can cover some distance.*

The marksman drew to a halt in front of them, sweat pouring down her face, the sheen of it glinting along her flanks. "There was a raid on Soleb," she said breathlessly.

"A raid?" Frost repeated. A cold prickle eased through him. "By who? Battleguards looking for us?"

"Worse. The Redthorns. Umesh Madara."

Gilda hissed. Frowning, Frost looked from her to Saba. The names meant nothing to him.

"Umesh is the gurash slavemaster your mother saved Nebsamu from," Saba said. "His Redthorns are part of a grand kora operation."

"He's massive, even for a gurash," added Gilda. "And he's a GUM."

The cold prickle became a tightness in Frost's chest. "Did Tia get caught in the raid?"

"I don't know," Saba said.

Frost stroked the aether ring on his pinky. A quest to locate Umesh Madara, Tia, and the others popped into his head. "Let's find out. And whether he does or not, I say we kill this Umesh Madara."

"Finding him is one thing. Killing him is another," Saba said. "We're not strong enough for that. We also need to be certain he has Nebsamu and Melori. If it was up to me alone, I would leave them. But Nebsamu still hasn't paid me for my help."

Frost almost said he didn't give a shit about Nebsamu or Melori. Or about Saba getting paid. He bit his tongue. "Let's get to it." Frost made to kick his mount into motion.

"Not so fast." Saba retrieved two bundles from her inventory. Blue clothing by the looks of them. "I encountered two Azureguard scouts. One dead, and the other on the brink of death." She tossed a bundle to Frost and the other to Gilda.

Frost caught his bundle.

Acquired armor: Azureguard uniform
Damage reduction: 3 percent
Stagger resist: 1 percent

Saba continued, "Get dressed. Before he died, the last scout said a Battleguard company is flying in to Soleb to investigate. The locals are the type who don't take kindly

172

to strangers. We'll need some sort of authority if we're to get anyone to talk to us so we can have an idea as to where Umesh has gone off to or if he even has Nebsamu, Melori, and your sister."

CHAPTER 14

Epic players do epic things, Frost thought with a smile. He was dressed in an Azureguard's hard leather cuirass over a sky-blue gambeson to match his hose. The insignia of Khertahka's Dual Katars adorned his sleeves, while the Coalition's Mountain and the Aetherstream emblazoned his cloak. With Noobstick in hand, he swore he could pass for a Vindicator, the Grendesh Coalition's most elite warriors.

Gilda rode to his left, garbed in a full set of cobalt robes that set off her cerulean skin. She looked none too happy about it. Her glum expression made Frost's smile widen.

Saba trotted on the other side in leather armor dyed in standard Coalition green and yellow. Her human half was in a gambeson with a cuirass over it. She had a flanchard to cover her flanks, peytral for the equine part of her chest just above her legs, and a crupper for her hindquarters. While Frost and Gilda both had the single stripe on their lapel and below the Khertahkan Dual Katars to identify them as mere soldiers, Saba sported a lieutenant's triple stripes below Nimri's Longbow.

Frost's smile lingered until Soleb came into full view. He stared, mouth agape. The village was in shambles. Most buildings were little more than burnt out husks. Blue, purple, and red blood stained the ground. Folk huddled outside their destroyed homes, many bawling like babes. Others hugged the remnants of their families. Forlorn gazes tracked Frost and his group as they rode into the village.

A few locals acknowledged them with bows and whispers, some with prayers and thanks to Nif, while others hurried along, gazes averted. Although some headed in the same direction as Frost and his group, double their number trudged in the direction from which the group had come, heads down, backs bent, clothes covered in soot. The murmur of mournful voices floated on a breeze that carried the overbearing stench of char.

"Split up and gather the information we need so we can leave before the Battleguards fly in," Saba said. "Meet back here in an hour."

They went from home to home, questioning survivors. On many occasions Frost had a sinking feeling in his stomach, the one he got whenever he heard a tale about a child dragged off by the slavers, slaughtered during the raid, or burned to death in a home.

Each story reminded him of his experience in Niba, made him more desperate and worried for Tia. As did the black patches that scarred the ground. The blood-soaked bandages of survivors. The tears of a hapless mother. An orphaned child's sobs. Frost was the last one back to the meeting spot.

"A few mentioned seeing Nebsamu, Melori, and Tia," Saba reported. "But none knew what became of them. They said we should ask the village Elder. An erada named Amun. How did you do?"

"Heard pretty much the same thing," Gilda said.

Frost gave his account. "Most were concerned with their own tragedies. The ones who said more mentioned Amun also. Said we could find him at the village square."

He jutted his chin toward the dirt road winding its way into Soleb.

"The village square it is, then." Saba trotted in that direction.

Though he tried to ignore it, Frost couldn't help but see the remnants of destruction around him as they rode through the village. Nor could he stop the growing urgency and dread in his gut.

They arrived at the square where people lined the left side of the area, heads bowed in prayer, voices murmuring in unison. But it was the entire right side that held Frost's attention. Bodies lay in neat rows. All of them were erada. Someone had cut off their horns. Frost swallowed hard against the urge to puke.

"Umesh Madara's work," Saba said, voice gruff. "He slaughters those who are too much trouble to enslave and takes their horns for the grand kora markets."

"That many horns would be worth thousands of credits," Gilda said. "Tens of thousands. Either to be ground into powder to be added to healing potions for a more powerful brew or to treat rare ailments. The finest looking ones would be sold to rich grand korae as pieces of art."

A coffee-skinned erada departed from the front of the mourners and shuffled toward them, his light-colored robes stained with soot and blood. His horns were thick, majestic, curled back and then down and around before ending in a point. A hint of hope shone in an otherwise bleak face touched by at least ten decades.

"Lieutenant, Soldiers, I am Elder Amun." The Elder dipped his head while wringing his hands. "Praise be to Nif for your speedy arrival." He made the sign of the X on his forehead.

"Nif's name be praised," they said as one.

"You must hurry if you are to save the children and

the others the Redthorns took," the Elder said. His eyes pleaded as much as his tone.

"Must?" repeated Saba in a stern voice.

Frost scowled despite knowing the dresdor was only playing a part. A quest line for freeing the captive villagers became available.

"Sorry, sorry Lieutenant." The Elder bowed several times. "No insult was intended. I just—"

Saba waved him off. "Just be careful. Another lieutenant might not be as forgiving as I am."

"Yes. Thank you." Amun dipped his head again. He swallowed. "If I may ask, is the rest of your company close behind?"

"Not far," Saba answered.

"Praise Nif." Elder Amun looked toward the heavens and drew an X over his heart.

"I'm Saba." The centaur gestured to Frost and Gilda. "This is Soldier Frost and Soldier Mordian. Do you know where the Redthorns went?"

"Our last scout report said they took the captives north along Apep's Belly, most likely headed to Marna in the Gerza Valley."

Frost lost his patience. "We're also looking for two eradae who may have been here at the time of the raid: a scar-faced man with one horn and a young girl. A gurash was with them, one with marbled blue and green skin."

Immediately, Amun's features became guarded. He shook his head. "I would remember a gurash outcast other than Umesh Madara, and an erada with one horn would stand out also. Sorry—"

"You're lying," Gilda said.

"I—" began Amun.

"She's my sister," blurted Frost. "Help us, please."

Saba leaned down and whispered something into

177

Amun's ear. The Elder's eyes opened wide. His face brightened for but a moment before his mouth downturned into sadness.

"All three were here," the Elder said. "The Redthorns captured them and mentioned that Umesh had been after Nebsamu for some time and would make him suffer a slow and painful death. A few hinted that the chance of taking Nebsamu had been the only reason for them to be around Soleb."

Frost sensed the bitterness in the reply. The hint of blame. "This Marna in the Gerza Valley. Where is it?"

The Elder pointed to the mountains. "Head north until the end of Apep's Belly. Follow the range until it curls back south into the valley. Marna sits up against those slopes."

"Why go there?" Gilda asked.

"Flightmaster Matahu's Aviary," Saba said. "Soleb was to be our first stop for supplies. Then we were to head to the Aviary once we met Nebsamu.

"Umesh's choice makes sense. Even if he wanted to, he can't cross the mountains with so many slaves. And he can't go the other way back into the Lothal dominion. His own people hate him for practicing slavery.

"He also can't take his prizes overland across Khertahka, for fear of being caught. So, he'll use Matahu's collection of flying mounts to ferry them into Puria to the grand kora markets."

Elder Amun spoke, his expression distraught. "And there is a very good chance most of them will have their horns taken before or close to Marna."

"Then why're we still standing here?" Frost hefted Noobstick. Objectives for Matahu's Aviary became available. "Night's almost here. The Redthorns gotta stop to rest because of the children and chained prisoners. I say we get fresh mounts and ride all night."

A lament of drakes' gurgling shrieks cut through his words, cut through the people's fervent prayers. High in the sky, appearing more like black, blue, green, and red birds with webbed wings, rather than scaled beasts three times the size of a man, at least thirty of the creatures banked before diving toward Soleb. Their riders were barely visible as they leaned close into their mounts' necks.

"So much for that idea," Gilda said.

"Let's go now, while there's still time before they land," Saba said.

"No." Gilda shook her head. "It's already too late. And since we're dressed like them, it'd be strange for us to leave now. There's also no way we could outrun them. We need a believable story for being here."

"I agree with Gilda," Frost said. "Gotta play our parts until we find a way to escape."

"What if someone talks." Saba eyed the Elder suspiciously.

"You have nothing to fear from me or mine." Amun lowered his voice and stared at Frost. "Your friend told me who your mother was. The Hand was a dear friend."

CHAPTER 15

While Saba went to greet and report to the Azureguard company's Major, Frost and Gilda busied themselves by assisting with burials. Whispering to each other, they discussed how they might resolve their current dilemma. Not long after, Elder Amun arranged for food and drink to be brought to the Azureguards in celebration of their arrival, subsequent aid, and the battle to come. Frost and Gilda offered their help.

Sunset bled into the night's dark embrace as the Azureguards set up camp on Soleb's outskirts and deployed scouts at several locations. They roped off an area for the drakes, who often blared like discordant trumpets. Campfires blazed to life.

The Azureguards settled in, singing raucous songs while drinking and enjoying the constant stream of food. A few danced, blue garb limned by flames. The night wore on.

One by one, the Azureguards headed to bed. Campfires began a slow death, leaving behind the glowing orange eyes of embers. Perhaps two hours passed amid the drakes' earsplitting calls and the fading revelry.

Saba joined Frost and Gilda where Frost had set up their sleeping area beyond earshot of the closest Azureguard. "Did any of the Sky Swords ask about you?" She kept her voice low, barely audible above their campfire, whose flames crackled and capered with the wind.

"A few did," Frost answered. "I told the story we agreed on. I'm just a lowly Soldier from Benna, a town in the western part of this nome."

"Adak." Gilda sat with her back against a pile of bags. "Northwest, a few towns beyond Benna."

"Good, good." Saba nodded. "This is one of the few times I can say it's a blessing that Exarch Bakui Assam has Azureguards posted all across Khertahka."

"You think they bought it?" Frost asked.

The centaur smiled. "I'm certain they did. Since the voidstorm that created Maelpith Island, it's not uncommon for the Coalition to send out scouts to track reports of draconids beyond the Front. Typically, it might be someone of lesser rank than myself… but for one thing… I'm a woman.

"And because of that, Major Neferna and I got to talking. We were able to relate as women who struggled through the ranks, who had to take on tasks below our station in order to advance. To gain respect." She scowled. "The conversation went rather well when I mentioned where I trained, my old colonel, and a brigadier who had more rules than commandments in Yarl's scriptures. And the trials of having to work three times as hard as men to please a Drillmaster."

"Sounds all too familiar," Gilda said acidly.

"Did you find out where this company came from?" Frost studied his surroundings, one finger stroking his aether ring. The other ring was a weight on his chest. "Any chance they know about Niba?"

"The Sky Swords are from Aprunis," Saba said. "Part of Nomarch Setnana Botros' cohort. And they know about Niba."

Frost hissed at the Nomarch's name and the news.

"Don't worry." Saba shook her head. "Neither you

nor our patron is their concern at the moment. Major Neferna let it slip that the Exarch sent the Nomarch on some urgent business to the Ignis dominion. A mission to Maelpith Island, launching from Kituan."

Frost breathed a bit easier but not by much. "What's the plan now?" He noted the numerous mounds of slumbering Azureguards. "The longer we wait, the worse it gets for Tia and the others."

"We have no choice but to wait." Saba shook her head of short hair and let out a sigh. "The guards would see if we snuck off in the night. Besides, the major plans to fly to Marna before dawn breaks. If we're lucky, we'll catch Umesh and his Thorns unprepared."

"Or we could steal a few drakes." Frost could not see himself sitting idly by all night. Not with Tia in harm's way. Not with her plight being his fault. And he did not intend to. "Some villagers said if we flew east from here, over Apep's Belly, we would get to Marna."

"You speak as if there aren't any guards," Saba said.

"We could take care of them," Frost countered.

"Even if we managed it, where would that leave me?" Saba arched a quizzical brow, face highlighted by moonlight and the campfire's orange glow. "Have you ever seen a centaur fly a drake?"

Frost fought back a grin at the image. "I once heard dresdori are fleeting like the wind. Even more so with you being a marksman. Use Streak a bunch of times, and you wouldn't be far behind."

"Anyone ever told you you're an asshole?" Saba asked.

"Me?" Frost feigned being hurt. "I wasn't the one bragging about my prowess."

Saba rolled her eyes. "Anyway, let's say we did this, there's the little problem of an entire company against us."

Saba eyed the Azureguards in the encampment. "I studied both of you." She nodded at Frost. "I doubt you tested Void Legion before, which makes you almost a complete noob." She ran an appraising gaze over Gilda. "You have some skill. But both of you are level ten or less and most likely lack the strength or will to control a young drake. Even if you could, then we'd have to deal with the scouts raising the alarm."

"I had a feeling you were a player." Frost nodded. "But I wasn't certain, especially with the way you talk all prim and proper sometimes."

"I like to role-play, to keep with the spirit of the game."

"Where're you from?" Gilda asked.

"Out West. California. BioGen flew me to New New York for this phase."

"Cool," Frost said.

"Not as cool as playing beside two of the best," Saba said. "Even if you overestimate what you can accomplish at your levels. But I guess that's why you are who you are... the risks you take... I was always a cautious player."

"Cautious, huh?" Frost smirked. "Some people call that fear."

"Whatever."

Gilda spoke. "Frost and I already thought the plan through. The Battleguards won't be an issue. As for the drakes... the reins alone will keep them docile."

"Reins won't shut them up or make the scouts not sound the alarm." Saba tilted her head to one side, eyes reflecting the dwindling flames.

"Not a prob," Frost said.

"Not a problem?" Saba fixed them with a searching gaze. "What am I missing?"

"Most soldiers find it hard to resist a good drink... the horrors of war and all that." Frost cast a lingering look out into the encampment. There were numerous mounds. Abundant snores drifted on the brisk night air, the wind carrying the stench of unwashed bodies and piss. "Even the ones who insist on keeping a clear mind still need to eat. Or drink water."

"The right dose of ground dreamweed goes a long way," Gilda bragged.

"Now, we wait for all the campfires to go out to be certain they're fully asleep." Frost was proud of the plan. It had worked better than expected.

A Way Past The Guards
Objective Complete.
Incapacitate the Azureguards:
1000 experience points
Gained 100 Khertahka dominion credits

"You claimed you thought it through," Saba said quietly, an edge to her voice. "But did you also consider that when these drake riders wake up, they'll know exactly what transpired and blame the villagers?"

Frost puffed up his chest. "We did. Which is why we made certain to be seen helping with the food and drink. And we also fed the same dreamweed to the villagers."

"We'll be the three who're missing," added Gilda. "Trust and believe, any officer with an ounce of sense will blame us first. When Elder Amun mentions that we asked after the people Umesh Madara took, and describes Nebsamu, the major will know who we really are."

"Even if Major Neferna insists the villagers played a part," Frost said, "I doubt she'll order the Azureguards to butcher them. They're eradae. Not grand kora murderers. But as a precaution, we had Amun send a raven off to the Coalition leadership to let them know what happened and that Setnana's cohort is here handling the issue. He'll casually mention it to the major."

Their campfire flickered and died. The sole light was that of the moon's glowing silver disc. Frost clicked and waited for the answering forms.

"What are your plans afterward?" Saba asked. "For the Redthorns and rescuing the captives."

Frost shared a look with Gilda and then sighed. "We didn't quite have a solution for that prob, but our hope was to sneak them out."

"An absurd hope, at best." Saba's face was mired in shadowy highlights. "I have a bad feeling about this. But you've placed your cards on the shevla board. All we can do now is play." The centaur got to her feet.

Frost also stood. "Just keep an eye out while we get the drakes. Then you can head off."

"I thought your plan was foolproof." Saba pawed at the ground with her front hoof.

"Nothing wrong with extra caution," Gilda said.

"That, I can agree on." Saba eyed Frost. "But I heard it was fear." She scowled in his direction and then melted into the darkness, Concealment hiding her completely.

Relying on echolocation, Frost and Gilda picked their way among the sleeping Sky Sword company. They nearly jumped out of their skins on more than one occasion when someone grumbled, snorted loudly, or turned for a more comfortable position. They stopped at a group of Soldiers and took two drake reins: circular metal collars with one end open. They were as wide as Frost could stretch his hands out to both sides of his body. Frost placed his atop his left shoulder and let it fall crossways to his right side.

Acquired item: young drake reins
Allows for basic flight
Young drake required

A drake rider stood. They froze. The man walked around aimlessly for a few moments before he lay back down in a different spot and promptly fell into a snore. They sighed in relief.

At the roped off area housing the chained drakes, the guards were also asleep. Dozens of bright eyes watched Frost and Gilda. A few drakes snorted their displeasure. One of them trumpeted. Most others made softer gurgling sounds of contentment. A wind gusted, bringing their musky fetor with it.

Frost located the metal tubs filled with cervin meat to feed the drakes. He scooped out chunks and tossed them to the beasts. A scramble followed as several rushed to feed.

Frost picked out two of the more docile drakes, one blue and one green, and approached with meat in his hand. Gilda followed his lead. The drakes in question shied away at first but soon took the offering. After a few more morsels, they allowed Frost and Gilda to rub their long noses, gurgling their acceptance.

Whispering soothing words, Frost lifted the reins from his shoulder. He shifted to the side of the drake's neck while it busied itself with the meat, reached up and out, and pressed the lever to snap the reins shut around the drake's neck. The beast gave a little shake and got down on all fours, webbed wings folded back to hug its sides.

Acquired Young Drake
Skill available:

Basic Flight
Flying Mount Speed 100
Effect: Allows for short flights before needing a rest. Young drakes can be grown and trained to increase their stamina, flight speed, and ability.

Frost grabbed a firm hold of the reins and swung himself up onto the drake where its long neck and back met above its forelegs. Gilda did the same not far from him.

Gripping the reins with both hands, he pulled back hard as he remembered from the old version of Ataxia.

The young drake did not budge.

"Shit." Frost tried again. And again. He glanced toward Gilda whose efforts were similarly futile. He made to give it another go, but the drake screeched.

Frost swallowed. He had thought this would be simple, similar to being able to ride the crevid the first time. But he knew now, as much as he didn't want to admit it, he knew Saba had been right. Neither he nor Gilda were strong enough to be seen as dominant. Void Legion had changed the flight ability to one requiring specific physical strength and will.

He climbed off the drake, mind racing as he considered their next move. He studied the Azureguards, praying the dreamweed's effects had not somehow worn off from any of them. None moved. He let out a slow breath, and although a weight lifted from him, there was still a sense of urgency. A need to be away from Soleb. A need to reach Tia.

"What now?" Gilda asked as they left the pen.

"No choice but to ride as hard as we can for Marna. We're dead if we stay here."

The sound of padded footsteps resolved into Saba at the camp's edge. She had two crevids. Strong looking bulls. Frost's heart leaped. He and Gilda hurried to the centaur.

"I tried to warn you," the marksman said when Gilda and Frost had mounted. "In Void Legion, there's more to drake riding than the reins and the ability to climb on its back. The beasts are particular. You'll both need to work with them, be around them, grow stronger for them to deem you worthy."

Frost did not argue the point despite feeling the need to wipe the smug expression from the centaur's face. He had greater concerns. "The company's gonna wake up by sunrise. Can we make it to my sister and the others before then?"

"I'm not sure," Saba said. "All we can do is try." She turned away and headed out onto the moonlit plains and the deeper darkness beyond.

Escape from Soleb
Objective Complete
Escaped Soleb:
1000 experience points
Drake mount acquisition:
Failed
Gained 100 Khertahka dominion credits

The failure was a lump in the back of Frost's throat. It chased him as they fled into the night.

CHAPTER 16

Exhausted to the point his surroundings became a blur, Frost clung to his crevid's reins and lost himself in the rhythmic thud of its hooves, the constant yet uncomfortable jounce of its powerful strides. A cool wind was his sole respite in the mad dash to reach the Redthorns and their captives before sunrise.

Sweaty and hot, this was one of those times he wished the game did not emulate reality so well. His ass was sore, his legs stiff, but still he willed himself to stay upright, to deal with the discomfort. Tia's life depended upon it. As did Mom and Kai. He shook off the thought of the last two, fearing his feelings for them would interfere with his need within the game.

He glanced over his shoulder. The moon was a distorted silver disc behind growing storm clouds on its descent in the west. He whispered to himself, praying they would soon discover Umesh Madara and the Redthorn camp. Daylight meant the death of hope for their rescue. Either because Umesh would make it to Marna or the Sky Swords would fly in and ruin everything.

Dismissing both fears, he tried to concentrate on Saba, whose form was a mere silhouette cutting through the grass in front of him, darkness no hindrance to her vision. Neither was it for him when he relied on echolocation. Gilda was on his right. Beyond her was the black-cloaked slopes of Apep's Belly.

Saba drew to a sudden halt. She raised a fist. Her tail swished in agitation.

Frost yanked hard on his reins, which brought his crevid to a grinding stop. An action that made him painfully aware of the abrasions on his ass. He winced. The crevid snorted its displeasure, sides heaving with exertion. Gilda stopped beside him.

"Something's wrong." Saba's head was cocked to one side.

Fatigue vanished, replaced by a tightness in Frost's gut. Discomfort forgotten, he peered into the deeper darkness, one hand reaching down and back to grasp Noobstick's handle. His ears twitched as he tried to discern any unusual sound. Only to be greeted by a sighing wind, the grassland's susurrus, the crevid's labored breaths, and a chorus of chirping insects.

He clicked and waited, ready to attack. But there were no other forms within a hundred feet that might be players or NPCs. Such absence left a sour taste in his mouth.

"I smell something dead nearby," Saba whispered, tail swishing a bit faster. Her tail stopped. "Wait here." She became one with the shadows.

Long minutes stretched in her absence. Frost sat, stiff as a corpse, eyes narrowed and straining to see, echolocation stretched as far as he could manage. He licked his lips. He brought Noobstick up to rest across his lap, one hand on the carry handle and the other on the back grip, finger hovering over the trigger.

"Someone's approaching," Gilda said, a hair above a whisper.

Frost let out a series of clicks. Almost immediately, he had the impression of a large object in the dark, gliding swiftly toward them. He aimed Noobstick. The shape was roughly Saba's size and shape. He squinted.

Saba reappeared in the same spot from which she had left. "The village scout is about a thousand feet ahead of us and another four or five hundred to our left. Took an arrow in the eye."

"Means we're close." Frost eased his finger away from Noobstick's trigger and lowered the weapon a bit. Though some of his tension had abated, he still did not relax.

"Perhaps," Saba said. "The scout's been dead for a while."

"Any sign of the Redthorns?" Gilda asked.

"They definitely passed by here. The scout was flanking their trail. Like Frost said, we're close, so I'd be careful. We wouldn't want to run head first into them."

"I say we push harder." Frost wasn't about to let up now. "Not much time left before sunrise."

"Fine." Saba turned to lead.

A burst of moonlight illuminated their surroundings. An instant later, they were mired in darkness once more.

"Wait." Frost frowned. Saba stopped and faced him. Frost nodded up ahead to where the silhouette of the mountains ended. The land flattened to rise again in the distance. "Is that the valley entrance?"

"Yes," Saba said. "Not far from where I found the scout."

"Makes sense," Frost mused. "Looks like the beginning of a plateau up there. Great place for a marksman or two."

Saba shifted to regard the shadowy slopes. "You sure?"

"Definitely." Frost wondered if Saba's concern was more for their well-being or the fact that she'd missed something he'd seen. Or just plain fear.

"If they're watching the entrance, how do we approach the valley?" Gilda asked.

"Leave the mounts here and use every bit of cover to get closer," Frost said. "If I'm right about the plateau, then Saba, you're the best suited to climb up and deal with any lookouts." The centaur glared at him but offered no protest. Her kind were by far the better natural climbers than eradae. "From up there, you should also be able to see the Redthorns' campfires. After you've killed the lookouts, you can lead us to the camp."

"Sounds like a good plan," Gilda said.

"Maybe." Saba's tail swished. "But it also means we might not make it before daylight."

Frost heaved a sigh. "Maybe not, but daylight won't matter if we're dead."

"Fine, I'll go." Saba pawed at the ground before she trotted off toward the slopes and disappeared into darkness.

Frost and Gilda dismounted. They took a moment for a much-needed stretch. When they were ready, they left the crevids munching on grass and headed in the same direction as Saba. At the base of the slopes they kept low to the ground and crept from boulder to boulder, to clumps of bush or grass, to stunted trees, to long shadows. Whenever the moon shed its cloak of clouds, they waited until the return of night's inky blackness.

Frost surveyed the route ahead in those moments, picking out the next best spot to hide. He also kept an eye on the ledge but discerned no movement. On occasion, he hoped for a glimpse of Saba up on the mountain's shoulder. The centaur was nowhere to be seen. Time dragged, progress excruciatingly slow. The need for caution gnawed at him.

He and Gilda reached the end of Apep's Belly. The

Gerza Valley yawned before them, illuminated by a brief spike of moonlight. Far to the east towered Mount Setep and the rest of the Bakare range, peaks crowned in storm clouds. To the south, clothed in night's rags, was the expanse of small rivers that fed fertile lands and forests. On their right was the plateau and the Apep's peaks. Standing out miles ahead were the lights of Marna, the town built in the Apep's shadow.

"Looks to be a little over forty miles away." Gilda was looking toward the town. "Even if we ran nonstop, it'd take over two hours."

"I'm tempted to go for it." Frost ground his jaw. The longer they took, the more his mind conjured images of the erada captives slaughtered for their horns. Tia's face was among them.

"I'm right with you. But we can't. Not until Saba returns."

"Not even then," Frost said.

"Why not?"

"The same reason we're creeping along here. If the Redthorns aren't at Marna yet, then they're gonna have other lookouts who're sure to spot us if we don't sneak in."

"No doubt." Gilda nodded.

Knowing the dilemma did little to curb Frost's need. He wracked his brain for another alternative. There had to be a faster way.

"What do you think of her?" Gilda asked.

"Who? Saba?"

"Yes."

"She seems a capable player," Frost said, "if a bit too shook over every little thing."

"Yeah," Gilda said. "I couldn't imagine playing the way she does… second guessing everything… always afraid."

"Neither could I, but it's worked good enough for

her to make the alpha. And she's been useful. Just gotta mind our mouths around her."

"No doubt."

A cold prickle ran down Frost's neck to his spine. His inadvertent echolocation activated. Someone approached from behind. He snapped his head around, expecting an enemy. It was Saba, dark, silent, and swift.

"You were right," she said upon reaching them. "There were two lookouts up on the ledge."

"What about the Redthorn camp?" Frost asked.

"It's on the other side of a small wooded area about halfway to Marna."

An objective completion for finding the Redthorns popped into Frost's head.

"Finally, some good luck." He'd scarcely said the words when the gray pallidity of a new dawn seeped into the eastern sky. Lightning radiated among the clouds. Thunder grumbled. "Shit."

"Yarl's backside," Saba cursed.

"We might still be able to pull it off." Frost squinted as he tried to study valley. But the land was little more than silhouettes and shadows.

"How?" Saba looked at him askance. "Even if we did something as stupid as running right now, we won't make it to the camp before it's bright enough for them to see us coming for miles."

With his pointer finger, Frost indicated himself and Gilda. "See us? Sure." He pointed at Saba. "But it's no prob for you and your sharded Concealment and Streak. You can get to those woods you mentioned in less than half the time it'd take us. Get rid of any lookouts and–"

"And what?" Saba screwed up her face. "Take on the entire Redthorn company? I'm only level twelve. They're stronger than those Battleguards we fought."

"I was gonna say signal to us." Frost shrugged. "With the storm clouds, it'll still be dark enough that if you shot a single Aether Arrow low to ground, we should be the only ones to spot it."

"Risky," Gilda said, "but it can work."

"It will," Frost said. "While Saba does that, you and I can run back to get our mounts. Knowing crevids, they're still in that same spot. Or close to it. Any objections?" He looked to Saba.

She rolled her eyes then grumbled, "Let's just get it done."

Frost smiled. When Saba trotted away and melted into her surroundings, he and Gilda set off in the opposite direction.

Without the need for caution, the return trip was a short one. They retrieved the crevids and raced back to the slope overlooking the valley. The eastern sky now blushed, hues bleeding into the storm-laden quilt, revealing more of the ground below. Fog crept across the land, draped the fields like a sheet.

Frost made out the woods halfway to Marna. He waited, breath expectant. Lightning flickered. Gilda's crevid stomped its hooves.

A tiny azure bolt streaked from the woods, burned through the mist. It lasted but an instant.

Frost yanked on his reins and sent the crevid darting down the slope. He leaned forward into a wind thick with the crevid's musk and the valley's freshness. The wind streamed by him, flapped his cloak. Within moments, he'd reached the valley floor. Wearing a shroud of fog, Frost pushed hard, knowing the window to cover the distance on the open grassland was small.

"Faster, damn it, faster." He flapped the reins.

The crevid snorted. Its jounce became more violent.

Frost was only too glad for the soft earth and the grumble of thunder to muffle the mount's hooves.

Fog dissipated, inch by creeping inch. The woods loomed larger. Frost focused on the birth of morning, the misty remnants, and the tree line. He could just make out Saba with her back turned, watching for any unwanted approach.

Heart thundering, Frost smiled. He would make it in time. They would somehow sneak Tia and others out of the camp.

A drake's shriek shattered the dawn. Another answered. And another. The trumpeting cries of the Sky Swords became a chorus.

Frost balled his hands into fists. He glanced toward Apep's Belly to where he thought the shrieks originated, but only a sky wreathed in storm clouds greeted him. He flapped his reins harder against the sense that they might be too late.

CHAPTER 17

Frost reached the trees and leaped from the crevid's back just as the heavens opened. The first patter of rain fell. Lightning lit the sky. Thunder crashed. He snatched Noobstick from its harness and nodded to Saba. "Lead us to the camp."

"It's too late," Saba cried.

"No, it isn't," Frost snarled. "This fight, coupled with the storm, might work in our favor."

"How?" Grimacing, Saba threw her hands up in exasperation.

Frost took a breath to fight his trepidation, nostrils filling with the scent of fresh rain. "If Umesh Madara sends all his men to fight the Sky Swords, we're gonna sneak in, free the prisoners, grab some mounts, and make a run for Marna."

"And if they don't?" Saba arched an eyebrow.

Frost sighed. He didn't wish to be the one, but he could think of no other way. "If Umesh keeps some men in reserve, then I'm gonna help the Sky Swords by attacking the Redthorns from the forest. That'll force his hand. Then it's up to you and Gilda. If we do it that way, I'll meet y'all on the camp's far side, and we run for the Aviary."

"Even if we accomplished all of that, how do we

signal to you?" Saba asked.

Frost folded his lips and gave it some thought. "Cause a stampede. Find a bull, send it running out of fear, and the others will follow."

Saba shook her head ever so slightly. "I don't think I've ever met a person as stubborn or as reckless as you."

"Thanks," Frost said. "But I prefer persistent. Now, the camp. Quickly."

Saba turned and galloped deeper into the woods among dappled shadows. Frost and Gilda followed. Drake calls rang out. The Azureguards would be there in minutes.

"Way to assume I can handle what needs doing," Gilda said as she ran beside him.

"A friend of mine claimed you were one of the better players he'd seen. He's usually trustworthy. Feel free to let me know if he was wrong."

"One of the better players?" Gilda scoffed. "If we weren't pressed for time." Her voice trailed off.

Frost smiled. "I actually look forward to the day."

"So do I."

Through the light drizzle and the trees ahead, Frost discerned tents and a flurry of movement. Saba had stopped behind a large trunk. Her tail swished. Crouched low, they came up on either side of the dresdor.

Dressed in crimson and black, the Redthorns were comprised of two companies, one mainly made up of grand korae. A few dozen gurashi towered among them, each with marbled skin, either blue and red, green and brown, or some other combination that marked them as impure among their kind. Outcasts. One full company had gathered weapons and were rushing outside the camp, facing away from Frost and the others, attention riveted on the storm-wreathed sky.

Saba pointed toward a stockade on the left. "Over there."

The vast majority of the slaves were eradae. The gurashi among them stood out, taller than the closest eradae by some two feet. Frost concentrated on the gurashi. Soon enough, he picked out Melori. Nebsamu and Tia were beside him, heads barely visible above the stockade. Tightness eased from Frost's shoulders at the sight of Tia.

Drakes screeched and trumpeted. The beat of wings accompanied the dissonance. Drake riders burst from the storm clouds. The drizzle became a downpour.

"I'll meet you in that stand of trees." Frost pointed to the stand in question several hundred feet past the encampment. "Wait for me to attack. That should bring the second company out. Good luck."

He waited for them to engage Concealment. Clicking, he tried to get a sense of their forms, but it was odd being told something was there that didn't seem to exist. He watched as the rain peppered their invisible shapes, creating ripples in the sheet of water, and hoped no one else would notice. He counted to ten before slinking through the woods to flank the Redthorns.

Magical booms echoed in concert with thunder's peal. Men roared. Drakes shrieked. Scores of Flame and Ice Globes and Infernal Spears shot up through the rain from among the Redthorns. Diving drakes banked this way and that, twisting to avoid the onslaught.

The Sky Swords answered with their own magical barrage. Cyan, bright white, or purple radiated among the clouds. Thunderbolts spilled forth.

Aether and Ice Shields and Aether Barriers sprang up around casters from both factions. Most warriors brought their shields to bear if they had one. Some combatants tried to dodge the magical assault.

Drake rider spells blasted aside Redthorns lacking the appropriate protection, but those victims staggered to

199

their feet moments later. A second or third strike put them down permanently.

Successful Redthorn first attacks against similarly unprotected drake riders elicited pain-filled screeches from drakes and sent the beasts spiraling down before the riders brought them under control. Subsequent blasts either knocked the riders from the mounts or saw the drakes plummet head first from the sky to crash into the ground.

Frost crouched in the brush and aimed Noobstick above the Redthorn formations. He chose Aether Bomb and squeezed the trigger.

"Sixty," he said under his breath, beginning the recharge countdown.

A round cyan luminance formed at the cannon's tip, growing until it was the size of a basketball. It launched from the barrel with a whoosh. Leaving a trail behind, it shot up into the sky.

"Fifty-five."

Frost took off running through the wet forest to a different location.

"Forty-five."

The blue Aether Bomb soared up to its peak. It began its descent.

While running, Frost snatched glances to determine the bomb's trajectory. Mentally, he continued the countdown.

He'd barely gained the next chosen spot twenty feet away when the Aether Bomb landed on a Redthorn. The moment the ball hit the grand kora, it exploded with a ring and a roar. The Redthorn was blown from his feet. Flames shot out. Anyone within ten feet of the impact zone was afire. They staggered about, screaming and swatting at themselves as if caught in a swarm of stinging insects.

Cannon Kata kicked in. Frost used the speed burst

to dash to another location. Exp gained was a distant thing in the back of his mind.

He waited the additional recharge time, snapped a look toward the Redthorns, aimed, pulled the trigger, and began another countdown. He repeated the sequence half a dozen times, pausing for longer periods, for minutes if needed to add to the confusion.

But eventually, the Redthorns caught on. The second company charged outside to reinforce the first. A barrage of Flame and Ice Globes, Infernal Spears, and Thunderbolts ripped through Frost's last location. Flame Columns burst from the ground. They set the woods ablaze. Several Redthorns zigzagged toward the forest.

The ground quaked. Animals bellowed. Over a hundred mounts galloped from the camp, charging toward the Redthorns. Chaos ensued as the Redthorns scattered.

Using the last bit of Cannon Kata's influence, he sprinted toward the area where Saba and Gilda had left the woods. Heart racing, hair plastered to his face, he grinned. *Damn, I love this shit.*

He dashed from the trees toward the rear of the encampment, away from the battle. Echolocation picked out a small object moving incredibly fast. Something blurred in his periphery. By sheer instinct, he twisted and dropped to the ground. And felt a tug as something sheared through his leather cuirass and the gambeson beneath. A burning sensation across his shoulder and chest elicited a yelp.

He came up on one knee, brought Noobstick to his waist, and faced the direction in which he'd discerned the motion and the object. Squinting through the downpour, he tried to make out any movement among the woods he'd vacated.

All he saw was the flames. Several more spells ripped through the forest. Breathing heavily, he tried to ignore the rain in his eyes, the stinging in his shoulder and chest. He fought the urge to wipe away the water or touch his wound.

And then he saw it at the same moment echolocation revealed it. A humanoid ripple in the downpour. Rain falling on something that was not quite there.

He fired. Korbitanium Projectile. Aether Shot. Divergence. Then an Aether Bomb for good measure.

He was up and running before impact, Noobstick held with both hands across his body. Cannon Kata and exp gain told their own stories. His legs pumped even faster through the wet grass.

Assuming there were several marksmen or cutthroats chasing him, Frost wove a haphazard pattern toward the distant stand. At the tree line, Tia and the others waited atop mounts. Saba stood with them, arrow nocked and aimed. A spare mount awaited his arrival. Gilda, Tia, and Nebsamu were waving him on frantically.

His heart skipped several beats when enemy arrows sliced through the air past him. He almost jumped out of his skin when a Flame Globe did the same, its scorching heat sending steam into the air before the globe fizzled out some distance ahead. He dared not look back.

Up ahead, Gilda's chakrams lit up. Red and blue. Fire and Ice Globes hurtled from her and blazed arcane trails past him. Her spells boomed behind him with their impacts. Saba loosed a Triple Barrage followed by an Aether Arrow.

Frost chose that moment to skid to a halt. In one motion, he turned, dropped to a knee, took quick aim at his pursuers, and loosed Divergence. A second trigger squeeze fired off an Aether Bomb. An Ice Pillar burst from the ground near him. He leaped to his feet and fled.

"Go! Go!" he yelled when he had but a short distance to cover.

Saba and the others wheeled around. All but Gilda,

202

who kept her hands on his crevid's reins. The other four bounded away along the trees.

Frost reached his mount. "Thanks."

"Don't thank me yet." Gilda fired off a few spells in the direction from which he'd fled.

Frost slid Noobstick into the harness on the mount's side and quickly climbed into the saddle. A moment later, he was flapping his reins and kicking his heels. A glance behind revealed Redthorns on foot dashing among Gilda's Stalag-mites.

"Got them." Gilda's chakrams radiated blue.

The Stalagmites exploded as she activated Glacial Eruption. Every single Redthorn was frozen in place. A blanket of ice covered the ground, powdery snow drifted down. Within minutes, the frozen Redthorns were distant forms. Frost let out an elated whoop.

"Now, you can thank me," Gilda said.

Frost grinned at her. "Thank you."

"Here." She held up a vial. "This should take care of the wound from that marksman's Aether Arrow." She tossed it to him.

He caught the vial, popped the cork with his teeth, and downed the potion. Within moments, it refreshed him.

Free the Captives

Objective Complete

Rescued group from Redthorn slavers:

2500 experience points

200 Khertahka dominion credits

The IM did nothing to ease Frost's sense of urgen-cy. He pushed the mount hard, wind and rain streaming by as they surged up the slope toward Marna's walls and front gate. Despite the escape, they were not yet truly free.

By now, the Sky Swords knew who they were, and most likely had been joined by the other Battleguards Setnana Botros had sent to hunt them. Whenever the Battle-guards were done with the Redthorns, Frost and the others were next.

He and Tia had to reach Marna and take a simurgh to Kituan before then. Or to anywhere away from Kher-tahka and Puria. He hoped Nebsamu had already made ar-rangements with this Flightmaster Matahu. Now was not the time for negotiations.

The race up to Marna seemed to take forever. Mag-ic still boomed behind them. Piercing drake trumpets and shrieks continued to ring out. Minutes later, there came a lull in the cacophony.

Up ahead, the town's gates loomed. Nebsamu, Tia, Melori, and Saba had stopped upon reaching the entrance. Saba was pawing the ground and swishing her tail.

Frost and Gilda drew to a halt at the gates. He im-mediately glanced toward Tia. She was wet and bedraggled, one sleeve of her tunic nothing more than torn cloth, her hair a tangled mess. Her face radiated fear.

"How you doing, sis? Did they hurt you?" he asked. She nodded numbly. Frost tried not to imagine what she must have suffered, but dark thoughts and darker deeds crept in.

From behind and below came a roar of a thousand voices. A quick look back at the Redthorn camp revealed victorious Battleguards.

"Time to get moving," Nebsamu said.

"Why'd we stop anyway?" Frost asked, frowning. Then, he noticed. "Why no guards? In fact, where's every-one?"

He turned slowly, taking in the town, the nearby homes lining the cobbled avenue. Beside him, Gilda twirled her dagger. Frost picked out movement behind curtains, shadowy forms pulling back from windows to hide, faces peeking from cracked doors.

"I asked the same thing," Nebsamu said. "It's why we waited. Something is not right."

Frost eased a hand down to grip Noobstick. "Doesn't matter now. Either we reach the Flightmaster and get out of here or the Battleguards catch us."

"Perhaps the Battleguards didn't notice us or don't know we're here," Saba argued, tail swishing. "They were concerned with the Redthorns. Whatever has frightened these people can't be good for us. We should just find another way down. A way out of the Sky Swords' sight."

"Even for you, that's kinda far-fetched," Frost said.

Drakes shrieked. At the Redthorn camp, several drake riders took to the air, headed for Marna.

"So much for that first idea," Gilda said.

"The Flightmaster, it is, then," Nebsamu declared. "The Aviary is on the north side of Marna, a big field on the outskirts."

"What if Matahu is already gone?" Saba asked.

Nebsamu shook his head. "He would not have been scared away like these folks. And not only is he loyal to Blue Sky but I paid him a small fortune."

Frost smiled. "I could kiss you right now, homie." He took one look at Nebsamu's scarred face and added, "Well, not really, but… bah, forget it. Lead the way." Gilda and Saba chuckled.

With a snap of his reins, Nebsamu sent his crevid bounding forward. They galloped straight ahead before veering north onto another street. A few more turns found them riding along an avenue close to the town's wall.

Frost kept a wary eye on their surroundings, expecting Redthorns to appear at any moment. At every corner he was ready for an ambush. He tensed when coming upon alleys. He peered toward roofs for marksmen or casters.

Through the driving rain, he tried to discern any tell-tale shapes. The downpour itself only served to increase tension, making echolocation even more difficult. His obscured surroundings brought a weight down upon his chest.

Splashing through puddles, they galloped the entire length of the town, chased by the drakes' trumpets. Not once did they encounter Redthorns or guards. The only people were those peeking from the safety of their homes.

The weight in Frost's chest built. His heart thudded to match. And then, over drumming hooves, over the beating rain, over the crash of thunder, over the drakes' encroaching shrieks, came the ring of steel.

Up ahead, several bodies were strewn about an intersection. They were eradae dressed in green uniforms.

Nebsamu turned right without slowing and headed toward an open gate. More corpses were near the opening. The gate itself hung by a hinge, creaking in the wind.

They bounded through into an open field. And drew to a halt.

Near the Aviary's stables, ten green-uniformed eradae faced off against a humongous marble-skinned gurash in baggy trousers and a silver cuirass. A litany of tattoos snaked up the gurash's over-sized arms. The gurash had to be at least twelve feet tall and broad enough to carry a wagon on his back.

Frost gaped. He'd seen gargants. He'd read the lore about the colossuses. He'd even fought his share in the old version of Ataxia. But never had he encountered a gurash this huge.

"Take a breath," Gilda said from beside him. "What you feel is the effect of Total Immersion. And before you ask, yes, that's the GUM, Umesh Madara."

Find the Slaver
Objective Complete

Umesh Madara located:
500 experience points

Umesh Madara certainly lived up to the reputation of Giant Ugly Mofoes. Scars crisscrossed a face twisted with rage and bloodlust. His eyes were deep dark pools that radiated hate. He bore a quaker axe only a person his size or larger could wield. One swipe of the double-bladed weapon could shear two men in half. A dozen bodies littered the ground around him. He brought the axe up and deliberately licked blood from one of the blades.

"There's no way we're beating him." Grimacing, Saba shook her head.

"Nif blind them," Nebsamu cursed. "Nif blind them all."

"What's wrong?" Frost asked.

"Behind the guards." Nebsamu pointed to where a woman cradled a man in her arms. "The two humans on the ground. That's Matahu and his daughter, Nepia."

CHAPTER 18

"Shit," Frost said. "What now?"

"The Flightmaster could still be alive," Melori said. "Perhaps, we can help him."

"Not with that monster in the way." Saba jutted her chin toward Umesh Madara.

IM made Frost aware of an objective to help Flightmaster Matahu and Nepia. "I don't think we have much choice but to try," he said as he studied the fight before him.

The guards had split up and were attacking in twos from several directions at once while their tank, a marauder with a great axe, held aggro, thus keeping Umesh focused on him. He turned Umesh Madara away from his fellows. The warriors among the guards dashed in to strike. Without shields, they could not afford to parry, but their armor was capable of absorbing splash damage when the GUM used Earth Nova, punching the ground to send out a circular blast of dirt and stone.

Sword-bearing reavers relied on quickness. They attacked with combinations of Eviscerate, Malignant Strike, and Mortal Wound, hoping to slow the GUM with bleeds and infections. Those Damage Over Time abilities stacked and often resulted in debilitation and health loss at a steady rate. But on Umesh, the DoTs appeared to have little effect.

Marauders were more direct, their aim to do as much damage as possible with single blows. Armed with two-handed axes, they led with Raging Rush to get in close before unleashing Cyclonic Strike, weapons extended as their bodies spun for several revolutions. One attempted a Staggering Blow, but the GUM resisted the stun. Another leaped away from a quick succession of Umesh Madara's slices to unleash an Aether Cleave, blue arcane energy extending away from the axe's double-sided blade.

The two casters among the guards worked in tandem, a windwalker with his warfan, and a sorcerer with a disc-shaped chakram in each hand. A flick of the windwalker's warfan produced Gust, clear air becoming translucent. A mix between fog and water. The spell shot across the distance.

The sorc fired off Flame and Ice Globes, quickly followed by a Flame Column, an Ice Stalactite from above Umesh, and a Stalagmite from below. Arcane red, blue, white, and hellish flames illuminated the area.

For a colossus, Umesh Madara was quite nimble, leaping away from their attacks, countering with arcing swings of his weapon. The blows and spells that did land only seemed to enrage him. Mud and water careened into the air when he dashed this way and that, his weapon seeming to slice the rain itself.

The ground trembled with each thudding footstep. He was a blur of violence whose attacks weren't limited to his axe. His kicks and punches snapped out with equal venom, the trademark of dementers.

Frost was amazed at the skill on display from the guards, at their ability to avoid the GUM. He tried to tell who was faring better, but it was difficult without Hit Points. Instead, he tried relying on the reaction to blows and spells, the effects a wound had on a person and on the GUM in particular. An arm hanging limp. Favoring a leg. Gripping one's side. That sort of thing.

Umesh Madara bellowed once, stomped the ground, and sent up a shower of mud. The Shockwave staggered two guards. He finished them with an Aether Cleave. The blade itself never touched them. The aether, honed into a thin blue edge, sheared the guards in half, cutting through armor, flesh, and bone like paper.

"We might not need to beat him," Gilda said.

Frost smirked at her optimism. He wanted to say they couldn't defeat the GUM even if they tried, but he bit back his words.

Gilda pointed. "There's a simurgh left. A young one, but it'll do."

"I like your thinking," Saba said. "Fleeing is our best chance."

"I'm certain it's what Umesh wants also," Frost said. "And he'll get it as soon as he's done with those guards."

The great beast-bird occupied the last stable, silver and black wings folded against its body, tongue lolling from its jaws. It cocked its lupine head to regard the battle. The fact the beast was still there spoke to impeccable training by the Flightmaster.

The shrieks and gurgling cries of Sky Sword drakes grew closer. Frost looked back the way they'd come, expecting the drake riders to be close, expecting them to come soaring through the sky on the leathery-winged creatures. Storm clouds greeted him. Spell blasts reverberated from the same direction. The effects illuminated the air above Marna.

"You don't have time for this," Nebsamu said. "Tia told me about Anefet's letter."

Frost shot his sister a look. *When had she read the letter? And why would she tell anyone?* Tia averted her gaze.

"This is bigger than this one fight," Nebsamu

continued. "Bigger than myself. You have to get to Adesh Hamada in Kituan. You will find him in the Gregis District at a tavern called the Wyvern's Eye. Show the barkeeper the ring Anefet gave you and tell him you're looking for a hammersmith.

"I owe my life to Anefet. And to you after today. Melori and I will help the guards and keep Umesh distracted. You three, see to Flightmaster Matahu and Nepia." He held out his hand. "Give Noobstick to me." Frost hesitated. "With Stand and Deliver and Aether Overload, I can put it to better use than you right now. If your concern is not having a weapon, you can buy a better one in Kituan."

Frost pulled the cannon from its harness and held it out toward the scavenger. "Is Stand and Deliver really that potent?"

Nebsamu climbed off his crevid. "You will see for yourself when I glow like a blue god." He took the weapon, hefted it, limbered his shoulders, and nodded to the gurash.

Melori followed his boss' lead. But when he dismounted, he tore away the sleeves of his shirt to reveal silver korbitanium vambraces. Dementer's weapons. Frost was certain Melori would have matching greaves on his shins.

"It was a pleasure helping Anefet's seeds," Nebsamu said. "Forgive your sister. She only did what she thought was right."

"She's already forgiven. And thank you." Frost dipped his head. "We wouldn't have made it here without you."

Melori placed a fist over his heart. "May Deluth and his warriors keep you strong."

"Anefet would be proud." Nebsamu eyed Frost, expression inscrutable. "Coming all this way to rescue us was brave."

"I was just trying to do the right thing," Frost said.

"Which is admirable." Nebsamu's lips twitched ever so slightly. He grew serious. "But it tells me you're still attached to your feelings. While I'm grateful you risked your life, the choice might still prove to be your downfall. Hopefully, it is not.

"You must realize not everyone can or should be saved. You must learn to let go. An inability to do so will fester. Before long you'll be that person mumbling to yourself about the world's ills. Don't be that person. Nothing good comes of it."

Frost nodded. "I'm gonna keep that in mind."

Nebsamu bowed and then stalked toward the fight, sloshing through mud and water. Melori followed in his wake.

Judging from Umesh Madara's earlier speed, Frost realized they could not attempt to get to Nepia and the Flightmaster before Nebsamu and Melori engaged. Even then, he and the others only had as much time as those two could survive.

"Get ready," he said to Gilda, Tia, and Saba.

Nebsamu stopped his advance perhaps three hundred feet behind Umesh Madara and stood with his legs spread, Noobstick held waist high. Lightning coruscated among the clouds. The rain seemed to fall harder. Thunder bellowed.

Noobstick coughed out a whomp, this one louder than its predecessors. A thicker, wider pulse spat from the barrel. The air itself glowed bright cyan as a skill Frost could only assume was a sharded Aether Shot hurtled through the rain. A split second later Noobstick spat a second burst, this one a deep, dark blood clot red.

"Now." Frost flapped his reins. His crevid leaped forward.

Through the beating rain, Frost watched as Umesh

212

Madara shifted at the last second before the sharded Aether Shot struck him square in the back. Instead, the pulse hit the GUM in the left arm. Umesh bellowed, the force of the blow twisting him. The second shot, the deep red one, struck his pauldron on the same side and burned into the silver armor. If he hadn't moved it would have been a clean headshot.

Umesh snatched a corpse and flung it at Nebsamu, but the scavenger was already sprinting away from his former position. A barrage of Korbitanium Projectiles spewed from Noobstick. They kicked up mud and water from the spot Umesh had been moments ago. The gurash had leaped into the air toward the strafing Nebsamu.

Melori roared. His marble skin reddened as he engaged Dementia. For the next thirty seconds his speed and power were multiplied tenfold.

The gurash vaulted up, higher than Umesh. He Spurted forward while in midair, covering the distance between them in a blink. He delivered a punch, Gravity Bomb, to Umesh's midsection. The blow knocked Umesh from the air.

Arms spread, Umesh flew backward down into the ground. His impact sent up a great splash of mud and brown water. The colossus skidded some twenty feet on his back, carving a path through mud and grass.

Umesh slammed his massive clawed hands into the ground. The move left rents and brought him to a stop. Roaring, he bounded to his feet and charged through the mud and rain toward the two men.

Frost and the others reached Matahu and Nepia. The girl was rocking back and forth while holding the wizened old man. The water around her was a bloody pool.

Gilda was the first off her mount. Frost dismounted and then helped Tia down. His sister clung to him, buried

213

her head in his shoulder, and let out a whimper.

Frost squeezed his eyes tight while whispering soothing words to Tia, telling her all would be well now, that she no longer had to fear the evil men. Tia held his arm in a death grip when they followed Gilda to Nepia's side.

Gilda touched the girl's shoulder. Red-rimmed eyes in a face framed with dark hair stared up. "Let me take a look at him."

The girl shied away at first. Her mouth opened and closed. She burst into sobs.

"Nepia, we're here to help," Frost said tenderly. "Trust us." The girl nodded but her eyes were still fearful.

Flightmaster Matahu's eyes fluttered open. Recognition flashed in them when his gaze passed over Frost.

"Anefet's first born," he wheezed. He reached a trembling hand up to his daughter. "Nep-Nepia."

"Yes, Papa?"

"Do as I begged you."

"Papa, you're going to be fine."

"Just... just say yes, my rose. Fulfill... my dying wi–" His body went limp. A last breath escaped his lips. He stared up sightlessly.

"Papaaaaa!" Nepia bawled.

"I'm sorry," Gilda said. "I'm so sorry."

But it was as if Nepia hadn't heard. She climbed to her feet, her gaze riveted upon Umesh Madara. Her face contorted from a mask of grief to one of hate. Pure odium. "I will do as Papa asked on one condition."

Frost frowned. He had no idea to what she referred but a part of him said to agree. "Name it."

"Promise that one day you will kill that monster." She had eyes only for Umesh Madara.

Nebsamu and Melori were still fighting him. Only three guards remained.

"I promise," Frost said. Immediately, he had a quest for killing the GUM.

Nepia's shoulders slumped. She let out a deep, shuddering breath. She got down on her knees in the mud and muck and kissed her father's pale lips. She stood. "Follow me."

She led them through the drumming rain to the simurgh's stable. A whiff of rankness and shit carried on the wind. The great beast-bird cocked its head and regarded them with intelligent eyes.

Frost had seen simurghs grow to over two hundred feet from snout to tail. This one was perhaps half that. Yet, the rows of teeth lining its jaws were anything but friendly. On one side of the stable were man-sized droppings. Frost grimaced.

Nepia closed her eyes and held up her hand. Long moments passed. The simurgh made a chattering sound. As if on command, the simurgh lay flat on its belly in the grass. Nepia directed them to climb atop its back.

Frost couldn't help his chuckle when Saba complied. Despite his years playing Ataxia Online, he'd never seen a centaur ride a simurgh. Or ride anything, for that matter. And though Saba had been deft enough climbing atop the simurgh, she looked utterly ridiculous as she folded her legs under her to lie down. Frost kept seeing a horse riding atop a bird.

If looks could kill, the glare Saba shot his way would have made him keel over right there. Frost covered his mouth in a half-hearted attempt to stifle his mirth.

Folding his lips before he burst into a cackle, Frost waited for Tia and Gilda to get aboard before he scrambled onto the simurgh between the sorcerer and his sister. He wasn't new to the experience, yet he couldn't help but marvel at the difference in the feel of the creature under Total Immersion. The mixture of feather and fur was soft yet pliant and had a strong odor that reminded him of a dog.

Nepia was the last to join them. She sat close up to the simurgh's neck. "Get comfortable before I give the command to harness."

Frost wiggled about for a bit before voicing his readiness. Ahead of him, both Saba and Gilda did the same. Tia wrapped her arms around Frost's waist and buried her head in his back. Frost fought his own small trepidation at the idea of harnessing.

But a moment passed before the feathery fur elongated and twined together. It was as if it grew on the spot. It coiled up and around Frost's legs, ankles, and his waist. Frost leaned forward to grab a bunch of the feathery fur and wrapped it around his hands. The fur tightened on its own.

"Hold on tight," Nepia said.

Drakes shrieked. Half a dozen of them soared up from the direction of the town's gate. Frost had no idea what took the Sky Swords so long to reach nor did he care.

At the battle with Umesh, only Nebsamu and Melori were left. Both had sustained wounds. Their chests heaved.

Umesh bled from a few cuts. His armor was singed and battered in several places, but he appeared unperturbed. His body blurred. And abruptly, there stood a dozen Mimics of the GUM.

A blue glow emanated from Nebsamu. Legs spread, he pointed Noobstick at the GUM. An Aether Shot burst from the cannon. Korbitanium Projectiles followed. Then Divergence. Aether Bomb. And the red shot.

The attacks were slow at first but steadily increased in pace. The buzzsaw bled into whines and whomps. They alternated. In moments, the separate discharges blurred into one, became a solid roar, a rain of metal and aether that was Stand and Deliver.

216

Umesh's Mimics separated. They leaped into the air above Nebsamu's onslaught and flung their quaker axes. A dozen of the weapons spun end over end toward Nebsamu.

Melori roared. He spun and punched up, all in one motion. The crescent-shaped wave of a Sonic Blow sliced through the air toward the incoming axes. In the same instant, a blue-tinged, oval-shaped Aether Barrier sprang up around him and Nebsamu.

With a screech, the simurgh lurched upright. It beat its wings. A musty wet wind buffeted Frost like a storm. After a final cry, the simurgh took flight.

The Flightmaster objective completed.

The ground, the town, Nebsamu, Melori, and Umesh dwindled, smaller and smaller, magics and aether and cannon fire streaking between them. The Sky Sword drakes had almost gained the landing. The view widened to encompass the verdant Gerza Valley. People became specks. Clouds blotted out Frost's view. Soon, they were flying above the storm, above clouds crowned in sun gold.

Khertahkan Trials
Objective Complete
Survived Umesh Madara:
1000 experience points
Saved group from slavers:
1500 experience points
Khertahkan Trials passed:
4000 experience points
Gained 500 Khertahka dominion credits

For the first time in a while Frost felt himself relax. He took in a deep breath of clean, cold, yet fresh air. Solemnity ate at him as he considered Nebsamu and Melori's fates. And yet, he was safe. So was Tia. But most of all, he had direction, a path to Adesh Hamada. In Kituan, he would grind out quests until level ten or eleven, and then head to

Maelpith Island.

And though a part of him feared the thought of failure against GUMs similar or worse than Umesh Madara or Emperor KiGyaba, there was something about the chance that lit a fire within him. And not just the prospect of helping his mother, Regi, Rayne, and Kai and eventually seeing them all free. He relished the challenge of the battle itself. The learning. It was as if he was raiding again for the very first time. His lips twitched with a small smile.

Until six drake riders speared through the clouds behind them. Their drakes shrieked.

CHAPTER 19

The drake riders flanked them, two to either side, and two above.

Frost gritted his teeth against the swirling wind. "This is what I get for giving up my fucking cannon."

"It wouldn't have made a difference," Saba said, voice a bit disorienting since she'd engaged Concealment. Frost imagined she was smirking. "Simurghs hate an aether cannon's discharge. And a cannoneer noob like you hitting anything while flying is unlikely. The wind and movement would throw off your aim. I've practiced and I'm barely decent at it."

"But you're not a cannoneer," Frost pointed out.

"Same principle," Saba retorted.

Frost almost argued the point, but it seemed childish. He had supreme confidence in his skill and knowledge from years playing gun sims, first person shooters, extensive firearms experience, and excelling at 3-Gun tourneys.

Saba continued, "Even if you got lucky, all the riders would have to do is dive as soon as the muzzle lit up."

"I woulda lowered the power and taken my chances." He chided himself for answering.

"Remind me how well lowering the power worked out in Snakewood Forest."

Frost scowled. "You can sit here and do nothing, but

219

I'd rather not be target practice if one of them happens to be a caster."

"I'm hardly doing nothing," she said. "I'm waiting for them to get close enough. They won't see my arrows coming. And for any casters to be effective, they'd also be putting themselves within Gilda's spell range."

"She's right," Nepia called from up front. "Tenefer would have tossed you from her back. Low power or not, the noise upsets her all the same. And those riders are smart enough to be cautious about a caster themselves. Doubly so if they caught sight of your dresdor friend before she Concealed. None of which will matter in the next few moments."

Won't matter? Frowning, Frost opened his mouth to ask Nepia if she'd lost her senses when the simurgh swelled beneath him. His unspoken question became a grin. In his absence from Ataxia, he'd forgotten about the simurgh's ability, its magic, the reason it was the preferred vehicle for long distance travel. The Velocity Surge.

Bracing for the Surge, he leaned forward, his face touching Gilda's back. He relished the perfume of her muskiness. He sucked in a breath and pushed hard against his midsection, stiffening his abdominal wall.

With a screech, the simurgh beat its wings and shot forward as if it had been fired from an aether cannon. The sudden acceleration drove Frost further into Gilda, made his stomach lurch up into his throat.

Behind him, Tia let out a strangled cry. Her grip on his waist tightened.

Frost's skin tingled. The world blurred. Frost cackled. He would have looked back if he could, but the velocity pressed down on him. He imagined the drakes as mere specks. And then completely gone.

He reveled in the adrenaline rush as the simurgh repeated the process again and again. Its speed increased every time. The trip brought back memories of the few times Pops had taken him to Hell's Descent, a roller coaster atop a skyrise Downtown Brooklyn with a drop of some thousand feet. A smile touched his lips before melancholy stymied the recollection.

In an hour, the simurgh burst through the clouds and into the glare of the afternoon sun above the human dominion of Ignis, the Grendesh Coalition's birthplace. A myriad of cities, towns, and villages dotted the landscape. Rivers snaked through lush plains. Forests, both great and small, marked the land in a thousand green shades. Far east, the Empyrean Sea was a rippled reflection of the bowl of heaven.

Frost's hands grew clammy at the sight of the ocean. He struggled against memories of almost drowning. Helplessness in water's embrace. To fight his fear, he focused on the peninsula known as the Glaive. Northeast of the Glaive was Sippar Island, and directly east of Sippar lay Maelpith Island and its cloak of mist in which lightning flickered in fitful spurts.

With a screech to announce itself, the simurgh began its descent toward the capital city of Kituan. A few beats of the simurgh's wings and Velocity Surges made Kituan grow from a speck to a vast citadel built upon the River Segia's delta. For the first time since he had taken her from atop the crevid back in Marna, Frost felt Tia relax.

Below, Kituan was as rife with villas, spires, avenues, and streets as it was with canals and waterways. A great curtain wall surrounded the noble acropolis, which had once been the city entire before the days of Commander Aureliano Grendesh and the Coalition. Now, the wall served as a barrier between nobility and lesser folk.

Buildings sprawled far beyond the acropolis' rich ac-

221

coutrements in the Tiberium District, to modest affairs in the Limne and Sumne Districts, to the jumble of structures in the Gregis and Caesia Districts, which extended to the city's outskirts dotted with homesteads, farmlands, and vineyards. Great time towers reached into the sky in each district, their timespheres glowing with aether as they rotated.

The metallic glint of the Aetherium dominated one end of the Tiberium District. Wrought from korbitanium, the collection of spires and buildings was said to hold the greatest magical secrets and powers in Mikander and claimed the best hierkaneers. Within its walls the Vindicators learned their trade. The trade of death. The wielding of aether enough to challenge the draconids and their advanced technology. Rumor had it that deep beneath the Aetherium, the Coalition had hidden away a Genesis Engine.

They were gliding down to the citadel, the air thickening with the Segia delta's briny scents, when Nepia spoke. "Which district do you want? I can land at any Aviary outside the Tiberium District."

"Nebsamu said Adesh would be in the Wyvern's Eye in the Gregis District," Frost said. "That'd be our best bet."

"Do you know someone there who can protect you or act as your guide?" Nepia asked.

"Why?" Frost furrowed his brow.

"Because," Saba said, "the Gregis District has become home to every criminal you could imagine. It's a hard place. I personally wouldn't go in there before level twenty without guards."

"There's four of us." Frost shrugged. "We can hold our own."

"I doubt it," Saba said. "Especially since you don't have a weapon. What will you do if we're attacked? Kiss someone? Punch them? Are you adept in Hand-to-hand combat? As it stands, it's more like two and a quarter of us because your sister is absolutely no help in a fight."

"I don't like agreeing with her, but she's right," Gilda said.

Frost glared at Gilda's back. "You're supposed to be on my side," he grumbled.

"I am, trust and believe," Gilda said, matching his timbre.

Saba spoke again. "Back at the mines, Melori was actually saying it'd be better if we left your sister at a Temple of Nif with some mystics."

"Not gonna happen," Frost growled.

"I'm not setting foot in the Gregis District without proper protection," Saba said. "Either we do something easier to level up and then return. Or we hire guards."

"Guards, it is," he said grudgingly.

"Then that leaves three districts to choose from," Nepia said.

Tenefer banked to begin a circular path over the city. Other simurghs floated higher up. Drakes flitted this way and that below them on their descents to various Aviaries.

The most prominent of all the sky traffic were zephyrs, the humans' favored flying mount. They came in various shades or mixtures of white, brown, and black. They were as big or bigger than drakes, with muscular bodies, diaphanous wings, and faces like owls.

"Limne would be your best choice," Saba said. "It's home to most eradae in the city. You might even find a protection guild like the Granite Order that will take KDC rather than rip you off in converting them to IDC."

"Protection guilds used to be pretty expensive." Frost took a look at his Khertahka dominion credits.

"Still are," Gilda said.

"How much KDC do you have?" Saba asked.

"Fifteen hundred."

"Might be able to get one level thirty guard at that price. Or two level fifteens."

"I still need a new aether cannon." He felt naked without a weapon. And Saba's earlier jab didn't help. He would have to do something about unarmed combat when the chance and the credits presented themselves.

"I could loan you some credits," Gilda said. "I've got about a thousand to spare."

Though grateful for the offer, Frost shook his head. "You need them to advance as much as I do."

"No doubt," Gilda said.

"I got a better idea." Frost eyed a human Bloodguard atop a zephyr. "I know a friend who plays the Auction Markets. He'll be able to help. Head to Caesia." Frost fully expected an objection from Saba and was surprised when she offered none.

Nepia had the simurgh veer off its line and glide down to the Caesia District and its red brick streets and buildings. A maze of waterways and canals intersected those streets. They headed directly toward a Landing: a large roped off field where runners dashed this way and that, directing incoming flights by waving short phosphorescent glimmerwands. Tenefer glided down, then beat its wings not far from a runner, kicking up a cloud of dust and debris as it slowly lowered to the ground.

Trek to Kituan
Objective Complete
Arrived safely in Kituan:
1000 experience points
250 Ignis dominion credits
Level 5 Gained.

With the addition of stats, namely two more strength and agility, IM made Frost aware that Concussion Blast was available. He took out the shard and absorbed it.

Skill unlocked

Concussion Blast

Cast time: 1 second
Recharge Time: 30 seconds
Consumes: Aether
Available shard slots: 3
Effect: Fire a blast of aether up to 250 feet that detonates on impact, stunning enemies in a five-foot radius and knocking them into the air. Builds 5 percent aether for a direct hit. 1 percent for each additional enemy in area of effect.

Frost smiled at the skill. He needed to find time to practice at some point.

"What'll you do now?" Gilda asked Nepia when they landed and had dismounted.

"Return to bury my father and to rebuild and run the Aviary." She eyed Frost from atop Tenefer's back. "Don't forget your promise."

"I won't," Frost said. "I'll bring Umesh's head for you one day."

Nepia nodded. "I look forward to it. May Nif and Kitu bless your quest." She drew an X over her heart and made a circle on her forehead.

Frost repeated the gesture and added, "May Nif and Kitu keep you safe."

He frowned when he'd done so, pondering the interaction. But it felt like the natural thing to do. In ways, the game's relation to real life was as wonderful as it was frightening. He led the others away and stopped at the edge of the roped off Landing to watch as Nepia and Tenefer took to the skies once more.

When Tenefer became a speck, Frost headed out onto the bustling Via Iridius, which was split by lanes and waterways. Frost was certain if Hughey was playing Meritus

Killgain, then he would be at the Auction Market this early in the game, acquiring credits for weapons, skills, and items before heading out to do any sort of leveling. Preparation was Hughey's middle name.

As he walked, Frost stroked his aether ring and took in his surroundings. Shops and taverns made up the brunt of the buildings along the Via Iridius. Criers shouted out their wares or tried to usher people into the associated businesses. Most of the people along the avenue were humans, but there was the occasional sprinkling of Marang's other playable races: grand korae, eradae, dresdori, and gurashi. Dressed in fine garb, they strode down the avenue as if they owned it.

There were more also, mostly elementals: a few dryads with vegetation growing from their bodies; an undine whose translucent watery form distorted things beyond it; a gang of diminutive swaggering rock-form dvergar, their skins the color of stone. Frost couldn't help gawking at one or the other. They were everything he could have hoped for if he truly lived in a game.

As Gilda had warned him, one aspect of the crowds was quite disturbing. The number of people and things played havoc with his echolocation. It took a supreme effort of will to tune out most of it. Even then, he found himself distracted.

Frost frowned. His group was making way at a faster pace than anyone else. Space had opened up around them. Realization dawned. People were avoiding them. Some pointed. A few whispered to each other. One erada woman turned up her nose.

He glanced down and growled. "We should split up."

"That makes no sense," Saba said. "We're safer together."

"We're supposed to be, but look around."

After a few moments, Gilda spoke. "It's our appearance. All the dirt and blood."

"Exactly." Frost nodded. "Saba... Major Neferna told you Nomarch Setnana was headed to Kituan before Maelpith Island. She might still be here. From the way the Sky Swords chased us, it's safe to assume that our plan worked and Neferna knows who we really are. Most likely she sent word ahead by Communication Orb in case this was our destination.

"Which means there's a chance Setnana already has people on the lookout for us. All we need is for the casual mention of three dirty eradae and a dresdor strolling along the Via Iridius to fall on the wrong ears."

"Point taken," Saba grumbled.

Frost glanced toward the district's time tower. The massive aether-infused timesphere read two hours past noon. "Gilda, you and Saba go buy a change of clothes and meet us at the intersection of Libris and Iridius in an hour."

"At least allow us to escort you and Tia to the Auction Market," Gilda said.

"Alright, but don't walk with us. One of you go on ahead; one stays behind."

They did as he asked. Saba in the lead with Gilda trailing. People still continued to offer scornful looks here and there, but the reactions weren't nearly as prevalent. Slowly, the space around them closed to more normal proportions, with him and Tia at times having to shift a bit to avoid someone in a rush.

Before long, they reached the bustling square building that was the Auction Market, where many a player sought to buy or sell the rarest goods. Saba and Gilda went in search of new outfits while Frost headed up to the second floor where he was certain he'd find his best friend.

Meritus Killgain was sitting at a table in one corner,

seemingly staring off at nothing. Skin a deep bronze, his face that of a young man who would easily be overlooked, Meritus was the same as Frost remembered when they played Ataxia together. He was dressed in a satin shirt with frilly sleeves and dark-colored pants. Right now, Meritus was most likely sifting through sales and purchases and credits. Frost made to approach his friend.

"Just a moment, buddy," a deep voice said from down below. "The boss is busy."

Frost looked down. Face looking quite disinterested, despite the fact he stood no higher than Frost's knee, was a green-skinned goblin. He was dressed in black robes with a bar of gold thread running down the short sleeves. Which was how Frost saw his bulging biceps. A folded scarf was tied around his forehead. His hair was done in a top knot, and he had a wispy beard. The goblin promptly began to clean his nails with a tiny haladie: a wavy double-edged, double-bladed dagger.

"You gotta be kidding me." Frost almost burst into laughter. "I understand you gotta do your job, but Meritus and I go way back."

"Still have to wait."

"This is an emergency." Frost made to take another step. His leg froze. Literally. A block of ice encased his leg.

"Not trying to be mean; let's not make a scene. I don't know why you people always act like this toward the Little People, but I'd hate to have to put the rest of you on ice." The goblin's yellow-toothed grin belied his words.

The room cleared in their immediate vicinity. But for one other person. Frost didn't know how he'd missed him, but against the wall behind Meritus was a crimson gurash dressed in chain mail and leaning on a massive crescent axe. The gurash had eyes only for Frost. Eyes that said he was going to put a hurting on someone.

"Frost!" Meritus exclaimed. "Ryne, knock it off, you bully." Meritus shot a glare at the goblin.

Ryne scowled at Frost. The ice dissolved and left a puddle on the stone floor. After one more venomous glare, Ryne stalked away, took up a position beside the gurash, and stared at Frost. Frost had the sudden urge to stick his tongue out at Ryne but resisted. Barely.

Grinning madly, Meritus got up and walked over to Frost. They gave each other a dap by gripping fingers right hand to right hand, releasing, then slapping that right hand over their hearts. Not until that very moment did Frost fully realize how much he missed gaming and how much he missed his best, and maybe only true friend.

"Come. Sit." Meritus pointed to two chairs opposite his. "And your lovely lady as well."

Frost and Tia sat. That simple act in the confines of a comfortable room brought exhaustion crashing down on Frost. He took a deep breath. He could use a nice long sleep and some food.

"Kinda surprised to see you this soon," Meritus said. "You look like shit."

"Shaddup." Frost forced a smile. Meritus chuckled. Frost sighed. "Been having a rough time of it. Rougher than I expected."

"Who's she?" Meritus jutted his chin at Tia.

"My sister, Beketia. I'm currently trying to keep her and myself safe after our mother was killed."

"Sounds like the kinda trouble you always find yourself in." Meritus produced two rejuvenation potions and handed one to Frost and the other to Tia.

"I know, right?" Frost chuckled. He downed the potion. In moments, he was refreshed. He took in Meritus' fine clothing. "Looks like you're doing well."

"Yeah. Kinda loving it here. Makes you wonder if we

even need the real world to enjoy life."

"Good question," Frost said. "I'll let you know when I find the answer. Anyway, I'm here because I need your help."

Meritus spread his arms. "Whatever you need, homie. I'm always here for you."

"There's a lot going on," Frost said. "I can't give all the details right now." He leaned in close so only Meritus could hear and whispered, "My mother was the Hand of Freedom."

"Wow." Meritus leaned away, brows raised.

"Yeah. Now, we've got some erada woman, No-march Setnana Botros, hunting us with Battleguards."

"That's the least of your worries," Meritus said. "If the people believe all the recent stories about Blue Sky, it'll be the rest of the Coalition soon enough. How the hell did you get caught up in this madness?"

"Just trying to follow the quests."

Meritus' thick brows climbed his forehead. "You? Questing? And saying us? I woulda expected you to be off grinding solo somewhere. I remember you had a saying... what was it again?"

Frost smiled. "Whatever doesn't kill me gives me exp."

"Yeah, that was it."

Frost shrugged. "Just trying an easier way now. One thing led to another. Whatever is going on, the plot runs deep. The way they're after us says there's something more." He frowned. "If I could only figure it out."

"How can I help?" Meritus asked.

"I gotta go to the Wyvern's Eye to meet someone. But I heard the Gregis District is a lot tougher now. Especially for a noob like me. We need an escort. Someone about level thirty. And I also need an aether cannon and some ammo."

"Oh shit, you chose cannoneer?"

"Yep. Wanted something different."

"They kick ass."

"So, the demo said."

"Nah, you don't understand," Meritus said, waving his hands, "they have this skill at level ten, called Stand and Deliver, which is insane. I already picture you using it." Scowling, Meritus simulated holding an aether cannon. "Be like Neo in the Matrix saving Morpheus. The helicopter scene when he's tearing the building up with the minigun."

"You and those old ass movies." Frost shook his head. "But, yeah, I recently saw that skill in action. It *is* epic. But for right now, I just need you to help me get a new cannon and an escort."

"I got you, homie. You can take my guards with you." Meritus flicked his thumb back toward the two men. "I can hire more. The goblin's an NPC. He's thirty-one. The other." He paused. A light smile curved his lips. "First, promise you won't trip."

Frost gave Meritus the side-eye. After a moment, he said, "I promise."

"The gurash is an old guildie. The best tank we had in Soldiers of Chaos." It looked as if Meritus was doing his best to keep a straight face, but there was a twinkle in his eye.

Frost shook his head and smirked. "You just *had* to go get him, didn't you?"

Meritus shrugged. "He was looking for an easier job outside his main quest. Hint, hint. Besides, I never had the issues with him that you did after SoC broke up."

"Come on, dawg. Dante *was* the reason for the break up and us losing number one rank across all servers."

"Let that old beef die, homie," Meritus said. "With the things I've heard from a few testers since I started playing, we're gonna have to. And you gave your word that you wouldn't trip."

Frost glanced over at Dante Blackblade, who was watching them with narrowed eyes. Then he returned his attention to Meritus Killgain. "Alright. You get to be the one to tell him. And you also need to let him know that Gilda Mordian is with us."

Meritus' brows shot up. "Just Blaze?"

"Yep. And not only is she playing a sorc, she's also a pretty light blue erada."

"This is gonna be interesting. You're in a group, which is unheard of, and with two people who probably wanna kill you." Meritus shook his head. "And there's this quest line you're on. Something epic is gonna go down. I can feel it. And I wanna be there for it. I might have to roll with y'all once I get all the skills and gear I need."

"You're always welcome," Frost said. "If I gotta group, it might as well be with someone I don't mind being around. But I'm letting you know now that eventually I gotta head to Imanok Sanctum."

"See!" Meritus exclaimed. "Epic. Just epic. There's been so much talk about Maelpith Island. All kinds of nice loot. A gatherer's dream, too. From herbs to korbitanium. It's got the market buzzing. Heard there might be hierkas and rare schemas. Even saw a reaver showing off a sharded Necrotic Slash he said he picked up from a GUM. Been a few guilds sending groups too, but no one has beaten Emperor KiGyaba."

"So, I've been told," Frost said.

"No wonder you got Gilda."

"Not exactly how we met, but I guess." Frost shrugged. "Since you mentioned nice loot, hustle me up that aether cannon on the Market. Oh, and some armor. I got fifteen hundred KDC and two hundred and fifty IDC to

232

spend. I'd prefer if the weapon has increased duration on Cannon Kata."

"Why not just find you a side quest to get a new cannon?" Meritus sat back. "Save your credits for skill shards? Talking to almost any random NPC like a vendor should start a quest. You can actually haggle for what you want your reward to be."

"Don't have the time for that with these people on our asses."

"Alright," Meritus said. "But this works easier if you'd just run the Auction Market tutorial and open a warehouse rather than have me buying for you."

"Just reached level five when I got to Kituan," Frost said. "Haven't had time to do either. And don't have the time now."

"No worries. I got you." Meritus stared off at nothing again. After a moment, he said, "I think I found the perfect cannon. Level five. Named Deadeye. Extends Kata by six seconds."

"Sounds good. And the armor?"

"Nothing you or I can afford. Not to worry, though, you can pick up some Coalition standard-issue from the armorer."

Frost groaned. "It'll have to do."

"Snagged your cannon and ammo. I'd tell you it's on me... but you'd still send me the credits anyway."

"As long as you know."

"Got you something else too." Meritus was grinning.

"What?"

"Shaddup."

They both laughed.

"Let's head to my warehouse and you'll see." Meritus stood. "I'll tell Dante and Ryne Waldron that their contracts have passed to you."

"Pay you back for them too."

"Yeah, yeah." Meritus waved him off. "Oh, I forgot to mention. They got a lil feud going. Dante's mad because Ryne gets to do most of the dirty work." He went off to speak to his guards.

Voices rose. Mostly between Dante and Meritus. While Dante gestured vehemently, Ryne just shrugged and nodded. Dante scowled in Frost's direction.

They left the Market and headed to Meritus' warehouse. On the way, Frost and Meritus discussed the differences in the game. Both were completely amazed by the sense of being a part of the world. The old VR engine was like Pops' stories of playing games on televisions or computer screens. Frost couldn't even begin to imagine what that must have been like.

"Really makes you wonder if things like Total Immersion will replace real life altogether one day," Meritus said.

"Yep." Frost nodded. "Even the feelings in game are ridiculous."

"Could you imagine?" Meritus shook his head. "It's crazy enough already with so many people always hooked in to VR. What type of world would it be if that was all of us in SR? Better? Worse?"

"Who knows?" Frost shrugged.

At the warehouse, Meritus retrieved Deadeye and passed it to Frost.

Acquired weapon: Deadeye
Level: 5
Damage: 50 – 75
Force: 10
Special: Extends Cannon Kata by 6 seconds
Available shard slots: 1

The cannon was similar in style to Noobstick but

with a shorter barrel. It had a button next to the trigger that emitted a light to mark a target. The battery was also smaller.

Meritus held something else out to Frost. A skill shard. Frost took it.

Skill acquired

Stand and Deliver
Cannot absorb
Requires ability to activate Aether Overload.

Frost grinned despite knowing he needed to be level ten. "Damn, homie. Thanks. For real, thanks."

"It's all good. Just hurry and level up so you can use that bad boy."

"No prob," Frost said as he dreamed of using the skill.

Their next stop was the armorer. The merchant was a stocky dryad. After looking over the merchant's wares, Frost dismissed the idea of the green and yellow Coalition standard-issue leathers. Instead, he settled on a black gambeson and mahogany colored brigandine. He also picked out new leather greaves, cuisses, and bracers to match.

The armor set him back four hundred KDC, but the random pieces were an improvement over the old stolen Azureguard fare. With the new kit, he had four percent damage reduction and two percent stagger resist. Frost was able to sell the old stuff for fifty IDC.

"I still think you shoulda went with the Coalition standard-issue," Meritus said when they stood outside the armorer's metal and brick facade. "Or at least kept the cloak. Those colors can make people with bad intentions think twice."

"True. But I doubt it works in my favor if it's all I have when I head to the island. Most likely the inhabitants won't care what I'm wearing. The ones that do won't be praising the Coalition. We both know how the Coalition goes about their expeditions."

"Soldiers on the ground. Blood, fire, and magic negotiations," Meritus said. "The Coalition way or the grave."

"Exactly."

"Well, good luck, homie." Meritus reached out and they gave each other a dap, ending by tapping palms over their hearts.

"Thanks again, dawg," Frost said.

"It's all good." Meritus smiled. "If you need anything else while you're here or run into trouble, I'm staying at the Cobalt Talisman. Third floor, middle room to the rear. And, Frost?"

"Shaddup," they said as one and burst into laughter.

After a few moments, Meritus turned and strode back toward the Auction Market. Frost watched his friend until Meritus stepped through the Market's doors. Then, with Tia beside him, and his two bodyguards following, he headed in the opposite direction.

"Dante," he said, "I dislike this as much as you, but if we're gonna make this work, we gotta let bygones be bygones."

"I can do that," Dante said, his shrill voice out of place coming from an eight-foot gurash who weighed a good four hundred pounds. "But when we're all max, we'll settle up."

"No prob," Frost agreed. "As for you, Ryne Waldron."

"I'm here to serve you, my good man." Dante had the voice Frost would have expected from Blackblade. Deep. From the chest. "Any enemy of yours is an enemy of mine. And unlike Big Foot," Ryne jutted a tiny thumb in Dante's direction, "if you say jump, I'll ask how high."

"Just remember, the gnome can only jump but so

high," Dante quipped.

"Gnome." Ryne grimaced, took a long slow breath, and shook his head. "Always the disrespect in every aspect. At least I can jump, fat man."

"I. Am. Not. Fat." Dante glared at the goblin.

"Of course not, you're big-boned."

"At least I can reach around to scratch my back." Dante snorted. "Arms like a baby raptor." He imitated his statement.

Frost chuckled. "Alright, alright, you two, cut it out. Ryne, what class are you?"

"Shadowmancer."

"Ah." Frost nodded.

The class explained the goblin's cockiness. Shadow-mancers were as difficult to play well as they were potent.

Frost recalled the many times he'd fought one. Each had been challenging. And annoying. Necrosis was one of their favored spells, dealing increasing Damage over Time before a final explosive burst. If that DoT wasn't bad enough, they had other direct damage spells, summonses, Haunt, and the ability to go into Ethereal Form, which reduced all incoming damage while increasing their output. And Phase. How could he forget Phase? It made them invulnerable for a short time, although they couldn't attack in its duration. The downside was their low vitality and the huge consumption of aether.

Frost stopped and frowned. He glanced down at Ryne. "A shadowmancer with an ice spell. Interesting. Mind if I ask how you picked it up?"

Ryne smiled, rolled his right hand, and dipped his head as if he just completed a performance and was recognizing the crowd's adulation. "A wizard never gives up his secrets."

Frost shook his head. "Whatever."

"The gnome has always been cocky," Dante said. "Swears he's a poet, too. Don't let him get to you."

"My name is Ryne, Big Foot. Ryne. Say it more than one time." The goblin glared at Dante and added something else unintelligible that sounded very much like a string of curses.

"I see," Frost said to Dante, then continued down the Via. "What level are you, Dante?"

"Fifteen."

Ryne snickered.

Frost scowled. *I coulda sworn I told Meritus*—he dismissed the thought. Giving him Dante meant Meritus believed the gurash was more than up to the task. Especially with a level thirty-one shadowmancer, Gilda, and himself. Not even counting Saba. *I hope your faith isn't misplaced, homie.*

Soon enough, they reached the intersection of the Via Iridius and the Via Libris. Gilda and Saba were already there. They both smirked at him. Saba reached up to her neck to a chain and flipped open a timeorb. She shook her head for good measure.

Gilda was wearing a black studded jacket that ended mid-thigh. Underneath was a white cotton shirt. She had replaced her star-shaped chakrams with circular ones done in gold and silver. Her loose-fitting pants matched the jacket. Her cerulean skin absolutely glowed.

Frost found himself drawn to her horns again. Gilda's dagger appeared in her hand. She twirled it. He shook off the thought.

Saba had shed the gambeson for a coat of plates, its deep brown leather accentuating her bronze skin. Her flanchard, peytral, and crupper were all the same type of leather material and color. Her short hair was slicked back. She had a new bow made of some dark wood.

"What's up," Frost said cheerily. All he got in return

238

was a roll of Saba's eyes and a shake of Gilda's head while she twirled her dagger then put it away.

"And men like to say we take long getting ready," Saba said under her breath.

"I heard that," Frost shot back.

"You were supposed to." Saba pranced impatiently. "Can we get a move on?"

"Let me introduce our escorts first," Frost said.

"Escorts?" Saba repeated. "There's just the big fellow."

"The disrespect," Ryne huffed from down below. "Always disrespect in all aspects for the Little People."

"Oh, damn. I'm sorry." Saba cupped a hand over her mouth. "I didn't–"

"See me," Ryne finished. "I know. People always overlook me or see me last. Until my foot is in their ass. I'm Ryne Waldron and am only too happy to be escorting you five ladies."

The girls outright laughed or giggled. Frost and Dante scowled at the shadowmancer. Ryne shrugged.

"I'll show you lady when I get to your level," Dante said.

Frost gestured to the marauder. "This is–"

"Dante Blackblade," Gilda finished. "We crossed paths."

While Dante was glaring at Gilda with clear bad intentions, she seemed unimpressed. Frost hoped Dante wouldn't try to call her out right there and then.

"Like I told your boyfriend, here," Dante said, nodding to Frost, "we're all good until we're max. Then all bets are off."

"No doubt. But he's not my boyfriend." Gilda's dagger appeared again. She made a show of cleaning her nails. She blew on them. "I heard the idea of men... I mean, boys, getting mad because they got beat by a girl was so 2010."

Frost fought down a smile. "Alright, alright. Enough pleasantries. We got some place to be."

Following his lead, they crossed the intersection where the Via Iridius became the Via Arcadius and the start of the Gregis District, buildings casting long shadows in the evening sun. Frost tensed, knowing a crucial part of their journey had begun. He sensed the same from Gilda and Saba. Even Tia had gotten closer to him.

"We're being followed," Ryne Waldron said. "At first I thought it was coincidence. But through my concealed defiler, I confirmed their lack of innocence. Two Azureguards on a parallel street. Two on this one. Alternating in an attempt to remain inconspicuous."

CHAPTER 20

"Let's go over there and kick their asses," Dante said as they strode down one side of the Via Arcadius.

"The idea is *not* to draw attention to ourselves," Frost said. "Meritus told you what the issue is, the position we're in. Making a scene in the heart of the Coalition would be pretty dumb."

"You're the boss," Dante grumbled.

"I have to agree with our patron," Ryne said in that disconcertingly deep voice of his. "Kalarch Voculo passed a new law against fighting in Kituan. Get caught starting a fracas and you'll face a trial no defendant has ever won.

"Punishment is a year spent mining korbitanium, which most don't return from. Death from the fumes in the mines or the spriggans that live there is often the outcome.

"Unless you're a lucky one. Lucky ones get to toil in the Kelsial vineyards. Of course, the guilty can always choose the Fighting Pits of Bastards."

"I enjoyed my time in the Bastards," Gilda said.

"A woman after my heart." Ryne chortled. "I could marry you."

In a flash, Gilda's dagger appeared. She regarded Ryne, expression flat. "I've killed for less."

The goblin smiled his yellow-toothed smile. He took out his haladie and imitated Gilda.

Frost grinned. He could picture it now. Seven-foot Gilda with a goblin barely three feet tall, the goblin muttering bad poetry into her ear. He shook his head ruefully.

"Let me handle our followers." Ryne's gaze was still on Gilda.

"Not gonna happen," Frost said.

"You hired the world's best goblin. Now, you refuse him?" Ryne pouted and put away his haladie.

Frost smirked at the goblin. "You just said—"

"I know what I said. Did you *listen?*"

Frost narrowed his eyes in contemplation. He considered everything Ryne had mentioned about the new law. He snatched a look at Ryne as he understood the suggestion. The goblin wore a small smile.

"Now, *that's* what I'm talking about!" Grinning, Dante clapped a hand to his thigh like an overly excited schoolboy. "I'm all about that action. Pew! Pew!"

"No. No. No fucking way." Frost shook his head vigorously.

"I agree with Frost this time," Saba said. "That's a bad idea."

"Only if we get caught," Dante said with a sly smile.

"The goblin has a point," Gilda chimed in. "What's the plan otherwise? Let them follow us all the way?"

"We can't do that either." Frost tried to think. "There's gotta be another way to get them off our tail."

Ryne cleared his throat. "I keep hearing 'we'. Who is this 'we'?" He peered all around, even up into the sky.

Frost stopped at a stall where a vendor was selling roasted beardbeak. Fifty credits got enough of the meat for everyone. Stomach grumbling as he took his, he used the time to shoot a quick glance to their left.

A male Azureguard across the street was paying way too much attention to some female gargant's underthings at a linen seller. The Azureguard held up the underpants, arms spread wide to accommodate their size.

The group set off again. Chewing the succulent meat, Frost crossed the next intersection. Sure enough, the same Azureguard crossed the other side a moment later. Frost also picked out one more trailing the first, mingling with the crowds.

"Alright, Ryne," Frost said. "Take care of them. We're gonna pop into that apothecary over there." Frost nodded to the establishment in question.

"No fair," Dante whined. "I'm an escort also."

"And you're escorting," Frost said. "Ryne's level thirty-one and something tells me he knows exactly what he's about."

Dante grumbled something unintelligible as they headed toward the apothecary. Frost ignored him. When they reached the shop, Ryne was still with them. Frost, Tia, Saba, and Gilda entered the apothecary. Ryne stood with Dante outside, on the opposite side of the door.

"Gnome, weren't you supposed to be taking care of the problem?" Dante asked aloud.

Frost stopped just inside the door where the Azureguards would not be able to see him when he spoke to Ryne. "Wanna explain why you're still here?"

Ryne offered no response. Not even a smart remark at Dante's quip. He just stared off at the crowded street.

Frost frowned. He made to speak again when he noted the unnatural stillness of a few stray strands of Ryne's hair. Ryne's wispy beard was the same. As were his robes. This, despite a breeze that swirled dust out in the street, ruffled cloaks, loose clothing, and rattled the store's sign.

"A Mimic," Gilda said from behind Frost. She rested

a hand on Frost's waist.

"A good one, too," Saba added.

Frost smiled. The goblin might be worth his weight in whatever price Meritus had paid. "Nothing to do now but wait." Frost turned to the shop's interior and offered a warm smile to Gilda. "See if there's anything you'd like to pick up from here for any of your concoctions."

The next fifteen minutes passed with Gilda and Saba haggling with the merchant about his prices for simple herbs. They finally settled on a few.

Frost kept an eye on the Mimic while also perusing the apothecary's goods. He paid three hundred IDC for an entire batch of vials and potions, including health, rejuvenation, and sanctification. Before he stashed them in his inventory, he checked to make sure their effects were the same as the old version of the game.

Health Potion

Regain 500 health instantly

Reuse: 2 minutes

Rejuvenation Potion

Regain 1000 health over 30 seconds

Reuse: 2 minutes

Purification Potion

Cleanse one adverse effect

Reuse: 2 minutes

The vials were on three-minute reuse timers.

Aether Power

+25 to Aether effects

Protection

+500 armor

Agility

+ 10 Agility

Colossus

+ 10 Strength

Elements
+25 to Elemental Power
Aether Resist
+25 resistance to Aether effects
Elemental Resistance
+25 resistance to all elements
Fortification
+50 Health
Aether Protection
Absorb 1000 to 2000 Aether Damage
Elemental Protection
Absorb 1000 to 2000 Elemental Damage

Satisfied, he nodded to himself.

"That went rather well." Ryne's voice originated from the Mimic, which meant it was the goblin himself. There was a distinct difference now, a more lifelike skin texture and natural movements of clothing and hair.

"How'd you get rid of them?" Frost asked as he, Saba, Gilda, and Tia stepped outside.

"A Mirage of us to convince them we'd gone down the alley to the canal that runs behind the building."

Frost gaped. "You did it behind the apothecary?"

The goblin pointed down with his index finger. "Below it, technically. Stairs lead down into the canal's artery."

"You couldn't pick some place farther away?" Saba scowled.

The goblin let out an annoyed breath. "The nature of a Mirage means I have to remain close to those it imitates. Or else it dissipates." He paused, a thoughtful look on his face. "Perhaps, I should become a bard. Anyway, no one saw me."

"But someone's likely to spot the bodies," Frost said under his breath.

"What bodies?" The goblin shrugged and spoke in

a deep sing-song lilt. "This canal is a deep one. Its waters are stygian. Fun fact: Azureguards wear heavy armor. Armor like an anchor.

"Gave my defiler a hard time to drag. Had to summon a second one to get the job done. Now… I'm pooped." Ryne let out a whoosh, emphasizing his exhaustion.

"Seems Gnome is about that action," Dante said, nodding his approval.

"He certainly is," Frost agreed. "Well done." He dipped his head to Ryne.

"Thank you." The goblin rolled his hand and bowed from the waist.

With a shake of his head at Ryne, Frost set off toward the Wyvern's Eye. They discerned no other followers the rest of the way. They entered a large, crowded square where Ryne pointed toward a four-storied building. A sign depicted a black wyvern with a red eye. Hanging from chains connected to that sign was another with the establishment's name.

When they entered the tavern's smoky interior, Frost couldn't help his sense of relief. Finally, he would complete the quest given to him by his mother.

A chubby serving girl in a cut-off shirt met them. She directed them to a long table with a bench on either side near a wall. Glasses and silverware clinked. The murmur of conversation drifted on the air along with the coiled smoke and potpourri of pipes, cigars, and incense.

Bloomglobes hung along walls and from the ceiling, most of them white or a pale yellow, illuminating patrons from all across Mikander. There was even a brown-furred gargant from the Ostenia dominion in the Korbash continent, so massive he was seated on the floor and still towered over everyone. The gargant was picking bugs from his

246

fur and popping them into his mouth while he waited to be served.

"Order some food." Frost stood. "I'm going to see the barkeep."

On his way over to the bar, which was neatly positioned on one side of the room close to a doorway and a set of stairs, Frost removed the chain from his neck. The barkeeper was a human with black hair and a thick mustache. His corded arms and boulder shoulders said there was more muscle than fat beneath his apron and shirt than his wide form suggested. He was cleaning a glass with a cloth and eying Frost.

"Good afternoon," Frost said.

"Afternoon to you, too, friend." The barkeep dipped his head as he spoke in a silvery voice. "New around here, I see. What can I get you?"

"Some plum wine, if you have any."

"Course, I do. I had pegged you for a beer man. I'm usually right." The barkeep put the glass he had cleaned on top the bar. "Name's Hardizan."

"Frost." Frost stuck out his hand. "Beer's always been too bitter for my tastes."

Hardizan stared at Frost's hand, frowned, then finally shook it. "Nice to meet you." The man's grip was firm, his skin rough.

Hardizan turned away to the bottles lining the shelves behind him. He picked out a green one with a white label, its contents dark. When he came back to Frost, Hardizan found the chain with the aether ring sitting beside the glass. He paused for a mere second before he poured the red plum wine.

"I'm looking for a hammersmith," Frost said, keeping his voice low.

"I see." Hardizan's eyes looked past Frost, and Frost

got the sense the man had just scanned the room. "Give me a moment." Hardizan shuffled off toward the door and stairs at the end of the bar.

Frost picked up his drink and took a sip. Swilling the sweet wine around in his mouth, he casually turned to where he could survey the room and keep an eye on the doorway. Everything was as he recalled: people busy drinking, eating, and talking. His group shot looks his way without making it obvious.

Minutes later, Hardizan returned in the company of a coffee-colored erada a little taller than Frost. The man was dressed in plain black robes, his horns as dark as his skin, his eyes piercing black beads. His dark hair was done in neat cornrow braids. While Hardizan went about his business, cleaning more glasses, the man stopped in front of Frost, his hands clasped behind his back. He looked down at the chain and aether ring.

"Put that away," the man said in a soft-spoken voice.

Frost picked up the chain, put it back around his neck, and tucked it beneath his gambeson before he said, "How do I know you're–" The newcomer arched an eyebrow. "The person I was sent to meet?" Frost finished, meeting the man's studious gaze with a searching one of his own.

"You're alive and still have your tongue." The man put his left hand on the bar and leaned forward. An aether ring adorned his left thumb.

"My mother sent me," Frost said.

"May Nif keep Anefet's soul." With his right hand, the man made the sign of the X over his heart. "And yes, I am Adesh Hamada."

Information Memory clicked.

Locate Adesh Hamada
Objective Complete
Found Adesh Hamada:

2500 experience points
250 Ignis dominion credits

Frost closed his eyes for a moment and let out a slow, relieved breath. Then he spoke so only Adesh could hear. "She left a letter saying you could help me. My sister and I need some place safe to hide from Setnana Botros and her Battleguards. They chased us all the way from Niba."

"I will try, but on the same day they killed Anefet," Adesh said, "there were multiple attacks on Blue Sky across Khertahka, Ignis, and Lothal. Most of the Blue Sky leadership died or were captured. I came here to gather information and to pick up the pieces."

"Who exactly is responsible for killing her?"

"A sect within the Coalition seeking to grab power for themselves in these chaotic times. We call them the Black Hand. Anefet named Exarch Bakui Assam, Nomarch Setnana Botros, and Nomarch Aishani Chaten among the conspirators. But myself and a few of the surviving leaders think it runs deeper."

Frost nodded. He took note of a new quest. Scourge of the Black Hand. He'd thought there was something odd going on when Nebsamu mentioned no response from the Exarch or directly from the Coalition. In the back of his mind he saved the two additional names for retribution. He already knew of a way he might get to Nomarch Setnana Botros.

"Nebsamu had explained how they came after Anefet again despite her exile. How'd they manage to get the Coalition to do the same to the rest of Blue Sky?" Frost asked.

"Your mother's group was regularly destroying the sect's secret mining operations and their slave camps," Adesh Hamada said. "So, they framed us for attacks on Coalition supplies meant for the Front, an assassination attempt on Kalarch Voculo, and for the spread of the Gray Death."

"Spread of a plague? How?"

"If you get enough mystics, hierkaneers, and common folk repeating the same thing to the right ears, someone with authority is bound to believe."

"Still—" Frost began.

"Perception is a palette," Adesh said. "Blending it is art. Lies become truths. Ugliness becomes beauty. Evil becomes good. Up is down and left is right. Master the colors of perception to make the world your canvas."

Frost couldn't argue the point. Pops used to say something similar. But with less words. With the explanation came a quest completion.

Circumstances of Anefet's Death
Objective Complete
2500 experience points
300 Ignis dominion credits
500 Khertahka dominion credits

Frost shook his head. "What now, since everything's stacked against us? Anefet wanted me to make sure my sister was safe. It's the reason she sent me to find you."

"We have two strongholds of which the Coalition and the Black Hand are unaware. One in the Nimri dominion and the other across the Empyrean Sea on Korbash, where we have the protection of the gargants and the yurids."

"Korbash is best. The farther away she is from all this, the better."

"And you? What is your plan?"

"Become stronger so I can get justice for Anefet."

"Vengeance, then." Adesh nodded once.

"Fulfilling the promise I made to her," Frost said.

"Don't turn around," Adesh said under his breath. "Someone followed you."

"You sure?" Worry stirred in Frost's chest. "I swore we got rid of them."

"Seems you missed one. Because Khafra the Mad, one of Setnana's personal Blackguards, is here with several Battleguards." Shifting his head a bit, Adesh spoke to the barkeeper. "Hardizan, tell Marivelle to go to his friends' table and insist they join us at the bar." He focused on Frost once more. "Keep talking to me as if I gave you no warning." The barkeeper signaled to the serving girl.

"Is he looking our way?" Frost tried to think how they could escape the situation. If they should fight or try to flee.

"I can see your mind working. You are far from being strong enough for Khafra. He is at least thirty. A dementer of considerable skill. I doubt I could take him."

Frost swallowed. Just when he thought he'd saved Tia and made some headway, everything seemed to be falling apart. Still, he had his new cannon, Deadeye. He could turn and unleash a combo when his friends got to the bar. There had to be a backdoor to the tavern. *But what then? Where would we run to?*

CHAPTER 21

"First, they escaped Khertahka." Setnana sneered at the drake rider captain down on bended knee before her. "Then, you lost them when their simurgh landed here in Kituan. You found them again... *and* lost them again? Are the pictures you have of them not clear enough?"

"I blame myself for this failure," Major Neferna said. Standing a few feet behind Captain Tisheru Chuma, the Sky Swords leader kept her head suitably bowed. "I should have been here, but I took it upon myself to try capture or kill Umesh Madara rather than chasing after the Hand's children."

"Shouldering some of the blame is only right, Neferna. It *is* a company in your command." The Nomarch strode to a nearby table and picked up a glass of wine.

She threw her head back, emptied the blood red vintage, and replaced the glass. The wine was smooth and rich. Expensive. Kelsial Valley, if she wasn't mistaken. She nodded her approval.

Setnana stared Major Neferna in the eye and continued, "But you offset your failure with Umesh Madara by capturing Nebsamu Tadros and one of his Blue Sky helpers. That is worthy of praise. Captain Chuma, on the other hand, failed at the simplest of things. Several times. How difficult is it to catch two children when you have them in your sight? Forget catching them… how difficult is it to keep an *eye* on them?"

Captain Tisheru Chuma glanced up and made as if to speak.

"Captain Chuma… that was purely a rhetorical question." Setnana stared the man down. Any defiance fled his eyes. He averted his gaze.

She let out an annoyed breath. For months, she'd refused to promote the captain despite his many successes in the field against poachers, slavers, and bandits. He had even defeated grand kora raiders before she had allied with Aishani and Exarch Assam. But his short thin horns, wiry body, and forgettable face did not meet the alluring beauty she required of her officers. *I should have known better.*

"Neferna, you've been far too forgiving with your men. Leniency is weakness. Demote this man to Soldier. The others who failed with him… they were riders, correct?" She eyed the Major, who nodded. "Have them whipped, demoted, and paraded before the army in Aprunis. Let them know what incompetence can buy them."

"Yes, Nomarch." Neferna bowed.

Setnana waited for them to leave before taking a peek at her timeorb. The day was wasting away. *What was keeping the man?*

To calm herself, she strode out onto the balcony overlooking the Tiberium District's estates. Fiery hues seeped across the sky like fading remnants of an explosion. She inhaled the rich, briny scents of the River Segia, upon whose estuary the humans had built Kituan.

Off to her right, and continuing behind her villa, rose the tiered buildings and pillars of the Kituan acropolis, home to Kalarch Stadius Voculo, the waddling, stern-faced human who had the most influence in all the Coalition. One

253

day she would hold sway over every erada as Kalarch Voculo did for every human. Kalarch Setnana Botros of Khertahka had a nice ring to it.

"All in due time." She stopped before the balustrade.

First, she had to deal with the Blue Sky Network fugitives. The surviving Frosts, in particular. And whomever had helped them at Marna. They were the reason she was away from Perihy, away from Aishani's loving arms, the reason Exarch Bakui Assam had punished her with this forsaken mission.

She clenched her fist. Knowing Nebsamu Tadros was currently suffering in a dungeon back in Aprunis assuaged her anger somewhat. But capturing Anefet Frost's children, Beketia and Drelan, and the instructions they carried, would redeem her.

She wondered as to the content of those instructions. And to whom they might be delivering them in Kituan. She would know soon enough. Their fates were all but sealed.

Images of Drelan and Beketia Frost bloomed in her mind. An artist's rendering delivered to her from Exarch Bakui Assam's people. Both children were less than stellar looking, Drelan being ordinary if not ugly. There was nothing remarkable about him. Nothing appealing. Not his dark magenta skin, slim body, his large horns, or bulbous nose. He was the opposite of her Perihy. Not surprising considering his lack of pedigree.

Thoughts of the children brought her to the mission itself. Far ahead, beyond the acropolis' curtain wall and the flagstoned avenues overflowing with folk from every corner of Mikander; beyond the numerous bridges over waterways and canals occupied by watercraft; the granite and marble buildings; the Aetherium's foreboding giant pillars, walls, and arcane secrets, was the River Segia's delta where it bled into the sapphire of the Empyrean Sea.

Maelpith Island sat within that sea. A mystery shrouded in mist that radiated with voidstorm lightnings. Reports she'd gathered said to be wary of the storm's remnants.

Which part of the island held Imanok Sanctum? The seemingly abundant greenery that were forests? Or the lone cloud-cloaked mountain? Could these rumored schemas, skill shards, and this zhua, Benediction, really provide a cure for the Gray Death? A cure for Perihy?

The click of the door opening and closing reverberated. Confident footsteps headed toward her. As did the soft tap of a staff on the carpeted floor. She could recognize that gait anywhere. As she could recognize the person's form. The footsteps and taps stopped outside the balcony.

"Ihuet, did you locate the sceeves?"

"Of course, my Nomarch," answered Ihuet's quiet, almost bored voice. "They're hiding at a tavern in the Gregis District. The Wyvern's Eye. Khafra is keeping them in his sights."

"Good." She looked to her left, far in the distance beyond the curtain wall, where the city's architecture changed from granite and marble to limestone. The waterways became narrower canals. The wide flagstoned avenues meandered into cobbled or dirt lanes, except for the Via Arcadius: the thoroughfare leading into the heart of the Gregis District and its numerous small buildings and open-air markets.

Kituan's criminal underbelly thrived in the Gregis District. Even if vigorously denied by Ad Mauros' nomarch, Demipho Pansa, a furtive little beast of a man who made her skin crawl.

"Get a coach ready." She could not stand the idea of Exarch Assam seeing her as a failure after the events in Niba. He had already sent word by Communication Orb, blaming her for Soleb and Marna also. *And now, these children. Children! I will not have it.*

"Khafra and I can handle it," Ihuet said. "You should head to the island. We'll catch up."

"After I see to this."

"But what of little Perihy?"

She heaved a slow breath. "We don't know for certain if the cure is on the island. But we *know* where Anefet's bastards are. We can take care of them and leave for Maelpith tonight." A big part of her wanted to find Imanok Sanctum right now, but she also did not wish to miss out on a perfect chance at the remaining Frosts.

"As you say. Still, your presence—"

"I want to be there. I want to look Anefet's children in the eye when they die." In truth, she wanted to do more than that. She would take their lives with her own hands. She saw Papa's smiling face. "Now, hurry, prepare a coach. I won't forgive anyone who causes me to miss this chance."

"Taking a coach into the Gregis District might be a giveaway," Ihuet said in the same bored tone. The man could be unnerving. "Alerting the vermin that nobility is among them might only serve to make them overly cautious. Disguising ourselves as sceeves is the better option."

She grimaced at his suggestion. Still looking out over the city, she waved a dismissive hand. "I might don a less colorful dress, something with less shimmer and frills, but making myself appear like the lowest of the low is something I will *not* do. Nobles are known to have darker sides and desires and are sometimes in need of things from the criminal element. I will be one such, interested in goods I could not otherwise acquire in a more reputable place. And you will be who you are: my bodyguard."

"As you wish, my Nomarch. But there *is* one thing I will not budge on."

Setnana sighed. "Go on."

"We'll abandon the coach a few streets away, take a gondola down the nearby canal, and approach the tavern on foot amongst the locals."

She nodded. "That, I can do."

"How will you deal with not having Kalarch Voculo's permission for military action in his dominion? In his home city? What do I advise Major Neferna to tell the Battleguards should the humans interfere?"

She shrugged. "It's the Gregis District. Place the blame on a thief's guild thinking I was an easy mark. We were defending ourselves."

"I'll make the necessary preparations." His footsteps receded. The door clicked shut.

A smile curved Setnana's lips. Her gaze remained on the Gregis District, her thoughts on the satisfaction to come. A thrill eased through her body.

✶ ✶ ✶ ✶ ✶ ✶

Bands of hazy flame limned the western sky as they made the last portion of the trip in a gondola. Nose wrinkled at the effluvium drifting off the canal's dark green water, Nomarch Botros sat facing away from the gondolier, a wiry human who'd bowed profusely and introduced himself as Piero.

Ihuet sat opposite her, one hand on his staff, seemingly disinterested, but she knew he saw and heard everything around them as evidenced by his ears' slight twitches and his shifting eyes. They passed buildings and homes that seemed to sprout from the canal itself, foundations stained with water marks. Passersby crossed over a bridge ahead of them.

"We disembark on the other side of that bridge,"

Ihuet said. "The Wyvern's Eye is directly down the lane and across the market square. Our men are disguised as some of the local eradae, either in the market acting the part of shoppers or visitors, or inside drinking with the patrons."

"And Khafra?"

"In the tavern, ensuring our targets do not escape."

Setnana sat up a bit straighter. Her heart fluttered. Soon, she would have redemption and a measure of vengeance, of justice for Papa. And then she could head to Maelpith Island for hierkas and shards to save her Perihy. She pictured Perihy's smiling face, his unblemished skin, full of life and vigor.

They pulled into the bridge's shadow, the splash of the gondolier's long oar echoing, as did the lap of water against the walls. The gondolier maneuvered the boat until it drew alongside a set of stairs. He tossed a rope over a hook in the wall and tied it off.

Ihuet was the first off the boat, causing the vessel to rock. The gondolier reached a hand out to help Setnana but pulled it back at the scathing look she shot his way. She raised her gossamer hem and followed Ihuet as if she'd lived on the canals.

Setnana and Ihuet ascended the stairs and were soon among the bustle and murmur of the throngs entering and leaving this section of the Gregis District. Criers shouted out their wares, offering sales due to the pending close of the day's business. Being an erada, taller than most races, had its advantages. Her height provided her with a good view of her surroundings.

A panoply of peoples from numerous races and dominions went about their business. There was even one of Korbash's colossal gargants and a male yurid with his majestic wings folded behind his back. Her eyebrows rose at the presence of a dryad: a green-skinned delicate flower of a woman about half her height.

Yet, for all the variety, most of them were little more than sceeves. Not one among them had as splendid a set of horns as she, nor wore a gossamer and velvet dress that accentuated their svelte form. *I am a goddess among mere mortals.* She flicked her hair into the space between her horns.

Head high, chest out, she strode purposefully across the square. People pointed and whispered. Many bowed. A path cleared ahead of her and Ihuet. She basked in the attention.

A sooty-faced little human boy stepped from the crowd, begging as much with his eyes as with his open palms. She grimaced and shot him a glare that could crack rocks. Ihuet had his body and staff between her and the boy before she could utter a word. The boy yelped and scurried away. Ihuet bowed to her in apology. They continued on, Ihuet's staff tapping the ground with his every step.

Perhaps two hundred feet away, a sign hanging from the front of a four-storied sandstone building depicted a wyvern. The winged two-legged cousin of the dragon was done in black. It had a single fiery eye. Hanging from chains below that sign was another, a board with the words: The Wyvern's Eye.

Her heart skipped a beat. She was as a child, rapt in dreamy fulfillment. She could picture the Frosts cowering before her, begging for their lives. *Which one do I kill first? Drelan or Beketia? The boy or the girl?* She licked her lips.

She'd barely had the thought when people fled through the tavern's front door and into the street. Several windowpanes shattered. People fought to scramble through them, slicing their hands and arms in the process.

Arcane red glowed within the tavern's black recesses. Cries and screams echoed from inside. As did a pulse of power.

The crowd outside scattered. They scrambled in every direction away from the establishment. By instinct, she summoned an Aether Barrier.

"Khafra!" Ihuet cried. He bounded forward.

The remaining windows on the first floor exploded outwards. A roar followed. Flames burst through every opening. The spell blasted scores of people from their feet. Heat washed over her.

Ihuet stood a few feet ahead of her, staff planted on the ground. His robes billowed. A translucent blue Aether Barrier surrounded him.

The building's second floor exploded. And the third. And then the last. Flames engulfed the Wyvern's Eye.

A large figure stumbled through the inferno at the front door. A figure Setnana recognized all too well. *Khafra!* She hissed.

Ihuet let out a choked cry. He Flickered to his friend.

Khafra's body deflated, the duration of his Dementia expiring. He was a mass of scorched flesh, black and red and angry. He managed one more step before collapsing toward the flagstones.

Ihuet caught Khafra before Khafra struck the ground. He cradled the dementer in his arms.

Setnana Flickered to them. She swallowed against the lump in her throat when she took in Khafra's charred body, the wet purple flesh exposed through cracked skin, his blackened horns, the melted clothing and armor sticking to his body. He reeked of cooked meat.

Khafra's lips moved. The voice that uttered words were a hoarse croak. Nothing resembling its former deep resonance. "Ad... Ad... Adesh... Adesh Ham... Adesh Hamada. The... the Frosts. Greg... Gregis Aviary." Khafra's head flopped to one side.

"GET ME A MYSTIC!" screamed Ihuet.

Information bloomed in Setnana's head.

Locate Adesh Hamada
Objective Complete
Found Adesh Hamada
3000 Experience points
Save Khafra: Failed
Capture the Frosts: Failed
Gained 500 Ignis dominion credits

Setnana snarled. "Stay here with Khafra until the mystic comes." She signaled to Major Neferna, who had the Battleguards form a defensive perimeter around them. "Bring your men. We're going to the Gregis Aviary."

CHAPTER 22

Atop some Azureguard's smelly female lupine that made her miss Wenet, Nomarch Setnana rode with over a score of her Battleguards, galloping down the Via Arcadius as evening donned night's cloak. The encroaching darkness made her glad for the white arcane bloomglobes and glimmerstalks illuminating the avenue. Some of her men waved glimmerstalks, the short, illuminated wands intended to give ample warning for people to clear the way.

Despite the Battleguards' efforts, Setnana and the others still had to weave their way past occasional wagons and coaches. People scrambled from their path. Some swore at her. She growled under her breath, ready to ride over anyone if necessary.

She had the Battleguards cast aside all pretenses of the district's sceeves. They had their full erada regalia on display, complete with Khertahka's Dual Katars on their sleeves. Major Neferna had tried to argue her out of this action, claiming the political ramifications would be massive.

Setnana cared for none of that. She would deal with any repercussions later, pay the necessary reparations, but she could picture nothing worse than bruised egos over her infraction. A pittance when placed beside her goal.

All that mattered in this very moment was Adesh Hamada and the Frosts. Getting to them before they took flight. In her mind's eye, she saw Khafra's scorched body. She recalled the gashes and burns on Papa's corpse.

She kicked her bolsters harder, driving the lupine forward. Her quarry had to be close.

An offering of a thousand credits had brought forward a few sceeves who'd survived the beginning of the fight inside the tavern. Adesh Hamada, the Frosts, and four people, a gurash, another erada, a dresdor, and a goblin, had fled upstairs. Further inquiry while waiting for mounts had revealed the fugitives escaped across the roof of an adjoining building. Most likely to mounts waiting somewhere, but they would have to navigate around the throngs.

As if on cue, Major Neferna was galloping back toward her. One reason alone would warrant such an action. Neferna had spotted the targets.

Major Neferna fell in beside Setnana and yelled, "Nomarch, seven people on crevids two intersections ahead. I've sent my fastest men forward."

Setnana fought against the sense of triumph. "How far until the Aviary?"

"Six, perhaps seven more intersections."

"Then we have them!" Setnana could not help her grin.

"I believe we do. The Battleguards I sent ahead should catch up and prevent them from taking to the air."

"Good. Now, let's get these sceeves. Yah!" Setnana yanked on the braided grips woven into the lupine's hackles and dug her heels into the bolsters.

Soon, she picked out the lead Battleguards and the fleeing mounts, the closing space between them. Vengeance was almost hers. For Papa. And for Khafra. And then she could see to Perihy and return to her path to rule.

This success and the impending one at Imanok Sanctum meant Exarch Assam would have to acknowledge her prowess. She pictured it. Heard his compliments. Tasted his regret. His humiliation.

Three more intersecting streets before the fugitives reached the square that held the Gregis Aviary. The Battleguards were less than two hundred feet behind them. She leaned forward, focused like an arrow.

The fleeing crevids bounded across the second to last street before the Aviary. Her lead Battleguards followed moments later. The fugitives were all but captured.

A horn's bray cut through the night, long and loud and lingering, above galloping hooves and lupine howls. An animal's scream echoed and sent a chill down her spine. People scattered. The streets emptied. Not just around her on the Via Arcadius, but also all the way to the Aviary. They ran inside any open building.

"No. Not now." Desperate, she squeezed the grips, kicked the bolsters. The lupine growled beneath her, but she could coax no more speed from the beast.

Lance-wielding human warriors jogged out into the intersection at the cross street where the Aviary began far ahead of the fleeing mounts. Bloodguards, clad in their infamous knee-high soft-skinned boots and red uniforms trimmed with black. They blocked off the Via Arcadius, their forms casting long shadows. As one, they slammed the butts of their lances into the ground. The sound reverberated.

The fugitives kept riding toward the humans. But her Battleguards had pulled up sharply. She wanted to shout at them to continue forward but knew such a command was pointless and would only worsen the situation.

When the fugitives got to within a few feet of the Bloodguards, they drew to a halt. They dismounted and got down on their knees with their hands raised. Several Bloodguards took them into custody, pushing and shoving them back through the formation. The ranks closed.

The animal scream echoed again. She glanced up. A zephyr was silhouetted against the moon, diaphanous wings spread wide. This one matched a drake in size. A human rode atop its back. The wings beat once and then the creature glided down to land in front of the Bloodguards.

The man dismounted and took a moment to stroke the zephyr's owlish face. The creature shook its muscular body and settled down on all fours. Setnana sighed. Although halfway down the avenue, she still recognized Nomarch Demipho Pansa.

Setnana and Neferna reined in their mounts upon reaching the Battleguards. Still eying Demipho Pansa, she said, "Major Neferna, come with me. The rest of you stay here." She nudged the lupine into a walk with a tap of the bolsters against its flanks.

Shoulders back, head high, she approached Nomarch Demipho Pansa. When she was perhaps twenty feet from him, she dismounted. Major Neferna did the same.

Setnana strode forward with all the grace she could muster and stopped in front of the scrawny human whose robes looked as if they would swallow him. His mount snorted and shook itself, its reins jangling.

"Nomarch Setnana Botros," Nomarch Pansa began, his high-pitched lilt almost condescending. "Military action by any outside force is expressly forbidden anywhere in Ignis. Even more so in Kituan. Not only have you broken the law, you've insulted Kalarch Voculo. I should have you arrested where you stand." The beady-eyed little man spoke as if he did not recognize his betters.

Setnana smiled but did not let it touch her eyes. "We both know that is an empty threat." She flicked her hair behind her horns. "Besides, this was not a military action. My men and I were chasing after Blue Sky operatives who stole credits from me, blew up a tavern, and severely injured one of my personal guard."

Demipho gazed past Setnana. "My men are investigating that very incident as we speak."

"This crime to my person cannot go unpunished. I demand the thieves be handed over to me."

"They will be punished. That, I can promise you."

Setnana arched her brow. "You're denying me my rightful justice?"

"I wouldn't dare." The look in Nomarch Pansa's eyes said otherwise.

"Then—"

"Here's what I'll do," Demipho Pansa said. "You can show me which one of them was the thief. I'll hand that one to you to do with as you will. The others belong to us."

"Eradae belong to no one," she said flatly.

"Be that as it may, not all of them are eradae. Also, their crimes were committed here, in the Ignis dominion." He wore a smug look. "Human law takes precedence in the matter. And I *will* file a formal complaint with the Coalition about your action."

"Then you leave me no choice but to call an assembly." Setnana spoke in the same controlled tone from earlier but underneath she seethed. "Where I will make it clear that stealing from a noble was overlooked by you. That despite appearances, Kituan is *not* safe. It's infested with Blue Sky operatives. Convincing the assembly would be easy once I present my personal guard burned beyond recognition." She surmised that such a hit to Kalarch Voculo's reputation would certainly dent his influence with the Coalition.

"Fine," Nomarch Pansa grumbled. "No formal complaint."

"And I get two of the thieves if I let you have the main culprit, Adesh Hamada." She knew he would not have given up Adesh anyway, but she had to make him feel as if he had won.

"Agreed." Nomarch Pansa nodded and puffed out his chest, looking for all world as if he had just received a gift.

Her quest completed.

The Kituan Debacle
Objective Complete
Fugitives captured
1000 Experience points
Win negotiation with Nomarch Demipho Pansa
1500 Experience points
Avoid conflict with Ignis dominion
1000 Experience points
Gained 1000 Ignis dominion credits

"Take me to the captives so I can choose my two," she said. Nomarch Pansa did not move. Setnana frowned. "Well?"

"You didn't say please."

Scowling, she said, "Please." In her mind, she added, *you son of a motherless sceeve.*

Demipho smiled and turned away. The Bloodguard formation parted before him. He strode between them. Setnana and Major Neferna followed, Setnana not so much as sparing a glance for the humans. The seven prisoners were on their knees, hoods covering their bowed heads. Several Bloodguards stood at their backs.

Her heart fluttered with anticipation. It was amazing how a person could expect the worst but receive Nif's blessing instead. Moments like this were to be savored.

Nomarch Pansa strode in front of the prisoners and made to speak. He paused, mouth agape. Consternation bunched his features. "I thought you said one of them was Adesh Hamada?"

Setnana's stomach clenched. It could not be. She quickened her pace and reached Nomarch Pansa. The prisoners stared up at her.

None of them was Adesh Hamada. And not only did none of them fit the descriptions of Beketia and Drelan Frost, but none were erada. She cursed herself for not realizing the ploy. The lack of a dresdor should have alerted her.

Setnana balled her hand into a fist until it hurt. She stifled both the need to scream and the arcane energy coursing through her. "They must know something," she growled. "Put them to the question."

CHAPTER 23

Frost and the group disembarked from the gondola amid the canal's briny stench, night's murmur, and the gentle lap of water against a bridge. A zephyr's beastly scream pierced the relative stillness. Adesh Hamada held up his hand. They froze. He peered at the sky. After a moment, he signaled for them to move on.

Cloaked in darkness, they hurried up a set of stairs and kept to the lanes off the Via Iridius. Frost was glad Adesh's ruse had worked, but at the same time he hoped the people the sorcerer had paid would not be punished too severely. If at all. They knew nothing other than a stranger hired them to ride hard toward the Gregis Aviary and surrender to the Bloodguards.

Stroking his aether ring, he reminded himself that he was in the game. But worrying came so naturally. Those feelings extended to the patrons of the Wyvern's Eye. He could only imagine the numerous dead or injured by the explosion triggered when Adesh Hamada cast Inferno. At first, he'd been horrified, until Gilda told him most of them were likely to be NPCs. Thinking of them that way helped.

But what about players like me? Players under Total Immersion? Their deaths. The effects of it IRL. He cringed to think of his heart or brain functions stopping even for a second.

Recognizing his concerns would change nothing, he forced them to the back of his mind. Of more importance was completing the current quest to see Tia to safety. Once they reached Adesh's secret Aviary, all would be well.

Frost stopped in his tracks, struck by a sudden realization. The others bypassed him before coming to a halt also.

"What's wrong," Gilda asked.

"We gotta get Meritus at the Cobalt Talisman," Frost said.

Adesh Hamada shook his head, eyes reflecting a nearby bloomglobe's light. "Our decoys have been caught by now. Setnana most likely has the Coalition completely on her side after what happened at the Wyvern's Eye. The Bloodguards will lock down the city soon enough. Deathguards will be dispatched, if they have not been already. Our window of opportunity is small. We must go to my Aviary now. Staying isn't only risking yourself, but also your sister and everyone else."

"He's right," Saba said. "This is our best chance to escape."

Frost glanced from one to the other. His gaze lingered on Tia and Gilda. As much as he wanted to go to Adesh's private Aviary and take the simurgh to Korbash with Tia and the others, grind out some levels, and return stronger, he also knew he had to help his friend.

"I understand, but I gotta help Meritus. Like Ryne said, whoever followed us musta been Concealed from the start. A Concealment spell not even Ryne's summoned defiler saw through. Which means they saw us with Meritus. I won't leave him to die or be tortured. You can go on without me." He'd take his chances solo on the island.

"That isn't happening." Gilda stepped over to him.

Tia smiled at him, but her eyes shone with fear. She

270

followed suit. Saba's tail swished once before she did the same.

"Gnome and I are under contract." Dante strode over. "Besides, Meritus was always a cool dude."

"Ryne. My bloody name is Ryne. Call me gnome one more time." The goblin shook his fist and stalked across the threshold. He stood, fists bunched, neck craned to stare up at Dante.

"Don't do it," Frost warned as a smiling Dante opened his mouth. "We don't have time for this nonsense now."

Dante closed his mouth. He and Ryne continued their staring match.

"It's decided then." Adesh Hamada dipped his head in surrender. "Come, I know the fastest way to the Cobalt Talisman."

Adesh Hamada led them through a maze of dark alleys and lanes, avoiding the Via Iridius. They stopped at the rear of a building. He made his way to a shed from which wafted a pungent odor. When he pulled open the door, Frost and the others shied away at the vile stench. Adesh stepped inside.

A moment later, a light sparked to life. Adesh Hamada held a glimmerwand, the thin aether-powered hierka revealing a set of stairs. Without pausing, he descended into the sewers, where water bubbled and dripped, and unseen things scurried and squeaked in the inky blackness beyond the reach of his glimmerwand's luminance. Faced with little other choice, they followed the sorcerer.

Adesh navigated the sewer tunnels as if he'd lived there. From time to time, they emerged to travel the streets for a bit. Bloodguard presence slowly increased as they wove their way to their objective. Adesh made them pause whenever a zephyr's cry echoed.

271

On one occasion, Ryne called forth a Mirage of a guard to distract a patrol. Soon enough, the sewers became Adesh's only avenue of travel. A while later, they made it to the sewer shed behind the Cobalt Talisman. Adesh snuffed out the glimmerwand, leaving them mostly in darkness. The slit of the barely open door provided the sole illumination.

Ryne summoned a defiler. The wraith-like creature had long claws and wore black hooded robes that trailed behind it. Green eyes glowed within the hood. Ryne Concealed the defiler and sent it out to make certain no guards were in the backyard. The building's rear was clear. As was the front of the Cobalt Talisman.

"Most likely they're watching the place, hoping we show up," Saba said. "Or they already have him."

"I say we just storm in, smash some heads, rescue him, get the hell outta here." Dante hefted his crescent axe.

"I'm with Big Foot," Ryne said. "Unfortunately."

Dante shot him a glare. Ryne offered a smile, face more mischievous by the way the light fell across half of it.

"Nah." Frost shook his head. "We might never make it out the city, then. Gotta do this quiet. Gives us a better chance." He glanced at Gilda. "You're gonna have to use Concealment to get in there and tell him."

"As much as I dislike volunteering," Saba said with a sigh, "my skill is most likely better than hers."

"But Meritus doesn't know you," Frost said. "I told him about Gilda. All she needs to do is say her name."

"How do we even know he is there," Adesh Hamada asked.

Frost peeked outside the shed. Bloomglobes mounted on the rear of the building lit the yard. There were alleys to either side of the tavern. He could see part of the way down one. It appeared to be empty. Echolocation told him he was correct. Light shone through the window of the third-floor middle room. Someone passed by the curtain.

Frost pulled back inside. "He's there. Third floor, middle window."

"What about guards?" Tia asked. "He said he was going to hire new ones."

"If he's in his room now, he woulda dismissed them," Frost said.

"Or so you hope," Saba added.

"This is where I wish I was a cutthroat again," Gila said. "I could've just climbed up there and got him. Well, a girl's gotta do what a girl's gotta do." And with that, she stepped past Frost, glanced over her shoulder to him, smiled, and added, "I'll be back with your friend." Then she was gone.

Frost stood to one side of the slightly open door with a view of Meritus' window. The others crowded around him, their breathing heavy. He fully expected for them to have to rush outside to the sounds of battle. Trying to calm his nerves and resist the urge to go out was an exercise in discipline.

The wait seemed to last forever. At the point when he was ready to tell Saba to head out or for Ryne to send out another concealed defiler, the lights in Meritus' room winked out.

Someone swept aside the curtain. The window cracked open. Then it swung wide.

Framed by bloomglobe light, Gilda pulled herself up onto the window ledge, crouched, then jumped. Frost held his breath. Someone behind him hissed. Gilda hit the ground with a slight thud, rolled in the grass, and came up ready, head on a swivel from one alley to the next. She eased back perhaps ten feet and then signaled up to the window.

Meritus was there. He appeared uncertain at first. Then he took a breath, teetered, and jumped, arms flailing.

He landed with a heavy thud and stumbled forward before falling face down. He just managed to get his hands beneath him.

Frost let out a breath he didn't realize he held. Gilda led Meritus to the shed. Frost kept an eye out to make certain no one came to any windows.

"My man," Meritus said once he entered the shed. He coughed, covered his nose and mouth with one hand, but still managed to give Frost a dap in the dim light. "That explosion and fire in the Gregis District was you, wasn't it? I knew things were gonna get epic."

Frost chuckled. "And I shoulda known you were gonna love this. I'll fill you in with the details later. Right now, we need to get outta Kituan as fast as possible."

"Lead on, homie," Meritus said.

Adesh Hamada activated the glimmerwand. They descended the stairs to the sewers. The trip was a longer one, filled with twist and turns, and the sewer's effluvium. When they exited at one of the many canals, the relatively fresh air was a welcome respite.

Frost got his bearings as they hurried across the bridge. They were somewhere deep in the Gregis District, near the city's outskirts. They went down the stairs on the other side and entered the sewers again.

Less than fifteen minutes later, Adesh led them to a blank wall. He pressed some unseen switch. The wall slid aside to reveal stairs.

They ascended into a dimly-lit building that could have passed for a large barn. Instead, there were several pens. A few held drakes. Three had zephyrs. Two simurghs occupied the biggest area.

"Welcome to Blue Sky Headquarters," Adesh said proudly, gesturing around. "Pashere, Nofre, it is time," he shouted.

An erada man and woman emerged from the back of the building near the simurghs. The man, Pashere, had skin like smooth mahogany and was dressed in dark trousers and a sleeveless tunic. Nofre's complexion was a bright electric blue, in stark contrast to her dark robes. They hurried to the beast-birds.

"They are Blue Sky's last riders left in all of Ignis," Adesh Hamada said. "Made to stay for instances such as this one. Everyone else is gone. The activation of any trap at one of our safe houses like the Wyvern's Eye was the signal to flee. We will soon be safe in Korbash."

"Not exactly," Frost said.

He'd contemplated how they would take his next words. Gilda might want to join him. He wasn't certain of the others. Not that he needed them. He believed he could go at it alone.

"Meritus." He turned to his best friend. "I'm going to trust you to see Tia safely reaches the Blue Sky stronghold in Korbash."

"No prob. I got you." Meritus puffed out his chest.

"The rest of you can choose what you want to do," Frost continued, "but I'm going to Maelpith Island."

"Drelan, no, you can't," Tia exclaimed. She grabbed his hand and looked up into his face with pleading eyes. "Why do this when you have a chance to be free of it all? Besides, I'm going to need you."

He gazed down at her. "I won't be free of anything 'til I get the people responsible for Mom's death. You read the letter. You know what she asked me to do. I promised. And a man is only as good as his word.

"My best chance of fulfilling her last wish is to clear the Sanctum, hopefully come away with some shards, and maybe an epic hierka weapon. It's the best shot I have to get back at Setnana."

"You're chasing rumors about Sanctum treasures, now?" Saba asked, brows raised.

"Not all are rumors," Adesh Hamada said. "I can confirm that the Coalition found weapon and skill shards and at least one schema from a GUM in the Sanctum or on the island itself." He turned his attention to Frost. "Anefet also spoke of a need to secure a special hierka from the Sanctum, but unlike her, you are not ready for the island, the Sanctum, or Nomarch Botros."

An objective popped up called Sanctum's Secret Hierka.

Frost shrugged. "I gotta do this now." How could he tell them that the well-being of his IRL family relied on him doing this? He felt as if time was running out. Saving Meritus had set off a sudden urgency. Worry for Kai, Mom, Regi, and Rayne filled his head.

"Even after you saw Khafra the Mad's power?" Adesh Hamada gave Frost a dubious look. "Setnana is more powerful than he is."

Frost swallowed at the reminder. Khafra had killed a dozen Blue Sky operatives in the Wyvern's Eye with a single combo of Dementia, Shockwave, and Sonic Blow. With his speed and power enhanced tenfold by Dementia, his Shockwave had staggered everyone within fifteen feet. Sonic Blow had exploded through anyone lacking heavy armor who was standing directly in front of him in a ten-foot range.

"I'm not stupid enough to fight her head on," Frost said. "But if I get the chance to ambush her, thwart her plans, or steal anything she finds, I'm gonna make it happen."

"I'm coming with," Gilda said.

"You don't have to."

"I know. It's my choice."

"Shiiitttt." Dante rested his axe handle on his shoulder. "I'll be damned if I let y'all have the fun of all the action and bragging rights to a world first."

"As much as I would love to venture out on the island," Ryne said, jutting his chin toward Meritus, "my place is with my employer."

"It is." Meritus pointed to Frost. "And he's your boss."

"It's settled then." Ryne grinned.

"You guys realize we have terrible group composition?" Saba screwed up her face.

"There's that 'we' again," Ryne said.

"Whatever." Saba rolled her eyes at the goblin and continued, "First, we have no mystic. And since the Sanctum scales in difficulty to match levels, Ryne can't enter with us. Hell, having Dante and me in the group will be pushing it."

"Guess it means you're in?" Frost arched a brow.

Everyone laughed when Saba's tail started to swish.

"I'll come, too," Adesh Hamada said. "Although I will be unable to aid in the Sanctum. But I, too, gave you my word. I also want to help fulfill Anefet's last wish. I should be able to convince the island's dvergr tribes to lend us a hand. They have no love for the Coalition."

Frost glanced down at Tia and gave her shoulder a reassuring squeeze. "See, sis, I'm gonna be fine. Now, let's get you and Meritus on a simurgh to Korbash."

Gilda leaned over to Frost and whispered, "I'm surprised you didn't just sneak off so you could try solo it."

"I thought about it. Believe me. But then I remembered a friend told me sometimes you have to do things you don't like to get what you want. Or to save people you love. My mom IRL said something similar the night we had the accident."

Gilda smiled. "Sounds like a smart friend. And a smarter mother. Let me see what reagents they have for potions in this place and then I'll be ready." She touched Frost's hand and then strolled away.

While the others made preparations, Meritus came over to Frost. "I picked up a lil something for you, homie." Meritus held out his hand.

Frost opened his palm. Meritus dropped a translucent blue orb into it. The orb sunk into Frost's skin, became a part of him. Information Memory flashed.

Acquired Communication Orb

The device grants the owner the ability of text or voice communication by way of its connection to the Aetherstream. Requires recipient's orb address, which begins with @ followed by their name.

Meritus' IGN was already listed as @MeritusKillgain.

"Damn." Frost shook his head. "That had to cost you."

"Worth every credit," Meritus said. "Just make sure you use it."

"I will."

After a final hug and reassuring words to Tia, Frost watched her and Meritus climb atop the first simurgh. Nofre was the rider. Frost and the others did the same on the other beast-bird. Gilda mounted behind Frost.

As Frost wondered how they would fly out of an enclosed building, there came a great churning of gears and a repetitive metal on metal clank. The roof creaked. Dust fell. The roof split down the middle and slowly opened inward, folding down into the building itself to reveal the impenetrable black of a desolate night sky.

Frost looked on in awe. He waved to Tia just as Nofre took flight. Beneath Frost, the simurgh tensed, and then leaped into the air with a beat of its great wings. In moments, they were soaring above Kituan.

Eyes closed, Frost relished the feel of the cool air

against his face. He opened his eyes and marveled at the numerous lights beneath him, the canals and streets and lanes that were Kituan's veins. Finally, he allowed himself a true sense of relief. He smiled.

A zephyr screamed. Then another. And another.

"Deathguards!" Adesh yelled.

Diaphanous wings tucked, a half dozen armored zephyrs dived toward the simurgh carrying Meritus and Tia. Atop the zephyrs' backs were the black clad, human elite Deathguards, heads down, bodies low to the back of their mounts. Another six zephyrs repeated the maneuver toward Frost and his group, but he had eyes only for Tia.

"Go, go, go," he urged, neck straining forward, hands clenched into fists as if he could will Nofre to be faster.

The distance closed. Frost's stomach clenched. He reached a hand out, his eyes wide. And then Nofre's simurgh swelled, beat its wings, and shot forward.

Frost barely had time to let out a relieved breath, register the IM of exp and credits gained from securing Tia's escape, as well as quest completion for Kituan Trials, when a blue streak of light and heat seared his vision. His simurgh let out a pain-filled shriek. And tumbled from the sky.

"Hang on," Pashere yelled.

Winds buffeted Frost. Teeth gritted, he clung to the fur handholds, tried to press his legs and body tighter against the simurgh as it plunged. If not for the creature's harnessing, he would have toppled from its back. Gilda clung to Frost with her face buried into his back.

The beast-bird spun. Frost's stomach knotted. His heart raced. Thundered. The frothy gray glint that was the ocean raced to meet them.

He imagined himself pulled beneath its surface, an ending far worse than the blaze of Aether Shots exploding into the water. Frost closed his eyes, took a deep breath, braced for pain, for the cold unforgiving sea. For a watery grave.

And then, the falling stopped. The simurgh screeched. Leveled out. Glided.

Frost opened his eyes. The ocean sped beneath them, a fathomless expanse glinting with moonlight. A speck floated out where the solemn gray sea swallowed the deathly black sky. He sucked in a shuddering breath, his eyes wide with the thought of the ocean's closeness. Gilda's hold on him eased.

He managed to pull his eyes away from the fear-inspiring spectacle and glance over his shoulder. Zephyrs and their Deathguards were still in pursuit. A dozen of them at least. They were too far away for ranged attacks but were closing the distance. He forced a smile. One Velocity Surge and the pursuit was over.

The simurgh wobbled. Then steadied again.

"She's hurt," Pashere bellowed over the wind, his voice strained. "We won't be able to outrun the Deathguards. Our best chance is to climb, but I doubt we'll be able to land without crashing."

"Land?" Frost repeated. "Where the hell are we gonna land? Please tell me you're not talking about the sea."

"He meant crash," Ryne yelled. The little green bastard actually sounded excited.

"Over there." Adesh Hamada pointed toward a curtain of gray mist that swallowed a portion of the gray sea and sky. Lightning flickered within it. "Maelpith Island."

The simurgh screeched and ascended at an angle. It climbed. Higher and higher. Far below, the mist was a stain upon the ocean, sporadic bursts of lightning radiating in azure, white, and hellish hues. The simurgh leveled off for an instant, banked, tucked its wings, and plummeted. They dropped faster than the first time.

Frost's stomach lurched. He gripped the fur so tight his hands hurt. Gilda's arms were cinched around him. Frost's eyes teared up. The wind howled. But there was another sound, long and protracted. It took him a moment to realize it was him. Screaming. So were the others. Except for Ryne. The goblin was cackling.

They plunged into the mist, the air abruptly cold and clammy. The silent lightning flickered all around, causing Frost's hair to stand on end. He shut his eyes against the glare. Against his clenching stomach. Against the fall. The fear. Abruptly, the cold clamminess was gone, replaced by heat like hell itself.

Frost forced his eyes open. Plains stretched beneath them, the ground a blur that made it impossible to discern any details. The simurgh's wings spread wide, decreasing its speed, its furred feathers ruffling in the wind. It gave a piteous cry, slammed into something, and tumbled.

When the simurgh struck the ground, Frost's world became a tumbling haze of pain, the taste of blood, and fear. Fear of death. Fear for himself. Fear for his family.

CHAPTER 24

Sidrie tapped her lips with her forefinger as she perused the attendee names scrolling down the upper right side of her HUD. A dozen senators and every person of importance from the most influential corporations made up the list. They were due in the Grand Ballroom for Equitane's Annual Gala at 7 p.m.

"Estela, have all the reminders been sent out for this evening's party?"

"Yes."

"The security measures… are they all in place?"

"Yes, madam. And coordinated with every guest who has a security detail."

"Excellent. Please inform me of any changes."

"Yes, madam."

A message from Zhi Yin appeared in her HUD. A progress report on the algorithms to track the anomalies.

Sidrie flicked to her next issue: video of C9040's failed assassination attempt. Gun aimed, her hand trembling, the young red-headed DeGen stood before Shane Constantine, brilliant young senator and lead AI engineer at Sunrise Systems. C9040 lowered the weapon and fled Shane's apartment. Shane burst into sobs. Then he bent down, unclenched the arms of his four-year-old daughter from around his leg, picked her up, and hugged her tight.

Sidrie sighed. She'd hoped for better from C9040. The woman had been one of the best gameborn among those taken in their teens and had not made a false step in all five years she had been in the Total Immersion Program.

"Estela, report on the cause of C9040's failure." She was certain she knew the reasons, but Estela's confirmation was necessary for the records.

"A hormonal and emotional spike when she saw the child," Estela said.

Sidrie shook her head. "Five years down the drain."

"We can still use her." Dr. Redmond's voice piped through Sidrie's aurals. His image was in the opposite corner of her HUD.

"Not this argument again." Sidrie sighed.

"That's millions of credits in TNT," he said. "Why let it go to waste?"

"It has already gone to waste. She failed. She succumbed to her humanity. None have ever recovered."

"We could give her another role," the doctor insisted. "Make her a permanent fixture in Void Legion. With her vast experience and levels, she could be pitted against other gameborn or the testers."

"And waste more resources?" Sidrie scowled. There had to be a way to cure the doctor of his attachment to some of his patients. "Total Immersion is a means to an end, a means to cut away humanity's flaws. We've met failure with too many of the older models like her. I'm of a mind to destroy most of them and only keep the ones brought in when they were five years and younger."

"That's several thousand people, many of them children." Dr. Redmond's voice was quiet. "Not to mention billions of credits to grow them."

"Several thousand people who are mostly DeGens," corrected Sidrie. "And reminding me of how much we have spent on failure does nothing to help them. It achieves the opposite. I can cut the corporation's losses in the name of progress. From here on, it must be about perfection." She had ideas of where perfection would begin.

A beep echoed in her aurals. A message flashed telling her it was an incoming secure communication from Senator Kirkland. "A moment, doctor." She waved a finger to shut off Dr. Redmond and to accept the communication. "Senator, tell me we won the votes."

"I'm sorry, Miss Malikah, but we didn't." Senator Kirkland's nasal voice sounded more annoyed than disappointed. "What happened to your surefire reason to sway Congress?"

Sidrie frowned. "Constantine didn't report an attempt on his life?"

"No. Was there one?"

"Apparently not."

"I could leak it."

"And give away everything? What are you? A fool?"

"I–"

"Answer and I will have your throat slit." Sidrie set aside her annoyance to think. As much as she disliked the idea of changing her mind, now was a prudent time to do so. "Congress and the City Board will have a reason to convene soon enough. There will be no question as to the vote."

"Yes, Miss Malikah."

She severed the communication and resumed her line with the doctor. "I will go with your recommendation on C9040 this time. And only this time."

"Thank you, Miss Malikah."

When the call disconnected, Sidrie contacted her Chief Security Officer, Keenan Costace. The former Special

Forces team leader would be able to arrange exactly what she had in mind. The misdirection would be perfect.

Dressed in a curve hugging magenta and ivory halter-style gown adorned with dazzling sequined and lace embroidery, a deep V neckline, and a satin cape, Sidrie Malikah strode among the patrons after arriving fashionably late. Intimate details for every guest scrolled across the upper left quadrant of her optics. Not that she needed the help. She knew them all. She made certain to smile just the right amount. Offer a nod here. A wave there.

Her words, she reserved for the important folks, the most prominent of them being Governor Richard Morrison. For in words, there was power. And people were tools. With the right combination of words, she could have anyone do her bidding. Add money to the equation and the possibilities became endless.

The Governor fancied himself a ladies' man. And like many a man, he enjoyed the idea of a chase. The idea itself made Sidrie sick, but her feelings did not matter. Only the goal.

Tonight, the governor was wearing a royal blue Belucini suit that she was certain he thought made him quite refined, if his smile and confident demeanor were any indication. But the suit did little for his battle ax of a face and receding hairline. It *was* of a nice cut, but that too was ruined by his less than flattering build. His lone admirable quality were his eyes. They were hard gray pebbles. Trying to appear inconspicuous behind him were two of his personal security detail, a man and woman, in dark suits that screamed bodyguard.

"Richard." Sidrie smiled and held out her hand. "I'm

honored you could make it tonight."

He took her hand and kissed it. She cringed inside but smiled all the same. "The honor is mine, my dear, Sidrie. I wouldn't have missed this or you for the world." He stepped back, still holding her hand, eyes twinkling as his gaze followed her neckline for the merest second before he caught himself. "Stunning, as usual."

She gave his hand a slight squeeze before easing hers away, gently so as not to make him feel put off. "Thank you. You flatter me." She let her smile broaden and hoped he interpreted her blush as embarrassment.

He grinned, most likely pleased with himself and the effect he imagined he had on women. Her, in particular. "Just giving a well-deserved compliment."

"Thank you, again."

"It's nothing." He leaned in a bit. "Now that you're here, I'd like your company for the grand re-opening of Hamilton next week Friday."

"I–"

"Don't turn me down this time."

"I was about to say I'll clear my schedule."

"You were?" His brows shot up.

"Have our secretaries work out the details."

"Just like that?" His eyes narrowed. "It's been what… four years of me inviting you to different functions only for you to turn me down? What changed?"

She scowled. "I resent your implications. If I wanted to hold something over you, or expected a favor in exchange, I would have made such a request when I had my hydroponic silos resolve the latest food shortage after the DeGen attack. My fault for deciding I made you wait long enough." She turned to walk away.

"No, wait." He touched her arm.

She glanced down and faced him, regarding him

with dead eyes.

He withdrew his hand. "I'm sorry. I didn't mean it like that. And I wouldn't dream of accusing you of such a thing."

Liar, she thought.

He threw his hands up in a helpless gesture. "Just surprised you came around."

"I surprise myself sometimes."

"So, we're on then?" His eyes were soft. Hopeful.

She nodded. "My parents always raved about that musical. I'm excited to see it. I have to run now, but we'll chat before the night is out." She turned and strolled away, leaving him with his mouth open. Her stomach churned. Still, she managed to smile and continue her greetings.

She had done her rounds, speaking to senators, investors, CEOs, VR developers, AI engineers, all the brightest tech industry minds across the NAR, when her aurals beeped. The call was from Chief Security Officer Keenan Costace.

"Yes, Mister Costace?"

He appeared in her HUD. The burly, coffee-skinned man was standing with his back to a set of holos. He stared straight at her with gunmetal eyes. "There's been several De-Gen attacks, Miss Malikah."

"And you feel the need to inform me because?"

"They struck two of our hydroponic solos in Manhattan and one of our water reservoirs in Prospect Park. They also hit similar assets belonging to the other major Corps. All of them in Manhattan."

The news must have spread. Almost everyone was engaged in ways that said they were listening to communications via aurals. An agitated murmur rippled through the room. The murmur quickly became an uproar.

She frowned. "So many places at once? In two boroughs? They have never done that before."

"Exactly. And that isn't all."

"Go on."

"We captured one of them and got him to talk. He claimed they have the backing of the SAC."

"The cartels?" She refused to acknowledge the South American Conglomerate as any form of government.

"Yes. At first, I thought it was a stretch. That he might've been at the point of saying anything just to end the pain."

"But?"

"Some of the enemy had P56Zs. Most toted BR18s."

"You're speaking gibberish right now."

"P56Zs are SAC pulse guns, ma'am. BR18s are their standard-issue assault rifles."

"See what else you can get out of him," Sidrie said.

"Yes, ma'am."

Sidrie tried to think. The number of attacks were truly unexpected. "How are our security forces holding up?"

"Well enough. The DeGens captured a few floors, but we're pushing them back. The fight in Prospect Park is a tougher one. They came in numbers. It's First Ward level, so easier access for them. They used the old abandoned subway tunnels to burrow into the park past our security teams and droids."

"Thank you, Mr. Costace. Pull men from wherever you need and keep me posted." She headed for Governor Morrison, barely hearing Keenan's reply.

"Yes, yes," the Governor said as she drew close. The man in his personal security detachment stepped in front of her. She looked him up and down and smiled icily.

Governor Morrison continued. "Send everything we have and crush them. I want the NYPD, NAIL, and the SDF out there. Hop to it. We can't afford to lose any more assets." When he finished, he strode over to her. "Sorry, Sidrie, but duty calls."

"I understand completely. Go. Go."

"Thank you." He strode away with his security detail in tow. He began gathering his aides and other cabinet members.

"Estela," Sidrie said, tapping her pointer finger on her lips, "route the current news reports to the holos on the stage."

The holos changed from showing new Equitane properties, new vehicles, and Total Immersion, to the De-Gen raids. News, police, and military drones hovered over several locations. Pulse and projectile weapon fire blazed a trail between the battling forces. The police and military drones unleashed missile salvos. Above the dissonance of their discharges came the staccato bursts of old-style gunfire.

One holo displayed police and military EVTOL PTs and Airbuses flying across the Hudson River into Manhattan. Another followed a long line of Hover Type vehicles, sirens wailing, emergency lights blazing, as they sped across the Brooklyn Bridge. Soldiers in gear emblazoned with NAIL, SDF, and NYPD had landed on a building's rooftop. In Prospect Park, the fighting was taking place at different sections of the wall surrounding the lake from which a few silos got their water supply.

Transfixed, everyone stared at the holos. Cheers went up when DeGens fell. Gasps when it was one of the good guys. More than a few folks were pointing and yelling whenever they saw a DeGen try to snap off a shot from cover or attempt an ambush. As if the intended targets could hear them.

Something boomed within the building, startling Sidrie. The lights went out. A klaxon wailed. People screamed.

From somewhere close by came the burst of pulse weapon discharges and stutter of assault rifle fire.

"Estela, what was that?"

No answer.

In fact, Sidrie's optics were completely dark. No information scrolled across her HUD. Something was wrong. Very wrong. A tightness gripped her chest. A foreign yet familiar feeling. One she hadn't felt in years. Decades. One that still haunted her. A memory of terror from the night some DeGens broke into their house in Dumbo, right off the Brooklyn Bridge, and killed her parents. Raped her. Left her for dead.

She sucked in ragged breaths, chest heaving. *God, this can't be happening. Not here. Not now. Why didn't I bring security? I should've brought security!* A part of her wanted to flee through her secret passage in the back. In less than two minutes she could be upstairs in the most secure quarters in New New York. *Stop it, woman. Breathe. This is your place, your home.*

"We have to get out of here," someone yelled.

Beams of light emanated from the few people who had worn Smart Glasses rather than implants. A commotion ensued. In the spasmodic lighting, there came a mad scramble for the door amid shouts and screams. She could imagine the crush of people, some falling, only to be trampled by a hundred feet. More screams. Some of which cut off abruptly.

Closing her eyes, she forced herself to breathe long and slow. Her thundering heart slowed. "You are in control. You are always in control." Over and over she whispered to herself.

Red and white strobe lights flashed on. Flickering spasmodically, they cast an eerie glow over the crowd struggling to get out, made them into a frenetic mass. But full security measures had kicked in. The door would not budge.

Her optics flickered to life. "Mic for this room." It clicked on. "Everyone stop. Be quiet." Her voice echoed.

The room froze.

"You're safer in here than out there. This room is sealed."

Conversation picked up. Someone shouted a question that she couldn't discern.

"Some people got trampled just now," she said. "Help them."

People acted on her words. They assisted the fallen who could not stand on their own. Others who got up, groggy and bleeding, were led to the stage. A few waiters and waitresses retrieved first aid kits. There were a couple doctors and nurses among the crowd. They got to work.

Sidrie turned off the mic. "Estela report."

Still no answer.

Her aurals beeped. It was Keenan. "What the hell is going on?" she asked.

"DeGens attacked us here. They got inside the Towers and set off an EMP," he said. "Knocked out everything. Most of our systems are still down. I'm leading a full company down to you."

Grimacing, Sidrie shook her head. "Here? How did they get past the security droids and cameras downstairs?"

"We were hacked."

"Hacked?" She frowned.

"Yes. Cyber caught it before they got deep but not before they managed to shut off the cameras and disable the MX5s."

She shook her head. The DeGens were a bunch of cast offs, the worst society had to offer. Surely, none among them were capable of getting past the building's encryption protocols. And yet they had.

The weapons fire escalated. It grew closer.

"Hurry."

"Almost there, ma'am."

Governor Morrison and his detail approached, emergency strobes casting them in a macabre mix of red, white, and shadow. Accompanying them were a dozen other men and women with handguns, security for several other important patrons. Their employers were right behind them.

The Governor stopped before her and asked, "Are you certain they can't get in here?"

"I'm positive, Governor. Sit tight. My men are on the way."

"Miss Malikah," Governor Morrison's clean-shaven bodyguard said, "I'm Henry. I think we should prepare just in case things go badly."

"What do you need?"

"Tell everyone to fall back from the door. Tell them to help us stack up these tables and chairs close to the doors and back this way." He pointed. "Then the rest of you head toward the side of the stage so that you can put it between you and any fire."

Sidrie did as he asked and made Keenan aware of the plan. People rushed this way and that to comply. Within minutes, the area near the entrance was an obstacle course of monstrous chairs and heavy tables under the capering strobes. The armed men and women split up to either side of the room with a few tables as cover.

The dissonance of pulse weapon and assault rifle fire raged. Right outside now. An explosion roared, its reverberations felt within the floor.

A hush fell over the room. A breathless murmur of suppressed fear. Dread. Whispered prayers for the room to be impregnable, for the authorities to arrive in time to prevent a massacre.

The pitch of the firefight changed, pulse bursts and

assault rifle chatter ringing out in measured intervals. A chaotic fusillade answered. The pattern repeated several times. Fire and response. Then the bursts grew slower and singular. Sporadic. Soon, all that was left was silence. An eternity of emptiness.

Crouched behind the stage with Richard beside her, Sidrie peered toward the door. The expectant breathing and whispered prayers of numerous guests filled the air. As did their perfumes and colognes.

The door slid open to reveal the hall and its spasmodic lights. A body was on the floor.

"Miss Malikah, it's us." Keenan's voice chirped in her aurals.

Tension fled Sidrie's body. She exhaled long and slow. She stood. "Henry, don't shoot. My men are at the door."

The building lights flashed on. Someone yelled, "Hell, yeah!" Cheering followed.

A moment later, two dozen heavily armored and armed men of Sidrie's security company entered. Assault rifles and long pulse guns aimed, they surveyed the room. Once certain all was well, they lowered their weapons.

Sidrie's aurals beeped. Dr. Redmond.

"We have a problem," he said. "Void Legion went offline. And DeGens got into the Total Immersion room. They took several players."

Breathing deep, Sidrie schooled herself to calm, to not curse, her balled fists trembling with exertion. She strode over to Keenan Costace and pulled him to the side. "DeGens infiltrated the Total Immersion room and took several assets. Do not let them get out of the building. Find them. Now." She turned and headed for the Governor to have words. One way or another he was going to have to do something about the DeGens.

CHAPTER 25

Dre tried to make sense of his circumstances. Not long ago, he was in Ataxia Online. The wounded simurgh on which he rode had crashed on Maelpith Island and sent him flying. He remembered the in-game agony. Some of it was still with him.

In the next moment, he had woken, cold, groggy, disoriented, and under strobe lights. An alarm was blaring. Hands grabbed him, pulled him out of the Total Immersion pod, and hustled him from the room.

Now, a man was helping him down stairs, a man with a black-painted face, dressed in tactical armor. The man had an assault rifle slung over his back. A HK433 if Dre wasn't mistaken. A dozen men and women, similarly armed and dressed, and roughly ten half-naked alpha testers, were ahead of Dre and the man.

Why were they all doing that weird fucking dance?

Dre tried to clear his head. To think. But thinking was so difficult. The klaxon worsened the effect. It was as if he was in a fog, the world, lethargic. Except for his seemingly drunken companions who capered in the strobe lights. Shivering, he continued down the stairs, his feet moving of their own volition, one after the next, following the lead of the dancers ahead of him.

Time and the number of flights were a foreign thing. He grew weary, his legs wooden. Numb. But the man around whose shoulder his arm was tossed would not allow him to slow down.

Someone else complained. They stopped, the group spread between two landings. A few testers huddled together for warmth. The alarm stopped blaring.

Dre's head cleared a bit. He took his arm from around the man. Dre shook violently.

"You alright, buddy?" The man's voice was gruff.

"I-I'm freezing." Dre's teeth chattered. "But at least you guys stopped dancing."

"Dancing?" A pause then a chuckle. "Oh, the strobes. Your vision had to adjust."

"Who're you guys?" Dre asked. "Why'd you take us from the pod room?"

"We're your rescue."

"Rescue?" His heart leapt. "You're the police? Someone knew what Equitane's been up to?" Dre felt like he could hug the man.

"Yeah, someone did."

Dre frowned at the testers. "There were a lot more of us."

"I know. We got who we could and split into groups. The important thing now is to get you out of here." The man gestured with his head for Dre to follow the others.

"But my mother and sister," Dre pleaded as he reluctantly obeyed.

"One of the other groups probably has them," the man said unconvincingly.

"Dion, either you shut him up or I will," said one of the closest policemen. "This fool's gonna give us away."

"You heard the man," Dion said.

Dre lowered his voice. "They weren't with the players. My mother was—"

"Right now, there's no going back," Dion hissed.

295

"Our focus is to get you guys to some place warm and safe. Once we've accomplished that, we'll see what's what. Now, shut up before you get us all killed."

Resigned to his current fate, Dre hugged himself against the cold and trudged down the stairs. But he could not stop thinking of his family. They were all he had left.

What if the police were too late in getting to them? Were they alright? Is Sidrie gonna think I violated our agreement? Would she try to get revenge by hurting Kai? Mom? The twins?

On and on, his fears haunted him. He blew into his hands and stopped at the feel of his aether ring. Stroking it, he tried to think of a way out. Maybe it was better if he ran from the police and returned to Sidrie. The more he thought on it, the more that last became the best option.

Once more, they stopped, most of them on the stairs between one landing and the next. Someone touched his hand. A girl tester. Asian. If the emergency lights weren't playing tricks on him again. He did his best not to let his gaze rove to her bare chest.

"Hey, Frost," she said in a low voice. "Or Andre, rather, it's me, Just Blaze."

Dre's brows climbed his forehead. Just Blaze certainly wasn't the girl he'd imagined. Neither were the circumstances of their first meeting. He frowned.

Matching her timbre, he said, "How do you know my real name or that it's even me?"

"Because you just gave it away?" She shrugged.

"I'm serious," he said.

"The same way I knew where to find you in-game."

Grimacing, he shook his head slightly. "Wanna explain?"

She held one finger up for a moment, head tilted slightly to the side. Then she said, "Damn it. They're on to us."

Before Dre could question her words or reaction, a deep baritone below them spoke. "Listen up, people. We thought we had more time before Equitane's security discovered we might be using this stairwell. We don't. Our best option now is for you guys to hide among the droids stored in the rooms on this floor and the one above. The doors will be open. Pick a room, no more than two of you to a room. We'll draw away Equitane's guards and fight them off. We'll return for you as soon as we've cleared a way."

Dre frowned at the instructions. Something wasn't right.

Dion opened the door to a hallway behind Dre and Just Blaze. "Half of you come through here. The other half go downstairs."

Amid fearful murmurs and his own worry, Dre headed into the hall with Just Blaze on his heels. Several other testers followed. Together, they stood there, uncertain of their next move.

"What're you fools waiting for?" Dion scolded. "Find a room and hide before the lights come back up."

Just Blaze grabbed Dre's arm. "Let's go." She hurried down the hall.

Still shivering, Dre ambled after her, using her white spandex shorts as a guide. He took a quick glance back at the others heading the opposite direction. Something about the situation left a sour taste in his mouth.

When he caught up to Just Blaze, he said, "This doesn't make sense."

"What doesn't?" Just Blaze stopped at a room, opened the door, and peered inside.

"Their orders. Cops wouldn't leave us to fend for ourselves. And none of their gear had any police decals. Something's off."

"Maybe, it's a secret op, and they want us out of

harm's way during the firefight. I don't like this room. Let's try another." She continued down the hallway.

"That's the thing," Dre said, brow furrowed, cold all but forgotten. "Would a company like Equitane openly attack the police?"

She checked another room. "Judging by how they got some testers, I'd say yes."

Dre screwed up his face. "At the risk of losing their entire company? The government would crush them. Sidrie didn't come off as stupid."

"I doubt they see it as a risk." At the next room, she said, "This one looks good. MX1s are in here." She shot him a look. "It seems like Equitane's willing to do whatever to get us back... in the same way they were willing to do anything to force some of us to alpha test. Also, you said it yourself, our rescuers didn't have police decals. The guards could claim they figured them for thieves."

Just Blaze had a point, but Dre still had his doubts. Dre followed her into the room where it was colder than out in the hall. Neat rows of MX1 androids filled the space. Dre was certain they were all decommissioned.

"Let's say this *was* a government raid," Dre continued. "There'd be a search warrant and plenty news media to cover it. That's how the government always works in the big Corp cases. Which means they'd want everything to be official." He paused for a second. "What if those men weren't cops?"

Brows furrowed tight, he added, "Come to think of it, why were they carrying Heckler and Koch HK433s? That's a very old gun and was never used by the American police. The Next Generation Squad Assault Rifle is standard-issue for the cops. The NGSAR4, to be exact.

"Also, I was the one who asked about police. All Dion answered to was someone knowing about Equitane's dealings." He stopped and stared at her bare back, a prickle easing through him. "You said they were on to us before one of them did. How'd you know?" He paused. "Same thing with my name."

Just Blaze stopped, turned to face him, and sighed. "I was wearing an earpiece. And you're right, they weren't cops."

Dre opened and closed his mouth. Finally, he whispered, "That was your crew?"

"Not exactly. They're people I know who were trying to save us."

"How'd they know exactly where to look?"

"We have someone on the inside. And." She held up her hand. Under the strobes, Dre could just make out a ring. "My Three Ring."

"What? I don't understand." By sheer instinct he touched the Two Ring on his pinky finger.

"Your father had these made."

"Pops?"

"Alphonso. Yes."

"How you know him?"

"He was also an alpha tester. But my people discovered he was more than a player. He was one of the main engineers behind Void Legion's AI, Estela. They led me to him in game, and we became friends. But he soon found out I was a hacker, that I knew about the experiments, the secrets behind much of what BioGen was doing with Void Legion's tech and Estela."

"Pops designed the new AI? He worked for Bio-Gen?"

"Yes. And Equitane by extension."

Dre shook his head, trying to make sense of the news.

Just Blaze continued, "BioGen was using Estela, the

299

game, and TNT, to experiment on players, recording improved skills, physical prowess, and intelligence, and how it translated to real life. For what purpose? We're not certain. But if the end is a reflection of the means, then it can't be for anything good. BioGen called them gameborn."

"Pops would never be involved in anything like that. I'm not listening to this nonsense." He made to walk away, but she grabbed his wrist.

"At the time, your father didn't know Equitane's real purpose as owners of BioGen." She let go when he glanced down at her hand. "It was by chance that he discovered DeGen children hooked up to the game, immersed into the world for development over years. The first batch were placed in the experiment as teenagers. When the desired results weren't met, BioGen sought out toddlers and pre-teens, often paying poor and desperate DeGen parents for their children. At other times, they simply took the ones they desired.

"Top players like us are used to test the gameborn. They're sent to hunt us in-game. Sometimes, we're recruited through alphas and betas or offered money. When those methods fail, Equitane resorts to other means. Means you know well."

Dre shook his head. "How's any of this possible? Someone woulda reported it."

"Who would report it?" Just Blaze scoffed. "DeGens paid by Equitane? Ones who could finally live a decent life, escape disease, crime, and death? Ones who could now live a cushy life in a higher Ward? There were rumors that some were awarded Citizenship.

"As for complaints... who would listen to DeGens? Does anyone listen now? If you let society and OneWorld tell it, DeGens are the worst of us... disease-carrying monsters... gangsters... criminals... illegal aliens."

"But they're other testers like us who aren't De-Gens," Dre argued. "Regular people. I was a Mid Warder."

"Most DeGens *are* regular people," she snarled. "Mothers, fathers, sons, daughters… hard working people trying to scrape together a living in the worst conditions."

"But," he began.

"There are no buts." She shook her head and scowled. "One thing I learned long ago is that social media has stopped being very social. It's been used to divide us. The First Ward's the way it is because of the Corps and the government. Because of the Seven. Trust and believe, there's as many criminals living in the Upper Wards as down below."

Just Blaze's tone carried the fire of conviction that smoldered in the glint of her eyes. "Any time one of you norms has some serious disease and can't afford healthcare, they send you down to the First Ward. Pregnant Bottom Warders often flee down below to avoid the FPC." Dre made to speak, but she continued on. "As for you being a Mid Warder… I doubt it was true when they got you to test. Equitane is meticulous. And more ruthless than you got to experience. Most of all, they have the money and power to make trouble disappear."

"There's gotta be something, somewhere… someone who knows," Dre insisted.

"Not people that matter. Which is why Alphonso was trying to expose Equitane. I introduced him to some people who could help. They decided to work together with members of your father's team that he trusted.

"Using the team's expertise with Estela, they developed a way into Ataxia and then Void Legion. From the game, we could gain access to BioGen and Equitane's systems to acquire evidence and release it publicly.

"He was on his way to us with the final ten protocols

to bypass Estela's security as well as other files he down-loaded. He didn't trust sending them over the Grid.

"That's when he had the accident. We think Equitane killed him. The same way they killed off other team members. Same way they caused your accident."

Dre felt numb. His mind reeled. *Pops was murdered? The crash wasn't an accident?* Dre saw his father's accident replay, then he saw the drone replay of his own, the wrecked Camry, Mom and Kai unconscious, Mom hooked up to the machines, fighting to survive.

"We know he logged into Ataxia from his Holo Tab just before he died," Just Blaze said. "We believe he hid the protocols and files somewhere in the game. They're the keys to everything."

The strobes stopped flickering. Soft white lights flashed on. Pulse and assault rifle fire echoed.

CHAPTER 26

Hugging himself to keep warm, teeth chattering, Dre sat in the shadow of stacked MX1 boxes. Mist coiled into the air with Dre's every breath. Soft, white overhead lights bathed the room. Bursts of energy weapons and firearms came and went like specters in the night.

Just Blaze sat not far from him, knees to chest, dainty chin resting on her folded arms. Under the lights, she was quite the picture. She wasn't anything like he'd imagined, her build more athletic by far. Her skin was lighter than his caramel, more in the area of honey, which made her long black box braids stand out. Her face was small but somehow suited her perfectly. Her slightly angled dark eyes watched him watching her. He averted his gaze.

Dre considered her story yet again. For perhaps the twentieth time. *Did someone in Equitane… No. Did Sidrie have Pops killed? Did she arrange the Camry's crash?* Neither was beyond the woman he'd come to know. Proving either, however, posed a problem.

Despite lacking such evidence, a part of him still wanted the woman dead. It's the least she deserved. And anyone else involved with the Camry's crash, with Mom's current condition.

All the other stuff about gameborn sounded like something from a movie. But then, he'd thought the same

303

about TNT and Total Immersion. The game itself was proof of greater achievements and tech than he imagined.

Still, something bothered him. Something that didn't quite add up. If Equitane was capable of everything Just Blaze said, then how was it that they hadn't caught her? The Corp had gone to such great lengths to acquire top players but were willing to allow her to roam freely?

Brow furrowed, he considered conversations with her in game and how she had given him the vaguest of answers at times. *Had she been so careful that she'd never given away anything to GMs monitoring chat logs?* She claimed to be a hacker. Perhaps, that was the answer. Still, she must have made a mistake at some time.

And why didn't she tell me about Pops in game? I was honest with her from the start, when this whole time she was hiding things from me.

"Why… why didn't you tell me all this when we were playing?" he asked.

She looked at him over her arms. "I wasn't certain how to approach you. Or if you'd even believe me. I tried several times."

"And you think I believe you now?"

"Maybe you do or you don't, but there was something your father said to tell you when we met."

He perked up. She unwrapped her arms and straightened her long legs before crossing them at the ankles. He glanced away from her bare chest, a lump forming in his throat, and focused on her dark eyes as a way to prevent his gaze from wandering.

She held his gaze. "Stand on your own two. Nothing worth doing is easy."

Dre stiffened and squeezed his eyes shut. When he opened them, Just Blaze was studying his face. "Thank you." A weight lifted from him. She nodded.

"I assume they're more people like you in game," he said. "People in this fight against Equitane."

"No doubt. Some are players like us. Others are NPCs like Adesh Hamada. NPCs programmed by your dad."

"How do y'all hide from the GMs?"

She held up her hand. "While tracking may be near impossible to avoid, we can mask our chat and whereabouts with our aether rings."

"How? What do they do in game?"

"When activated, they create a zone that scrambles the game's monitoring."

Dre's brows climbed his forehead. "Really?" Just Blaze nodded. Dre tilted his head to one side. "Wouldn't the admins see when that happens? Be able to pinpoint the disruption?"

"Your father said security would see an anomaly. But most times it would be in a completely different region or even continent from where the safe zone activation took place."

"That's amazing."

"Your dad truly was."

Hearing those words hurt. And yet they felt great. "Why not keep it on all the time?"

"After ten minutes, they can pinpoint the anomaly. Same with using the same ring more than five times in a nome in a day. Leave it on any longer and they'd be able to find the person using it."

Dre studied the small 2 engraved into the middle of the ring along with a pattern of lines and marks like runes. "How do you turn it on and off?"

"Spin left twice to activate. Opposite direction to de-activate." She emulated her words.

Dre nodded. He recalled her doing just that on more than one occasion. "Not long after I logged into Void Legion, I ran across a few people who I'm sure were NPCs that seemed to believe they were in a game. Hearing them say it was strange. Nebsamu and Tia called them dreamers. Are those the gameborn?"

"Some might be. Most aren't," she said. "The name dreamers came about when a few players began a cult. They convinced some NPCs they were part of a game played by the gods, and everyone were its pieces. The story spread, eventually being connected to shevla. Gameborn don't know they're playing a game. For them, Ataxia is life."

Dre smiled. "Leave it to us players to influence the game in ways the devs probably didn't consider."

She returned the smile. "We do what we gotta do. It's why we're the best."

"We?" He glanced around.

Just Blaze giggled. "You big dummy."

"I couldn't help it. Ryne's funny. And he had a thing for you."

"Pfft. You mean *you* had a thing for me."

Dre glanced away. "You wish."

"I'm not the one blushing. And I'm not the one who can barely look at the other person."

"You're naked!" Dre exclaimed.

"Half-naked," she corrected.

Dre cleared his throat and looked directly at her but tried not to *see* Just Blaze. The chatter of distant weapons fire echoed. "How do you think your people are doing?"

"Well… I hope."

"If they can't help my mother and Kai, I got no choice but to stay," Dre said. "I gotta at least clear Imanok Sanctum."

"You know Sidrie won't stop with the Sanctum. And probably won't ever let you and your family go."

"That might be true, but I agreed to do something."

"She forced you. It's not the same."

"But I still gave my word," Dre said. "Not just to her, but I promised Mom also. I'm gonna keep my word. For my family's sake. I'll see what Sidrie does in return. If this rescue fails, it's the only hope for Kai, Mom, and the twins."

"Personally, I wouldn't trust her."

"I don't." But inside, Dre had to make himself believe Sidrie would keep her end of the bargain.

"Good," Just Blaze said. "The truth of the matter is that both my people and Sidrie think you can help locate the protocols. That you might figure out where your father hid them. The rest of his team who survived Sidrie's efforts hope you can too. They're currently hiding down in the First Ward."

"I can try," Dre said.

Weapons fire reverberated once again. Assault rifles and pulse guns. Closer and louder this time.

"Should we head out when they're almost here?" Dre asked.

"No. Someone might shoot us in the confusion of a firefight. If Equitane wins, let them come get us. Once surveillance is back online, they can see every room in the building and detect heat signatures. We can play the victim then. Claim we escaped our would-be captors."

Dre frowned. "Why would they believe that?"

"Because the people fighting to free us are mostly DeGens. I'm a DeGen."

Dre gave her an incredulous stare. His natural thought was to shy away, but he didn't. He stopped to think. Her anger over people's opinions on DeGens made sense now.

He recalled the DeGen who'd jumped in front of the Maglev. The DeGens on the news. He couldn't reconcile her or their would-be rescuers with either of those memories. Those DeGens on the news barely seemed human, had faces covered in lesions, misshapen bodies, and stank of death and worse. He abruptly noticed the cold again. He hugged himself.

"We might end up waiting here most of the night," Just Blaze said. "The only way we don't freeze to death is if we make a little hut out of these boxes of MX1s and stay close to each other. Use our body heat."

Despite his trepidation only moments ago, Dre's heart sped up at the prospect of being close to her. But not out of fear. Or loathing. Deciding that the best way to control himself was to work, he got up and began the process of moving the boxes containing the androids. The boxes were relatively heavy and soon he was focused on the task.

Just Blaze did the same. He couldn't help but to sneak glances at her. She seemed to be having an easier time than he was, picking up the boxes and stacking them. Her arms and legs were quite toned, muscles bunching while she worked.

She soon had a sweaty sheen, which became intoxicating to watch. Once, she caught him looking. And smiled. He returned it. Barely. His face grew hot.

He cleared his throat. "You work out often?"

"Not often enough," she said.

He nodded to her body. "Sure looks like you do."

"I used to at one point. I had to. Staying fit went hand in hand with being a thief."

"Looking at you makes me wish I did more often." Dre stacked another box.

"I'm lucky if I get to work out more than once a month since I became a tester a year ago." Just Blaze bent to pick up a box. Dre stared at her ass in the white spandex. "I spend almost all my time in-game."

"And you still look like that?" Dre shook his head.

She shrugged. "Good genes. Despite what the government and social media would like you to believe about DeGens. You're not too shabby looking yourself for a sixteen-year-old."

"Thanks," Dre said. "And I'm almost seventeen." Frowning, he considered the days and nights in Void Legion. "How long do you think we were under?"

"One day in-game is like three days IRL, so you do the math."

Dre gaped. "That's like nine days. My sister must be worried sick. And then there's Mom and the twins." Panic rose in his chest.

"Nothing you can do about it now. At least you know they're in a safe building under the care of the very best doctors."

Thinking of it that way eased the pressure from Dre's chest. Still, the worry lingered in the back of his mind.

Soon enough, they had built a hut tall enough to duck inside. He entered first and sat. She followed.

"We're gonna have to spoon," she said.

"Spoon?"

"Yeah. Lie on your side, facing me with your legs curled a bit."

"I know what it is, but—"

"Just do it."

He did as she asked. Working to build the hut had already eased the chill from his body, but he was warmer still.

"And now, my turn." She scooted around until her back was to him, her butt in spandex brushing against him, then positioned herself so her back was to his chest. The rest of her body fit like a glove against him.

Dre swallowed. His heart thumped loud in his ears. He begged himself not to rise to the occasion, to the raw emotions running through him, the emotions that dwarfed those he felt when he dove into VPorn. His body refused to listen. He got so hard it hurt.

Pulse assault weapon fire echoed again. Farther away.

"Hmm," she said, voice low and husky. She reached behind her and grabbed his butt and pulled him closer onto her, nails digging into his flesh. "It's ok. Trust me. You trust me, right?" He nodded numbly as she continued to whisper. To coax. "This will be the best way for us to stay warm. Take off my pants."

Dre's hands shook as he complied. Just Blaze coached him in that low voice of hers. The rest was a blur. A dream of sensations, primal instinct, pleasure, moans, heat, and slick wetness unlike anything he had experienced in his entire life.

He thought he knew what sex felt like, what sex would be like. But the examples and experience in VPorn were a pittance compared to this. Just Blaze felt so good. So perfect. Beyond perfect.

"Harder! Faster!" She cried from on all fours, head down, back arched.

He rammed into her. She thrust back with each slap of his hips against her ass. Sweat poured down his face, its taste salty in his mouth. A feeling overcame him, from deep in his gut. His soul. His toes curled. With a final drive, he experienced ecstasy.

When he was spent, he hunched over her, trembling. And then he slid off to the side and sprawled next to her, the perfume of their sex thick and musky in the air. She placed her head on his chest and kissed him. She worked her way down, her mouth soft and warm.

And then she took him into her mouth. Her mouth!

His eyes bulged. Within seconds he was hard again. But she kept going. Sucking. Licking. Kissing. Stroking him with both hands. If he thought his first release had been ecstasy, the second was beyond as she made love to him with her mouth, lips, tongue, and hands.

The act left him shuddering, caused him to make guttural sounds, sounds he didn't recognize as himself, even as he threw his head back, eyes closed. A part of him wanted to pull away. The other part didn't want the feeling to end. He felt as if he could break something. And then, it ended. He felt… drained.

But she wasn't finished. In turn, she showed him how to kiss her, lick her. The smell of her privates was intoxicating. Her reactions drove him. Her moans. Her cries. Wetness. She grabbed his hair tight in her hands; her back arched; she shook; and with a final moaning whoosh of breath, her body went slack.

Afterward, they spooned.

Dre traced a line with his index finger down her toned arm and leg. "Why?"

"Why what?"

"What we just did. And with me."

"Why the question?" she said.

Dre shrugged. "I wanna know. And I won't know if I don't ask."

"A girl's gotta do what a girl's gotta do," Just Blaze said.

Dre chuckled. "Nah, seriously."

"I wanted to. And we needed to generate more heat so we wouldn't freeze to death. Also, I had to make you see us DeGens in a different light. Most of us are as normal as you norms."

Dre made to speak.

"We can talk later. Let's get some sleep."

Hours later, a man's voice shouted, "This is Equitane security. Come out with your hands up. Don't make any silly moves."

Dre and Just Blaze pulled on their spandex and went out to meet them. They were greeted by soldiers in full tactical armor toting NGSARs and AVP41B pulse guns. EQUI-TANE CORP or NYPD was emblazoned upon their chests and backs.

CHAPTER 27

The Upper Ward floors were abuzz with activity when Dre and Just Blaze arrived with the other testers. On the way up, Dre found himself snatching glances at her and smiling. He felt like a new man. He couldn't quite put a finger on the difference. Describe it. But it was there. Intangible. So was the memory of their time together. It was intoxicating. And quite unlike anything he had experienced after a VPorn session.

He could still feel Just Blaze. Smell her. Touch her. Taste her. The soft silkiness of her skin, her warmth, her breath, her voice, her salty sweetness. He sighed.

Techs and security hurried along the corridors, scanning Holo Tabs. Equitane guards, in tactical armor and armed with NGSAR5s or AVP41Bs, stood at every entrance. Doctors fussed over the testers, making certain they were in good health. When a doctor finished, a tech led the tester in question back to their pod.

All except for Dre. He was to wait for Sidrie. The thought of the woman curdled his insides, twisted him into knots.

His ire was almost forgotten when Just Blaze smiled at him as she departed and mouthed that she would see him in game. He blushed. Once again, he relived their night.

And nearly jumped out of his skin at Sidrie's voice. "You look better than I might have expected after your ordeal." Sidrie was wearing a gray and black knee-length pencil dress with three quarter sleeves and a scoop neck, the gray portion sitting within the black, which followed her curves.

Dre's lip curled, his loathing for her a tangible thing that crawled across his skin, left a sour taste in his mouth. The heat of his emotions rose. He balled his hands into fists and forced himself to calm by stroking his aether ring.

"Tut, tut." Sidrie gave a slow a shake of her head. "You have such hate for the person who saved your life twice."

"Saved me from my rescuers?"

"Is that what they told you?" She chortled. "And you believed them?"

"Why shouldn't I?"

"Oh, I don't know, maybe because they were De-Gens?" she said with a wry smile. "Human traffickers? They planned to harvest your organs. My security team is the only reason you are alive."

"Bullshit."

She arched an eyebrow and made a steeple of her fingers just below her waist. "You should be thanking me."

"Thanking you?" He grimaced. "For being the reason I'm here in the first place? That my family is here? That they're hurt?"

Her lips twitched but the smile did not touch her eyes. "The reason for their injuries? No. That was you."

"Liar."

Her hands dropped to her sides. She stared at him, unblinkingly, her predatory eyes obsidian beads. When she spoke, her voice was flat. "You really think it wasn't an accident, don't you?"

"You tell me." Dre didn't believe her. Not for one minute.

"I have no reason to lie to you," Sidrie said in the same monotone. "You already have little choice but to do as I wish. So, I will tell you this now. The crash *was* an accident. Part of the reason I called it fate or luck."

"If you say so."

Her face went slack, her eyes dead. "You forget Theresa and the twins are under the care of the very best doctors in the world. My doctors."

Dre bit back his next rebuttal and controlled his tone. "I just want to return to Void Legion to fulfill our deal."

She nodded once, but her expression did not change. "And you shall. I actually came to ask your opinion of Total Immersion. Seeing that you doubted its capabilities."

A part of him wanted to lie, but he could not. Doing so would be childish. "It's impressive. A little scary and disorienting all at once."

"And amazing," Sidrie added, her face lighting up. "This is why Total Immersion is better than reality in every way." She raised her hand and gestured, her tone filled with conviction. "When perfected, it is the only experience any man will need to live his fullest life. Take you, for example, you were in Total Immersion for nine days, and yet here you stand with no ill effects."

The mention of time brought worry surging back again. Dre fought down his concerns. "I guess." He shrugged.

"You disagree?" She appeared taken aback.

He met her questioning gaze with a straight face. "The last thing I remembered was crashing, pain, and blood. Soon after, I was out of the pod. No downtime. No pain in the real world. No experience to draw from it. What did I learn? What did I gain?"

She folded her arms at her midsection, left index

finger tapping her bicep. "Another bit of luck on your part. The game went offline at the same moment your simurgh was crashing. Before TNT registered any major injuries, before it left an impression." A distant expression encompassed her face.

Dre frowned at her knowledge of his whereabouts in Ataxia. "I guess it's good to have dumb old luck. Can I go now?" He wanted so badly to ask to see Kai and Mom, but he was certain Sidrie would use any sign of desperation against him.

Sidrie smiled wryly. "A moment ago, you seemed to have a high opinion of the DeGen attackers. I wonder how you would feel knowing Equitane was not their only target. That they struck several other skyrises and hydroponic silos."

"I don't care," Dre said. "None of it had anything to do with me. Or my situation."

"Really?" Sidrie's brow arched. "They murdered dozens of people. Even a senator. Their EMP shut down Equitane's systems, including the medical facilities."

It took but a moment for the implications of her words to dawn on Dre. His chest grew heavy with dread. "Mom. The twins. Are they alright?"

Sidrie gestured to the closest guards. "Return this boy to the pod room."

Dre made to rush toward Sidrie, but the guards intercepted him. "Talk to me, please!" he shouted. "Tell me... tell me they're alright. Please!" His thoughts spun. He imagined the worst of things.

"Let this be a lesson to speak to me with the utmost respect." Sidrie's voice was steel. "To curb your tongue in my presence. I hold your futures in my hands. You can discover their condition if you manage to clear the Sanctum. Fail and you would prove useless to me. So would they." She turned on her heels and strode away.

Dre was left weeping. His legs were weak. A guard took him by the arm and led him to the pod room. He felt lost as he climbed into the pod, the polymer cold against his skin, his mind occupied by Mom, Regina, Rayne, and Kai. Forcing himself to think good thoughts, to imagine them together somewhere free and safe, he waited for Total Immersion to kick in.

CHAPTER 28

Frost opened his eyes. Only to discover Ryne's hideous green face looming over him. Frost shied away. "What the hell are you doing?"

"Checking on you." The goblin leered, exposing yellowed teeth and noxious breath. "Frost's awake," he called out.

"So are the others," said Adesh Hamada's voice.

Frost sat up, head filled with thoughts of Mom, the twins, and Kai. Filled with worry. Dread. *I gotta find out how they're doing.* And he had an idea of how to achieve just that.

Eyes narrowed, he took in his surroundings. He was on a straw bed laid out on hard-packed dirt in a long, narrow abode of some sort, its walls a combination of wood and straw. Near Frost was a totem carved in a vague resemblance of a chimera and a drake locked in battle. Cool air entered by way of open doors, one at each long end, a lone window, and a hole in the roof.

Gilda was in the act of sitting up on a bench a few feet from him. Dante leaned on a nearby wooden beam. Frost saw no sign of Saba. Someone had stacked their weapons, armor, and clothes in a corner.

A dark-complexioned man, no taller than four feet, dressed in skins and a cloak, fussed over a cauldron at the center of the house. His body was powerful and stocky, his legs disproportionately short, his gangly, muscular arms reaching to his knees. He sported a wooly beard and green eyes. Frost frowned at the man's skin. It had a strange texture. Stony in appearance.

A bouquet of spices and the mouthwatering scent of food filled the air. Soup, if Frost wasn't mistaken. His stomach grumbled.

"Where are we?" he asked.

"A hut," Ryne said matter-of-factly.

"No shit." With a sigh, Frost climbed to his feet. "I can see that. But where exactly?"

Adesh Hamada spoke. "We're among allies on Maelpith Island. One of the dvergr tribes I spoke of."

"What happened?"

"You four were knocked unconscious when the simurgh crashed," Adesh said. "We searched all night for you and did not find you until this morning. It was as if you disappeared. Strangely enough, we found you all in places we swore we had already looked. Unfortunately, such a fate was not to be for Pashere. He did not make it."

"I'm sorry for your loss," Frost said.

"He died doing what he loved." Adesh Hamada drew an X over his heart. "May Nif keep his soul."

Frost repeated the gesture. He took in the home once more, stopping at the stone-skinned dvergr. "Where's Saba?"

"Outside. She woke before you did." Adesh gestured to the dvergr who put a wooden spoon to his lips to taste the soup. "Einarr is the leader of this particular tribe. He and his shamans took care of you."

"Thanks." Frost dipped his head to Einarr.

"You are most welcome," Einarr said, voice a low rumble. "Any enemy of the Coalition is a friend of ours."

"Speaking of enemies... what happened to the Deathguards?" Frost eyed Gilda, who'd gone over to the pile of belongings to retrieve her clothes and disc-shaped chakrams. A certain warmth rose when he took her in, her sky-blue skin, the shape of her face, her mouth, the curve of her horns.

"We lost them in the storm," Ryne said. "Hopefully, they're dead and gone."

"It does not matter if they met their end." Adesh Hamada shook his head, braided locks as neat as ever. "Nomarchs Botros and Pansa will send more men to hunt us."

"Just means we gotta be ready," Frost said. "Gilda, can I have a sec?"

"Sure." Gilda had put on her white shirt, black-studded jacket, and matching pants. She hung her disc-shaped chakrams from the loops on her belt at either hip.

"You should eat first." Einarr indicated the steaming cauldron. "A man cannot function properly on an angry belly."

"Alright," Frost said. Not that he needed much encouragement. His stomach had already decided.

Soon enough, he, Gilda, and Dante were wolfing down bowls of spicy soup. It was thick and filled with vegetables and bits of meat. And it was utterly delicious.

While on his second helping, Frost asked Gilda to join him outside. He finished up, wiped his mouth with the back of his hand, thanked Einarr again, got dressed in his gambeson and brigandine, and headed for the door with Deadeye in hand. He ducked through the opening.

The air outside the hut was cool, fresh, and damp. Frost found himself among a dozen identical homes built on a ridge overlooking a forest. Dvergr men and women

320

went about their business, not even sparing the two eradae a glance. Children, however, pointed and giggled. A few of them were over in an open space playing with Saba.

Frost tried to get his bearings amid the day's gloom. The sky had thrown on a gray blanket, blotting out the sun, while the nearby mountain had donned a matching cloak and hood. Clouds argued with each other in a display of radiating thunderbolts; their voices cracked and rumbled.

"What's up?" Gilda asked.

Frost twisted the Two Ring twice to the left. A part of him wanted to lash out, to blame her and her people for endangering Mom. Another part of him wanted to touch her. Hold her hand. Kiss her.

He sighed. "I doubt they coulda expected it, but when your people used the EMP to shut down Equitane's systems, it did the same to my mother's medical equipment."

Slack-jawed, she covered her mouth. "I'm so sorry. I'm sure they didn't know." She shook her head vigorously. "They couldn't have." She touched his hand. He found the touch comforting. "You have to believe me."

"I do." He twined his fingers with hers for a moment.

"How is she and the twins?" Gilda asked.

"Sidrie wouldn't tell me. She said I'll find out if I clear the Sanctum."

"That bitch is evil."

"That's too nice a word for her." Frost let out a breath. "You said you had someone on the inside. Think you can contact them to find out how my mother and sister are doing?"

"I could pass word to one of ours who isn't playing in Total Immersion, but that won't be until we're off the island. I have to meet them in person."

Frost sighed. And then had the spark of another

321

idea. "Give me their IGN. I could use the Communication Orb."

She shook her head. "The ring's masking effect doesn't work for messages. The admins would see. And before you mention using some kind of secret message, there isn't any code Estela couldn't crack. It would expose all of us."

Deflated, Frost closed his eyes for a moment. Worry for his family hung like a weight upon his shoulders. There was but one thing left to do. Level up and beat Imanok Sanctum. He turned the aether ring the opposite direction to deactivate.

A ding in Frost's mind announced a message via Communication Orb. A voice recording from Meritus. With a mere thought, Meritus' voice piped into Frost's ear.

"Yo, homie, it's ya boy, Meritus. We got to the sanctuary in Korbash without any issues. The gargants have been very welcoming. You should see the size of some of them over here. The Blue Sky members have also been gracious. Tia is settling in nicely. Blue Sky has a crazy operation over here. Can't wait for you to check it out. Stay safe and kick some ass for me."

Family Trials
To Save a Sister
Objective Complete
Tia's safety acquired:
3000 experience points
Family Trials Passed:
7000 experience points
Gained 500 Khertahka dominion credits
Level 6 gained

Frost smiled. His chest swelled with the sense of accomplishment and relief. "Tia and Meritus made it."

"Awesome," Gilda said.

With that task completed, there came a certain freedom. "Time for me to focus on leveling up."

"I know you like soloing, but it'll be better if you and I group up. Exp will be faster," Gilda said. "Remember, the mobs are elite," she added, even as he opened his mouth to protest.

For all of a moment Frost thought about still denying her. But he knew he'd enjoy her company. With the way Mom's condition weighed on him, Gilda's presence would be a welcome distraction. Not to mention her fighting skills and knowledge of the island. And the fact that she was right about the exp.

"Alright." He envisioned only himself and Gilda in the group and IM made it so.

"We shall all go," Adesh Hamada said.

Startled, Frost turned. He hadn't heard the sorcerer approach. Ryne and Dante stood behind Adesh.

Einarr was off to one side speaking to two dvergar, a woman armed with a sword and a man with a bow. Both of them were dressed in gray-green shirts and wide-legged trousers. Their boots were leather.

"Einarr's warriors will show us to a good hunting area," Adesh Hamada said. "They will also ensure we are not ambushed by the Coalition. When you reach the desired level, we will head to the Sanctum. In exchange, they want our help to solve a problem with some monsters."

Frost frowned. "What problem? What kinda monsters?"

"Korbitoises. They are part of the secret to the dvergar's korbitanium stockpiles. The creatures eat korbitanium, and the metal becomes part of their shells and armor-like skin," Adesh Hamada said. "The dvergar typically harvest them, but of late the korbitoises have bred faster than they can be killed because the tribes have sent off the majority of their casters and marksmen to fight the Coalition. Now, the dvergar are low on metal for weapons and armor."

"So, they want us to kill a bunch of these things?"

"Yes."

"No prob." Frost nodded. The moment Frost agreed, he became aware of a quest line for the korbitoises.

Frost and the others got their backpacks while the dvergar prepared for the mission. Gilda and Saba went about preparing potions and vials with the herbs they'd purchased in Kituan. When the two women finished, they handed some out to their group. They all filled the pouches on their belts with the corresponding consumables and put the remainders in their inventories.

When the dvergar were ready, the two expedition leaders introduced themselves. The green-eyed woman was Dagrun. She wore her hair in a spiked mohawk. The man, Gunarr, had bright red braids and a bushy beard to match. His bow was twice as tall as he. In half an hour they set off, Dagrun and Gunarr leading a company of twenty warriors clad in mismatched bits of armor.

"Saba, Dante," Frost said, as they wove their way single file down a rock-strewn path. "Because of the Sanctum's scaling, we can't afford for either of you to level up, so I'm gonna keep y'all out of the group. Plus, I need as much exp as I can muster."

"Lovely," Dante grumbled. "I get to watch you two have all the fun."

"There's gonna be plenty for you once we're inside," Frost said.

"There better be." Dante scowled in Ryne's direction. "Gnome's been getting all the good action."

"I *knew* you were jealous of me, Big Foot." Ryne grinned mischievously. "Not my fault you don't get a treat. That you aren't light on your feet. I'll let you in on a secret."

Ryne lowered his deep voice. "You need to go on a diet." He made a circular motion in front of his belly to imitate an oversized gut. "And your armor is too shiny."

Frost, Gilda, and Saba chuckled. Dante grumbled something obscene. The banter between the two continued, helping Frost to push the real world to the back of his mind.

They soon descended onto grassy plains surrounded by hills. Dagrun and Gunarr dispatched the dvergar to act as lookouts. When satisfied with lookout positions, the two headed over to Frost and his group.

Dagrun pointed. "There. Up on the slopes. Do you see them?"

Frost squinted. Scores of huge slow-moving four-legged creatures traversed a hillside, skin mottled dark green and gray. Spiked shells formed humps upon their backs. On all fours, they were as tall as an average man.

Some got up on two legs to survey the land, elongated necks stretching out, triangular heads ending in thick pointed black beaks. The korbitoises stood at least eight feet tall then, revealing that the spiked shells also covered their underbellies.

Several plodded over to a cliff-face glinting with metallic deposits. They gouged the formation with their beaks and proceeded to chew. Others entered caves along the slopes.

"Looks like Bowser had babies," Dante said.

Frost smiled at the comparison. He jutted his chin toward the beasts. "Dagrun, those things look pretty tough. How do you kill them?"

"The head and neck are their weaknesses," the woman replied, voice raspy. "Especially the neck. Our sorcerers or archers wait for one to stand, then they shoot it when its neck is stretched. A perfect shot below the chin kills it instantly." She pointed to her jugular notch, the dip where her collarbones met.

"Any other place on the neck means a wound that prevents the creature from withdrawing into its shell, which sends it into a frenzy," she continued. "Our warriors have to get in close to finish them, then. And it usually gets messy."

"You're not killing them with one shot, Frost," Saba said. "Not at your level. Not without a more powerful weapon. This sounds like a job with my name on it."

"Except we can't have you leveling up," Frost reminded her.

"Oh, yeah." Saba sighed.

"Any other options?" Frost asked Gunarr.

"No. Fail to hit the exact spot and the thing pulls into its shell, rolls into a ball, and attacks," the red-bearded man said. "The only way to stop it then is to strike its head while it spins. Some of them also spit chewed korbitanium the size of a fist. Seen it knock a man dead or pierce armor. Some can hurl the spikes on their backs."

Frost could picture the horror. A massive spiked ball of near-impenetrable korbitanium crashing into and rolling over someone. Or those thick bits of metal hurtling through the air to pierce someone's chest. He multiplied the scenario by dozens. "Do they defend or attack as a group?"

"Yes. But only if you make the mistake of attacking one that is too close to another, incurring the hate of the second," Gunarr answered. "Or if you use an Area of Effect ability that hits more than one."

Frost sighed. "No AOEs, then."

Saba was right, although he would never admit that to her. It would take him several shots to finish a korbitoise, particularly since he was forced to use single target attacks. Also, to get proper credit and full exp for the kill, he could not have any of the warriors finish the job. This had to be done by himself and Gilda. He began calculating.

"What're you thinking?" Gilda asked.

"A combo between us. You cast Stalactite or Stalagmite, since both stun for six seconds each."

"Mine stuns for eight seconds," Gilda said. "They have Duration and Tenacity shards."

"Even better." He stroked his chin. "And if I'm understanding IM correctly... Tenacity means damage doesn't break the stun."

She nodded. "You got it right."

"Here's the plan," Frost said. "You cast either stun first. Then follow with Fire or Ice Globes since they're instacasts with no recharge like my Korbitanium Projectile. After you cast the Globes, I'm gonna fire off a Projectile followed by an Aether Shot, both of which have greater velocity than your spells. Timed well, they should strike almost simultaneously. We'll continue with a couple more instacasts.

"Then you stun again, and we repeat. That should do the trick. Nice and simple."

Gilda nodded. "I can also throw in a Flame Column and an Infernal Spear since they're both single target."

"Sounds good," Frost said. "Alright, Dagrun. Let's go."

"Follow us." Dagrun waved Frost on and headed left toward one of the lesser populated hillsides. "We'll show you how we do it."

Soon enough, the group was creeping along the slope, utilizing rocks, shrubs, and sporadic trees for cover. Whenever a korbitoise stood, everyone froze in place as instructed by Gunarr. They set off again when it dropped back onto all fours.

Gunarr and Dagrun had them stop behind a massive tree. A korbitoise was on the trunk's other side less than fifty feet away.

"Watch. Learn," Gunarr said. The short, stocky

dvergr unlimbered his bow. He nocked an arrow and stood with his back to the bole.

Dagrun was on his other side, peeking at the korbitoises. Frost squatted down to make himself roughly the same height as the dvergr and eased his head over until he could see. The korbitoise was busy chewing on korbitanium deposits. It stopped and stood on its hind legs, its neck outstretched.

"Now," Dagrun hissed.

In one smooth movement, Gunarr stepped from behind the tree, aimed, and loosed. An arrow streaked through the air and plunged into the korbitoise's neck several inches up from where the shell ended, a spot where the gray and green merged to form a darker blotch. Green blood spurted into the air. The creature pitched over on its side and rolled end over end down the slope until it settled at the bottom. It did not move again.

"Incredible shot." Frost stood, in awe of the dvergr's prowess.

"Thank you." Gunarr slung the bow over his shoulder.

Frost could think of no way he could improve upon the kill. Or equal it. "Why do you need our help again?"

"Only aether or korbitanium can harm them," Gunarr said. "The five arrows in my quiver are all the korbitanium we have left. The rest was sent with our warriors who fight the Coalition invaders. The casters who remained with us are not strong enough."

"Oh, alright." Frost nodded.

"Your turn," Gunarr said. He and Dagrun stepped back to give Frost and Gilda some space.

Staying low, Frost moved up close to the tree trunk. With Deadeye held across his body, he took a peek. He picked a korbitoise a good distance from any others. "Fifty feet up from where they got the last one. Whenever you're ready."

Time dragged as Frost waited. He kept his sight focused on the dark blotch. The jugular notch.

"Now," Gilda said.

Her Stalactite dropped from the empty air and pierced the back of the korbitoise's neck. The beast froze. A moment later, an Ice Globe streaked through the air.

Frost stepped from behind the tree and squeezed the trigger. As a burst of Korbitanium Projectiles spewed from Deadeye, another Fire Globe shot past him. Frost fired off an Aether Shot.

The result was as he'd envisioned. Gilda's spells and his shots landed almost simultaneously. Frost repeated his attacks as Gilda cast another Ice Globe. A Flame Column burst up from the ground, engulfing the beast. The korbitoise crumpled before Gilda needed to use a Stalactite. Aether swirled into the air, split evenly, and darted into him and Gilda.

"Not a bad kill," Dagrun said. "Took some time, but you did the job. Beware the guardians, though. They are much stronger than the others. Bigger too. And more gray than green."

"Will do." Frost nodded. The kill had netted him three hundred exp. He did some quick math. "A hundred more kills to level. You?" He jutted his chin toward Gilda.

"Another fifty and I'll be twelve. There'll be diminishing exp returns for me once I level up, which works in our favor for the Sanctum."

"Watching you guys makes me want in on the action," Dante said from where he squatted near the tree. Adesh, Saba, and Ryne were close to him.

Frost opened his mouth.

"I know. I know." Dante sighed. "My level. You two

carry on then." He pulled a deck of cards from his pocket. "Saba and I'll play a few games of shevla while we wait."

"No, we won't," the dresdor marksman said. "I saw some rare herbs I can use." She trotted in the opposite direction toward the field.

"What about you, Adesh?" Dante held up the cards toward the sorcerer.

Adesh shook his head of cornrow braids. "I need all my attention for our patron."

"We got this, Adesh," Frost said. "You can relax."

Adesh Hamada bowed. "Even so, I shall remain vigilant in case you need me." He turned back to Dante. "Perhaps later."

"That leaves you and me, Gnome." Dante smiled sheepishly at the goblin. "Care for a game? If you even have a deck, that is."

Ryne cracked his fingers, then grinning madly, he reached into the folds of his robes and came away with a little ornate box. He opened it and carefully removed a deck of shevla cards. "I'll enjoy beating you like the child you are, Big Foot. But we must have a wager."

"Name it."

"I win and you stop calling me Gnome. I'm not one of those cheeky, thieving beasts."

"Some people would say you just described goblins. Not gnomes," Dante said.

Ryne smirked. "I bet those people just waltzed into a goblin's home, as if it were their own. When gobby shows up to defend his territory, he becomes the bad guy in the story."

Dante stroked his chin. "I never thought of it like that. Still, the way you talked about gnomes… whatever happened to respecting the Little People?"

"Rules are different for gnomes," Ryne growled.

Dante chuckled. "Sounds personal."

"It is. Do we have a bet?"

Dante nodded. "You got a bet."

While the two of them settled down to play, Frost turned to Gunarr and Dagrun. "What do your people do with the dead korbitoises?"

Dagrun answered, "When we've cleared enough of an area, the skinners come in to collect the carapaces and skin. Our metalsmiths have a special process to remove the korbitanium from the shells. From the skin, our leatherworkers make some of the strongest light armor. We dry and preserve as much of the meat as we can. What we can't eat, we take up into the Daggerspine and feed to the drakes that live near the peak. We let nothing go to waste."

"Drakes?" Frost repeated. The mere mention of the beasts got him to thinking. "Do your people ride them?"

Aghast, she stared at him. "In the name of Pyrini, no! We worship them. They help keep us safe from the chimera guards that sometimes fly up from the Sanctum."

"Ah," Frost said, disappointed, his hopes of learning to ride drakes abruptly dashed. He gestured to the korbitoises. "We're gonna be here a while, so send the skinners over when you're ready."

"As you wish." Dagrun signaled to Gunarr and the two headed down the hill toward a few waiting dvergar.

Frost hefted Deadeye. "Time to get to leveling."

"No doubt," Gilda said.

They spent the next hour and a half working their combo until it became second nature. He was on his seventieth kill when they found a cannoneer skill shard on a carcass.

Skill Acquired

Staggering Shot
Cast time: Instant

Recharge Time: 10 seconds

Consumes: Aether

Available shard slots: 3

Effect: Fires an Aether Shot which explodes on impact and stag-gers an enemy for 6 seconds. Accurate up to 300 feet. Replenishes 1 percent Aether.

He told Gilda about the ability. "I'll initiate with Staggering Shot from now on, so I can get some practice and experience with it. I'll follow with an Aether Shot. You time your stun so it hits right after my Aether Shot then we continue as normal."

"Gotcha."

They resumed the grind. They were hiding behind some brush when they encountered a new korbitoise, one much bigger than the others, its skin almost completely gray. It also had a short point on the end of its rump like a tail.

"This gotta be one of the guardians Dagrun warned us about." Frost scanned the area to make certain no others were within the vicinity. "Same plan, but add Infernal Spear, and whatever spells that are recharged at the end."

"Got it." Gilda's chakrams glowed.

When the korbitoise guardian stood, Frost began with Staggering Shot followed by Aether Shot. A second lat-er, Gilda stepped around the brush and cast her spells. The timing was impeccable. The abilities blazed a trail through the air and struck true.

Frost gaped. Unlike its predecessors, the korbitoise guardian didn't crumple to the ground. Instead, it strode through the Flame Column like a towering gray giant. Gil-da's Infernal Spear exploded into its chest.

The korbitoise guardian let out a bellow, its eyes fo-cused in their direction. Even as Frost prepared to fire off another Staggering Shot, the creature snapped its head back and then forward, its beak wide open. It spat out something gray, glinting, and the size of a man's head.

Frost made to leap to the side when Gilda's Ice Pillar burst up from the ground ahead of him. The guardian's metal chunk slammed into the thick, circular Ice Pillar. The Pillar disintegrated, and the korbitanium chunk fell among the icy remains.

Frost fired off a Staggering Shot. They worked their combo a second time, but Gilda added a Stalagmite to keep the beast stunned. The korbitoise guardian died to the second Infernal Spear.

"Phew." Frost shook his head. "That was close."

Gilda checked the carcass and came away with a skill shard. "Aether Barrier," she said as she absorbed it. "And I already have the effect that makes it cover one additional person."

"Awesome. Wanna kill another?"

"Only if we're forced to," Gilda said. "Twenty more exp and the chance of a regular skill shard isn't worth the trouble. We need to kill faster to get you leveled. We can always return to farm them later."

"Agreed," Frost said.

They'd practically cleared the entire hill when two new spawns appeared. Frost picked the first of the two and waited. When the korbitoise stood, it did so more cautiously, pausing several times before it reached its full height. Frost fired. His eyes widened as the creature attempted to withdraw its neck. But it wasn't fast enough.

"Did you notice?" Frost asked Gilda after the kill.

"Yeah. They're adapting already."

"Makes me wonder just how much and how quickly the AI functions."

"In my experience, elites and GUMS are the fastest to change," Gilda said. "They're also the most complex. But even they become limited after a while, especially in a case like this where we have the utmost advantage, where we're the predators."

Frost decided to test the next respawn, but there was little difference. They continued on, clearing the second slope. None in that group had changed at all, making Frost conclude that old mobs did not automatically gain new behavior. Only respawns. They stopped to rest when the dvergr quest ended.

Help the Dvergar
Objective Complete
Depleted korbitoise infestation:
1000 points
Objective Complete
Resupplied the Dvergar:
1500 experience points
Gained 250 Ignis dominion credits
Level 7 gained.

Four dvergr skinners showed up to work on the carcasses. They were quick and efficient. Another two dvergar appeared with two carts pulled by unguls, the creatures looking for all the world like donkeys but for the three short tentacles that made up their noses. Frost chuckled at the sight of the dvergar commanding beasts so much larger than themselves.

"Level seven," Frost announced, wiping sweat from his forehead. "Let's keep at it."

"Grats," Gilda said, beaming. "I made twelve a little while ago."

"Thanks. And grats to you, too." Frost returned her smile.

With the stat increases from the new levels, the fights became easier. Normal korbitoises no longer lasted until a second Aether Shot. The guardians died before they could spit their abilities. If Gilda landed a critical hit, she could kill a korbitoise with her globes.

Morning dragged into afternoon with their grind. Frost was seventy-five percent of the way to level eight. He aimed at a guardian. The korbitoise brayed, dropped back to all fours, and rolled into a ball. The other creatures in its immediate vicinity did the same. Some rolled into nearby caves.

A shadow swept across the slope. From the air came a cracked howl, a bleat, a roar, and a great beating of wings. Red and tan streaked down from the sky. Massive webbed wings spread to slow the newcomer's descent.

A chimera landed less than a hundred feet from Frost and Gilda. Its body was a burgundy mass of scales like dried blood and ended in a long, thick, spiked tail. IM named it Azonoth.

The GUM was massive, some hundred feet long from head to tail. It had three heads. Lupine. Dragon. Crevid. In that order. Azonoth threw back its dragon head and roared, filling the air with the miasma of brimstone. It focused on the korbitoises; the lupine head darted forward and snatched a guardian up in its jaws.

CHAPTER 29

"**D**ante! Saba!" Frost yelled.

"Already right here," Dante said from directly behind him.

Saba was beside Dante. As was Ryne and Adesh Hamada. Farther down the slope, a few dvergar had gathered to watch.

"Gilda, did you fight him in the other alphas?" Frost studied Azonoth as the chimera's tail whipped out to impale a korbitoise and hold it in place for the lupine head to savage. The dragon head spewed fire and smoke.

"Once. He's a lot like the old chimeras but stronger than Emperor KiGyaba's twin guards. From the damage he did, we figured he's about level fourteen. He–"

"Level fourteen," Dante interrupted, grinning. "Right where I need it to be."

"As I was saying," Gilda continued, shooting Dante an annoyed look, "he has pretty much the same old abilities but with a Flame Wall and a Wing Blast added."

Frost stroked his chin, thinking back to all he could remember about the old chimeras. "So, the dragon has Hell

Breath, which is a multiplicative DoT; the lupine can Howl, which silences us, preventing any ability use and causes us to run around disoriented for ten seconds; the crevid can Charge and knock back or damn near kill someone in a single blow; and any of the three heads can use Smoke Screen to blind us or summon a Flame Pillar for direct damage. All that to go along with their basic melee attacks, right?"

"Yeah."

"What're the mechanics of Flame Wall and Wing Blast?" Frost asked as he watched the dragon's red maw spew Hell Breath's infernal flames. The korbitoises caught by it immediately unfolded. Liquid fire dripped from them.

"Like Flame Pillar, both can be done by any head," Gilda said. "Flame Wall targets two random people who aren't the highest in aggro and leaves a debuff that triples all damage taken. So, we need to make sure none of us pass Dante in threat. Him getting Flame Wall would be pretty bad."

"Pffft, as if that will ever happen." Dante scowled at her. "You forget who was the best tank in all of Ataxia. Disrespectful."

Gilda shrugged. "Anyway, the two targets will feel their skin get uncomfortably hot. The ground will glow red beneath them. They have three seconds before the Flame Wall springs up between them, shooting from one to the other. If they're not paying attention, they'll leave Flame Walls in the raid."

"What if they run away from each other? Does it stop the wall?"

"No. They have to stay within ten feet of each other. Then run just as the flame touches them. Done right, you might get singed or a little initial burn. As long as there's no damage taken afterward, there's no need to worry about pots or heals unless you really feel like crap, which is a cue that you're hurt badly. The Flame Wall itself stays on the ground until it burns itself out. Also, please call out a direction for your partner to run."

"Sounds manageable," Frost said.

"Would be good if we treat the Pillars the same way," Gilda said. "You'll know they're coming when you feel heat beneath your feet and see a more orangish glow on the ground."

"What about Wing Blast?" Frost asked.

"Azonoth flaps its wings and blows us back. If it knocks a person into a Flame Wall or a Pillar, they take quadruple damage."

"Damn," Saba said, tail swishing. "That means death. I think we should just leave it alone."

"I say we kill it." Dante hefted his axe. "Think of the loot. And getting a World First kill."

"No World First, unfortunately," Gilda said.

Dante sucked his teeth. "Still worth the kill. Both for exp and gear."

"I agree with Dante." Frost nodded. "And this is our best shot to learn what the chimera guards are like before we get to Emperor KiGyaba."

"We could make it easier and have Ryne and Adesh help," Saba argued.

"And diminish our exp?" Frost grimaced. "Nah, I need as much as I can get. Besides, they won't be with us in the Sanctum." He eyed Ryne and Adesh. "You two can keep an eye out, though, in case Azonoth kicks our asses."

"You're the boss." Ryne shrugged but disappointment was etched on his face.

A tingle of excitement ran through Frost. He grinned madly. "Moments like these are why I loved VRMMOs. And now SRMMOs. It's hard to see how real life can top this. We're about to fight a chimera. A fucking chimera."

"No doubt about the love," Gilda said, eyes twinkling, "but I know ways real life can top it."

Frost flushed. He smiled and did his best to fight down the images his mind conjured.

"I'm with you both," Dante said, his skin brightening from crimson to scarlet, a sure sign he'd engaged Frenzy. "Now, let's do this." He took a step forward.

Frost grabbed Dante by the arm. "Wait, fool. We gotta lay out the strat first."

"Oh, yeah." Dante smiled sheepishly. The scarlet bled from him, his chest heaving as the rage subsided.

"Before I turn it over to Gilda." Frost met their intense gazes. "I hate saying this, because we aren't noobs, but I often say it anyway. The most basic rule of a boss fight. Don't stand in shit. Shit kills. So please, don't stand in shit."

"Shit?" Ryne asked. "Monsters poop while you fight them? I never noticed."

Frost gave the goblin a blank look. Ryne's expression was one of genuine confusion and curiosity. Frost was the first to let out a guffaw. The other players joined him.

"Shit," Frost finally managed between wheezes, "is anything that can harm you or the raid." He paused to gather himself. "Like fire, poison… that kinda stuff." He heaved a sigh.

"Oh." Ryne appeared particularly embarrassed.

"Gilda." Frost shook his head, still grinning at Ryne's question. "Go ahead."

Gilda wiped a tear from her eye, straightened her face, and then spoke. "We have to rotate stuns on the dragon, so it doesn't Hell Breath while all the heads are alive. A brief glow at the dragon's mouth is the tell for Breath.

"If the lupine throws back its head to Howl, then whoever is last in the rotation has to stun it. We can't mess that up. Ever. We can survive Hell Breath, but we can't survive Hell Breath *and* Howl at the same time."

"What about diminishing returns on stuns?" Frost asked.

"Diminishing returns have been changed on interrupts like stun and silence," Gilda said. "They start after the first rotation."

Frost's brows bunched. "So, for us four, diminishing returns start after the fourth successful interrupt, but if it was just one of us, they'd start after the first?"

"Yes," Gilda said.

"Is it the same type of diminishing return?" Frost asked. "As in, if we stun again within twenty-five seconds of a stun, the next stun duration is diminished by a second? And if we keep going in the twenty-five second window, then the GUM becomes immune to stuns?"

Gilda nodded.

"For each individual head, right?" Frost asked.

"No. The heads are treated as one monster."

"One monster," Frost repeated, eyes wide. "That can't be right."

"It is," Gilda said. "The good news is we can damage any of the other heads but the stunned one and we won't break the stun."

Frost grimaced. "That sounds nearly impossible. Typically, a chimera like this will Hell Breath or Howl within every twenty seconds. The importance of interrupting Howl cuts down our time even more. Unless we decide to rely on RNG and *hope* he doesn't Howl one of those times, wait the twenty-five seconds, which resets diminishing returns. If we maintain every stun, it means two and a half rotations at best. That's like two minutes to kill a head. And that's with counting your Duration shard."

"Means we have to do insane damage." Dante beamed. "My kind o' work. DPS for the win. Pew! Pew!"

"Don't get so crazy about DPS that you forget your real job," Frost warned. "Whenever that crevid uses Charge, you gotta be ready with Soul Scream to pull aggro back to you."

"Yeah, yeah, mess it up and one of you glass cannons is a dead man. Er, woman." Dante smirked at them. "The reason I love heavy armor and lots of stamina." He slapped his chainmail chest.

Gilda continued, "No attacks during Smoke Screen so we don't mistakenly knock the dragon or lupine out of a stun. Whomever is next up for a stun after Screen, please be quick about it."

"First stun is yours, Dante," Frost said, pushing his doubts to the back of his mind. "Then Gilda, then Saba with Paralysis Shot. I'm last. Gilda, you have the extra stun and effect shards, so you'll double up or be ready for emergency.

"We're gonna risk resetting diminishing returns at the start of the third rotation. We wait it out even if we get Hell Breath. The only way we break that rule is if he tries to Howl during those twenty-five seconds. Go it?"

"Got it," they said.

"Relying on good old RNG." Smirking, Dante shook his head. "You know I hate relying on luck, right?"

"Sometimes, it's better to be lucky than good," Frost said.

"I'd argue that point," Dante said.

"Says the man who often rushes in headfirst without thinking."

Dante grinned. "You got me there."

"As soon as you feel any weakness, pop a health potion first then the rejuvenation about twenty seconds later," Frost continued. "Keep them cycling since we don't have a mystic. Should keep us at maximum fighting ability for long enough." It was the best workaround he could think of for the lack of a mystic and visible Hit Points.

"Don't forget to use sanctification pots as soon as Hell Breath touches you," Gilda said. "Four ticks of the DoT it leaves is death. One tick, if you have Flame Wall."

"Kill order?" Saba asked.

"Lupine, dragon, crevid?" Frost looked to Gilda who nodded her approval.

"Why not the dragon first since he does the most damage?" Saba asked.

"'Cause we can survive a Hell Breath by itself," Frost reminded her. "A missed Howl stun and any combo of Wall, Pillar, Breath, or Charge means someone dies. And that means a wipe."

"We're popping vials, right?" Saba looked on, hope shining in her large round eyes.

Frost shook his head. "Not on a first try. I'd rather save them for the Sanctum."

"So we're going to risk one of us dying on this?" Saba's tail swished violently.

"Preventing that is where Adesh and Ryne comes in," Frost said.

Saba rolled her eyes. "Fine." She muttered something unintelligible under her breath.

"We got everything covered now?" Dante hefted his axe. "Like, can we start?"

"Whenever you're ready." Frost gripped Deadeye tight, his pulse quickening. He could already imagine the fight.

Dante's skin bled from crimson into bright scarlet as he once more engaged Frenzy. His eyes shone with intensity. Rage. With his power and speed increased, he dashed forward into a dead sprint, arms and legs pumping, crescent axe swinging up and down in rhythm. His body blurred as he employed Raging Rush, covering the remainder of the distance in a flash. He leaped high into the air, axe cocked back in the iconic form of Death From Above.

Time slowed. Dante hurtled down, eight-foot frame a pittance against the backdrop of the GUM's scaled body. He buried the axe into the dragon head. Blood fountained. Azonoth let out a cry between a roar and a screech.

The lupine head tried to snatch at Dante, but the marauder had already yanked the axe out and dropped to the ground. Dante went into his next ability, Cyclonic Strike, his body spinning, axe held out before him, the blue glow of aether flowing from its edge. Chop. Chop. Chop. Chop. Each revolution was an impact on Azonoth's chest. Blood flowed.

The dragon roared. Its mouth glowed red.

"Hell Breath incoming," Frost shouted.

Dante's body stopped spinning. He struck with Staggering Blow and stunned the dragon head. He Soul Screamed, the sound tearing the very air, forcing the other two heads to attack him.

"Turn it," Frost said to himself.

Dante complied as if he could hear Frost, stepping a bit to the side to turn the heads away from them. The lupine and crevid snapped at him. The tail whipped out. Dante shifted just in time to dodge the tail but absorbed the damage from the heads.

"He should have good aggro now," Frost said.

"Yeah." Gilda nodded. "All the heads look pretty pissed at him."

"Our turn." Frost opened with Aether Shot then followed with as many Korbitanium Projectiles as he could pump out in the two-second recharge window before he could fire another Aether Shot.

Beside him, Saba nocked and fired arrows. The twang of her bowstring played a tune. A rhythm. A marksman's symphony of deadly accuracy and effortless speed.

Gilda's Ice and Fire Globes lit the air, arcane trails blue and red. Her Infernal Spear followed close behind, dissecting those trails with its length of billowing flames in hellish hues. Even as the attacks exploded into the beast, the dragon's maw glowed. A Stalactite impaled the dragon head.

Azonoth threw back its lupine head to the sky. "I got lupine," Frost yelled. He hit it with Staggering Shot.

Azonoth pawed at the ground. The crevid head shifted to stare at Gilda. Frost swallowed, knowing the deadly Charge was incoming.

Dante Soul Screamed. The crevid snapped its attention back to Dante. But even as he retained aggro with the taunt, Dante bellowed, his body swelling to match his use of Sentinel Shout, which increased his health and defense. A second yell was for Enfeebling Bellow, decreasing Azonoth's power.

A shadowy doppelgänger of a crevid the size of Azonoth charged at Dante. It slammed into the marauder. Dante staggered for but a second, the combination of fortification from Sentinel Shout and weakness from the Enfeebling Bellow serving their purpose.

"My Paralysis Shot was resisted," Saba cried.

Gilda's Stalagmite burst from the ground, signaling the start of the second stun rotation. The dragon head froze.

A tendril of smoke drifted from the crevid's nostrils. Dante Staggered the crevid before it could cast Smoke Screen.

"Shit," Frost said, "you weren't supposed to do that."

Moments later, the ground beneath Gilda glowed like molten rock. She leaped away. A Flame Pillar shot up from the vacated spot, heat waves spilling from it. It lasted three seconds before dissipating, leaving behind a blackened, smoking spot.

And so, the battle went, all of them working in unison as if they'd done so for years. By the start of the third rotation, Dante's armor was torn in several places. Blood leaked from a gash on his leg and one on his shoulder. Undaunted, the marauder continued to chop at Azonoth.

Frost counted down the twenty-five seconds to reset diminishing returns. He wondered how they'd know if they were close to success. Despite the scorched fur and numerous wounds on the lupine head, Frost couldn't tell exactly how effective their attacks had been. Not without Hit Points. Panic stirred in his chest.

He reached fifteen seconds. Spurred on by the chance of success, he fired again and again at the lupine head.

A thrill rose in him at the prospect of the reset.

And then the lupine threw back its head. Gilda's Stalactite stopped the Howl.

"Shit." Frost deflated.

In that moment, Frost noticed the changes. Discoloration in the lupine's flesh, its sluggish attacks, the lack of roars, snarls. Aggression. When the next blow landed, the lupine head flopped to the side.

The dragon head roared.

A sudden heat emanated from Frost's body and beneath his feet. A quick glance down revealed a ruddy glow. Its twin was around Gilda. Frost's heart sped up. "Flame Wall, Gilda! Left!"

They sprinted off to the left. They'd gone perhaps five steps when the Flame Wall ignited between them. Fire raced across the ground, a literal wall of it. They timed the flames and leaped away at the very last moment. Crackling, the wall of fire stayed in place. The debuff rose from Gilda and Frost like a heat haze. They drank rejuvenation and sanctification potions.

They rejoined Saba. The marksman's hands were a blur as she worked her bow, firing arrow after arrow, sweat pouring down her face, brow furrowed in concentration. Grinning at Gilda, Frost added his firepower to Saba's fusillade.

Azonoth's maw glowed red.

"Hell Breath incoming!" Frost shouted the warning, knowing the GUM was now immune to stun.

Dante Soul Screamed the crevid then used a combination of Enfeebling Bellow and Sentinel Shout. He threw his arms up in an X across his chest, the crescent axe jutting above his head. A skill Frost knew to be Crossguard, which boosted the marauder's defense yet again.

And as if Crossguard wasn't enough, a blue glow flashed across Dante's skin. From the empty air stepped a spectral golden-armored warrior. A copy of Deluth's protectors. A Warden. The level ten marauder Overload skill. The Warden mimicked Dante.

"Burn this bastard!" Dante shouted. "I ain't got much left."

Even as Dante yelled the words, Azonoth unleashed Hell Breath. Flames engulfed Dante. The ground underneath Frost's feet grew hot. Steam rose. As did liquid fire. Thousands of tiny red and orange globes of it, popping as they elevated, casting a heat haze upon the air itself.

When the first tick of Hell Breath hit Frost's arm, he almost screamed. It was as if someone had splashed that small area with boiling water.

Teeth gritted, Frost reached down to his belt loop, took out a sanctification pot, flipped the cork with his thumb, and emptied the contents into his mouth. The burning subsided. Frost steadied Deadeye and discharged every skill he had in rapid succession.

The thrum of Saba's bowstring was a distant thing

346

in Frost's mind. Gilda's chakrams were alive with radiance. Spells zipped from them.

Explosions rocked Azonoth. Both heads. Its body. In the midst of the conflagration stood Dante and his Warden, arms crossed in defiance. Azonoth's body shuddered. And then the GUM collapsed.

The group stopped firing. The Warden dispersed. A cheer echoed from the dvergar at the bottom of the slope.

"Hell, yeah!" Dante shouted. He keeled over onto his back.

Frost bolted toward Dante, ignoring any information of exp or quest completion. But Gilda and Saba were there first, Gilda having Flickered, and Saba by way of Streak. They stood over Dante but made no other move. Frost swallowed, praying it wasn't an outcome he feared.

When Frost reached them, Dante was still on his back, blank eyes staring up at the sky. His armor was dented, gashed, and blackened. His skin was scorched, raw, and red. Blood leaked from too many wounds to count along his arms. Bruises and soot marred his face.

"Thought I was dead, didn't you?" Dante grinned. His eyes focused. "You did. Look at your faces. Haaaaa! Got you."

"Not funny," Saba said.

"From down here it sure as hell is."

"You're a damned fool." Frost shook his head but smiled. "You alright?"

Dante nodded and climbed wearily to his feet. "I doubted the doctors and techs about pain in Total Immersion. Hadn't noticed anything worth thinking about 'til now. Damn, some of that hurt. If I wasn't desperate for credits I might not be doing this." He paused then shook his head. "Who am I kidding? This shit is epic. I'd do it for free."

Frost strode over to Azonoth's carcass. The massive

creature stunk of fire and blood. "I think you just did. No loot."

"Now, that," Dante said, "is some bullshit."

"Got exp, though." Frost analyzed his IM. "Loads of it. I leveled off the kill and completing two quests. Saving the Korbitoises. And Making the Dvergar Hunting Ground Safe Again. Anyone else had those two."

The others had cleared the quests. Thankfully, none of them had leveled up.

"Kinda ironic," Gilda said. "We were here wiping out the korbitoises but get a quest completion for saving them."

"I would've still preferred some loot after the beating I took." Dante sighed. "I'll need either a mystic to heal me before I do anything else, or to drink a ton of pots and get some rest."

"Well, Frost," Saba said, "I hope that fight changed your mind about the Sanctum. Facing *two* of those things *and* Emperor KiGyaba is a bit out of our league."

"I think we'll be fine if we take a mystic," Frost said.

Before anyone else voiced an opinion, Adesh Hamada, Ryne, and the dvergar joined them. Frost got a dvergr mystic to work on Dante. The dvergar gathered around Azonoth's corpse, talking amongst themselves.

"We're indebted to you," Gunarr said. "Azonoth and his brothers have terrorized us for a long time. It's good to see one of them fall for all the dvergar they have taken."

"The chimera's scales are special." Dagrun ran her hand lightly down one of Azonoth's legs. "Our smiths can craft rare armor out of it for you. It will take some time, but it will be done. It's the least we can do."

"Thank you." Frost dipped his head. "But it was a team effort. I just played my part. As for the chimera plate armor, give it to him." He nodded to Dante. "He more than earned it."

348

Frost was about to deliver the good news when a distant pall of smoke caught his eye. Billowing black smoke mixed with blue. He frowned.

"What's that?" He pointed.

Both Gunarr and Dagrun hissed. Their reactions gave Frost and ill feeling in the pit of his gut.

"It means the Coalition has attacked our village." Dagrun had eyes only for the smoke.

"Then we should head back," Frost said.

"No." Gunarr pointed. "Listen. Look."

Distant shrieks and screams mingled with the rumble of thunder. High above the smoke, but beneath the gray quilt that radiated with thunderbolts, were over a dozen tiny forms of drakes and zephyrs.

"It is already too late," Gunarr said. "Those who could have escaped would have done so already. We knew this could happen. Come, we make for the Sanctum now before they head this way. And hopefully before the might of the next storm."

CHAPTER 30

Nomarch Setnana Botros strode around the stone slab that was sticky with fresh blood. The naked dvergr chieftain was spread-eagled upon it. Restraints kept his head, arms, legs, and waist in place, yet he tried to buck against them.

Setnana grimaced at the creature. The reasons the gods would create such abominations as the dvergar were beyond her. They were ugly little things. Smelly too. Undeserving of life. No wonder these particular dvergar were relegated to such a godforsaken place, a place formed from the voidstorm responsible for Perihy's sickness, the place keeping her away from her son.

I shouldn't have been the one sent here.

Scowling, she had to remind herself that Maelpith Island possibly held the cure to the Gray Death. That she would salvage much from this trip. Perihy would be beautiful once again. She would slay Adesh Hamada, Drelan Frost, and go on to crush Blue Sky. Here, she would begin the next step in her rise to Kalarch.

Perhaps, it was meant for me to be here after all. She smiled grimly.

"Where are they?" Nomarch Setnana put her index finger beneath the dvergr chieftain's chin and tilted his head up. Defiance lived in his eyes. And fear. She could understand that last. "Tell me and I will set you free. Or you can have their fates." She did not look directly at the people to whom she referred. But she saw them all the same, smelled the fetor of their bodily fluids.

The chieftain's eyes shifted. To either side of him were the flayed bodies of three dvergar. Two men and a woman. Their blood, piss, and shit stained the stone slab, trickled onto the chieftain's side. They still breathed but were unconscious. The pain. The pain had been too much for them to bear.

A little blood magic, so they would not bleed out, and Life Link to one of the other captives cowering on the ground was all Setnana needed to give them a living hell. The lost art of the vampire god, Bodek. The greatest shadowmancer to ever live.

The chieftain's shoulders slumped. A bleak expression crossed his face; his eyes shone with wetness. A solitary tear trickled down his cheek. And then he stiffened. Nostrils flaring, mouth twisted into a hateful rictus, he gazed up at her, his eyes tiny black pebbles.

"Have it your way." She shrugged.

In one motion, she turned her hand, allowing her haladie to drop into her palm. She cast Immobilize then Life Linked to a shackled warrior, directing his vitality into the chieftain. She got to work. Humming a tune, she peeled away his skin with the wavy double-bladed dagger, her hands becoming slick with blood. Soon enough, as with the others, his eyes rolled back in his head.

It took but a moment to realize she had allowed the heat of her emotions to take her. The chieftain was dead. Scowling, she had Ihuet untie the little beastly creature and roll it off the slab.

"Bring me another," Setnana ordered even as she

washed the stickiness from her hands in a bucket filled with water stained a bright crimson.

Ihuet chose from the line of dvergar on their knees before her Battleguards. He grabbed a woman by the arm. A young girl cried out and reached toward the woman.

"No." Nomarch Setnana pointed. "Bring the girl."

Ihuet tossed the woman aside. Khafra snatched the girl by her head. Setnana smiled. It was good to have Khafra back, even with all his scars. Too bad the Vindicator who had healed him could not have gotten rid of them.

"Nooooo," the woman bawled. "Please, spare her. I will tell you what you wish to know."

"Go ahead."

And so she told, detailing where Adesh Hamada, Drelan Frost, and the others had gone to hunt. When the dvergr finished, she regarded Setnana with hopeful eyes.

"Thank you." Setnana turned and strode away. "Bring the girl. Get rid of the others. Make it quick."

Screams and cries chased her. Then the sound of spells. Of horror. Smoke hung thick in the air, a miasma of burnt wood and cooked flesh, rising to join the sky's gloom. For a moment she had considered letting them live, but long ago she learned the value of not leaving potential enemies who could one day return for vengeance, the value of showing no weakness.

When her Battleguards were done, Nomarch Setnana called for the drakes. They took to the skies, meeting with the black clad Deathguards on zephyrs. The Deathguards were Nomarch Demipho Pansa's way of acquiring some measure of justice, saving face after the events in Kituan.

Following the young dvergr girl's directions, they soon found the cluster of foothills rife with korbitoises. Battleguards and Deathguards landed first to make certain no one waited to ambush them from the caves along the slopes. Once the area was secure, Setnana followed Khafra and Ihuet, landing where there were obvious signs of a battle. Charred ground. A massive carcass. Close inspection revealed the corpse to be a skinned chimera.

"Not more than a few hours dead." Ihuet stooped over the carcass, studying it.

"A few hours too much." Setnana scowled. Every time she'd come close, her quarry slipped from her grasp. "Whichever way they went, we must be able to catch up to them. They're on foot."

"Let's hope," Ihuet said. "The locals know this land better than we do."

"Hope is *not* good enough."

"As you say." Ihuet bowed.

Silence stretched as her people searched the foothills. The wind ruffled the grass and carried with it the bloody scent of the dead chimera. She waited atop her drake, impatience growing with every lost moment.

One of her trackers approached. He dipped his head. "Nomarch, they headed east around the hills, toward the mountain." He pointed to slopes shrouded by thick mists that ascended into gray clouds where lightning radiated in a hundred hues.

"There's only one thing that way," Khafra said, voice hollow, his eyes dead things.

"Imanok Sanctum," finished Ihuet.

Setnana frowned, struck by a sudden thought. *Have I gotten so lucky as to already be chasing the very same Blue Sky group Exarch Assam sent me to stop? Supposedly, Blue Sky's best? Or were they simply fleeing? No. They could not know I'm here. When the Deathguards found them, they were already headed in the direction of the Empyrean Sea. They must be the group after the Sanctum's treasures.*

Her eyes widened. "We must stop them. If not from

entering the Sanctum, then from leaving it with anything. I prefer the former. To the air!"

"Wait," Ihuet called.

Clenching the drake's reins tight, Setnana shot the man a scathing look but she complied. "What is it? They have a good head start. I want them caught."

"And they will be," Ihuet said. "But we cannot fly to the Sanctum."

"Why not?"

He nodded to the chimera's carcass. "Them. They guard the skies above the Sanctum and for miles around it. And that is just the beginning. The Sanctum sits in the middle of the voidstorm's remnants. We would be dead before we got close."

"Can we fly off this hill down onto the plains below?" Setnana asked.

"We could, but that risks drawing the chimeras' attention."

She growled under her breath and almost gave the order anyway. Until she considered Perihy. "Have two men wait with the drakes. The rest with us."

"And her?" Khafra nodded toward the dvergr girl.

"What about her?" Setnana strode away. Behind her, the girl screamed.

CHAPTER 31

Frost's group and the dvergar had skirted the Daggerspine Mountain and progressed through a valley toward a lake upon which the Sanctum sat. The day had long since died, its corpse the fathomless black beyond the light cast by their glimmerwands. Pregnant clouds had given birth to a storm. Cold, soaked, and huddled in a hooded cloak that fought a relentless wind, Frost led his group after the dvergar, boots squelching through mud. He wrinkled his nose at a mustiness reminiscent of Kituan's canals.

Howling, the wind whipped raindrops diagonally into a million tiny opaque arrows. Lightning cracked. Again. And again. And again. Within minutes, the sky became a panoply of radiance as if the gods themselves did battle.

He and Gilda had hunted during the trek, and he was now almost level ten. Their group had killed two more chimeras at the valley's entrance. He'd picked up another skill shard.

Piercer
Cast time: 1 second
Recharge Time: 12 seconds
Consumes: Aether
Effect: Fire a piercing Aether Shot through a maximum of three targets in a line. Accurate up to 300 feet. Gain 2 percent aether for

first target with a 2 percent multiplicative effect per additional target.
Each additional target receives less damage but is slowed. Available
during Stand and Deliver when recharge is reduced to 2 seconds.

There was no hunting to be done at the moment.
Anything with half a brain sought shelter. Except for his
group. Even the Coalition's drakes and zephyrs had disappeared from the sky behind them. Their absence did little to
curb his fear of an attack.

"How much farther?" Frost shouted to Dagrun over
the wind and deep growl of thunder.

"We're almost there," she said.

Frost tried his best to see into the depth of darkness
beyond their light, to rely on his echolocation for a hint of
imminent danger. But there was just wind. And rain. A drum
that played havoc with his senses. The musty breath of the
lake hung thick in the air now.

Fifteen minutes trudging through mud and muck
brought them to a small, squat, stone building. Dante held
up his glimmerwand. They stood before a large solitary
opening. Darkness waited inside. From within poured the
musty stench. Earthy. Sulfuric. Frost grimaced.

"Imanok Sanctum is through there." Dagrun point-
ed into the foreboding dark. "This is as far as we go. We will
stay here to buy you time and for a chance to take revenge
on the Coalition when they arrive."

"Thank you," Frost said, "but you've done enough.
You don't need to risk anymore of your people."

"It's what Einarr would have wanted. Also, I watched
your fight with Azonoth and heard you and your dresdor
woman speak after." She gestured to a young dvergr woman
in blue robes whose skin was the color of desert sand. "Take
Sigrid. Although she's only level fifteen, she's the best mystic
we have left."

"Absolutely not." Frost shook his head. "You're

gonna need her here."

"I beg of you. She's my daughter. Her chance of surviving is higher with you than out here when the Coalition invaders arrive." Dagrun reached up and gripped Frost's hand, tearful eyes searching his face. "She can help you. She even has her Servitors."

Frost hung his head. He couldn't deny those pleading eyes, the desperation in her voice. Nor the request of a mother to save a daughter's life. "Only way I agree is if you tell me where you're gonna be after you survive here. Where I can return her to you."

"Praise be to Pyrini." Dagrun looked to the heavens. Beaming, she squeezed Frost's hand. "I am ever indebted to you for this. If any of us survive-"

"Not if. When."

Dagrun smiled. "After the fight here, we will head up into the Daggerspine. We can hide for years within the mountain itself."

"I'm gonna see you in the Daggerspine, then."

"I shall be waiting." Dagrun bowed. Then she strode away in Sigrid's direction.

Frost turned to Adesh and Ryne. "Help the dvergar but don't get yourselves killed. Make sure Dagrun gets to the Daggerspine."

"No problem, boss," Ryne said.

Adesh smiled in the glimmerwand's blue light. "I shall give a good account of myself for Anefet's sake. And for Blue Sky."

"Thank you." Frost looked to Gilda. "Anything we gotta worry about as soon as we enter?" She shook her head. "Good. We're leaving when Sigrid gets here."

Dagrun, Gunarr, and Sigrid hugged each other then stood for a while with their foreheads touching. After Dagrun planted a kiss on Sigrid's forehead, she led the young mystic over to Frost's group.

"This is Sigrid," Dagrun said. "My only daughter."

"Hello, Sigrid," Frost said. "I'm Drelan Frost." He indicated the others, each in turn. "That's Gilda Mordian, Dante Blackblade, and Saba Nerubi."

"Nice to meet all of you." Sigrid's voice was like wind chimes. Her smile was pure innocence.

"Be brave, daughter," Dagrun said. "We shall meet again in the Daggerspine."

Sigrid threw herself in her mother's arms for one last hug. Dagrun looked up at Frost and mouthed, "Take care of my baby." Frost nodded. Mother and daughter lingered in each other's embrace a bit longer before Dagrun finally released Sigrid and made her way back to the other dvergar prepping for battle.

"Let's go," Frost said.

Dante strode toward the opening with his glimmerwand held up. Its light revealed the hint of a hallway. The moment he stepped inside, the hall lit up. Bloomglobes lined walls upon which were numerous murals. The largest depicted Emperor KiGyaba the hydra god, a dozen scaled bodies with snake heads arrayed behind him.

A cobblestoned floor stretched ahead. The group made their way down the hallway, footsteps echoing. At the end, the passage opened into a lighted room. They stood at the edge of a field of emerald grass. Or so Frost thought.

Until the grass moved.

Not the shift of wind, for there was no wind, but an undulating sweep that spoke of water beneath. This was no field. It was a vast pool of algae.

"This is the place? The Sanctum?" Dante's voice echoed.

"Through there." Gilda pointed down.

Frost frowned. "Under the water? We gotta dive?"

The very thought conjured images of drowning. Images he knew too well.

"It looks worse than it is," Gilda said. "We'll be able to walk about two thirds of the way across." She pointed at statues of Emperor KiGyaba to the left and right of the room. "Until we're even with those. Then you dive forward and down and there'll be a large opening. Count twenty seconds and come up. If you try to surface too soon, you're likely to bump your head on the roof and knock yourself unconscious."

Frost stared at the algae-covered water. There were many things he could do. Fight GUMs. Duel players. Climb mountains. Trudge through storms and snow. Dealing with water wasn't one of them. He'd only cleared most of the oceanic content in the previous version of Ataxia after getting a water-breathing spell.

Old nightmares consumed him. Nightmares of the ocean in Barbados, of Hurricane Perol, of an inability to breathe, his fight to get to the water's surface.

Someone shook him. He glanced over. It was Gilda. "You alright?"

"Ye-yeah."

"Then why're you just standing there?"

Frost blinked. He realized then it was only the two of them. "Where're the others?"

"They went already."

"Even Sigrid?" Frost did a double take. He tried to picture the little dvergr diving into the murky depths. And simply couldn't.

"Even Sigrid," Gilda confirmed.

A path through the algae was slowly closing. He thought about making up a different reason for his stalling, his apprehension. But one look at Gilda's face, which closely resembled her real-life features, and he said, "Remember that story about Barbados? About almost drowning? And the one about Hurricane Perol?"

"Oh," she said. "I see."

"Yeah." His shoulders slumped.

"Having lived through Ezra, I can relate," Gilda said. "You remember when we were in Niba I told you the game takes some getting used to? That whatever they're pumping into us, that TNT stuff, can make things more than they are? Emotions and such?"

"Yeah… which kinda makes it worse," Frost said.

"Yes and no."

Frost frowned. "I don't get it."

"Those feelings aren't quite right," Gilda said. "They're turned up several notches, but they don't last that long. The emotion part of Total Immersion relies on the baggage we bring from IRL. It's a mind trick."

Gilda turned her aether ring. "Think about everything you've been through so far. How does Anefet's death compare to how you feel about your accident? About your family? How does it compare to when your father died? To how you feel about your father now?"

Brow furrowed, Frost tilted his head to one side. His real-life experiences were with him every day. Every moment. Depending on circumstance. Even when he didn't want to think about them, they were there. They drove him. Almost every decision he made hinged on them.

On the other hand, most of the emotions in the game hadn't lingered. And when he'd been out of the game for a few hours he gave little thought to the experiences within it.

"She's right," a deep baritone voice said.

A baritone that was all too familiar. A baritone Dre hadn't heard in over six months. For in hearing the voice, he was no longer Frost. Not in that moment. He was Andre

360

Taylor. Dre. Mouth agape, he turned slowly.

A holo of Pops hovered before the hallway. Frost shook his head. *I gotta be dreaming.* He squeezed his eyes tight and opened them again. The holo remained.

It was baldheaded, had a full beard sprinkled with silver, a large nose, and smiling eyes. An unassuming build. It wore Pop's favorite black Body Engineer sweatsuit.

"Son." The holo smiled.

"Pops!" Frost cried. "Pops, is that really you?" He covered his mouth, tears streaming down his face.

"Kinda… sorta."

"How?" Frost paused. His heart leaped with hope. His mind raced. "You're alive. This means you're alive!"

"Actually, son," Pops said, voice somber, "it most likely means that I *am* dead in the real world."

The words crushed Frost. Almost like the first time he heard them.

"But I'm in here," Pops said. "In Void Legion. Or at least an emulation of my brain is."

Grimacing, Frost shook his head, trying to reconcile himself with the statement. "Why didn't you show up before if you've been here all this time?"

Alphonso floated down to Frost and Gilda. His eyes were the same deep brown Frost remembered. He had the same bags under his eyes and smile lines creasing his face. He reached a hand out. Frost did the same. Their fingertips passed through each other.

Frost sighed. "They really killed you." Unbidden tears rolled down his face.

Pops nodded solemnly. "You asked why I didn't make my presence known before. Risk of discovery is the reason.

"I'm here now because the aether rings are linked to this version of me. I can sense when and where one is used, but there are only certain places I can materialize without Equitane's security seeing. I call such places voids in Mikander. Appearing any other place would expose the connection between the anomalies and the rings, and eventually, to me. I can't afford that. Not yet."

"Is there anything you need me to do?" Frost said. "Anything I can help with?"

"Yes. But first, how is the rest of the family, Theresa and the twins. Kai."

Frost told Pops much of what had transpired since Pops' death. At the end, Frost found himself apologizing for driving the Camry, for not being the man Pops wanted him to be, for making the game such a part of his life that he'd ignored so much else.

"It's not your fault, son," Pops said. "It's mine. Are they okay for right now?"

"That's the thing," Frost said, "I'm not sure. Mom and the twins might be worse off now because Just Blaze's people tried to rescue us. Sidrie claims their EMP shut down the TNT facilities. She wouldn't tell me anything else. Just sent me back into the game."

"Damn it." Pops pounded his ethereal fist into his palm. "I should've seen all this coming sooner. I should've seen Sidrie's actions for what they were. Seen the trap.

"But I was so fascinated by the research we were doing, the advances we were making, the credits she had poured into the project. I turned a blind eye to her plots for Equitane to be the top Corp, to destroy the other members of the Seven, the personal army she has at her disposal."

Gilda spoke, "All the more reason for you to lead us to the protocols and the file or give them to us if they're a part of you."

Pops shook his head. "It's not that simple. I knew Sidrie would spare no expense in trying to find out what I did with them. So I hid them in Void Legion."

"And?" Gilda tilted her head to one side.

"Each protocol is linked to one of the main bosses," the holo said. "Killing them while wearing one of my aether rings exposes the code. An additional step in a secret room within each boss area allows the ring to absorb the code and transfer it to the player's brain by way of TNT. Emperor KiGyaba is the first of those bosses."

Frost frowned. "You certain Sidrie doesn't know?"

"Positive. Why?"

"She specifically asked me to clear the Sanctum. Kinda suspicious in light of what you just said."

"She doesn't know for sure, but she's as practical as she is ruthless," Pops said. "She's covering every possibility. Everything's about numbers for her. Most likely she's also testing you to gauge if keeping you and the family alive is worth the expense."

"Then I can't afford to fail," Frost said.

"You can't," Pops agreed.

"Something always bugged me," Frost said. "What happened the night you... the night you died."

A wistful look crossed the holo's ethereal face. "When I discovered that Equitane's security was on to me, I knew it was only a matter of time before they tried to grab my research and my collection of data. But acquiring it wouldn't be enough for Sidrie. She was already taking out anyone with intricate knowledge of Total Immersion. She would have me killed to shut me up or to stop me from passing off the protocols and the file to Just Blaze's people. There was also the chance I might give it to the other Corps in the Seven to even the playing field.

"I remembered your ring and stayed late that night to create a set of them in game that would respond to others with data coded into them in the real word. All it would take was to connect them by way of TNT. You nor Gilda didn't happen upon your particular quest lines by chance. I designed those to be activated once both your DNAs were discovered together in game.

"But myself, Uncle Hank Kim, and three other engineers had made a discovery when studying and experimenting with TNT and Whole Brain Emulation. Memories and persona were stored within the nanites. We had a theory on how to upload that data, technically that consciousness, into the game, perhaps into a character to make it functional.

"We never got a chance to test it. Equitane sent their men to grab me. I took a car I'd pulled off the Grid and tried to make it home. They caught me on the highway. In desperation, I connected to Void Legion and uploaded my data. And a version of my consciousness. The car crash, pain, and the world going black is the last thing I remember."

Frost rubbed his aether ring. "I understand wanting to be the top Corp and the things Sidrie's willing to do to make that happen. What I don't get is why the game's so important in all this. She claimed it's the future of mankind, but it's just a damned game."

"Actually, it's more than a game," Pops said. "And its capabilities *are* the future. Because of me and your Uncle Kim. Because of the work we did interfacing TNT, AI, and Hank's work on brain emulation."

Frost frowned. "I don't understand."

"TNT itself isn't new," Pops said. "But the breakthroughs in combining those three things are. And it began with you, son."

"With me?"

"Yes." Pops stared at him, eyes intense. "All those years I made you play VR games and simulators, then Uncle Kim and I would test your retention afterward. To see what you actually learned. Part of your retention was due to our work. Especially your uncle's experiments with brain emulation and TNT. The easiest way to describe what Hank achieved would be to compare it to procedural memory. Muscle memory. Years of daily repetition like a bodybuilder.

"But it wasn't just the knowledge you gained. There's also the physical gifts. Strength. Speed. Skills. Things that would take a body, a mind, years to harness in real life could be achieved in a fraction of the time in VR linked to our TNT system. We lacked two things to perfect it. Financing and a working Simulated Reality engine."

Frost opened and closed his mouth. He'd jokingly asked Dr. Redmond about such a possibility, not knowing it was all too real.

"Total Immersion," Gilda whispered.

Pops looked to her. "It's why you've remained in such good shape despite not working out as much in real life."

Frost shook his head. So much made sense now. Technically speaking, he was the first gameborn.

His mind ran rampant with the ideas of how such technology could be implemented. In a person like Sidrie's hands, who craved power, not much of it was good. More than ever, he was intent on stopping her.

"The chance Sidrie would discover that you were among the first that I used a stable version of our tech on was why I made you stop playing the game," Pops said. "I was also afraid she would use you as one of her testers. I needed time to program the necessary precautions."

From outside came the clash of steel. Men shouted. Spellcasts echoed, their explosive impacts resounding down the hall.

"You have to go," Pops said. "Kill Emperor KiGy-aba. His treasure room will open. There, you'll find a Void Gate room where you can complete the first protocol. Gilda, you have a minute to deactivate your ring."

Back at the entrance, a line of dvergar flung spells at an unseen opponent, lighting up the night. Frost returned his attention to the water. The old nightmares came to haunt him tenfold. He glanced down at a tentative touch. It was Gilda. She was staring up into his face.

"You can do this." She twined her fingers into his, reached up on her tip toes, and kissed him.

He let himself melt into her kiss, into those lips, the feel of them. The feel of her. Her smell. Taste. She caressed one of his horns, sending a shudder of need through him, a barely restrained excitement. But his arousal stopped short of the hunger, the primal need from in Equitane Towers, the real-life breathless euphoria that made him giddy.

Gently, he pulled away. Looking down at her, he smiled as realization dawned.

For all the amazement and advantages of SR, how it allowed him to live in a dream world, it couldn't match reality's raw feelings. Yet, SR had its place, allowing him to do things he couldn't achieve in life.

But there was something missing. Something different. Something he couldn't explain. It was one of those things that simply... was. He understood now that SR and reality needed each other.

He looked to the holo that was his father. There was so much he wanted to say. He warred with himself, with the feeling that he wouldn't see Pops again, speak to him. Tell him how much he missed him. "I-"

Pops disappeared.

Frost squeezed his eyes shut. A tear trickled down his cheeks. He missed the old man already. And he was at once angry and yet saddened by his absence. The emotions fought within him. When he opened his eyes, he stared at the algae-covered water and focused on the game.

Epic players do epic things.

Still holding Gilda's hand, he leaped into the algae, pulling her with him. The water was cold and stink, the algae clinging around him as he waded forward. When he and Gilda got even with the statues, Frost stopped.

He looked down into her eyes and smiled. "See you on the other side."

She returned his smile. "No doubt."

Frost let go of her hand and dived. At first, the cloud green water felt as if it sucked at him. His aether cannon dragged behind, threatened to pull him down. He started to fight it. To fight the idea of drowning, the weight on his chest, the need to open his mouth to try to suck in air, the need to try kick to the surface, which seemed so far away, a dull glow above, darkness waiting beneath. He wanted so badly to flail. Blood roared in his ears.

It's all in your mind. Just kick your legs. Sweep your arms. Kick. Sweep.

He gave the idea life. Repeating the words became a soothing mantra. The aether cannon became an extension of himself as if it had always been. His mind relaxed, the water a comfort rather than a hindrance, an old acquaintance, the safety of Mom's womb.

IM clicked. Exp gained for a Reunion quest. Two hundred KDC and IDC. *Did Pops do that?* He dismissed the thought. It didn't matter. He was finally level ten. And a skill he looked forward to was now available.

Stand and Deliver
Requires Aether Overload activation
Cast time: 3 seconds
Recharge Time: 3 minutes
Consumes: Aether Overload
Available Shards: 2

367

Effect: Fires Aether Shots and Korbitanium Projectiles in a quickly increasing progression. Standing in position for 6 seconds brings cyclic rate to 100 revolutions per second. Slows enemies after 6 seconds. Moving cancels skill. Reduces recharge time for Piercer to 2 seconds for duration. 50 percent chance to eliminate recharge for Divergence, Aether Bomb, and Aether Fusillade. Continues firing until Aether Overload expires.

One part of the goal given to him by Sidrie was complete. Yet, he felt no joy. No fulfillment. He doubted he would until his family's well-being was assured.

Knowing at least thirty seconds had passed, he swam up and broke the surface of the water. He was greeted by Dante and Sigrid near the pool's edge, hiding behind one of several huge pillars at the start of a flagstoned path lit by bloomglobes along an adjacent wall. There was no sign of Saba. Sigrid's desert sand complexion was paler still. Sweat trickled down her brow. Dante wore a smile. Frost followed their gazes.

Less than two dozen feet ahead was a patrolling pack of ten gigantic scaled void wolves. The voidstorm's power leaked from their bodies in dark and light tendrils. On occasion, the beasts stood on two feet like men, snouts to the air as they sniffed.

Frost's breath caught at what waited behind them. At the start of a roofed colonnade was a man the size of a gurash. He wielded a mist sword to match his height, its namesake power coiled around the blade. His scaled metallic skin was the infection of gray, deep green, and electric blue possessed by draconid grunts.

CHAPTER 32

Sitting at her desk, Sidrie took a sip of sparkling water as she answered her comms. Senator Kirkland popped into her HUD. "Tell me we have the votes."

"We-we have the votes." Senator Kirkland dabbed at his sweaty forehead with a handkerchief.

His nervous demeanor said there was something more. Sidrie waited.

"To send the SDF supported by NAIL into the First Ward," he continued, "to capture or kill the DeGens responsible for the attacks."

"And the rest?" Sidrie arched a solitary brow. "The cartels' involvement?"

"Any action against the South American Conglomerate—um, I mean the cartels, have been shot down. I-I'm sorry." He licked his lips, the fear of delivering the report alive in his round eyes. "Neither Senator Constantine's murder nor the discovery of the cartel guns could convince those against. They require more proof. Proof the guns were supplied directly by the cartels and not bought off the black market. They weren't willing to take the words of some DeGens under interrogation."

"Then we can only hope NAIL and the SDF discover the proof during the assault in the First Ward," Sidrie said. "Send me a list of all those who voted against. If they are any you feel were close to seeing things our way, then offer them whatever they need for the next time."

"Yes, Miss Malikah. Right away." He dipped his head.

Sidrie severed the connection. She needed to see exactly which dissenters voted solely due to their affiliation with the other major corporations. Equitane's so-called competition. With Constantine out of the way, there were but six other competing AI and bioengineers or developers who could harness Estela and TNT if they got their hands on the protocols and the associated file. Five were members of the Seven. The last was an independent. She would make certain none of them had the chance.

She wondered if any of the opposing senators had connections to the cartels. It would not be the first time for that sort of corruption. The army, and the dead zone that was once Central America, had stymied the flow of drugs, but there were still billions of credits being made here and elsewhere in the world. The cartels were paying handsomely in an attempt to regain their chokehold on North American soil.

Although disappointed in the Senate's overall decision, she still had a first step. Assaulting and subsequently controlling the First Ward would provide her with an endless supply of test subjects for her newest gameborn. And she would secure a measure of vengeance against the DeGens. She smiled at that last. It was a beginning.

"I take it the Senate wussed out when it came to the SAC?" Keenan looked up from the tactical holo he'd been studying.

"Cartels," Sidrie corrected him with a scowl. "Drug cartels. Purely criminal enterprises. The worst kind."

"Pardon me, ma'am." The coffee-skinned man dipped his head, but his gunmetal eyes did not waver.

"It was as we expected," she said. "Which means you will turn over every stone for more evidence during the raid. And won't leave the First Ward until you produce some. And of course, you will discover where those ungrateful ex-employees of mine are hiding down there and get rid of them."

"Yes, ma'am."

"Good. Now, your theory on the assaults?"

"We have a spy."

"Explain." She had her suspicions, but knowing he had come to a similar conclusion said she was on the right path.

He pointed a thick finger at his tactical holo. Red, blue, and green dots and crosses marked positions from the assault. "There's no way whoever is leading the DeGens just happened to attack on the same night we planned to frame them for Constantine and the silos. Or that they happened to find the pod room. Someone told them. They added their assaults as a diversion for the authorities in order to get to you."

"It almost worked." Sidrie grunted. She respected the effort. "We will have to set up a decoy at some point. Until then, do what you can to discover who it might be." It troubled her that someone could get so close, but she kept her poise.

"Yes, ma'am," Keenan said. "But what troubles me more is that it all speaks to a level of organization we overlooked or discounted."

"Or maybe doesn't exist," Sidrie said. "Now, you're giving the DeGens too much credit. They were lucky. Find the spy, and we will be rid of the threat."

"Yes, ma'am." Keenan nodded toward his holo, which had changed to the Apex Solutions skyrise. "Which gameborn do you want me to send out on this one since C9040 died during the Sunrise assault?"

"D600," she said.

The gameborn in question would have been a Mid Warder. His pregnant mother had surrendered him to the FPC when her family couldn't afford to pay the cost for an additional child under Better Tomorrow.

"I'll have the techs get on it," Keenan said. "If there's nothing else, I'll go prep. With your leave, of course."

"You may go." She dismissed him with a wave.

"Ma'am." He stood and strode from the office.

A communication from Zhi Yin beeped in her aurals and flashed across her optics. "Yes, Zhi, what is it?"

Zhi Yin's pasty face popped onto the HUD. "There's been a dozen new anomalies, Miss Malikah," she said, voice breathless with excitement. "I was able to pinpoint two that spawned close together. Both not long ago. The only reason they stood out was their location at the time I was inputting a new tracking algorithm."

Finally, a mistake. And a bit of luck. "Where?"

"Maelpith Island."

Sidrie sent out a comm to Dr. Redmond. He appeared beside Zhi Yin seconds later. "Doctor, I need to get in the game."

"Now?" he asked.

"Yesterday. We have a good lead on the anomalies and possibly the hackers."

Dr. Redmond shook his head. "It'll take at least thirty minutes to prep you, Miss Malikah."

She scowled. "That's not good enough."

"It's the best we can do with the limitations Alphonso set."

Sidrie snarled. She wanted to order the man to do better but also knew it would be a futile demand. Inserting herself into Total Immersion without adequate preparation might be at the expense of her sanity. "Fine. Zhi, send in two

GameMasters to the locations and link me to their feeds."

A few minutes passed with Sidrie tapping her foot impatiently. Her pulse quickened at the thought of catching the hackers. Or better yet, if the anomalies were as Zhi said, a part of Alphonso's code, then they were a lead to unearthing the protocols. At worst, she hoped for better insight into the reason for the disturbances and how they functioned.

"Miss Malikah, are you ready? I'm sending the link," Zhi said.

"I am."

The link appeared in the HUD. Sidrie connected. She saw through the eyes of the GMs in a spilt screen as if she were in both places.

The first GM was standing among the ruins of a village. Dvergr corpses littered the ground. Several baby drakes were tearing at the bodies. One of them cocked its head to regard the GM before continuing to feed.

"Get me a record of who was here and who did this," Sidrie ordered.

The record popped up in another minute. She perused the list. Dozens of players had passed through the area earlier. But one set of names in a group stood out. Drelan Frost, Gilda Mordian, Saba Nerubi, and Dante Blackblade. Chasing them was Setnana Botros. It was she and her Battleguards who had decimated the village.

"Show me the minutes leading up to the anomaly at the village."

The video changed. Battleguards were slaughtering dvergar. Women and children tried to flee but were cut down. Setnana Botros was speaking to a dvergr who was spread-eagled on a stone slab, his arms, body, and legs bound. The Nomarch leaned over the man's chest and made an incision with her haladie–a shadowmancer's small double-bladed dagger–and proceeded to skin him. Her eyes were dead

373

things as she worked, humming to herself the entire time.

Sidrie's lips parted. She had eyes only for Setnana and the exquisite work the gameborn was performing. The Nomarch was an artist in a trance, drawing a masterpiece, bringing life to canvas. Setnana's breath caught.

"Dr. Redmond, Setnana is D1030, correct?" Sidrie whispered. "Developed from one of the FPC's Mid Ward babies? One of the first we had with her pedigree?"

"Yes."

She had not needed to ask. She knew all there was to know about the best gameborn. "She is perfect. When her task is done in game, prep her for some time out of it. We must acquaint her to this world."

"Yes, Miss Malikah," Dr. Redmond said.

"The anomaly, Miss Malikah," Zhi Yin reminded Sidrie.

Sidrie shook herself and tore her gaze away from Setnana. "Yes." She cleared her throat. "Yes." Squinting, she analyzed everything in the immediate vicinity but saw nothing abnormal. She frowned. "Everything and everyone is as they should be. I don't understand."

Dismissing the first feed, Sidrie focused on the second GM. She was inside the entrance to Imanok Sanctum, standing before a vast pool covered in algae. From outside came the sounds of a dying battle.

"Here?" Sidrie asked. "The other anomaly was right here?"

"Yes," Zhi Yin said.

"Show me a recording of just before and during the time of the anomaly. Add a timer to the moment it spawned. Tell me the exact second it did."

Another video feed appeared in her HUD. A clock counted down the minutes. Frost and his group approached the pool.

Two minutes.

Frost stood at the pool's edge, staring off at nothing. Saba, Dante, and a dvergr girl waded into the pool and then dived.

One minute.

Frost was still standing there in a trance until Gilda shook him.

Thirty seconds. Sidrie narrowed her eyes, her pulse quickening as she waited for an answer to a nagging problem.

Frost told Gilda something about Barbados and Hurricane Perol. Gilda mentioned the way TNT worked.

Ten seconds. Sidrie leaned forward.

Abruptly, the screen turned to a muddled bunch of waves, the voices to unrecognizable sounds.

"No. Damn it. No. What happened? Get the feed back."

"That *is* the feed," Zhi Yin said. "There was some sort of interference that scrambled the video."

"Can't we unscramble it?"

"I can try, but it'll take time. You should also know that there was a short set of code."

"Estela," Sidrie said.

"Yes, ma'am?"

"The code in question." Sidrie had a hunch. "Compare its signature to the tiny bit we pulled when Alphonso uploaded into Ataxia before his accident."

A moment of silence followed.

"It is a match."

"As I thought." Sidrie let out a heavy sigh. *You thwart me at every turn, even in your absence,* she thought. She could picture Alphonso smiling at her frustration. *But I have a lead now. And I will beat you yet.*

The feed cleared. Holding hands, Frost and Gilda

waded into the water and dived.

Sidrie turned at the sound of voices and marching feet echoing down the hallway. Nomarch Setnana Botros and her Battleguards entered Imanok Sanctum. Sidrie smiled. She anticipated the clash between the gameborn and the testers.

CHAPTER 33

Frost made to warn Gilda as she surfaced beside him. But she was already looking at the void wolves and the draconid. Keeping an eye on the pack, he waded through algae toward the pool's edge, careful not to make any sudden movement or splash. He and Gilda eased from the water and crept over beside Dante and Sigrid.

"Where's Saba?" Frost said, voice low. He peeked around the corner. The void wolves stalked back toward their master.

"Concealed in the space between this pillar and the next." Dante jutted his chin toward the area in question. "Arrow nocked and ready in case the pack got wind of you when you surfaced."

"Good thinking," Frost said.

"Didn't expect to see draconids here," Dante said. "Saba wasn't too happy about them."

Frost chuckled. "Saba's never happy about anything dangerous. Gilda, were they here last time?"

"Not when I ran it. But I've heard about the possibility."

"Alright." Frost took another quick peek then pulled back. "I got a feeling the dvergar won't be able to hold off

Setnana and her Battleguards much longer, so we gotta make this quick. I wanna be at least a few rooms ahead of her so they gotta fight off respawns. Saba, you can hear me, right?"

"Yes," she answered in little more than a whisper.

"Pull the lead wolf and run all the way to that wall." He pointed to the far right. "Dante, Raging Rush to intercept the grunt without engaging the wolves. Off-tank him while we handle the pack, then we'll finish him off."

"Got it," Dante said.

"Sigrid, once Dante goes, you're gonna take up a spot between him and us where you can focus on healing him but still be able throw us a heal or two if we need it."

"Yes, sir." She put on a brave voice and a serious face but her hands shook. She already had the blue nebulous motes of the Heal over Time spell, Mikander's Tears, hovering above her left hand. Above the right were the red motes of Mikander's Blood, a direct heal that granted a set amount of health in one shot.

"You'll do fine." Frost reached down and squeezed her shoulder. "You won't ever be in harm's way. I believe in you."

Sigrid's face brightened. She stood a bit straighter. "Thank you."

"Give us a countdown, Saba," Frost said.

The void wolves reached the top of their patrol, turned, and headed back down to the draconid.

"Three," came Saba's soft voice. "Two. One."

An Aether Arrow's pale blue glow streaked from the seemingly empty air of Saba's position. It flew across the distance toward the trailing wolf that was standing on its hind legs, sniffing the air. The arrow exploded into the back of the animal's head, leaving a burst of arcane sparks.

The beast yowled, staggered for a moment, and then spun. Its packmates also turned, fangs bared. The void wolves paused for all of a second before they threw their heads back, howled, then bounded down the flagstoned walkway toward Saba who had done away with her Concealment and was sprinting to the far wall.

Behind the pack, the draconid grunt roared a challenge with his arms spread wide. He took off after the wolves, long strides eating up the distance between the pillars, humongous mist sword in one hand as if it weighed nothing. His footsteps reverberated off the flagstones.

The moment the last void wolf passed the hiding spot, Dante stepped around the pillar, skin flaring from crimson to scarlet. He Raging Rushed toward the draconid, becoming an eight-foot red blur swinging a crescent axe.

Frost didn't wait to see the giants collide. "Get in position, Sigrid," he said as he strode in the opposite direction from Dante and the dvergr, focused on the void wolves.

The wolves were moments away from pouncing on Saba when white lightning surged around them. Ensnared and hurt by the marksman's Lightning Trap, they yowled and whimpered, trying for all they were worth to reach their prey but only able to move a few inches at a time.

Bracing himself for recoil, Frost opened fire with Divergence's five Aether Shot spread and followed with Aether Bomb and Concussion Blast. Even as the shots hit their targets, the Aether Bomb exploded among the wolves with a whomp. Covered in flames, they yowled and yipped, trying to run this way and that but unable to do so because of the Lightning Trap. Concussion Blast impacted a second later. A hollow boom. The ability staggered a bunch of wolves and knocked them into the air.

Beside him, Gilda was casting, her chakrams alive with blue and red luminance. Ice and Flame Globes shot forth, following their intended targets whether on the ground or still suspended from the Blast. In moments, the

379

pack was nothing more than a bunch of carcasses leaking dark and light tendrils. Aether drifted into the air, swirling, before zipping into Frost and the others.

Frost ignored the IM concerning exp gain and the building of Aether Overload as he and the others turned their attention to Dante and the draconid. The gurash wore a smile and appeared to be thoroughly enjoying the duel. The two circled each other, attacking and countering.

Sigrid flicked her hand out, sending a blue mote of Mikander's Tears into Dante. Mist rose from him when it landed. The HoT spell would rejuvenate his health periodically, ticking every few seconds.

Frost was tempted to allow Dante to solo the elite monster. The thought lingered for but a moment. Time was against them. Setnana and her Battleguards would have finished off the dvergar by now. Frost waited for Dante to turn the draconid until its back was to the group before he started his attack. The others followed suit. Between the five of them, they made short work of the creature.

"A ruined mist sword." Dante held up the only loot available from the corpse.

"You know what they say," Frost said, "a ruined hierka is better than no hierka."

Dante shrugged. "Maybe. But I got a thing for my axe. I'll keep the sword to sell on the Market." The mist sword disappeared into his inventory.

"I'll go skin those void wolves," Saba said. "I know a leathersmith who could craft me some rare armor."

"No time," Frost said. "We gotta get to the next room."

Even as he said the words, he checked the pool. An erada man's head broke the algae's surface. The man's eyes widened as he took them in. A moment later his hand rose, a glowing blue chakram in it. Before Frost could open fire

380

or shout, an arrow blossomed in the man's eye. He sunk beneath the algae.

"Nice shot," Dante said to Saba.

"Damn it," Frost growled. "Even if we clear the next room, they'll be here before this one respawns." He tried to think of a way to stall the Battleguards.

"I have an idea," Saba said.

"If it involves running away, there's only two ways to go." Frost pointed. "Deeper in or back the way we came."

"No running away this time."

"Really? No running?" Frost looked at her askance.

"I didn't say no running. I said no running *away*."

Frost blew out an exasperated breath. "Alright, let's hear it."

She pointed toward the roofed colonnade. "There's a niche in the wall on the other side of those pillars. Hide there. Let Setnana and her Battleguards come in."

"We can't fight them here," Frost protested. "Not if we wanna win."

"Who said anything about fighting?"

"Then what—"

"I'm going full Leeroy Jenkins in the next three or four rooms, running back here into Setnana's group, and then whoosh... Concealment."

"You're mad," Dante said. "And I like it." He grinned, showing his canines.

Frost wanted to tell her no, that they would clear the way as fast as they could then pick a better place to fight. But he knew the odds were against them. Saba's method would help with that. *If* she succeeded.

"What do you think?" Frost asked Gilda.

She shrugged. "I like."

"Alright, let's do it."

They headed to the roofed colonnade. From the

walkway they had a good view into the next room. Where the colonnade's pillars ended, there was another draconid grunt, two void wolf packs, and six nalarr. If a god had stripped the fur from a sabretooth tiger, made it stand on two legs, and carry a great axe, then he would have made the nalarr. Their red, white, or blue bodies rippled with muscle.

Dante whistled. "You said three or four rooms, right?"

"Yep." Saba was staring ahead, her face a grim mask.

"Either this is going to be epic," Dante said, shaking his head, "or you're going to be very dead. Go big or go home, I guess."

They continued to the wall and followed it to where it appeared to end in six joined pillars. But the wall formed a corner at the first pillar, continued on for about eight feet, then made another corner extending *behind* the six pillars and out over the pool. Saba's niche was the space between the pillars and the wall. They squeezed into that space.

"Don't peek out," Saba instructed. "No matter how tempting. No matter what you hear. You don't want the Battleguards or the mobs seeing you beforehand. I'll shout go right before I use Concealment."

"Yelling go is lame," Dante chided. "It ain't a Leeroy without the Leeeerrrroooyyy."

"You got it." Saba grinned. And then she was gone.

Silence followed. The quiet stretched like yards of linen wrapped tight around the mummified remains of sound. A rag stuffed into a mouth. Stifling. Within that quiet lived disquiet, their every breath loud to Frost's ears, his heartbeat a thunderous monotone, the stink of their bodies and sweatiness as boisterous as any noise. The silence spanned an eternity.

And then, a splash. A voice. Several voices. Many more splashes. The telltale sound of swimming. A deep male baritone shouted orders. Footsteps reverberated in a pattern that spoke of formations.

A chorus of howls and roars echoed from deeper within the Sanctum. Faint at first. But they grew. The howls drew closer and closer. Louder. Frost's blood curdled as he imagined the number of void wolves and nalarr needed for such a ruckus, the number of beasts chasing Saba.

Setnana and her people in the room must have heard the monsters because the baritone shouted for quiet. The howls and roars were clear now. As were the bellows and screeches of something or some *things* much bigger. Far more dangerous.

Orders for men to form up came in a flurry. Booted footsteps hurried to comply. Armor and weapons jangled.

The howls and roars echoed from the room before the colonnade. Frost felt the beasts through the floor, a re-sounding dissonance for which it was impossible to attribute an exact number. There could be dozens of elite mobs. The thought dried his mouth. And yet he wanted to laugh. A smile formed despite his racing heartbeat.

"This is going to be epic," Dante whispered, mirth in his voice.

"They won't know what hit 'em," Gilda added.

Seconds later, the enormous lure was galloping down the roofed colonnade. Their footsteps were thunder, joined by the raucous dissonance of their screeches, roars, howls, yips, and snarls. Frost felt the malevolence rolling from them, the violence, the need to rip and tear. Slaughter. He prayed that the waiting Battleguards did not open fire with their spells and aether cannons the moment they saw something, anything, between the pillars. That first thing would be Saba.

"LEEEROYYY JENNKINNNS!" Saba yelled above the tumult. Her scream was followed by the unleashing of spells and cannon fire.

Frost eased forward and peeked around the pillar. The room was chaos. Void wolves, draconid grunts, nalarr, and much larger draconid overseers with storm lances made up the brunt of the mobs. Towering above them was a hulking void revenant, its appearance that of a raven, its wings draped about it in a great tattered cloak, its face a skull of pure white bone, even its beak.

From within the void revenant's skull glowed four red eyes. Two dark horns protruded from either side of the skull, curling forward then up and back. Dark tendrils of void energy pulsed between the horns. The void revenant's wings spread to reveal a humanoid body. In one clawed hand it held a massive war maul. The creature beat those wings once, blowing back several warriors. It charged after them.

In the midst of the Battleguards and Deathguards was a beautiful erada woman in red robes. Not one woman. Six of them. Mimics. They cast Shadow Globe after Shadow Globe, quickly followed by Nether Lances which left black trails in their wake. Shadow Flame burst from several mobs.

Frost's gaze met hers. In those eyes and writ large upon that face was an air of command. Arrogance. She could be none other than Nomarch Setnana Botros.

Her face contorted into a rage-filled mask at the sight of him. She pointed her haladie in his direction. Shadowy tendrils of aether congealed around her hand and the double-bladed dagger.

"Run." Frost bounded from their hiding place out beneath the colonnade.

And barely managed to dodge an empowered Nether Lance, the bar of black aether and energy as large and long as a man. The alcove exploded. Stone and debris peppered Frost and his friends. Gilda threw up a blue Aether Barrier, saving them from the worst of it.

They sprinted between the pillars hellbent on reaching the now empty room. Frost snatched a look behind him. Several Blackguards had extricated themselves from the battle to give chase.

CHAPTER 34

Frost, Gilda, Dante, and Sigrid raced between the pillars at the start of the empty room. Saba waited up ahead, grinning madly beneath the light of several bloomglobes, proud of her contribution.

"Go! Go!" Desperate, Frost waved his hand toward her. "Take us through the rooms you cleared." He jerked a thumb to indicate their rear. "We got about six Blackguards coming."

"Six? On top of the eight or nine other enemies I counted? What the hell?" Saba unlimbered her bow. "Isn't that a full raid group?"

"Sure is," Frost said.

He had barely uttered the words when Saba brought her bow up and loosed. She followed up the quick successive shots of Triple Barrage with an Aether Arrow. Frost stopped and turned to see the Battleguards running down the colonnade. He made to launch Concussion Blast in their direction when he had an idea.

"Everyone, target the colonnade's roof and pillars with your most explosive spells. We gotta collapse it. Also, hit the Battleguards with anything that slows or stuns."

Frost unloaded with most of his abilities in quick succession. Projectiles ripped into the stone. Aether Shots exploded, showers of debris cascading out from their impacts. He saved Concussion Blast for the Battleguards. Saba loosed a constant stream of arrows, forcing the Battleguards to use Aether Barriers and Shields.

Stalactites and Stalagmites blossomed down the hall. Gilda exploded them by way of Glacial Eruption, coating the hall in ice. Her Fire Globes and Infernal Spears tore into the wall above where the hall ended and pummeled several pillars. Dante waited in case any Battleguards got through.

Debris and stone chips flew. The room shook. In the enclosed space, the barrage of abilities and their impacts became a roar. A spiderweb of cracks ran up several pillars. With a final groan, part of the roof collapsed, exposing bedrock. Moments later, the pillars fell and the rest of the roof with it. A cloud of dust burst outward. The group stopped the barrage.

Frost squinted. "Looks to be as good as it's gonna get. Between the lure and that, they'll be a while."

"I just have one question," Dante said. "How do we get out when we're done with the emperor?"

"Through here." Frost nodded to the piled rubble blocking the hall. He could hear the enemy on the other side. "They don't know it, but they're gonna dig our path out."

"I like that." Dante grinned.

"Gilda, lead us to the emperor," Frost said.

"We should really hurry." Saba was staring at the rubble, head tilted to one side, a frown etched on her face. "I don't think we have as much time as we'd like."

"What makes you say that?" Frost asked. "That void revenant was a GUM. Add it to all those mobs and the rubble…" He shrugged, palms up, as his voice trailed off, the conclusion obvious to him.

"I can hear them," Saba said. "They aren't fighting anymore."

"Nonsense. I know dresdori have a trait for hearing, but is it good enough to get through that all the way into the next room?" Frost gestured at the rubble.

"It is." Saba nodded.

"Her claim makes sense," Gilda said.

"How?"

"She did the pulls. Those mobs scaled for her level the moment she pulled. When she lured on Setnana's group, aggro transferred to them at Saba's level. Setnana and her Battleguards are several levels higher and will have killed them easily. Their only obstacle will be the blockage. At least until the respawns."

"You coulda told me scaling was based off who pulled and not by who entered," Frost said. "Adesh and Ryne could be in here right now with us clearing."

"They could've but the penalty for our level differences would've been no exp or loot from kills," Gilda said. "And the Sanctum also scales up in difficulty for numbers in a group and doesn't allow you to alter groups once inside.

"The emperor also has an additional check where he scales on the fly to compensate for any other exploit we might try. And you're sealed inside the throne room once the encounter begins."

"Wouldn't Saba's Concealment have reset the mobs?" Dante asked. "And made aggro transfer to Setnana's group at their levels?"

"Only if she pulled it off before Setnana's group attacked," Frost mused.

Everyone looked to Saba.

She shook her head. "They didn't give me a chance. They started firing the moment they saw me. I had to dive to get out of the way before I Concealed. Do you know what a centaur looks like diving?"

Frost chuckled as he imagined it. "We need the fastest way to the emperor, then. And we need to get moving now."

"No doubt. Follow me." Gilda headed toward the far end of the room where three doors waited. "Which of those rooms did you lure from, Saba?"

"All three and three more after this."

"Shiiiit," Dante said. "Six rooms? That's freaking epic."

"Thank you." Saba practically strutted.

"She surprised me too, Dante." Frost eyed Saba with a newfound respect. "I didn't expect it, not with the way she always runs from danger."

"Not always," Saba protested.

They all stopped and looked at her.

"What? I did the lure, didn't I?" Her tail swished.

"Which involved running from danger," Dante pointed out.

Gilda and Frost burst into laughter.

"Okay, okay," Saba huffed. And then mumbled something about dumb brutes and always wanting to fight.

"Which of the rooms after these three *didn't* you lure from?" Gilda asked.

Saba pointed at the middle door. "The two after that one."

They continued forward along a wall with bloom-globes at measured intervals. The yellow luminance highlighted the intricate designs and glyphs etched upon the marble walls. Gilda led them through the central door.

They emerged upon a balcony that circled the room. There were stairs on either side. At the far end was a door on their level and one below. They made their way across the balcony to the door where they could see down a short hall.

Four gray-scaled draconid overseers waited in the next room, a network of vibrant red and blue adorning their chest and muscular arms like nebulous veins. One had a mist sword, while the other had a storm lance, electricity running up and down its length. The other two had korbitanium vambraces and greaves.

"Lure this room and the next to buy us extra time," Gilda said. "This is the last place we can do it. In the previous alpha, not only did the mobs after the next two rooms see through Concealment, but there was no place to lure them to."

She pointed to the stairs behind them. "We'll hide below. Pull them all the way across the balcony and into the room we collapsed. That'll give us enough time to run through to a safe spot before the next group of mobs. We'll wait for you there."

"Sounds good," Saba said. She paused, brow wrinkled. Her tail swished. "Do any of the mobs leash?"

"Leash?" Sigrid asked.

"It means do the mobs automatically stop chasing and return to their original location after they travel a certain distance," Frost explained.

"Not in dungeons like this," Gilda answered. "They'll follow you until you find a way to drop aggro and reset them. Or until they kill you."

"I'll choose answer A for a hundred points," Saba said.

Frost gave her a tight smile. "Sounds about right because we need you. Be careful."

"I will."

Frost, Gilda, Dante, and Sigrid headed downstairs. Frost peeked into the bottom room. It held a dozen nalarr.

"Concealed defilers are with them," Gilda said before he asked the obvious question.

"Ah." He understood Gilda's choice now. Although the draconid overseers were more powerful by far, they were melee. Defilers were casters.

"Hope you guys are out of sight," Saba said from

above. "Because I'm going." The clip-clop of her hooves advanced and then faded.

"What's left after the two rooms she pulls?" Frost asked.

"Two more rooms and the maze."

"You've been through the maze, right?" Frost had not been a fan of mazes in other games. He found them annoying.

"Twice. But more by luck than anything else. The path changes every time."

"What's the maze like?" Frost asked.

"A series of tiny rooms with eight doors like so." With the tip of her dagger, Gilda carved a rectangle into the wall's stone bricks. She added eight points to indicate door positions, two per side. "A thirty-minute timer begins when you enter. No one has managed to clear the maze in the allotted time. Entering a door will teleport you into an identical room with various mobs. Each room has its number painted on the walls and a letter above each door. You can fight or you can leave through any door. But once you enter, the mobs are aggroed and remain that way. The only good news there is that the mobs don't or can't go through the doors."

"Sounds like a pain-in-the-ass," Frost said.

Gilda nodded. "No doubt. There's also a good chance you'll return to a room you were already in, either from the door you left, with mobs waiting to kill you, or one of the other doors, which gives you a chance to run to another one unscathed. Rinse and repeat until you end up in a hall leading to the throne room."

Frost's brow knitted. "So, we could end up running in circles."

"Players have gotten stuck indefinitely," Gilda admitted.

"Damn." Frost grimaced. "What happens when the timer runs out?"

"Nothing as far as I could tell. We just kept trying until we made it."

Frost glanced at her quizzically. "Nothing? That doesn't make sense. There's gotta be a reason for the timer."

"No doubt." Gilda shrugged. "But I've never been able to figure it out."

"Might be the reason no one's beaten the emperor," Frost said.

"Might be." Gilda nodded.

Frost checked his quests for a hint. He had new one under the chain for Imanok Sanctum. Into the Maze. As with any other quest, it gave no detail as to the objective.

"Anyone ever figured out the actual pattern for the maze?" Dante was frowning. "All mazes usually have one." Gilda shook her head.

"Do you think they'd change the path every time?" Frost asked.

"I doubt it," Gilda said. "But I have an idea for a pattern from a ton of research I did since the last alpha. I'm not trying to get stuck in there for hours again. Now that I think about it, we should've asked—never mind." She shot a regretful look Frost's way.

Frost let out a relieved breath that she'd caught herself before she said anything about Pops. Brow furrowed, he cocked his head as his echolocation kicked in. "You feel that, Gilda?"

"Yeah, Saba's on her way back."

Frost hefted Deadeye and pointed it up toward the balcony. "Let's be ready in case we gotta fight."

The distinct roars of draconid overseers echoed. Saba's hooves beat a frantic rhythm on the stone floor. But they were soon drowned out by the overseers' metallic footsteps. The pursuit grew louder and closer. As did the mass of bodies picked up by Frost's echolocation.

And then Saba and her lure were directly above, sending down a cascade of dust and stone chips. Saba appeared on the balcony to the left. She was galloping for all she was worth. Behind her came six draconid overseers.

Following them were small ghostly creatures. Five-foot imitations of long dead titans. Spriggans. Frost hissed. The spriggans were small now, but they could inflate themselves to the size of fifteen-foot colossuses.

"They're gone," Dante said, as the last spriggan disappeared through the door. "Let's go." He made to move.

Frost grabbed Dante's arm. He put his index finger to his lips. Dante froze. Moments later came the focus of Frost's concern. Two more spriggans.

When the ghostly creatures were gone, Frost said, "Now, we can go."

They sprinted up the stairs and into the next room. Not slowing, they headed for the hall. In the next area, from which Saba must have pulled the spriggans, were several treasure chests. Inside would be the loot the spriggans guarded.

A chance also existed for any of them to be a trap. Explosive. Poisonous. Or even a toothy mimic. As tempted as he was to take some time and try to open the chests, Frost forced himself on. They stopped in a small alcove before the next area, which held two raven-like void revenants and more spriggans.

Minutes stretched as they waited, Frost's thoughts preoccupied by the maze. Since Pops had helped design Void Legion and Estela, he must have known the pattern. Frost wished Gilda had remembered to ask. Or that Pops had thought to mention it. He tried to think of anything unique to his father that might lend a hand. He soon gave up. He needed to see the maze itself.

Saba's drumming hooves preceded the sense of her form. She galloped toward them, majestic in her armor on both the equine and humanoid portions of her body. From his vantage, Frost could see past her into the preceding room. A train of mobs followed. But they did not appear to be aggroed. They had reset and were simply returning to their places of origin.

"We have to hurry and clear," she said, breathing hard as she reached them. "Setnana has already made it through the blockage. The first room was just now respawning. I doubt they'll have to deal with any other new spawns. Even if they split up to try to find out which way we went, it'll only take them but so long."

"Shit," Frost said. "Did any of them see you?"

She shook her head. "I don't think so."

In the room behind them, the draconid overseers and spriggans had settled into their normal patrols. The sound of spells echoed from the room before it.

"Maybe they did," Gilda said.

CHAPTER 35

"They're too close," Dante said. "Our best shot is to fight them while they're dealing with the mobs in that room."

"How many of them were there?" Frost asked Saba. "About twelve."

Frost looked from the room with overseers and spriggans to the one before him with the void revenants. Both creatures wielded storm lances. White lightning crackled down the weapons' lengths and cast long shadows of the revenant's black cloaked forms. "Gilda, is the room after this pretty much the same? As far as mobs?"

"Mostly, but one of the revenants is a GUM."

"Shit." Frost wracked his brain for a solution.

Dante hefted his axe. "Make up your mind. We only have a few minutes."

Frost had the spark of an idea. "Does the maze require anything special to enter? Like, do we need to clear the room with the entrance to gain access?"

"No," Gilda said. "Just walk through the door."

"And this door, is it where we can clearly see it?"

Gilda pointed. "It's off in the right corner."

"You aren't going to do what I think you're thinking, right?" Saba asked, eyes narrowed. "Please say you aren't."

"I think he isss." Dante grinned, high-pitched voice a little *too* excited.

"We're gonna run through," Frost said.

"Yes!" Dante pumped his fist.

"God, no." Saba pawed at the ground. Her tail swished in agitation.

Frost jutted his chin toward the silver-armored gurash marauder. "Dante, you're gonna Sentinel Shout and lead us." He focused on Sigrid. "No heals at all until we're in the next hallway." The dvergr nodded timidly. "Just have Mikander's Tears and Blood prepped for emergency, but don't use them unless I say so."

"You think he'll be able to handle that much damage with just the increased defense and health from the Shout?" Saba shook her head. "Those revenants will be nuking the hell out of him."

"I'm hoping he will," Frost said.

"I'm a marauder." Dante rested his axe on his shoulder. "In chain armor. I think I'll be alright." There was a thinly veiled edge of sarcasm to his voice.

"And what about us?" Saba asked. "Some of those spells are AOEs."

"Use pots if you gotta." Frost shrugged. "Sigrid's the weakest of us. I don't want her drawing any aggro. Nor anyone else but Dante, for that matter."

"Fair enough, I guess." Saba pursed her lips.

"Don't forget I'll also be able to lessen some of our damage with my Aether Barriers and Shields," Gilda reminded them.

Sigrid spoke in that silvery voice of hers. "I can always summon one or more of my Servitors. The Bulwark can hold a monster and draw its hate away from me. The others can heal or attack. And I can give everyone Aura of the Nomarch, increasing all defense and the amount of vitalization gained from heals."

"I had forgotten about those," Frost admitted. He revised his strategy as he considered the Servitors' abilities.

Servitors came in many forms and had three major roles. Bulwarks took aggro and tanked. Duelists attacked with ranged and melee skills. Shamans healed and removed ailments. "If things get too dicey, then call the Bulwark. You can prep heals for emergency."

Sigrid nodded, then brought her palms up in front of her stomach, thumbs and forefingers forming circles. A translucent pale blue glow like living liquid emanated from her right hand, coiling down her arm. Coral red suffused the left. Five nebulous motes drifted out from each circle, their colors matching the aether of the respective side.

Sigrid splayed her hands out. The motes floated above her fingertips. Mikander's Tears were a soft blue. Mikander's Blood was scarlet.

"Now for the Aura." Her entire body glowed for a moment. A soft light appeared around the group.

Frost immediately felt stronger. He stood straighter. He noted the Aura's hour-long duration.

Sigrid dropped her hands to her sides to signal her readiness. The globes remained suspended from her fingertips.

"Alright," Frost said. "I'm gonna hit them with Concussion Blast as soon as we get to the hall." He eyed Gilda and Saba. "It'll give you two time to set up Glacial Eruption and a Chain Snare or Lightning Trap. That's gonna buy us the seconds we need for Sigrid to heal us up and cleanse any debuffs or DoTs. Then we'll make a run for the maze entrance, jump in, go through three random doors together, clear that fourth room, and figure out our next move. Sounds good, Gilda?" She nodded.

Frost looked to the others. "What do y'all think? It's either that or we fight Setnana and them right here."

"You know me." Dante ran a finger along the edge of his axe blade. "I'm all about the action. But I also love loot. I'm tempted to say fight here so we can go after the chests those spriggans are guarding." He sighed. "And I know doing so most likely means no emperor. So, I say emperor."

Frost agonized over parting with the loot, also. He tried to think of a way to clear the room before Setnana and her group arrived but knew the feat was impossible. Still… he took another envious look at the five treasure chests. He could only imagine their contents, which helped him to decide. As much as they might hold something epic, any of them could be a trap or a classic mimic complete with massive teeth and slobbering jaws.

"Saba?" Brows raised, he regarded the short-haired dresdor.

"You said I liked running, right?" Saba gave a weak smile.

"I am here to follow," Sigrid said when Frost looked to her.

The sound of spells had died from the room with the overseers. Setnana's group would be pulling the room right behind at any moment.

Frost took a deep breath. The air smelled of age. "Go, Dante."

"Stay close, people." Dante charged into the room.

The spriggans aggroed almost immediately, bellowing a challenge and waddling toward the group. A few of the ghostly creatures swelled in size. The void revenants spread their cloak-like wings and screeched. Black lightning crackled around their storm lances as they took aim and began to cast.

Dante unleashed a Sentinel Shout while he ran. Sigrid was close behind him on one side, followed by Saba and Gilda. Frost brought up the rear. The mobs closed from every side. Frost struggled with the urge to stop and open fire.

The hall seemed a great distance off as Dante wove a path through the room to draw the mobs away to the left. The group fled to the right. Dante veered back toward the hall entrance. Two bars of jagged black lightning shot from the revenants. Crackling, the bolts streaked toward Dante.

The hair on the back of Frost's neck rose at the sight of them. An Ice Pillar shot up from the ground to intercept one lightning bolt. The other bolt struck the marauder. Dante grunted and stumbled. But his legs continued to churn.

"That shit hurt," Dante shouted. "I doubt I can handle two more. And it left some type of DoT."

Frost snatched a look behind. Dante was right. The Damage over Time effect manifested as dark tendrils that throbbed around him every two seconds. There was no way to tell how bad the spell's effect was, but Dante was sweating, his crimson complexion paling by the moment.

Left with little choice but to help the lagging marauder, Frost stopped, fired off Concussion Blast up and over Dante toward the revenants, and took off running again. The mobs were gaining fast. Every spriggan had swollen to the size of a gargant. Behind him, the Concussion Blast struck with a hollow boom. Revenants screeched.

He was smiling at the successful attack when void lightning blasted into his back. Frost yelped at the searing pain. Spots danced in his vision. The impact partially spun him, but he was somehow able to stay on his feet.

Teeth gritted, he fought through disorientation and forced himself to keep going. A second sensation replaced the first. It was as if something was gradually sucking the life from him.

They made it to the hall. Dante arrived moments later, huffing and puffing.

Frost's vision was still a bit fuzzy, but he faced the

399

incoming mobs and snapped off an Aether Bomb. The revenants had recovered from the Concussion Blast and launched four more bolts. Void lightning raced across the distance.

An Ice Pillar rumbled up from the ground to block two lightning bolts. Gilda, herself, absorbed the others by way of her red and blue Aether Shields extending from her forearms.

Concussion Blast had recharged. Frost fired it off again even as Gilda cast Stalactites and Stalagmites. She waited for the Concussion Blast to wear off before activating Glacial Eruption. A mob tripped a Lightning Trap Saba had found the time to place. The creatures were now all considerably slowed and disoriented.

Sigrid tossed a red globe of Mikander's Blood at Frost, which immediately made him feel like new. The rejuvenation lasted for all of a few seconds as the debilitation from the DoT kicked in once more. Sigrid cast Purifying Touch. Frost's ailment and lethargy faded completely. Sigrid added Mikander's Tears to gradually heal the wounds caused before she had cleansed the DoT.

Beyond the snared mobs, Frost could just make out Setnana's group in the throes of their battle with the draconid overseers. He launched an Aether Bomb at the revenants and spriggans.

"Haul ass for the maze," he ordered. "We're gonna have to engage the mobs this time. Disorient them however we can. Heal us, Sigrid." He turned. And swore.

The new room had a gargantuan void revenant. Not just a GUM. A boss. Mezanir. Along with Mezanir, there were four groups of mobs, each with a draconid overseer, several grunts, and spriggans. Frost made to change his mind, to fight those behind them, and take on Setnana and her Battleguards.

He never got the chance.

Dante sprinted into the room and Raging Rushed at Mezanir. The moment he collided with the boss, he hit it with a Staggering Blow and released an Enfeebling Bellow. Even as the swing ended, he was dashing to an overseer.

But the Staggering Blow failed to stun Mezanir. The void revenant screeched. Its entire body lit up.

Frost shot off his abilities. Gilda and Saba did the same. Then they sprinted after Dante, who was three quarters of the way to the maze entrance with most of the mobs a step behind. Spells streaked toward the marauder, a kaleidoscope of elements intent on his destruction. Dante Sentinel Shouted.

Sigrid flung out her hands. Blue and red globes left from above her fingertips and zipped toward Dante. Mikander's Blood and Tears struck the marauder. Several spriggans and at least one overseer stopped giving chase to focus on Sigrid.

But Dante Soul Screamed. Immediately, the mobs snapped their attention back to him. He was within two dozen feet of the maze's entrance, a black doorway between two pillars set against an otherwise empty wall.

Don't go through, Frost said to himself. *Please, don't go through.*

He knew the consequences all too well. Aggro would fall on the rest of the group and the mobs were between them and the maze entrance.

Yet, he could see no other way for Dante to save himself. Frost snapped a quick look behind to see the mobs from the previous room boiling into this one.

Shit.

He turned back to the debacle ahead in time to witness a blue glow flash across Dante's body. A golden armored Warden appeared in the midst of the pursuing mobs.

Dante stopped before the maze door, spun, and threw up his arms in Crossguard. Then, he Soul Screamed again.

The Warden mimicked the skills. Every mob focused on the Warden.

"Are you not entertained," Dante hollered. He threw his head back and cackled maniacally.

Frost grinned like a big kid. This was the old brash Dante Blackblade, the elite tank that he'd known and loved. He and the others skirted the melee as the mobs tried and failed to destroy the Warden. Together, they stepped through the maze door.

IM warned Frost of a timer. Thirty minutes.

CHAPTER 36

Nomarch Setnana opened the second to last treasure chest, letting out a puff of air that smelled of age. She licked her lips in anticipation. From one of the earlier chests, she had acquired a shard for Empowered Ameliorate. Now, she prayed these last two contained Suppression and Rejuvenate. But the chest held only a glimmerwand.

Heaving a sigh, she approached the last chest. Her Battleguards readied themselves all around her. A precaution should the chest prove to be a ravenous mimic. They had already killed one such creature.

She paused a moment, a flutter in her gut that was equal parts anticipation and dread rising together. Clenching her stomach against the feelings, she flipped the lid back. There, lying on golden cloth was a glowing blue shard with Rejuvenate written upon it. As with the other spell, the three slots in it were already filled.

"Yes! Praise be to Nif." She took the shard and added it to her inventory.

The Cure
Objective Complete
Retrieve Empowered Rejuvenate
Acquire one of three skills to cure the Gray Death:
2000 experience points
2000 Khertahka dominion credits
2000 Ignis dominion credits

She let out a whoosh of breath. One more em-powered spell and the zhua, Benediction, and Perihy could be healed. She smiled. Finally, the mission was proving its worth.

A glance at the next room wiped the smile away. The group with Drelan Frost and Adesh Hamada had fled yet again. She growled under her breath. The way that group fought was revolting. They had no finesse. No beauty. Skill. They resorted to the cheapest of tactics—luring monsters onto her group, perhaps hoping her people might be over-ran.

"Fools." She studied the monsters in the room.

The largest was a dungeon guardian, Mezanir. A gar-gantuan void revenant. Revenants always seemed to be some god's grotesque imitation of a raven. At least in terms of the its cloak of black feathers that brushed the ground.

But no raven ever had a face that was a white skull with a bone beak. Nor did they possess two horns between which rose tendrils of dark void energy. Beneath those horns were four red glowing eyes. The mockery of a raven was complete with clawed hands and a humanoid body be-neath its feathers.

She frowned. *What other monstrosities waited in the next room after this one? How many areas were left before Emperor KiGy-aba?* The frown became a glower. *If only the stupid guide hadn't died to the dvergar outside Imanok Sanctum.*

"They must have gone through a door we cannot see from here," Khafra said from beside her, interrupting her thoughts. "We can catch them if we go now and skip the monsters as they did." His eyes glinted with the raven-ous need for vengeance. It had consumed him ever since he woke from a grand mystic's healing.

The temptation to do as Khafra suggested ate at her. Adesh Hamada had to pay for hurting Khafra. He had to pay for his role as one of Blue Sky's leaders, as one of the people who, along with Anefet Frost, had engineered Papa's death. Which brought her to Drelan Frost himself and her promise to wipe the Frost name from Mikander.

They had both made her look a fool, had brought about her current punishment, which had taken her away from her beloved Perihy. At every turn, when she thought she had them in her grasp, when she could taste justice, they employed trickery and deception to slip through her noose.

Not this time. This time she knew it was their group just ahead. And yet, there was the chance this guardian, Mezanir, might drop a weapon or hierka that could see her attain her other coveted goals, or better yet, the last skill shard needed to heal Perihy.

At the same time, she could not let them reach the emperor first. They could not be the ones to find Benediction.

She almost laughed. Almost. Perhaps the dreamers were right, and this was all a game. In it, the gods had chosen her to play. They had conspired against her but then brought everything she could ever want in one place, teased her with it, then told her to choose.

But there was only one real choice in this moment. No matter how much she wanted the others. No matter how much it hurt to give them up for now.

"We shall kill Mezanir, *then* we go after them." Her lips curved into a grim smile as she basked in her thoughts. *I will get everything I want in the end. Patience and strength. I have both in ample amounts.*

Khafra glowered at her but slapped his right arm to his chest, his korbitanium vambraces ringing against his armor. He bowed. "As you wish. Can we at least kill them all at once? It would save us time."

She considered the idea for a moment. The last

room with void revenants and spriggans had been a test when they applied the same strategy. The fight made her wonder exactly how the smaller and weaker group had managed to defeat any room. Perhaps their luring had been the better strategy. Making someone else do their dirty work. She ground her jaw.

"No. We kill them as they are. As four separate groups. Then we deal with Mezanir. I don't want any more deaths before the emperor."

"Understood. I will pass the orders." He stalked off to speak to the remaining Battleguards and Deathguards.

"Give him time." Ihuet leaned on his staff, his gaze riveted upon Khafra. "You must understand no one has ever hurt him as Adesh Hamada managed to do. Khafra wants to face him. He wants to be the one to deliver the killing blow."

"I will grant him that chance. But curing Perihy comes first."

"Of course, Nomarch."

Khafra returned to her. "We're ready."

"Proceed."

Khafra gave the signal. A marksman shot an arrow at the first group's overseer. The creature roared and charged toward the marksman. Its minions followed in its wake.

Setnana eyed the other groups of monsters, prepared to call a full engagement if they had noticed their counterparts' aggression. But none had. They continued with their business, talking amongst themselves.

The first monster group had covered perhaps fifty feet, when her plate-armored reaver, Djare, used Onslaught to charge across the distance at several times his normal speed. Shoulder first, he crashed into the draconid. In the same instant, Djare flung his two-handed sword past the creature. Aether emanated from the weapon like a cyan mist. The blade spun in an arc, carving a path through the minions, aether connecting one beast to the other like beads on a string in a skill named Boomerang Blade. The weapon returned to Djare's hand. With a snap of his wrist, he yanked every creature to him.

The remainder of her group engaged and killed the monsters. They healed and repeated the process until only Mezanir remained.

"Flawless," she said, beaming. "Now, for this brute. Two warriors to hold it as a precaution. One must be a dementer."

"That would be me." Khafra stepped up, resplendent in his blue, black, and purple armor. All the colors of erada elite. Splatters of blood and grime covered his korbitanium bracers.

Setnana smiled. "Good." She had hoped he would embrace the role. Return to a semblance of his former self.

He returned the gesture and nodded despite the tightness in his eyes. He faced the raid group. "Listen up. We haven't fought this one before. But as with any other time, we shall take the cautious approach."

"Mystics." He gestured to two robed Azureguards, Utunet and Ahaten, and to a human Bloodguard. "Djare and myself are your primary responsibility. We die. You all die. Utunet." He nodded to the erada man then indicated the reaver. "You're taking care of Djare." Khafra turned his attention to the female mystic. "Ahaten, you are on me." The two eradae bowed, but Ahaten's face had paled.

Setnana smiled at Ahaten's fear. The woman was right to be afraid. Dementers often took a great amount of damage. And Khafra was known to kill those he found lacking.

Khafra eyed the human, lips curled in distaste. "Your job is everyone else."

"Yes, sir." The man dipped his head several times.

"The rest of you… if this creature curses you or places some other type of ailment on you, run away from everyone else as a precaution. A mystic will purify you if the spell can be removed. Use any potions you deem necessary.

"If you're a sorcerer, stormcaller, windwalker, or shadowmancer, manage your damage. This is *not* the time to flaunt your prowess. If you gain the beast's hate, get your asses away from the group so it does not piss on everyone. Also, for you sorcerers, have Aether Shields and Barriers ready to protect the ranged group.

"Other than that, let's take this bastard down. And then see what treasure he holds. Ready?"

"Ready, sir," they yelled.

Nomarch Setnana felt a lightness in her chest. She actually grinned. It had been a long time since she had ventured out on a hunt such as this one. She missed those days. Missed this feeling. She reminded herself to see to it that she called weekly hunts.

Khafra and Djare strode ahead of everyone. They shared a knowing glance. Khafra nodded. They broke into a run. After the first seven or eight strides, Djare employed Onslaught, covering the distance to Mezanir in a blink. Khafra Spurted, his body a blur. Djare bellowed.

The revenant screeched. A piercing sound that echoed, felt as if it cut into Setnana's soul. For a few seconds, she could do nothing. It took but a moment to recognize the entire group was silenced. None of them could cast a spell.

Djare got to work, hacking away at the gargantuan revenant, his body reaching no higher than the thing's knee. He positioned it facing away from everyone.

Khafra took up a spot at an angle off to Djare's right. His vambraces rose and fell as he pummeled the beast. Their two mystics shifted into place between the main group and the two warriors.

"I think they have it," Setnana called out as the silence wore off. "Everyone attack."

The marauders, cutthroats, and dementers rushed into melee range. Their weapons rose and fell as they chopped and sliced into Mezanir's back. An array of spells shot across distance, lighting up the room. They exploded upon impact. Marksmen loosed arrows in quick succession.

Setnana waited. She was by far the most powerful of the lot. Allowing them a good lead before unleashing hell was only fair. She cast Mimic twice. Copies of herself appeared to either side of her. She summoned a defiler and a nightmare, the latter an ethereal black mass that constantly changed shape.

Mezanir spread its massive dark wings and flapped once. A great wind knocked back everyone in melee range. It kicked up dust and debris. But before Mezanir moved, Khafra had Spurted back to the revenant. Djare followed a moment later. The rest of the melee re-engaged.

Every melee must have taken damage, because the mystics hurled a wave of the red and blue motes of Mikander's Tears and Blood onto them. Setnana did not know the particulars of how a mystic perceived a wound. But somehow, they knew who and when to heal.

The revenant screeched time and again. Whether in agony or anger, Setnana could not tell. Nor did she care.

Mezanir spread its wings again. When it flapped, there was no wind. Instead, over a dozen black feathers streaked through the air like spears, headed for her group.

Sorcerers threw up a barrier of interconnected red and blue Aether Shields. The feathers smacked into the barrier and fell harmlessly to the ground. One of the sorcerers had not paid attention. The spiked end of a feather protruded from his back. He stared sightlessly then keeled over.

Between Mezanir's horns, the tendrils of void en-

409

ergy pulsed. The pulses grew faster and faster. Setnana had an ill-feeling.

"Everyone but Khafra and Djare, fall back!" she yelled. "Mystics, Mikander's Tears on them. Now!"

Blue motes flew through the air. They landed on Khafra and Djare, seeped into their skin.

All but two cutthroats in the group followed her orders. Those two continued to stab and slice into Mezanir. She prayed they were ready to engage Escape or Cloak, for the pulse was now too fast to separate the beats.

The pulse stopped.

A blast of void energy shot out in a circular wave from Mezanir. Khafra, Djare, and the two disobedient cutthroats screamed. But while Khafra and Djare buckled for a moment before continuing to fight, the cutthroats crumpled to the ground. Poisonous void energy rose like mist from the bodies of all four.

Mezanir was folded over like a great sleeping bird. Its chest rose and fell in a slow, steady rhythm.

"Purifying Touch," she yelled. "Vitalize and Suppression. Get that ailment off Khafra and Djare." The mystics ran forward to comply. "The rest of you... ATTACK!"

Setnana had a sense they would not survive another Void Pulse. She called upon Metamorphosis. Her horns grew longer. Her body swelled, her muscles growing bigger and stronger. Her robes adjusted with her new form. She was the image of a demon from the old tomes about the Titan War. Aether energy filled her to brimming.

She applied Necrosis to Mezanir to increase her shadow damage. Then, she let loose. Shadow Globe, Shadow Flame, and Shadow Flare shot forth in quick succession. She added Plague, an ailment whose damage increased with each tick until a final explosion. Teeth gritted, she cast and cast again as fast as she could.

Her mimics copied her every move. The summoned defiler's specialty was an empowered Shadow Globe, which it cast every few seconds. The nightmare flung Nether Lances.

Across the threshold, Khafra had employed Dementia. He too, was now in full attack mode. He was a raging, dark-skinned, blue-armored blur of destruction.

Mezanir shook itself. It let out a screech. One more round of the knock back and spears repeated. The Void Pulse built again.

Breathing labored, desperation clawing at her chest, Setnana continued to cast. Mezanir's pulse sped up. Setnana let out a primal shout, trying to will herself to unleash more spells.

The final pulse came. A pause. The world slowed.

Mezanir let out a plaintive cry and pitched backward. The melee scattered. The void beast hit the ground, cracking the floor, and sending up a shower of dust.

Cheers echoed in a deafening roar. People hugged each other. Setnana let out a long slow breath. And then, she grinned.

The Cure

Objective complete

Defeat the Maze Guardian

Defeated Dungeon Guardian Mezanir:

5000 experience points

5000 Ignis dominion credits

"Back here!" someone yelled. "The treasure."

Setnana approached tentatively. The area smelled of scorched flesh and spells. Behind the corpse were two golden chests. She wanted so much to open them but dreaded not finding that which she needed most.

"Go on," Ihuet said from behind her. "You deserve this."

Setnana flipped open the lid. A shard was inside.

Suppression. Try as she might, she couldn't help the tears that rolled down her cheeks. "Praise be to Nif." She drew an X on her forehead.

In that moment she heard Papa's voice. *A Botros shows no weakness. Strength always.*

"Yes, Papa," she whispered under her breath.

The Cure

Objective Complete

Retrieve Empowered Suppression

Acquire one of three skills to cure the Gray Death:

2000 experience points

2000 Khertahka dominion credits

2000 Ignis dominion credits

She dabbed her face with the sleeve of her dress, straightened her shoulders, and proceeded to the next chest. *Nif wouldn't smile on me so brightly as to allow me to find Benediction right here, would she?*

Whispering prayers, she eased the lid up. Her eyes widened at the sight of a smooth wooden shaft. Her belly fluttered. Wider and wider, she lifted the lid. Until she could see the entire weapon. Her breath left her in a whoosh.

Though the item was a hierka, it was not the one she sought. This was a rare storm lance named Mezanir's Coil. Made from polished korbitanium, the weapon was a bit over five feet, intricate designs etched into its length. A large yellow pear-shaped gem was set into the top. The bottom was where the weapon earned its name as a lance, the edge glinting in the bloomglobe light.

I should have known better than to think this would be so easy. She waved to Ihuet. "Hold it until we return to Aprunis."

"Yes, Nomarch." The storm lance disappeared into Ihuet's inventory.

Setnana did not allow her disappointment to linger. She strode past Mezanir's huge carcass and crossed the room to the door set between two pillars. Its surface was completely black. She could see nothing beyond. Draconid writing adorned a plaque above the opening.

Setnana closed her eyes and calmed her fluttering heart. All that was left were the fugitives and the emperor. Black emptiness stared back at her from the opening.

"Khafra, Djare, lead," she called. The two warriors stepped up beside her. "Everyone else, be prepared to either fight the master of this place, the fugitives we've been chasing, or both. Either way, we end this."

CHAPTER 37

After Frost's group cleared the first room, they avoided mobs by running to another door. On the fourth occasion, they emerged in a room they had already entered. One with void wolves. They killed the wolves and took the door directly across once more. They encountered nalarr, whom they dispatched with brutal efficiency.

"Twenty-five minutes left," Frost called out after they'd cleared the room of the tiger-like beasts.

His mind conjured ideas of the gruesome deaths awaiting them when the time expired. Either an endless zerg of mobs. Or traps. Maybe death by gas. Or an enraged Emperor KiGyaba would spawn on top of them. He refused to believe nothing changed.

"Room thirteen." Gilda indicated the numbers emblazoned in black on each wall. "I think we've gone far enough in."

"Agreed." Frost nodded. "Now, we just gotta be ready to run through another door if Setnana's group shows up. Everyone's gotta stay together. No matter what. If they show, follow Dante. Everyone got that?" He waited for them to acknowledge him with a nod or a yes. "Saba, place traps at every door."

The marksman set about the task. Frost eyed the doors. Above each was at least one letter etched into the stone. The two directly ahead had U and B. The two behind had D and A. On the left, the doors were marked L and Se. To the right was R and St. He had a strong suspicion as to what the U, D, L, R represented. He was uncertain about the others.

"What now?" He looked to Gilda.

"Now, I get to see if I'm as smart as I think I am."

"Do your thing."

Gilda closed her eyes. Her brow furrowed. "If I'm right, we return to room one, and the numbers to each room will change in some sort of sequence as we go." Gilda opened her eyes, the green of them as intoxicating as ever. "There should be ten rooms to solve. Then the next takes us to the hall before the emperor's throne room. We don't have time to clear, so we're going to run through. Dante, you'll lead to get aggro if needed."

"Got it." Dante nodded.

"Keep Tears and Blood ready, Sigrid," Frost said. His pulse sped up. He itched for the action to come. "Saba and Gilda, you're with me on snare and stun duty."

"Let's do this," Dante said.

Gilda led them to the door with an L. "Initially, we're just going in and out the same door. Give everyone a moment to get in then we step back. We'll do that until we're in room one again."

"Okay," Dante said. "Here goes." He stepped through.

Frost and the others followed. They appeared in room fifteen. Void wolves were at the other end and did not aggro. The group stepped back. Room eighteen. Growling nalarr rushed them. Frost fired off Concussion Blast. The group reversed direction.

Room 1

It was still empty from the earlier clear.

"Alright," Gilda said. "Down to business. Dante, pay attention. In this room and the next, you'll choose the door with U. Then it's D and another D. So, when you go through the second U door, wait for everyone. Then do like we just did: step back because that U will be a D on the other side. We then head down to the next D. After that, I'll call out the other doors. Got it?"

Dante smirked. "Start with U. Cross the room to U. Wait for y'all slow pokes, then step back into D. Cross the room to D. Wait for your calls."

Gilda nodded, brows raised, a certain sign she was impressed. Frost smiled, knowing she would not give Dante the satisfaction by admitting as much.

"Ready?" Dante asked, a twinkle in his eye.

"Good to go," everyone said in unison.

Frost's heart was thumping now. He held Deadeye firmly. He forced himself to calm.

Dante Sentinel Shouted and stepped into the doorway. The rest of them did the same.

Room 4

Nalarr roared and were charging Dante when they entered. He Raging Rushed into them then loosed an Enfeebling Bellow. He dashed to the left, taking every mob with him. Frost and the others ran by. Dante sprinted across to the other side of the room with the snarling mobs on his ass, then grinning, he dashed straight toward the U door. Frost fired off a Concussion Blast that streaked by Dante into the mobs, then he followed the others into the door.

Room 8

Gilda and Saba had the void wolves in the next room snared when Frost arrived. Dante stepped into the door through which they had entered.

Room 12

The next room had four black-cloaked defilers. They

416

were nuking Dante with their spells. Sigrid tossed heal after heal. Gilda spawned Stalactites and initiated a Glacial Eruption, freezing the defilers in place. The group crossed the room to the D door.

Room 16

In the next room were several spriggans. They were swelling to titanic proportions. Frost hit them with an Aether Bomb.

"L and R," Gilda yelled upon entering.

Dante led the way to the door with L. Saba kited around the spriggans, using a combo of Chain Snare and Lightning Trap to remain ahead of them.

Room 20

Plague wolves infested the next room. Dante Soul Screamed to get them all on him. Sweat rolled down Sigrid's face as she struggled to keep him up. She summoned a Shaman Servitor to help. It came in the form of an asrai, a winged fairy no larger than a dvergr who flitted over to Dante and healed by way of Mikander's Blood.

Dante pulled the mobs away then Raging Rushed back to the group to put some distance between him and the plague wolves. Concussion Blast kept the wolves disoriented long enough to head into the R door.

"L and R again," shouted Gilda.

Room 24

Basilisks attacked. The lumbering creatures looked for all the world like ankylosaurus. Or giant korbitoises. Bowsers. Frost smiled. The room shook as the basilisks charged, heads down, the great spikes upon their armored backs large enough to impale a man. Dante and the entire group ran for the L door.

Room 28

This room held a combination of void wolves, nalarr, and defilers. Before anyone could move, Battleguards entered through the U door. Nomarch Setnana Botros and Khafra the Mad appeared moments later.

"Run!" Frost yelled. Heart thumping, he fired off Divergence, Aether Bomb, and Concussion Blast. Aether Shields sprang up around the enemy.

Frost's group bolted for the R door.

Room 32

The room had no mobs. But the moment they entered, a foul-smelling red mist seeped from the walls and floor.

"B and A," Gilda instructed while cupping a hand over her mouth. "Hurry!'

Frost's vision doubled as they followed Dante across the room through the mist to the door with B etched into the wall above it. Sigrid quickly cast Tears and Purifying Touch. With Deadeye aimed at the L door, Frost backed in, hoping no one managed to see which door they had chosen. Battleguards appeared. Frost unleashed his entire arsenal and fled.

Room 36

The room held a chimera guard. The lupine head unleashed a howl.

"Madness," Saba said. "We can't just go through that thing."

"Go! Go!" Frost urged desperately as he entered the room. "A couple of Setnana's people saw which door we took. Don't know if I got them."

Dante Raging Rushed. Then he popped Crossguard and Enfeebling Bellow.

The rest of them hurried by while he tanked. Sigrid healed Dante until he dodged an attack, turned, and sprinted for the A door. He was cackling like a madman. They all scrambled through the opening.

Room 40

An empty room.

Dante stepped to the side of the door, which now had a B over it. The rest of them darted to the middle of the room and turned to face the door. They waited. Time stretched.

Three Battleguards jumped through the door. The first one caught Dante's axe in his chest. The blow lifted him up and launched him back through the door. The others died to a hail of Aether Shots, Gilda's spells, and Saba's arrows.

Chest heaving, Frost kept Deadeye aimed at the door. Dante was poised with his axe ready to swing. No one else came through the opening.

Dante burst into laughter. The others soon followed.

Frost basked in the moment. He had been so focused on his role that he had not thought about or acknowledged his emotions, the adrenaline. His entire body was electric. Slowly, it bled from him. He let out a long exhale.

"That was epic." Dante propped his axe handle on his shoulder. "Fucking epic. This game is insane."

"It was. It is." Frost hugged Gilda. She squeezed him tightly. He released her and looked into her green eyes. "You did good. How'd you figure it out?" He could not help thinking of the maze's solution as a secret code like the ones his father used to rave about. *Pops, you woulda loved this.*

"Not here," she said under her breath. Louder, she added, "Time enough to explain when we're done. I can't give away *all* my secrets." She smiled but a hint of caution resided in her eyes. Frost nodded.

"So, which door to the emperor's hall," Saba asked.

"Straight ahead," Gilda said.

They strode to the door with the U. They went in.

Room 1

"I don't understand." Gilda stared all around, utterly confused. "Trust and believe, I was right. I know I was. The

419

numbers were in sequence."

IM alerted Frost to the remaining time. Eighteen minutes.

"If I had to guess," Frost said, frowning, "I'd say it means we can't just pick any door in room forty." He stroked his aether ring. "Let's repeat the pattern and try another. Maybe the one with Se or St since we tried all the others." He nodded to the doors with the words above them.

"Se," Dante said.

"Why that one?" Frost asked.

Dante shrugged. "E before t."

"Good enough for me," Frost declared.

The rest of them agreed. They repeated the sequence of doors.

U, U, D, D, L, R, L, R, B, A, Se.

Room 44

Another empty room. Frost assumed Setnana's group must have passed through and cleared it.

"All that's left is St." Frost pointed.

Hoping for the best, he followed Dante through the St door. They reappeared in a long hall lit by bloomglobe chandeliers. The place reeked with the redolence of age. Ornate paintings adorned the walls. Gold and silver molding carved in a pattern of swirls joined the ceiling and walls, then repeated again in the middle of the wall and the base, running along its length all the way to two closed halves of a massive door. Protruding from each half of the door to form a complete statue was the likeness of Emperor KiGyaba, the hydra god.

Into the Maze
Objective Complete
Solved the maze before timer expired:
5000 experience points
1000 Ignis dominion credits

"That's some great exp," Dante said.

Gilda spoke as Frost made to agree. "But the timer hasn't stopped."

CHAPTER 38

Twelve minutes remained. They stood before the massive doors, the statue of Emperor KiGyaba staring down at them. Dressed in robes, the emperor had somewhat human features and carried a storm lance in one hand.

"I'm guessing the timer doesn't stop until we kill the emperor," Dante said.

"No doubt." Gilda nodded. "Which coincides with Frost's conclusion. The timer might be a big part of the reason he's wiped everyone who faced him."

"Let's get to it, then," Frost said. "Except for Sigrid, we're all experienced here. Among the best of the best. But from the looks of things, we're gonna really need her, so we do our best to protect her. As for the emperor, Gilda said the fight changed every time in the other alphas, so we go over what we can but still play everything by ear."

"Why couldn't they just make it a tank and spank after all we've been through to get here." Saba huffed.

"Nothing worth doing is ever easy," Frost said.

"We can try burn him down." Dante hoisted his axe onto his shoulder. "I'll grab all three, summon Warden, pop all my defensive skills, and y'all just focus fire that bitch."

Frost smirked. "Didn't I just say something about easiness?"

"Simple solution to a complex problem." Dante shrugged.

"Tried and failed," Gilda said. "The guards and the emperor are linked. As long as both guards were alive, the emperor was immune to damage. We must kill one of them.

"The good news is that the emperor doesn't start doing massive damage until he transforms into the hydra. That's when he used a reaver's melee skills. Malignant Strike, Necrotic Slash, Soul Rend. That type of stuff. We got no farther than that."

"It's gonna have to be enough," Frost said. "There's only eleven minutes left. We need as much time as we can to see what he does. And as I was saying before, we're good enough that we can wing it. Figure out the tells and patterns. Every creature has them, no matter how advanced the AI might be. We've all done plenty World Firsts. This is no different. We learn and adapt. Alright?" They nodded.

Frost smiled inwardly. His feelings mirrored those of his first boss fight in a VRMMO. An electric tingle. A hint of fear, yet the sense that something incredible was about to occur. Leading the group also reminded him of his days as SoC's guildmaster.

"Dante." Frost gestured toward the crimson marauder. "You'll stay on the emperor. Saba, I'd venture to guess you and I might naturally have more survivability. You, because of your level. And me, because of this armor I picked up in Kituan. We'll take the chimera guards.

"Saba, you kite yours around with your snares and traps while Gilda and I kill the one on me. Gilda, we're gonna be counting on your DPS."

"No doubt." Gilda nodded once.

"Saba," Frost continued, "we'll kill your guard right after. Then we take care of the emperor. Sigrid focus your heals on Dante. Use your Servitors to help me and Saba.

Everyone, remember to use potions to help her out."

Frost opened his inventory. He provided them with two of each type of potion. He took a peek at his stash of vials and considered their effects.

Aether Power:

+25 to aether effects

Protection:

+500 armor

Agility:

+ 10 agility

Colossus:

+ 10 strength

Elements:

+25 to elemental power

Aether Resist:

+25 resistance to aether effects

Elemental Resistance:

+25 resistance to all elements

Fortification:

+50 health

Aether Protection:

Absorb 1000 – 2000 aether damage

Elemental Protection:

Absorb 1000 – 2000 elemental damage

"These are worth at least five additional levels in stats." Frost handed them out, three to each person. "Keep them on your belt and pop them as soon as we engage." He slid his vials and potions into the little pouches on his belt. "Keep a sanctification pot handy if Sigrid can't cleanse you fast enough."

Frost placed his hands against the great door. His heart rate sped up. Finally, it had come to this. He imagined seeing Kai and Mom when it was all done. He clung to images of them smiling.

"Remember not to stand in shit. Let's do this." He pushed.

The door swung inward. The group strode into a massive throne room lit by chandelier bloomglobes. Roofless colonnades lined two sides of the room but left a large space in the middle where they stood. A carpet ran down the length of the area. The exposed portions of the floor were a mosaic of red and blue stone. Curtains draped from pillar to pillar. Someone had been speaking when they entered. The room fell into a deep silence.

Dressed in sleeveless gold robes, Emperor KiGyaba sat upon a huge throne. He could almost be mistaken for a human, except he had to be at least fifteen feet if he stood. His exposed arms were like muscular tree trunks. His skin was an odd mixture of metal, stone, and skin as if he were some creature in the middle of molting. To either side of him stood a chimera guard perhaps half the size of Azonoth.

"I thought the titans all got killed off," Frost whispered.

"Apparently not," Gilda said.

Gathered near the emperor was a group of people Frost assumed to be his court, a collection of richly dressed men and women of every race. They slowly backed away as Frost and the others strode down the central area.

"Intruders," the emperor called out in an appropriately thunderous voice. "Treasure seekers. Kill them, my slaves."

Small doors opened to the left and right. In rushed a zerg: a group of low-level people. Many of them were eradae whose horns had been cut off. But there were other races also. Gurashi. Gargants. Winged yurids. Dresdori. Humans. Grand korae. Dvergar. Asrai. Nalarr. Their voices rose in a roar.

They waved weapons as they came, but a mere look

425

at them said they were malnourished. Emaciated. Yet, Frost knew their blades could slice him all the same.

"I know you like to keep a certain reputation and all that." Dante's high-pitched voice rose above the clamor. "Being all noble. But I'm not about to let a zerg cut me down. Not now. Not ever."

"Neither am I," Frost said. "There's too much at stake. Besides," he added with a smile in Gilda's direction, "they're most likely NPCs. Light them up. The nobles and the emperor too."

He opened fire. The rest of the group followed his lead. Dante charged into the midst of the slaves and unleashed Cyclonic Strike. Threatening yells soon became plaintive cries. The slaves and the nobility turned tail before the onslaught.

"You dare harm me!" KiGyaba bellowed.

He stood to his full height, swept one hand out and knocked away several nobles. He Flickered from his position to the center of the room. The chimera guards galloped after him.

Dante Raging Rushed to meet the emperor. Sigrid followed him, hands flashing as she tossed Tears and Blood.

Frost hit the chimera guard on the left with an Aether Shot, Korbitanium Projectile, Piercer combo, the shots a streak of blue, molten fire, and deep red.

Saba picked up the guard on the right by firing Triple Barrage. She dropped a Chain Snare and led it away from the group.

Chakrams twirling as if she danced, Gilda called forth a Flame Column, flung Globes, Infernal Spears, Stalactites, and Stalagmites. The latter two exploded in Glacial Eruption, freezing the chimera guard for a few seconds and leaving the floor coated in ice. The move allowed Frost to kite the beast in a circle, keeping just out of its range while continually firing whenever an ability was ready.

His chimera guard pawed the ground. Frost stopped and braced for the impact of a charge. The crevid head bowed then pointed toward Sigrid.

"Shit!" Teeth gritted, Frost fired off Aether Shot and Concussion Blast, both to help slow the beast additionally and to return its aggro to him.

The guard ignored both skills. Gilda's spells blasted into the guard. But the beast charged toward Sigrid. The distance between them closed.

Until an armored gargant appeared as if from thin air, directly in front of the beast. The gargant bellowed. Immediately, the guard stopped to attack the newcomer.

Mouth agape, Frost stared. It took but a few seconds to realize the gargant was Sigrid's Bulwark Servitor. Even as the thought crossed Frost's mind, he looked to Saba. The asrai Shaman Servitor healed her as she kited around her chimera guard. Saba avoided Flame Pillars with deft skill and still managed to get off a Paralysis Shot when the lupine head tried to Howl.

Ignoring her, Frost peppered the chimera guard before him with skill after skill. Gilda's chakrams were blue and red blurs as she cast. Between them, they prevented the beast from using Smoke Screen or Howl. It got off a Hell Breath. The DoT it left behind burned. Frost grimaced. He and Gilda ran within range of Sigrid so she could cleanse them with Purifying Touch.

In this moment, he wished he could tell how close the chimera guard was to death. Desperation tightened his chest. The lupine head sagged, its roars became plaintive cries, but it did not stop attacking the Bulwark.

"You're hurting my sons," Emperor KiGyaba shouted.

He flung a hand out. Several blue motes streaked

through the air to the guard attacked by Frost and Gilda. A circular beam dropped down around the beast and the Bulwark. Within seconds, the lupine head stood straight and supple. The beam faded to nothing. A misty glow emanated from the chimera guard. It howled with renewed vigor.

"Shit. He just healed it," Frost exclaimed.

"Yeah, but what was the beam? An aura?" Gilda flung an Infernal Spear at the chimera guard. The beast barely responded when the fiery spell blasted into the lupine's neck.

"Might have been." Frost frowned. The mist surrounded the Bulwark also. "Sigrid," he shouted. "Your Bulwark... is it buffed?"

A moment passed before Sigrid answered. "Yes. Imanok Aura. Increases both physical and elemental defense. One-minute duration... one moment... there... I removed it."

The mist no longer drifted from the chimera guard. The Bulwark's remained.

"The emperor must heal and buff the guards at a certain percentage, right when he yells it," Frost said. "We won't get it done like this."

"We can try using line of sight against the emperor. He can't see it; he can't heal it." Gilda pointed to three of the colonnade's pillars that touched each other.

"Worth a shot. Sigrid," Frost called out, "have your Bulwark drag the guard behind those pillars but position the Bulwark where you can toss it some heals."

The Bulwark backed up to one side of the pillars, leading the guard. As the Bulwark retreated, the guard followed until the pillars hid them both. Moments later, the Bulwark's armored back appeared at the edge of the last pillar. Only the chimera guard's tail showed on the far side.

Frost and Gilda repositioned themselves behind the

chimera guard. In the middle of firing off an Aether Shot, Frost had an idea.

"Only stun him on Charge. Servitors are immune to Blind and Silence. So Smokescreen and Howl only matters to us. We just gotta run around the pillar, out of its line of sight for those and any AOEs. And since what we do has a real effect in the game, I say we blow off that thing's tail so we don't have to worry about its sweep."

"Sounds like a plan." Gilda nodded.

They worked in tandem to prevent Charge while delivering as much damage as they could manage. Whenever they saw the smoke or flames puff from a head, they ran on the other side of the pillars. Half a minute of focus fire on the tail saw it blasted off. It flopped to the ground uselessly.

The emperor bellowed out his healing and buffing cry but could not cast the spells on a target he could not see. Frost and Gilda attacked the guard's body. Kill the body, the head dies. Within another minute, the chimera guard collapsed.

"Seven minutes left," Frost said the moment the creature keeled over.

Emperor KiGyaba shrieked. The cry echoed throughout the throne room even as the ground and roof shook. Debris and dust fell. Nobles and slaves screamed. Whatever the ability, it stunned Frost and his group.

"You have killed my son," Emperor KiGyaba's voice boomed. "Now, you shall pay. Feel the true wrath of the Void Legion's First General."

The titan flung his hands up. Glowing azure mist seeped from the ground, coiled around his legs, and climbed up his body. Ebony and silver void energy crackled around him. His skin fell away in chunks. His body swelled. The mist enveloped him, a boiling cloud flickering with vibrant black, azure, and silver hues.

The cloud exploded. Wind from it whipped at Frost and the others.

In place of the titan was a thirty-foot scaled humanoid torso. But it's face, chest, and arms were the only things remotely human. The rest of the body was that of a gargantuan reptile, its scales tan and green. Where there should have been one tail, the body split into a dozen, each one with a serpentine head. Their maws were large enough to swallow a man in one gulp.

The stun expired.

"Sigrid," Frost yelled. "Put the Bulwark on Saba's chimera." He did not look to see if she did. He had faith she would.

Dante Raging Rushed into the emperor's body. The snake heads whipped and coiled in an agitated hissing mass. Dante Soul Screamed. He turned the emperor until Frost and the others were staring at the backs of a dozen hydra heads. Half the snakes twisted to face them, long forked tongues licking out.

"He hurts like hell," Dante shouted while Sigrid worked feverishly to keep him healed. "He started to hit harder each time he shouted about his sons. I don't think you should kill the other one. Might enrage him."

He grunted then continued. "Deal with those heads. I can handle his Necrotic Slashes and other melee skills by way of Shout, Bellow, Siphon Armor, and Reaping Blow, combined with Sigrid's heals and purifying. But those heads are constantly hitting me and spitting shit on me. I won't last much longer like this."

"You heard the man," Frost said. "Attack the hydras. Start with the one on the left. Sigrid, have your Bulwark and Shaman take the guard behind those pillars again. That way we don't have to worry about anything it does."

They spread out and concentrated their abilities on

430

the heads. Frost shifted at an angle that would allow him to use Piercer to its full effect, the red pulse striking several heads with one shot. Every so often, a snake head would dart at them. They avoided the attacks by way of dives, leaps, Flickers, and Streaks. Some snakes spat green liquid. A splash of it landed on Frost's arm. It burned through his armor.

"Remember not to stand in the shit, people," Frost said.

"Dante," Gilda called out. "At your feet, the hydra spit is poisonous or acidic. Maybe both."

But Dante had already moved away. The green puddles bubbled. Dante continued to shift whenever the spit landed near him. Soon enough he was dancing among puddles, weaving one way and then the next, making sure he did not stand in shit. Whenever the goo splashed on Dante, Sigrid purified him before the first tick of damage.

The first hydra head flopped to the side.

"We are immortal!" Emperor KiGyaba screamed in triumph.

A white glow emanated from the central snake head. The dead one writhed. Then it rose, swaying from side to side, and begun its attacks anew.

"The center one," Frost ordered. "Kill the center one first."

He marked the target with Deadeye's red beam, then opened with Aether Shot, followed by Divergence, and Aether Bomb. When the Aether Bomb exploded, most of the snake heads hissed and writhed, often twisting and spinning.

"Some heads can be staggered," Frost instructed. "While we're killing the center one, stun any of the others that you can. If another attempts to revive the center one when it dies, we gotta stun that one."

Gilda triggered Glacial Eruption. Ice exploded

among the snake heads. All but two were frozen. The freeze lasted eight seconds, enough to alleviate some of the damage Dante was taking.

"Come here, slave!" bellowed the emperor.

An erada woman stepped forward from among the people who were still cowering by the throne. She ran toward the emperor. A snake head snatched her up.

"Your soul is mine!"

The snake swallowed the erada.

A moment later, the emperor paused. He raised one hand. A beam of jagged dark energy shot from his hand into Saba. The dresdor screamed and was frozen, her back arched, her mouth open in agony.

Frost knew the spell all too well. Life Link. "The hand. Attack the hand. Stop the drain."

With Aether Shot on full power, he alternated between it and Projectile. Gilda flung Fire and Ice Globes, a series of Stalactites, Stalagmites, a Flame Column, and Infernal Spears. The emperor cried out; his hand dropped; the beam winked out.

Free of Life Link's drain, Saba collapsed to one knee, chest heaving. Sigrid healed her. Within moments, Saba was on her feet once more. She joined the fray with a barrage of arrows.

"Three minutes!" Frost called out.

Palms slick with sweat, body weary, he fired again and again. His heart raced as desperation crept in. Without an indication of Hit Points, the panic built. They had decreased the beating Dante took, but Frost felt as if they were not doing enough damage.

The central snake head died.

"My precious! My preciooouuusss." The emperor's wail cut through the room. It was both anguish and rage.

"Some kind of attack incoming," Dante shouted

over the tumult of cannon fire and spells. "He's pulsing."

Sure enough, a dark glow had eased through KiG-yaba's scaled skin. It beat a steady rhythm that slowly increased. Pulses of this sort were always bad news.

"Stop attacking him," Frost said. "Sigrid, bring out the guard just a bit. Everyone but Dante get within melee range of the guard and attack it with everything you have. Dante, pop Crossguard and Warden the moment you think he's gonna cast the new skill."

Frost led the way behind the chimera guard. He, Gilda, Saba, and Sigrid stood beneath its hulking body. The DPS unleashed ability after ability.

"You're hurting my son!"

No sooner had the emperor shouted than several blue motes of Tears flew across the distance to strike the guard. Imanok Aura followed. A beam of light in which the group basked. Frost immediately sensed the strength, the increased defense. Power. He felt as if he were invincible.

"DIE!" the emperor roared.

A blast of void energy exploded outward in a circle from the emperor. It swept across the room, a black wave that ate everything it touched. Even with the Imanok Aura buff, Frost felt as if his body had been torn in half. His chest and head burned. Darkness engulfed him. He felt himself fading away.

Frost snatched at his belt and drank several health potions. The sensation dissipated. But he still felt weak. Deadeye was a weight he could barely lift. Two minutes on the timer was a distant thing. In the back of his mind he knew they could not survive another Void Pulse.

"Pulsing again." Dante's voice was strained. "I'm fucking dying here!"

Now or never, Frost said to himself as he led the group back to the room's center. He thought of Mom, Kai,

Regi, and Rayne. *I can't lose here. Not now. Not after all we've been through. And I can't let my friends down.* "Gilda." Frost's voice was hoarse to his own ears. "Gilda."

"Yes."

"Protect me the best you can with your Aether Shields and Barrier but run out of the room when there's thirty seconds remaining. Saba get out of here. Save yourself. Dante, when the timer is up, use whatever you need to escape if you can."

"The throne room door is locked," Gilda said. "Not that I was going to leave."

"Neither was I," Saba added.

"I promised my parents to help you help me," Sigrid said.

Frost opened his mouth to demand that they save themselves.

Gilda pressed her forefinger to his lips. "A girl's gotta do what a girl's gotta do."

"I told you I'm all about the action, boss." Dante cackled. "Besides, do you really think I'd let you get all the glory of a sacrifice or a World First. Ha! Imagine that. We dine in hell together."

Frost smiled weakly. *Well, if I'm gonna die for the first time in Void Legion, there's no better way to go.*

He squared his shoulders. "Saba, attack with whatever you can. Gilda, the Shields and Barrier."

"I got you." Circular blue and red Aether Shields sparked to life above Gilda's arms. A cyan Aether Barrier appeared around her and Frost. The Shields shifted to her fists in accordance with her movements.

Frost positioned himself squarely behind the emperor. Gilda, Saba, and Sigrid joined him. His vision cleared a tiny bit. He saw a broad back partially hidden by a mass of swaying, hissing, spitting hydra heads.

434

He aimed Deadeye. "Everyone… use your Aether Overload skills. Either we burn this bitch down or we die." With those words, Frost drew on Stand and Deliver.

Deadeye glowed blue and hummed. A list of abilities became available. Korbitanium Projectile. Aether Shot. Aether Bomb. Divergence. Piercer. Staggering Shot. The first two had no recharge time. The others had shorter recharge times. Divergence and Aether Bomb had a fifty percent chance to have their recharge completely eliminated.

Beside him, Saba's body gave off a faint blue glow. She activated Arrow Battery. Her hands appeared to barely move as arrow after arrow, either empowered with aether or elements, streaked from her bow.

With a squeeze of the trigger from Frost, Deadeye unleashed the hammer drill and buzzsaw whine. Shots spewed forth like fire. Each ability, one after another, until they settled into alternating Aether Shots and Projectiles. Frost's arms jerked with each recoil.

The cyclic rate was slow at first. Whine. Whomp. Whine. Whomp. It built. A rhythm. Faster and faster and faster until it became a solid sound. The jet engine whine of a PT. A glorious dissonance of destruction. The rapidity eliminated the recharge time for Aether Bomb and Divergence.

The emperor's body pulsed. The effect increased until the beats were inseparable. Hydra heads hissed, spit, snapped out, and struck.

Gilda was a blur of action around Frost. She was the Gilda from Heroic Castle Dhoom. But this time she danced with an Aether Shield on each arm, knocking aside hydra heads, blocking poisonous spit. From time to time an Ice Pillar rose from the ground to block a striking hydra. She was a beautiful sight, darting around him as she employed the sorcerer's defensive Overload skill, Song of Ice and Fire.

But poison spit was landing in copious amounts. It coated the floor. Coated Frost. A snake head got past Gilda's defense, bit into Frost's shoulder. He cried out but still clung to Deadeye as it fired. Gilda knocked the snake away.

Frost's vision blurred. He wanted so much to rest. To simply lie down on the ground. Sleep. To lose himself in a never-ending slumber. The slumber of the dead.

"BURN HIMMMM!" Frost's voice echoed.

He and Deadeye were one. Fire and light spewed from the muzzle in an incessant stream, stretching up to the emperor, a fireworks display streaking through the air. Saba's arrows were multiple blurs. Even Gilda unleashed spells while using her shields. The attacks exploded in too many places to count. Too rapid to track.

"DI-" The emperor's voice cut off. He swayed. Every snake was but so much mush. Holes and exposed meat riddled the back of the emperor's body. Half of his head ceased to exist. Green blood spurted from the necks, from his body. It pooled beneath him. The emperor collapsed.

Even as Frost made to let out an elated yell, he sagged. Gilda and Saba were there to catch him. Sigrid cleansed Frost and healed him with Tears and Blood. She did the same for Gilda and Saba.

"If someone don't get this big sack of shit off me," called out Dante's muffled voice.

The group burst into laughter. Frost, Saba, and Gilda helped lift the emperor's midsection, while Sigrid had her Servitors drag Dante from beneath the hydra.

Frost let out a whoop. "WE DID IT! FUCK YEAH. WORLD FIRST, BABY! Epic players do epic things."

"What-what happened to the last chimera guard," Dante asked, squinting as he peered all around.

"He died when the emperor did," Sigrid said.

The group hugged and laughed.

Trials of Imanok Sanctum
Objective Complete
Cleared Imanok Sanctum
15, 000 experience points
1500 Ignis dominion credits
1500 Khertahka dominion credits
The Void Legion's First General
Defeated Emperor KiGyaba
15, 000 experience points
1500 Ignis dominion credits
1500 Khertahka dominion credits

Doors opened around the room. The slaves and nobles fled. Behind the throne, an even wider opening gaped. Despite where Frost stood, he saw the thing awaiting them. His mouth hung open.

CHAPTER 39

Frost's group stood before the machine. Housed within a korbitanium frame made up of six beams was a barrel-shaped glass container large enough to fit a gurash. Inside the container there was a platform two or three feet from the bottom. Translucent aether swirled within the glass, glowing a radiant azure blue.

"You certain it's a Genesis Engine?" Dante walked around the machine, thoroughly enthralled.

"Yes," Frost said.

Dante squatted and peered into the thickest swirls of aether. "How does it work? Can we make our own hierkas? Or empower shards with skill effects?"

"I suppose we could," Gilda answered. "If one of us was a hierkaneer. And if we had the necessary schemas and all the materials."

"Do you realize how much this is worth?" Dante caressed the glass.

"I wouldn't touch it, if I were you," Frost said. "As for worth… the fucking thing is priceless. I heard one's in Kituan. In the Aetherium, to be exact. Supposedly, it's how the Coalition supplies some of the Vindicators."

"Those were nothing but rumors." Gilda shook her

head. "I never saw anything remotely like this when I studied at the Aetherium."

"Well, now we have one of our own." Smiling, Saba had a dreamy look on her face.

"I wouldn't go so far as to say we got our own." Frost shook his head. "It's too big for any inventory. And how do we know we can move it? Suppose it's the purpose for clearing this dungeon? Clear, bring a hierkaneer, craft, and leave."

"How's it work?" Dante was still squatting and staring into the glass.

The aether coiled and shifted like a living thing. Frost could feel its power. It called to him.

"A retired Vindicator taught a class on draconid tech at the Aetherium when I was there," Gilda said. "Genesis Engines tap directly into the Aetherstream that runs deep underground, flowing through all of Mikander like blood. The largest branches of it are even called arteries. The smaller ones are veins. The Aetherstream is one of the reasons people started believing the religions that claim Mikander itself is built around the corpses of three Divines: Sienne, Korbash, and Marang, who fled here during the Divinity War."

"I always loved that bit of lore." Frost smiled. "Their love story was deep."

"And tragic," Gilda added.

"It got me into roleplaying," Saba confessed.

"Bah. Nerds," Dante huffed. "All that matters is that until we get a hierkaneer in here, we won't know if we should, or can, move it. Which means it's useless to us for now. Let's see the loot we actually got. You know, the stuff we can take with us." He indicated the four golden treasure chests in the room.

Frost strode over to the first chest, the longest of

the bunch. He flipped open the lid. A zhua rested in a velvet mold, the staff portion etched with various designs, ending in a polished korbitanium claw. He reached down and picked up the mystic's hierka.

Benediction
Level: Levels with the owner
Damage: 50 − 75
Force: 5
Special: Channels void energy to cure the Gray Death. Skill activation requires
Empowered Ameliorate, Empowered Suppression, and Empowered Rejuvenate.
Shard slots: 3
The Sanctum's Secret Hierka
Objective Complete
Acquired the zhua, Benediction:
2500 experience points
1500 Ignis dominion credits
The Cure
Objective Complete:
Acquired Benediction
2500 experience points
1500 Ignis dominion credits

He told his friends. And he noted the quest still required the necessary spells.

"The Gray Death?" Saba repeated in disbelief. "As in the plague that wiped out so many? That's still prevalent in parts of Puria, Lothal, and Nimri? *That* Gray Death?"

"Unless you know another Gray Death," Frost said. He recalled his talk with Nebsamu about the plague. "Is it really that widespread?"

"It's worse than most know." Saba's tail swished. "The Coalition's been keeping news of it from spreading as quietly as they can while the Vindicators search for a cure.

But they have their hands full. Not just with the plague, but also with the devastation left after the last voidstorm, and the random draconid appearances."

"Should we give this to them?" Frost held out Benediction.

"The Coalition?" Dante grimaced. "The people hunting us?"

"Right?" Saba scoffed. "I'm surprised you're asking that question. We should go find the other spells it needs, or someone who has them that we can trust, and use it ourselves."

Frost told them all he had learned from Nebsamu and Adesh Hamada about the Black Hand and the Coalition. "Right now, our enemy is the Black Hand. They're using the Coalition to do their dirt. I'm willing to bet quite a few people within the Coalition don't know they're being manipulated."

"No doubt," Gilda said. "And because of that, I think we need to discover all the Black Hand's members before we even consider giving up the zhua. Or informing anyone else. Whomever owns Benediction has a lot of power. Enough to make others do what they want."

"Alright." Frost put the zhua in his inventory. "We search for the spells needed. We might get lucky and come across someone in Blue Sky that has them. Also, we find out who we can trust in the Coalition. We also root out these Black Hand members. They killed my mother. They gotta pay."

"That will take some doing," Saba said. "You saw how powerful Nomarch Botros is."

"I don't care what it takes." Frost shrugged. "I suppose everyone has the quest for the Black Hand?" Sigrid was the only person who didn't nod.

Gilda leaned across to Frost and whispered, "Looks

like this might be your group for a while, Mister Solo."

Frost smiled. "A guy's gotta do what a guy's gotta do." Gilda giggled.

"Okay, you two, enough of the lovey-dovey stuff," Dante grumbled. "Y'all can get a room and play with your horns later." He chuckled. "Loot, man, let's finish the loot."

The next chest contained a schema on how to craft more Benedictions. Frost whistled. He tucked it into his inventory.

The next two chests contained four skill effect shards. Two were for marauder skills. Empowered Sentinel Shout increased the defensive and health capability and added an attack power buff. Empowered Reaping Blow increased the health it returned.

"That's what I'm talking about." Dante grinned when he received the shards. "Kicking more ass and taking more names."

The next skill effect shard was for Gilda's Infernal Spear. Not only would it now be able to home in on a target, but also she could pinpoint two more after the first and it would pierce all three albeit a bit weaker each time.

Lastly, there was one for Saba's Triple Barrage. It became Quintuple Barrage.

Dante strode over to Frost. "That was like old times. Gives me the itch to be in a guild. How would you feel about starting up Soldiers of Chaos again?"

"I don't know. Honestly haven't given it a lot of thought." Frost couldn't picture reliving the stress and hurt from when SoC broke up. Starting a new guild meant opening those old wounds. He'd poured his soul into their family. He didn't think he was ready for that. Being in a group this long was bad enough.

"While you think on it, I just wanted to say sorry about what happened before." Dante sighed heavily. "Things in SoC should've never ended like that. A lot of it was my fault. But if you'll have me again, I'm more than willing to be your main tank or whatever else you need."

Frost smiled. "Thanks. I'm sorry about how things turned out also. And I'll keep it in mind."

"If we're all done, there looks to be a portal over there." Saba pointed to a column of yellow light. "Saves us the trouble of running into Sidrie on the way out."

"What's that on the other side of it?" Dante asked. "On the wall."

Markings on the wall glowed a greenish blue. They were in the shape of a door. The group made their way past the portal to the wall. A phrase was written above the door.

Void Gate.

"Never seen one of those before," Saba said.

Frost's ring vibrated. He shot a knowing look Gilda's way. "Gilda and I'll check it out. The rest of you wait here and keep an eye out in case Setnana and her Battleguards show up."

"Don't be too long," Saba said.

"You should let me come." Dante rested his axe over his shoulder. "In case there's some action."

"We won't be long," Frost promised. "And the dungeon is cleared, so the only action will be from Setnana entering the room. It's better if you're here in case she does."

"You're the boss," Dante said.

Frost and Gilda approached the etching. He held her hand, took a breath, and they stepped through. Frost's heart leapt with joy when he saw Pops floating in the air above a map of Mikander.

"You don't have much time," Pops said. "Nomarch Botros is close to solving the maze."

"Speaking of mazes," Frost said, "you coulda told us the way."

443

The holo slapped a palm to its translucent forehead. "Slipped my mind. But still, nothing worth doing is easy. How did you figure it out?"

"That was all her." Frost jabbed a thumb in Gilda's direction.

Gilda smiled bashfully and said, "It was from all those talks we had and quite a bit of research. Took some doing, but once I realized Imanok was really Konami, one of the old game companies you often went on about, I dug up some archives on their games. Emperor Demon Gava or Tenno Ki Gyaba was one of their bosses in a game called Contra. A game you mentioned being in love with. A search on the Grid got me an old code they were known for. Although the last two bits of it were missing."

"Excellent." Pops smiled. "You were always a quick thinker. Too bad we no longer have access to the old internet databases. You would've found the entire thing." Pops hesitated for a moment, a frown creasing his holographic features. "Come, hurry. Extend your hands with the aether rings until they touch me."

When Frost and Gilda touched the holo, the particles swirled. They coiled around their hands, formed a thin line, then zipped into the rings.

Frost felt a flash of something. Something electric deep within himself. He had a sense of numbers. Instructions. Code. He couldn't tell what any of it meant, but if he focused he could repeat every line.

"Dre," Pops said. His translucent arm pointed down at the map. "These are the nine protocol locations. Myself and Uncle Kim built them into the quest lines. Do what I couldn't and expose Equitane. Help stop Sidrie."

"I will. I promise."

"Whatever you do, make sure Sidrie doesn't get her hands on the protocols," Pops said. "Without all of them,

444

she won't have full control of everything in Void Legion. It's one advantage you have. Keep it that way."

"Alright, Pops."

The holo's expression softened. "Son, I'm sorry I failed the family. Failed you. I always wanted you to be the best you could be. Sorry I left you like I did, but I see you've become more of a man than I could've dreamed."

Frost smiled. He wished he could hug his father. "Thanks, Pops. You don't know how much that means to me. I miss you so much."

"I miss you, too. All of you."

Warm tears trickled down Frost's cheeks. His voice was brittle when he spoke. "I blamed you for everything bad that's happened since you left. Even your own death. Which wasn't fair. You did the best you could for us. And sometimes, even when you're trying your best, shit happens." Frost brushed the tears from his cheeks. A weight lifted from his shoulders, one he hadn't realized he had been carrying for over six months.

"It does, indeed," Pops said, smiling. His face grew serious. "I'll see you around in game, son. Get out of here before the Nomarch catches you." The holo faded.

Frost took a final look at the empty space. Then he memorized the locations on the map. He and Gilda left the Void.

As soon as they reappeared, Dante was standing directly outside the door, eyes shining eagerly. "What was in there? Epic loot? Mobs? I tried to get in, but it wouldn't let me."

"Was an empty room with a map of Mikander," Frost said. "I'm thinking some kind of operations room."

"How come it let you in?" Dante gave them both a searching look.

"Hell, if I know." Frost shrugged. "I just tried."

"Could be that we're erada," Gilda said.

"Figures." Dante shook his head.

"Let's get out of here." Frost eyed the open throne room door. "Nomarch Setnana and her Battleguards might come through any minute now."

"What about the Genesis Engine?" Dante nodded to the machine.

"Not much we can do about it," Frost said.

"Like hell there isn't." Saba scowled. "If we leave, and Nomarch Setnana finds her way through the maze, the Black Hand will get their hands on it. Isn't that as bad as them getting the zhua or the schema?"

"Not really," Frost said. "The Coalition already has access to a few Engines in the captured areas beyond the Dagoda Front. Which means the Black Hand does also. Blue Sky could certainly use it, but there's nothing we can do about that right now. It's better if we don't risk the zhua or the schema."

Gilda spoke. "We can always put together a group to go into the Front and find us a Genesis Engine to use once we get some hierkaneers. We *know* more Engines exist. We can't say the same about Benediction or the schema."

Frost also hated the idea of abandoning the Genesis Engine. He also hated that he wouldn't get to fulfill Anefet's quest and take vengeance as yet. But deep inside, he knew he was nowhere near ready to face Setnana.

"We'll take Sigrid to her people in the Daggerspine," he said. "Hopefully, Adesh and Ryne made it out safely. Let's go." Frost took one last look at the emperor's corpse and smiled at the prospect of seeing his family, of Mom finally awake. He led them to the portal.

They reappeared on the lake's eastern bank. Sigrid told them she knew the area and led them to another dvergr tribe who provided them with crevids. Not long after, they

446

ascended the mountain and found the remnants of Sigrid's tribe, including Dagrun. Both Adesh Hamada and Ryne were also there.

In the midst of the celebration of their return and victory, Frost was pulled from the game.

CHAPTER 40

"No, no, no, no." Setnana shook her head as she hurried toward the corpse. Her stomach clenched.

The massive hydra was already rotting, but there was no denying its identity. Emperor KiGyaba was dead.

"Nomarch Setnana, over here," Ihuet shouted. "The treasure room."

Setnana prayed that the Blue Sky group had somehow missed the chance to loot the throne room. She and her people had been close to them. Surely, they lacked the time for the kill and to steal every bit of treasure.

She frowned at the machine beyond the open doorway where Ihuet stood. The korbitanium frame. The large cylindrical tube containing aether. The transmutation platform. A Genesis Engine. She'd seen its like once before in a stronghold taken by the Vindicators beyond the Dagoda Front. This was a priceless discovery. Her heart soared. Not only because of the Engine, but its presence meant Benediction was still here.

Nif shines on me. I didn't need to find a way to kill a beast who has defeated everyone else before, and now I get to take what is mine. Perihy will be cured. Cured! She saw his face, his beautiful face, his skin so dark and vibrant and full of life.

She hurried into the treasure room. And stopped dead. The chests were open.

No, no, no, no, no. Her hands shook. Her legs were jelly as she approached the chests.

The first one was empty. Inside was a velvet mold in the shape of a staff with a clawed hand at the top. A zhua. Benediction. IM made her aware of her failure.

The room became a blur. She found it hard to breathe. All she could think of was Perihy. Aether energy crackled.

"Nomarch, let him go." The voice was Ihuet's. "Please."

She shook herself and glanced over. Her arm was outstretched. Dark tendrils snaked from her to the closest Battleguard. He was a mere husk, his life drained by her Soul Leech.

"I have failed Perihy," she blurted.

"No, you haven't." Khafra was on the other side of her. "Whatever happens now, Blue Sky is to blame. As well as Adesh Hamada, this Drelan Frost, and his friends. We will find them."

"There's also the Genesis Engine," Ihuet said. "You have the spell shards. You brought hierkaneers, which means they will know how to safely detach the Genesis Engine from the Aetherstream and take it with us. Then they can experiment to recreate whatever else you might need."

"We can work on a cure as well as build an arsenal for ourselves," Khafra said.

She nodded numbly. "Yes. Yes, we can." Her voice was distant to her own ears.

* * * * * *

Setnana offered prayers to Nif as she and Aishani stood at the window of the observation room deep in Aprunis' Temple of Nif. Perihy was shackled to the bed. A precaution against his reaction to the healing.

The return trip had left Setnana haggard. And even more worried since no hierkaneer had any idea how to craft Benediction. Not without the missing schema.

But she had hope. Hope provided by Vindicator Dita's strength in spellcasting and her personal zhua. The woman's reputation as one of the greatest mystics preceded her.

Vindicator Dita had cast the spells upon Perihy the night before. It was coming upon the thirtieth hour that he had remained healthy, his skin vibrant. Pure. He had not opened his eyes as yet, but his face was serene. A few more minutes, Dita had promised. A few more minutes to know if the results would be permanent.

Timespheres throughout Aprunis gonged the first toll of the thirtieth hour. A long peal.

"Praise be to Nif." Smiling, Setnana raised her face to the heavens.

Aishani squeezed Setnana's arm. Hard.

Perihy's scream reverberated from the room, through the window. Setnana snapped her attention to her son. She gaped. Vindicator Dita had stepped well away from the bed. Aether glowed all around her, focused on the zhua the woman held. Beside the Vindicator stood a sorcerer and a shadowmancer, glowing chakrams and haladie pointed toward the boy on the bed.

Perihy writhed. His face contorted. He fought against the shackles, bucked and kicked and lifted from the bed, his back arched into an impossible position, leaving several feet of space beneath him. A C turned downward. Abruptly, his body smashed the opposite way of its curvature, slamming into the bed, buckling the metal frame.

Setnana's heart thundered. She clenched her fists. Her legs buckled. She stretched an inadvertent hand toward

Perihy. As if the hand could help him.

"Please, Nif, help him. Please, Nif, I beg you." Over and over, she beseeched the goddess.

Perihy's skin lost its vibrance. Its life. It became completely gray. His skin tore. Blood leaked. All along his body, his muscles bulged and shifted and moved as if something lived within his very skin.

His skin burst. Every inch of it. Blood splashed the window.

Nomarch Setnana Botros wailed.

Shackled to the bed was a draconid.

CHAPTER 41

Holding Kai's hand, his heart thundering, Dre approached Mom's medical quarters. He didn't know what to expect. He feared what he might find, yet he clung to hope. Sidrie's only words were to congratulate him and to order the guards to bring them here.

The door slid open.

Dre's heart leapt. Mom was sitting up against a pillow. Kai let go of his hand and ran toward the bed, laughing.

"Mommmmmmmyyyyyyy!"

Tears streamed down Dre's face. Nothing could replace the elation he had inside.

* * * * * *

Up on the two hundred and fortieth floor of Equitane Towers, in the most secure of quarters, Sidrie Malikah watched impassively as the holo displayed Andre Taylor leaning down to kiss Theresa on the cheek. The woman brushed her son's face, tears streaming down her own. Her other hand stroked her daughter's head, where Kai rested on Theresa's chest.

Sidrie considered dashing their joy with the news that Andre's services were still required, and in fact, had just begun. She decided to let them have their moment. For now. After all, she needed Theresa to give birth to healthy babies.

Communication from Zhi Yin flashed into Sidrie's

optics. "Yes, Zhi?"

"The programming team has it, Miss Malikah." The restrained triumph in her sweet voice was palpable.

Sidrie tried to contain her own thrill. She spoke calmly. "Have they confirmed that it is the first protocol?"

"Yes."

"Thank you, Zhi. I will be along shortly."

"Yes, Miss Malikah." The comms cut off.

Sidrie drew in a long, deep breath. She let it out slowly, chasing away her excitement.

Smart to hide it in game. As I suspected. But what else are you hiding, Alphonso?

She was missing something else. Something bigger. She felt it. Whatever the secret, Andre would lead her to it and all the protocols. With a thought, she changed the view in her HUD to another room on this floor.

In it, her clone was peering from an observation window down into an area where surgeons labored over Alphonso's body. TNT machines kept the man alive. Seven months had passed and they'd regrown much of him. But it still wasn't enough. Not yet. Not until she got her hands on Hank Kim's research or on Kim himself.

Until then, she hoped the clone standing next to her clone, twin to the one in surgery, could learn enough to be convincing. The plethora of information gathered from the extensive surveillance of the Taylors had to suffice. Her window of opportunity was never better. She needed all the protocols. Not three months from now. Not three weeks. Now.

* * * * * *

Late that night, long after Mom fell asleep, Dre was lying next to Just Blaze. They had been given leave earlier in

453

the evening. They had snuck off to a hotel in the fifteenth ward.

Staring at the ceiling, Dre thought about Void Legion. About Pops. About the family. His greatest wish was justice for Pops and the family and to be free of Sidrie. At the same time he really wanted to play the game. It truly blew his mind. He had so many questions and couldn't wait to see Pops again.

He was even more certain now that SRMMOs *were* the most perfect *entertainment* ever created. He was also equally certain they weren't better than sex. They weren't better than real life. Making love to Just Blaze was more than just entertainment. It was everything. He admired the smooth honey skin next to him, trailed his fingers down her shoulder and back to where her ass curved into a perfect onion.

"So, when are you gonna tell me your real name. I can't go around calling you Gilda Mordian IRL. Certainly can't introduce you to Mom by your IGN. And Just Blaze… well… that won't do either."

"Just call me Blaze," she said.

"Blaze." He rolled it around on his tongue. "Blaze. I like that. I really like that."

THE END.

Thanks for reading! A little message from the author.

If you enjoyed this book, then I humbly ask you to leave a review on Amazon. Visibility is everything. And it helps us authors know we're doing something right.

To chat, for ARCS, free swag, news, and to just hang out and talk to me, join the Storyteller Terry C. Simpson's Void Gate, my Facebook group.

If you're so inclined,you can check out some of my

other fantasy series. If you're all about LitRPG and Gamelit, be sure to join the thriving Gamelit Society community on Facebook

www.ingramcontent.com/pod-product-compliance
Lightning Source LLC
Chambersburg PA
CBHW051508250626
47156CB00001B/13

* 9 7 8 1 9 3 9 1 7 2 2 5 9 *